Buildin

"Nobody, and I mean nobody, has such a unique and varied, and frequently brilliant take on Lovecraftian influenced fiction as Don Webb. He somehow manages to strike the Lovecraftian mode without it being mere pastiche, and frankly, I like Webb's work better than Lovecraft. He takes the best from the old master, but the clothes he makes it wear are gorgeous, darlin'."

Joe R. Lansdale

"Originality is hard to come by, almost by definition, in the literary demimonde of Lovecraftian writers, but Don Webb is the go-to guy for revitalizing Lovecraft. Don't miss out on this book!"

John Shirley
author of *Lovecraft Alive!*

"With *Building Strange Temples*, Master Mage Don Webb has laid his unique binding seal upon the legacy of H. P. Lovecraft. He has leashed and commanded the squirming, bubbling, amorphous chaos that is the highly eclectic and inclusive twenty-first-century Cthulhu Mythos and elevated it to supernal heights. These touching, horrifying, comedic, bewildering, traditional, transgressive tales start from the foundational work of Lovecraft, Smith, Bloch and other classic authors and amplify their core conceits and tropes to realms previously unguessed-at. Whether set in Webb's beloved Austin, on the borderlands of the Dreamworld, or in European climes; in the past, present or future; among the brilliantly delineated lowlifes, academics, bohemians or the bourgeois, these stories all exhibit Webb's immense familiarity with the Mythos, his intense and fecund creativity, and his ability to plot like the demonic offspring of Rod Serling, M. R. James, Robert Louis Stevenson and Shirley Jackson. On the same plane as peers like Caitlín R. Kiernan and Nathan Ballingrud, Paul Tremblay and Jeffrey Thomas, Webb is a National Treasure, a one-man-army of Weirdness and Cool. Long may he continue to pullulate!"

Paul Di Filippo
author of *Cosmocopia*, *A Mouthful of Tongues*, and others

BUILDING STRANGE TEMPLES

DON WEBB

RAMBLE HOUSE
2020

First American trade paperback edition

Ramble House
10329 Sheephead Drive
Vancleave MS 39565 USA

www.ramblehouse.com

ISBN 13: 978-1-60543-990-7

Dedication

To my brothers and sisters, fathers and mothers, sons and daughters of the tribe that shares Wonder as the cure for the world's pain.

Table of Contents

Building Strange Temples 9

Doodles 14

Elegy (Denise Dumars & Don Webb) 24

Movie Night At Phil's 25

Fall in Carcosa 34

Out of Bondage 35

The Phantom of Truth 46

Like Comment Share 48

Robert W. Chambers 57

The Last God 58

The Stele 71

The Auction 72

And Other Horrors (Nick Mamatas & Don Webb) 74

The Egyptologist 87

A Tune From Long, Long Ago 88

The Cult 97

A Comet Called Ithaqua 99

The God 104

Unsung Heroes 105

The New Earth 116

Lute 117

The White Silk 126

Ophiuchus	128
Fine Green Dust	142
Ool Athag	152
Beyond the Rim	161
Tomahawk	162
The Red Rite	171
Nailing It Down	184
The Revelation at the Abbey	204
The Head of the Tree	216
Night Gauntlet (by Various)	223
Point Nemo	239
Tick Tock	253
Red, Green, Blink, Black (John Shirley & Don Webb)	263
Root Work Saves the World (Christopher Ropes & Don Webb)	277
The Waters of Dhul Nun	289
The Healing Power of Snow	299
Pumpkins	309
The Codex	318
The Future Eats Everything	329
The Hollow Man (H. P. Lovecraft & Don Webb)	339

Building Strange Temples

WE ARE TAUGHT not to steal the writings of another. We are taught to jealously guard our own. H. P. Lovecraft didn't learn these lessons. He openly raided the works of Ambrose Bierce, Robert W. Chambers, and Arthur Machen. He shared his works and words in a love-feast with fellow writers like Clark Ashton Smith, Robert Bloch, and Robert E. Howard. He planted his words in the stories he revised. The great fear in Lovecraft's writing is said to be miscegenation. Yet more than any writer he created a practice of contamination, a loosening of writerly boundaries. When most of us use August Derleth's term, "Cthulhu Mythos," we refer not only to Lovecraft's writings but all the ancestors and descendants of his writing—we can refer to Ligotti and King, Derleth and Pugmire, Schweitzer and Asamatsu, Kiernan and Schwader. We happily make lists of Lovecraftian games, music, comics, animation, toys and magic systems. He never grasped the basics of marketing, was disdainful of the genre outlets for his chosen writing and could spend hours engaged in answering letters from fans. The very social matrix he began remains. Some of the folks I learned writing from, learned from men and women whom had learned from Lovecraft. I am sitting at my desk in Austin playing a game that has its roots in amateur press associations and the first stirrings of fandom. I've been in the home of living humans who received letters from Lovecraft, I exchange silly art and comics with young men and women in Japan and Pakistan that derives from Lovecraftian themes, good friends of mine make and sell art (ranging from a Cthulhuvian bong made by Anne Koi in Oregon to Lovecraftian tattoos from Berlin tattoo artist Andre Harke). I have overheard Lovecraft jokes made in rural Texas, at a pub in London, while visiting the Guggenheim Museum in Manhattan.

The puzzling question is why? Folks in my city wear burnt orange t-shirts when the Texas Longhorns are playing football. Some are former students, others identify because they live here.

It's a fairly easy tribalism. I was a UT student and when I wear my UT gear, I get positive feedback—whether it's smiling from a 16-year-old African American who cuts my lawn or the 93-year-old white woman who is in front of me at the pharmacy. It feels good. When I wear a Lovecraftian t-shirt at a SF convention I get some smiles, but what is this tribe saying?

1. We like being scared? No, not quite. Reading Lovecraft—although there are moments of visceral horror—is not scary in the same way as watching a serial killer movie. No one reads 'The Call of Cthulhu' and worries about the sounds in the basement. No one reads 'The Dunwich Horror' and wonders if his cousin got knocked up by the Guardian of the Gate. At least no sane person.

2. Is it because we are fans of Lovecraft's racism, his sexism, or his often-terrible politics? No, the readers of HPL—at least the hundreds I have met—are very quick to either apologize for his attitudes or simply say that they are of strong enough mind to enter into the world of a writer and separate the wheat of wonder from the chaff of racism. Lovecraft did not write to advance these agendas (in his commercial pieces), nor are there any small presses out there that feature say Lovecraft and Madison Grant's *The Passing of the Great Race*.

3. Is it because we are unaware of quality writing and are drawn to Lovecraft as a cut above *Fifty Shades of Grey*? Although such differentiation did no doubt earn Lovecraft a readership in *Weird Tales* days, Lovecraft's readers are often the readers of Kafka (a writer who he is very similar to) or Borges. Many of the practitioners of Lovecraftism such as Ligotti (or even Borges) belong firmly in the literary camp.

My answer to the t-shirt question is that *we are in on the joke*. Lovecraftians wink knowingly at one another, smirk at their little pranks—such as dropping a Lovecraftian name in a corporate training manual, and (at the best of times) use Lovecraft's philosophical speculations as a way to explore and expand their own thinking. At the worst (that is to say the least creative) this is expressed as slavish imitation of the master—creating those endless pastiches that kept Lovecraft's writing in the pulp fiction ghetto for years. At the best it can create philosophy and magick. So, what does it mean to be "in" on the joke?

There are two levels of response. The first level, the fannish level, is to decode the material. This means activities such as finding which New England cities become which fictional cities and then recoding the world with these names. Thus we have

Lovecraft branded absinthes or “Arkham Asylums.” This is a religious activity which one can note in converts to new faiths. The new Jew, Buddhist, Satanist, etc. goes through the remapping of the world effecting clothing, diet, etc. The new Lovecraftian changes her types of play.

The second level is to adopt Lovecraft’s ideas of the disease and the cure. The disease is nihilism. Face it: we are temporary beings that can exist under a small set of circumstance (temperature, pressure, gravity). We exist on a small world circling a rather uninteresting yellow sun in a perfectly ordinary arm of (what appears to be) a rather conventional galaxy in a small local group of galaxies. I will be dust, you will be dust, this book will be dust, this language will fade in time (if mankind does not destroy itself), and even the mountains and seas of this world will take on new shapes in less time than a single nap of dread Cthulhu. Your politics, your religion, art, are tiny bubbles of foam on the oceans of eternity. It does not matter if you love your spouse, pet your cat, or pray today. It will be forgotten tomorrow, or if not tomorrow in weeks, months, years, decades, centuries, aeons . . . So knowing this—how do I get out of bed and type these words? How do you go to work Monday morning? Why should we care if the bridges and infrastructure of our cities become rust? Why should humans worry about continent of garbage that now floats over R’lyeh?

One could react to this undeniable truth in various ways. We could become hedonists of the most debauched sort. We could end our existence in a variety of either pleasurable or dramatic ways. We could simply sleep in . . .

Much of Lovecraft’s life, as pointed out by even his semi-favorable critics like De Camp, can be seen as a reaction to this truth. He barely made enough money to eat and eventually his malnutrition contributed to his demise. Finding typing a great chore he didn’t even type some of his best known tales, made small attempts at marketing them, didn’t buy a home—didn’t even see to his legacy. He should have been blown like dust save for the Cure (and conditions of the Cure).

The Cure—both for Uncle Howard and us—is *Wonder*. Lovecraft is firmly part of the gosh-wow tradition of American Science Fiction. He differed from his contemporaries in two things. He could not fake optimism. His heroes didn’t get to bed egg-laying Martian women with big tits. His sense of wonder was not attached to the wonders of human invention or human progress. Secondly, he was not motivated by money. He made the usual whining sounds all writers must make to each other—yet much of his output was geared to produce nothing of economic value. His wonderful history of weird literature, *Supernatural Horror in Literature*—which took decades to research, two years to write, and months to revise—was written for a one-shot non-paying fanzine. It was guided by a published work, Birkhead's *The Tale of Terror*, which, although never a bestseller, proved the existence of a paying market for such a piece of work. Lovecraft did not fail to make money because of lack of public interest, simply because of lack of motivation. This leads to the second question: Why did Lovecraft write at all? His literary output shows great craftsmanship—stories (as I am always discovering) do not write themselves. If *Wonder* was a self-sustaining state one need only have recourse to imagination. One could dream of sinister Egyptian pharaohs one day and killer cats the next.

Wonder is shared. *Wonder* has two moments. The first is that moment of joy where the work or Art or the beauty of Nature or the marvel of Science takes the psyche beyond the limited experience of the here-and-now. The second moment is witnessing another so transported. It is a feeling that all of you have. You are excited when you have your moment of transcendence, and then comes that second moment when you initiate another. You know the thrill of turning on someone to a writer, a film, a piece of music. All of Lovecraft's output is enshrined in this quest—not just his fiction, but also his essays and most importantly his voluminous letter writing. We are made ashamed by the common capitalist values of our time to admit this mood—because (by and large) we don't make money from it. If you talk your aged aunt into watching *Dr. Who* or lure your chiropractor into reading 'The Raven' you feel a thrill that hasn't put a dime in your pocket. You are being a bad modern.

Lovecraft initiated readers and writers into his sense of *Wonder*. In the Lovecraftian system it is better to momentarily fool some *Weird Tales* reader into believing there *is* a *Necronomicon* than to make a buck by copyrighting the idea. It is better to steal the Yellow Sign and therefore provide a backdoor into Chambers than to simply use your own words. This joy of intertextuality is what sets Lovecraft's work apart. His words blend into other's writing, whether the connect to a Borges short story or a third imitation of a Lin Carter story put on a blog that got two hits. I began writing as part of this mood and I am informed by this strange need.

One of my stories here, 'Night Gauntlet,' has the writings of both men that influenced me to write at all (Walter C. DeBill Jr.) as well a young writer I encouraged and mentored. I have included tales influenced by writers that influenced Lovecraft (William Hope Hodgson in 'Lute'), writing inspired by Lovecraft's friends (Clark Ashton Smith in 'Polarion' or 'The Red Rite'), writing derived from his students (Frank Belknap Long in 'Doodles')—I even incorporated an unfinished fragment of Lovecraft's own writing in one tale ('The Hollow Man'). I have worked with great poets like Denise Dumars, amazing literary critics like Robert Price, writers with very different literary aims than me (Nick Mamatas, William Pugmire, Jeffery Thomas). I have included in-jokes from Lovecraftians of other times (such as borrowing the rock group Electric Commode from the late James Wade). In 'Tomahawk' I give a story that began as a collaboration between myself and Michael Swanwick; we could not come to a single vision and so he let me have the words. There are still some of his sentences, the better ones I imagine, hidden in that work. In my last piece of play I took one of Lovecraft's unfinished stories and finished it.

My hope is that some of my pieces will give you the moment of *Wonder*, that change in your subjective universe that is neither terror nor ecstasy but a refutation of the concept of Order. And in turn that you spread some of that *Wonder* into the objective universe finding some other soul you can share it with. Maybe it will be story that you will tell by the campfire, maybe it's buying this book as a Groundhog Day present for your chiropractor. Then perhaps long after I am dust and you are dust and this book is dust—something a bit more durable than dust can recognize itself in worlds and ways literally beyond our current imaginations.

And if such is not to be, at least you and I were in on the Joke.

Nudge, nudge, wink, wink. *Ph'nglui mglw'nafh Cthulhu R'lyeh wgah'nagl fhtagn!*

Doodles

MY CHANCE TO be a great man finally appeared directly after the World Horror Convention. I had waited long enough. Years of writing—trying to give my pinheaded fans what they wanted, what they should want. I had gone to the Convention as one goes to all conventions, that despite two and half decades of writing certain that, out of nowhere, this time Opportunity would knock. A publisher—or better still a filmmaker would open his large purse and shower me with gold. It has been said that the definition of insanity is "doing the same thing again and again and expecting a different result." If 'tis so, then writers are insane. I had gone and expected a different result. I had sat on my panels, gone to hotel room parties and was no whit richer or more famous. The last evening a certain Canadian magazine had thrown a costume party. We could come as "Horrific figures". I had decided not to be lost among the Frankenstein monsters, the Draculas, the Freddy Kruegers. I had gone as "Maxwell" of the Beatle's song 'Maxwell's Silver Hammer.' No one got the reference.

I know that you, my gentle reader, will recognize the song as from *Abbey Road.* It tells the song of medical student Maxwell Edison who uses a silver hammer to kill his girlfriend Joan, then his teacher and finally the judge (during his trial). I had a large silver hammer in a medical kit. I had otherwise affected a Victorian gentleman's attire since the song had obvious reference to Jack the Ripper (and of course scientist Clerk Maxwell). Men more famous than me. I had been Steampunk before Steampunk was cool.

After the dreary little party I had sought to drown my sorrows in pasta. Liquor only makes me more maudlin, but comfort food works every time. I had gone to Romano's Macaroni Grill and treated myself to their scrumptious green-shelled lobster ravioli. If you know the chain you know that instead of tablecloths, white butcher paper covers the tables and patrons may amuse themselves by drawing upon it with crayons provided by the management. Pasta, Chianti, opera-singing waiters, and crayons—all-in-all

American culture at its best. I was sipping on my raspberry Italian soda and playing with a "Sea Green" crayon when Opportunity sat in an empty chair at my table. The Crayola® folk call this neon chartreuse shade "Sea Green"—a long call from Homer's wine-dark sea. I suppose Homer did not play with crayons—at least not from the 64-color box.

Opportunity proved to be a younger man than me. He was tall and thin and had flaxen hair and quite a ruddy complexion. His eyes were slate blue, and he had a small Hitler mustache. I have never in half a century had someone sit unbidden at my table, and I was (of course) unaware that he was Opportunity. He carried a small brown attaché case.

"Excuse me," he said. "I would like to celebrate with you."

"Of course," I said. "What gaiety are we celebrating? Have we won the lottery?"

"I was named to the Fifth Appellate Court today," he said.

I looked at him carefully. I had seen his face on the ever-present CNN flickering in the hotel lobby. He could indeed be the lucky Judge. Of course, he could have also been a serial murderer. He seemed to have friendly eyes for a serial killer. Or are they supposed to be charming? I specialize in supernatural thrillers and I am woefully ignorant of the important things of life. I decided that if his Hitler mustache had been dark rather than the color of tea with milk, he would have never made it in politics. One cannot have even the look of being Nazi.

"Congratulations!" I said. "You certainly look judicial! And how are we celebrating?"

"I noticed that you were doodling on your tablecloth."

"It is not a cloth, it's paper." For some reason I had turned into a schoolboy caught at something.

"Of course. I mean, aren't you somebody?"

"I think everyone is somebody."

"I mean your outfit."

I had not considered my costume. Others from the convention had crossed the parking lot to this restaurant. Next to me were a Snape, a werewolf, a George W. Bush, and a mummy.

"I was at a costume party."

"No. I mean you're from the writer's thing aren't you? Aren't you someone important?"

I knew my name would conjure no spirits from the vasty deep of his mind. So I decided to give our young judge a story that he could dine off on. And perhaps I would get an Irish coffee out of the charade. I thought of telling the dolt I was Edgar Allan Poe, but that was probably the only horror he would know—at least well enough to know as dead. Lovecraft flickered through my mind, but I decided that if he did not know Lovecraft, I would despise him even more. Then I thought of the one name that even the least well-read reader would know. I would be the Monster from Maine.

"I am Stephen King. Some of my novels have been made into films."

"Oh yes," he said. "*Blair Witch*."

"My favorite," I agreed.

"This is so great my cousin loves that kind of crap. Anyway, I have an odd request of you."

I was considering my Kinsey rating in regards this fellow. Hmm. No real interest.

The judge said: "I would like your doodle."

"Pardon?"

"I would like your doodle. You see I collect doodles from interesting people."

Few could deny the author of Blair Witch was interesting. Not to mention *Scarrie*, *Skeleton Brew*, *Salem's Slut* or my novel of extraterrestrial doorbell horror *Tom's Knockers*.

"How did you begin your collection?"

"I began collecting in High School. I sat behind Buzz Aldrin at a MacDonald's and saw him sketching something. When he got up to go the john, I must admit I took it. Afterward I have been a bit more ethical and asked for my specimens."

I wondered if Mr. Aldrin was as much of astronaut as I was a Maine-based bestseller.

At this point one of the further tables had finished with their cheesecake and Death-by-Chocolates and were going to the door. We had a mummy, Alex from *A Clockwork Orange*, Cruella DeVille and a Raven.

"What's with Big Bird over there?" Mr. Mustache asked of the tall fowl from Night's Plutonian shore. Only thus and nothing more.

I answered: "A Raven from Poe's Poem."

"Didn't he marry his child cousin?" asked Mr. Hitler Mustache.

"That is such an American response. Didn't Fitzgerald drink too much? Does that make *Gatsby* not great? Didn't Burroughs shoot his wife? Shouldn't we keep *Naked Lunch* from the bookshelves? Should we get rid of *Vampires* and *City of the Night* because Rechy is a cocksucker? What about suicides like Plath?"

"I wasn't making a judgment."

"Sure, you were. That incest is your first question. We Americans are provincial. Does a German ask about Goethe's inability to keep it in his pants? No, he says Goethe was a fine writer. Poe was the beginning of something fine—Baudelaire, Lovecraft, Ewers, Ligotti, even Borges. Does Poe's drinking matter? The fact that he opened Doors matters!"

My little judge was (hopefully) feeling chagrinned. "Outside of the Law I am not well-read," he said. "Sorry, Mr. King."

"It is not your fault as much as the school system."

"Your doodle will be the only writer in my collection so far."

A depressing fact in the litany of fame.

"Are you carrying your collection with you now?"

"Oh, this." He lifted the attaché case. "No, this is work-related. My collection is at home. I have over 650 items."

"Well, perhaps I will be your 666th item."

"I dunno. I mean I guess you could be."

I started to tear my doodle from the table "cloth."

"Oh no," he said. "I standardize things now."

He opened his brief case and handed me a sheet of standard typing paper. Ah my old Nemesis—the blank page. I had a moment of anger thinking of all the times I had failed to fill those. I thought of all the pages I had filled that had never been read by anyone than me. This guy had to be kidding. I really wanted to slap his silly mustache off his ruddy face. Oh well, writers write and often we are paid for it. So I sketched my favorite doodle, the one I had drawn again and again since Tascoa High School.

I added my signature: Stephen King, Author of *The Hashslinger*

"That will be twenty dollars." I had seen that he was going to be buying me rounds of drinks and that would cover my entree and tip.

The judge looked startled. "I've never paid for a doodle."

"You approach famous people and ask them for—em art and you don't pay them? Then you what—sell it on E-bay?®"

"No. I keep everything. I have them all in my apartment."

"I don't believe you. You just spotted me, Stephen King, sitting here in this posh restaurant after World Horror Convention and thought, 'Poor trusting guy. I can enrich myself at his expense.' Some fan of his *Firestalker* will part with some shekels tonight."

"No really. I would have never thought of it." He reached for his thin shiny black wallet, probably seal skin. I was angry on Mr. King's behalf. Ok, I was angry that I didn't win the Bram Stoker Award for my story, 'The Great White Couch.' But I was angry and someone should pay. That is the American way. Nicht wahr?

He fished out a twenty, which I lay across my bill. It would be a lightweight tip. Well then, King should have been a better writer. I expected my angry young jurist to stalk away, and considered that I had obtained the better story. But the anger left his slate blue eyes and friendliness returned like the clouds leaving the moon. See that last sentence—that's a simile so you will know I was a writer before I became famous.

My young judge smiled. "I am legitimate. Would you like to see my collection?"

I had nothing to go home to. My wife was in Oregon seeing after her mother. My cats would not mind a late feeding, no television had been recorded and I had (alas) finished the new Ligotti book. Besides aren't writers (by nature) open to new experiences?

He told me his address. Judging must pay well. I drove in my Honda and he in some sleek green car, and I found the apartment.

As we past his apartment complex's fountain I decided that a wealthy judge might be a good person to have on my side. I could confess my non-Stephen Kingness in some suitable way. I tried to win Mr. Mustache back.

"I love the idea of collecting strange things," I began.

"Like what?"

"Well, I know someone that collects random ephemeras found in used books—postcards and letters, tickets and coupons."

"Really. Why?"

"He thinks that it helps him understand the book and the person who owned it. A travel book with postcards could be the sign of someone that wanted to travel and lived through the journeys of his wealthier friends."

"Or maybe he had some life circumstance, like the ailing mother your wife is caring for."

I could tell he was trying to make a connection.

With Mr. King.

You make a connection with a storyteller you get a story.

"My grandfather," I began, "was a great lover between the world wars. He lived in Weimar, which was the height of depravity and one of his great boast was that he was the lover of certain Fraulein Liebenzufrei, of the musical theater. One day he had succeeded in seducing her maid as well and little Suzanne told him that her mistress had a secret obsession. She collected buttons. One from each lover. Would my grandfather like to see? But of course. And there they were. Hundreds. Some from waiters' frocks and some from privates, some with seven and nine pointed crowns, some from generals and some from ministers. When my grandfather saw his own tiny red button, he realized that he was not the great lover, certainly not one of the few who scaled the Matterhorn. He packed the next day, placing his hopes of being Hemingway or even Seabrook in his carpetbag. He returned to Doublesign, Texas and one wife and mediocrity."

"I thought your family came from Maine."

"Of course, his son Malcolm X. King moved to Maine. You know when he was there, he sent a telegraph to granddad. 'I've got a girlfriend in Maine.' And Granddad telegraphed back, 'Bangor?' and dad answered with, 'Heck, No, I hardly know her.' "

His laughter was polite, judicial even.

Soon I sat on his new lazy boy recliner while the judge provided me with volume after volume of doodles. If they came from whom they purported to come from he had an interesting selection. But then I was Stephen King.

Since it was Austin, Texas—there were many musicians, a handful of artists, some academics and (I saw with the grim appreciation of a horror writer) many Texan criminals that had died by lethal injection or electrocution. Texas puts more humans to death than any other state, and some wag has said that we have an electric couch rather than an electric chair. I was thinking of a story to sell about Judge Mustache. Hmm, "Hitler Mustache and his Crate of Doodles." Since it was still fantasy stage writing, I was seeing it on the cover of the *Texas Monthly*, in the real world it would be in the back pages of the *Austin Chronicle*.

He pulled on surgical gloves to handle his collection. I loved the mad light in his eyes as he gathered his great black binders. If only I could be truly obsessed I would have done so much better in my career. My ADHD keeps me writing short stories, my need for creature comforts keeps me busy with minor commercial writing. If only, I prayed to Thasaidon, Lord of the Seven Hells, if I could be as obsessed as this jerk. As soon as I made my wish, one of the fluorescents in his kitchen flickered and went. Had the great Dark One made a wish and blown out my candle?

I don't know if it was my days of low sleep, the novel situation or simply my own brilliance, but I begin to notice patterns. Maybe it was paraphrenia; I had been drinking lots of Dr. Pepper at the convention. (Go ahead Google it, I'll wait.)

"I can tell which of these came from evil or interesting humans and which came from virtuous but boring humans," I said.

"What do you mean?"

"There are some patterns. It is in the curves and the angles, but get some unlabeled samples, so I can see if I am right."

"I have never seen a pattern."

"That is because you read too little horror fiction. I will extend your education—if I am right. Damn Belknapius was right! Who would have guessed?"

"What's a——"

"If you say 'What is a Belknapius?' at such an important moment I shall know you for a triple fool. I am about to hand you a technique that could clearly tell the morons of your profession who to hang and whom to release. Go and gather ten samples, and let's see how well I can do."

There was an authority in my voice, a Power I had never heard. My breakthrough—if it proved correct—would change our world. And it would be mine. In fact it would make me better known than Mr. King since all humans are interested in justice (at least for other people). The very thing I had prayed for these many years—FAME—was just around the corner. Even Mr. Mustache would have some small ladling of it, more than Fifth Appellate Court would have ever fetched him.

He had taken several of his bound notebooks to his small kitchen where he was pulling sheets out of their protective plastic. He had been hurt by my use of the word "Moron"—no doubt he wanted to prove me some crank and banish me from his flat. Texan hospitality was keeping him in check. "Who are you supposed to be anyway?" he asked.

I had tired of Maxwell Edison, student of medicine. So I said: "I am Dr. Raymond, the transcendental surgeon from Arthur Machen's 'The Great God Pan'. He operates on a young woman so that she can see Reality or at least another reality. Something from there impregnates her. Her daughter is a creature of both worlds. Here she is murderer and a pervert and a sadist. In the universe next door, Helen is some horrid goddess or demoness. She is soulless, without good—because she knows a world where good and evil are as little different as two shades of green."

"A woman without a soul. That has a shivery romance to it. I can see a sort of dominatrix on steroids."

Mr. Mustache surprised me. Maybe I had misread him. Maybe he was of some heart. "Why aren't you married? I would think that a wife is an important part of the political process?"

"My two attempts at domestic bliss probably did have souls," he laughed. "Any way, Mary Lou was too countrified and I lost her for political reasons. She embarrassed me. I guess that would mark me as soulless. Belinda hated that I had this collection. She saw any free energy I had beyond my career as belonging to her by virtue of that golden band."

He had pulled his sheets out with gloved hands. He passed them to me as though they were rare works of art.

The first was a magenta crayon doodle—all made of graceful curves.

"Good," I said.

"You are right, she is an elderly museum docent beloved of thousands of Texas school children."

A Kelly green Sharpie® had traced spirals upon spirals.

"Good."

"You are correct. It came from Willie Nelson. I got after a benefit concert for the people of Bangladesh."

Orange colored pencil traced angry thunderbolts.

"Evil."

"You are right again. This was Billy Dee Jenkins, killed his wife, two kids and their dog. I think it was a German Shepard."

Someone had drawn a pyramid with cheap blue pen.

"Evil."

Mr. Mustache laughed. "I would agree with you. He's a member of the Texas school board committee. His claim to fame was almost entirely pulling references to Thomas Jefferson out of a history book. He claimed—with a straight face, mind you—that he thought Jefferson had had a bad influence on the Constitution."

So it went on. I identified child abusers and heroic social workers, evil lawyers and saintly nurses. We had done nine so far, when his amazement overcome the actions.

"How are you doing this? You haven't missed a reading. Do you know how this could change the world?"

"Frank Belknap Long wrote a story about good and evil called the 'The Hounds of Tindalos.' He imagined two sorts of time. Good/natural time is curved. It is curve of patient and good harvest. Education in youth means a happier adulthood. What you worked in the past will work again."

"That sounds lovely. Like the yin-yang symbol. But what's the other kind of time?"

I smiled my evil smile. "Angular time. The time of radical shifts, changing luck. The time where bad things can happen to good people and good things. All knowledge that fucks things up. Relativity would be radical angle from Newton, the notion of god-kings a radical angle from primitive communism, and George Washington would be an angular break from George III. People that support the good and natural order draw curves. They like the cycles and they work hard to further them. They are all structure. People that want to break the flow are the angular ones. Their doodles show that Long's intuition is right; at times the face of the Serpent is seen. They are all anti-structure."

"But George Washington was good."

"The British wouldn't have thought so. I bet if King George had collected his doodle it would have been all angles."

"Do you have any idea what we can do with this?"

"Several things come to mind from employment screening to blackmail."

"I'm not really happy with 'blackmail,' " he said.

"Oh, I was just joshing you. I wanted to be sure you were a good guy."

The young judge stared at me carefully.

"Of course, we will need more tests."

"Of course we will, but you have over six hundred samples here. We've got the database to change the world."

"I never knew that my little hobby might mean anything. I want to call Mary Lou and tell her off. The bitch. I will save the world; I mean *we* will save the world. Damn it's late, what I will do is get a beer. Do you like Shiner?"

"I would love one."

You simple-minded cretin. You will save the world. I will rule the world. The one-eyed man is king in the country of the blind.

I heard him popping the caps of a couple of bottles of beer. I took out my medical bag. Thasaidon had surely helped me pack.

"Didn't you have ten samples for me?" I asked.

"Oh, the last one is a joke. Well, it was my joke. It was your sample Mr. King."

He came in carrying two frosty beers and my sample. The moisture of the bottles was ruining my specimen. That was OK. I would need to destroy it anyway. I stood up and put my arm on his back.

"Set it down on your coffee table, let's look at it and confirm my theory."

He lay the beers down and then spread my damp sheet on the table.

A nice spiky angry line in sea green—nine acute angles tracing a demon hound without a single curve. I bet I had doodled that Hound a thousand times in my High School's study hall. He started to say something.

I hit him with my silver hammer. More than just the two hits from Paul McCartney's vaudevillian number. Bang! Bang!

Bang! Bang! Bang! Bang! Bang!

He had begun falling with the first two blows, so I had to lean in. I was glad to be wearing a costume; the blood splattered quite a bit from the last three blows. They connected well as his carcass was already lying on his gray-brown rug. I put the silver hammer back in my bag. I would throw the whole kit away. I made use of his gloves as I cleaned up his apartment, and carried the binders down to my car.

I haven't decided what to do with my great discovery. I am looking for a patent lawyer to start with. The trouble is they all think I'm mad when the first thing I ask them to do is doodle something for me.

(*zu Ehren der H.H. Ewers' Kurve 1910*)

Elegy for the Old Ones

(by Denise Dumars and Don Webb)

I have heard the chimes and flutes
Of secret places and dream spaces
That have never
Dreamt of man.

A dark breeze blows on me,
That no one else can feel.
And I smell incense lit
In honor of the dead.

They are gone, before
We even had a chance
To find them. As dead
As the poetry in poetry.
Should I sing to the bag lady
Of the Old Ones?
Can I raise my voice to the flower seller
And say, "We were not alone."?
What can I say of star winds—
Save that I smell a little brimstone
In the air today.
Or perhaps ozone from an unseen storm.

Movie Night at Phil's

ABOUT TWO YEARS after, in fact twenty-three months after the event, Phillip Saxon realized that he owed what was left of his sanity to BetaMax. When this silly thought flicked through his head he laughed for the first time since his stay at the hospital. News was even carried to Dr. Menschel that he might be getting better.

When Phil had a life, he had been a programmer and technical writer. He had the usual desirable furnishings of a life for a man of his education and intelligence. His wife Jean carried her stunning looks into her forties, even if her red hair relied on Loreal®. His red-headed daughter Susan enjoyed her second year at community college, and would have transferred to the University of Texas next year. As far as Phil knew his ginger-haired son Travis made the honor roll and lettered in track. Even his golden retriever Hawn was admired for her Frisbee catching ability. Their two-story brick façade home had a lovely xeriscaped garden, and all three family vehicles were in good shape. Life was good.

When Phil had gradated Rice University, he had only one regret. There had not been enough film classes to minor in film. Early on Phil worked with the best software for films. If you've done any editing on a professional level, you've used some of Phil's products. The guy loved movies. Foreign films, classics, noir, Westerns, Bollywood, grade Z horror—he had a place in his heart for all of it. Only one thing drove Jean crazy. Phil was a little OCD. When he got on a "kick," watch out. Phil was always on a kick. One month it had been Luis Buñuel. Jean had been horrified by the eyeball-slicing scene in *Un Chien Andalou* on day one and dismayed by the confused eroticism of *Cet obscure objet du désir* on the last day. One month it had been Godzilla films; did anyone really need to know that there were almost thirty? Jean and her children lost Phil as father and husband for two hours or more a night. But he was a kind man, a hard worker, and sometimes the movies could be fun. Phil had friends and they were all movie buffs as well. They admired his home theater. They drank his beer and ate his popcorn, and often thought to bring their own to share. Four or five nights a week, Phil watched movies. Sometimes he watched them by himself, blogging into the night.

Christmas, Father's Day, his birthdays were easy. Books on films, posters, or memorabilia. It was all good. Then Jean saw *666 Films to Scare you to Death* on Amazon. Although she dreaded that he might obsess on *all* of the films, she knew he tended to stick with directors or themes. It seemed to be a good piece of mom-engineering. She thought it would save her son.

Jean was a Texas mom of three generations of Texas moms. Worse still she was a Dallas Metroplex stay-at-home, big hair SUV Mom. This came with rules: Don't Disturb The Breadwinner. Secret Keeping Is Good. Phil and Travis hadn't really talked to each other since Travis played football at Sam Houston Middle School. Phil hadn't been a jock; he hadn't related to his son in scouts—he just did his best by having Jean buy the boy expensive gifts. God knew he hadn't any expensive stuff growing up in Doublesign, Texas.

Phil thought Travis was still in scouts, Travis thought Phil was a dickweed. Travis had been suspended twice this year from Crocket High (Go Coogs!). Once for "suspicion" of smoking pot, once for being in a fight with a Mexican boy that had "mean mugged" him. Posters for Naziesque bands covered his room, but also Jason, Freddy, Michael Myers and the *Saw* franchise. Jean thought that if her boys started watching scary movies together, the mysterious force of male bonding would take over and Phil would never need to know his boy was not heading to graduation.

At first it was failure. Phil was always very historical in his watching. "Did you know the first horror film was shot in 1896? It ran for two minutes." Breakfast conversation with Phil was seldom interesting. Jean hinted that more recent films might be something he would share with the boy. So, there was a month of Italian *giallos*. Phil didn't gain any points by trying to explain why the word for "yellow" in Italian stood for horror *cum* sex. But Travis had liked the cruelty and the outrageous sex-and-death scenes, until he figured out the plot keys. "Why is the killer always someone that wears black gloves? Why don't the police just search their houses and arrest anyone with black gloves?" Vampire movies didn't work. "Vampires are for fags." But an unexpected sub-sub genre really appealed to Travis—the Roger Corman Poe movies. There were 8 of them: *House of Usher* (1960), *The Pit and the Pendulum* (1961), *Premature Burial* (1961), *Tales of Terror*

(1962), *The Haunted Palace* (1963), *The Masque of the Red Death* (1964), *The Tomb of Ligeia* (1964) and *Edgar Allan Poe's The King In Yellow* (1966). Let's compare-and-contrast. All of the movies star Vincent Price, except for *Premature Burial*, which starred Ray Milland. Most were filmed in the US except the last three, which were shot in the UK. But what most often brings smiles to English teachers is that two of the films aren't "really" by Poe at all. *The Haunted Palace* (despite its title from Roderick Usher's poem) is a good adaptation by the great Charles Beaumont of H. P. Lovecraft's *The Case of Charles Dexter Ward*, and the last of the series *Edgar Allan Poe's The King In Yellow* was James Blish's adaptation of an obscure French play *Le roi jaune* which may have been written (according to *666*) by Lautréamont, a generally creepy French writer born in Uruguay.

Travis loved Price's portrayals of despairing nihilistic intellectual sadists. *Everything* he saw he loved. Roderick Usher's domination of his sister touched some long held fantasies. Travis came on to Susan one night and even tried to capture her in her room. A sisterly knee to the groin took care of his advances. Thank god Phil never heard about it. Jean convinced Susan that dad would not be able to handle it.

After *The Pit and the Pendulum* Travis and Cormac Jones, another "Aryan Youth" kid, had held down a black girl and made slow arcing swipes at her face with a Bowie knife. The tip got closer and closer, but never connected. The principal sent him home for three days. But Jean did see how much Travis loved to watch the movies with his dad, and in Phil's fantasy world Travis and he were bonding over the lush Technicolor sets and the costumes. Jean told her friends at the book club that her boys were finally friends. Actually, a stranger thing had occurred: each now saw a reflection of himself in the other, but as St. Paul would have it "Through a glass darkly." Phil hoped that Travis might be inspired to be an RTF major at the University of Texas. Phil could already see his son's name scrolling by in end credits. And Travis decided that his Dad was "really into it." "It" variously being DBSM, Satanism, or something vaguer and eviler for the lack of a name. This folly was best represented one night when Travis asked his dad if he owned a riding crop. Phil answered in the affirmative, thinking that Travis was getting together a list of props for a short movie, maybe some period piece on YouTube. Travis heard that mom's butt was made to grow rosy when the bitch stepped out of line.

Some of Phil's geeky programmer friends came to the screenings. Mike, Juan and Swen were totally despised by Travis. Juan for obvious reasons, since he had made the bad life choice of being born brown. Swen should be OK, but he seemed to demonstrate that even the best genes did not save you from being an absolute Tool. Travis felt a special disgust for Mike. For one thing he was losing his thinning brown hair and he had watery brown eyes that looked the color of baby crap. For another Mike was a hoarder. Much attention has come to these nearly three million Americans who can't throw anything, cluttering their houses with trash and junk and destroying their lives with the overflow of turbo-capitalism. Mike actually stank. Mike's "collection" of electronics equipment had long ago filled his shower and tub. He cleaned himself with baby wipes. Every gadget of thirty years were piled around Mike's domicile—floppy disks, laser disk players, hand-held diathermy machines, record polishers, modems, video games. His house was so full that only two chairs were clean—so Mike could only have one guest at time, not that he had any guests at all. Phil thought of Mike as a sort of reflection of himself, where he would be if he lost control of his movie madness. Travis fantasized about stealing from Mike's house but realized it would be too hard to shift through the junk.

Jean had little imagination, so she didn't see the signs of what she had started. For example, after *The Haunted Palace*, which dealt with revivification, a neighbor's calico cat had been gutted. Someone had placed Bootsy in an inverse pentagram made of salt and drain cleaner hoping to make it a sort of feline Lazarus. Jean discovered the corpse in their alley after her morning jog. She certainly suspected her son; there had been other animals' deaths, but the crack-pot alchemy meant nothing to her. Just something else to hide in the garbage. Poor Bootsy!

Getting the first seven films had been easy. *Edgar Allan Poe's King in Yellow* seems to be the only AIP film not made into DVD. So Phil's film festival lagged a few weeks. Let's look at that entry in *666 Horror Films to Scare you to Death* shall we?

Edgar Allan Poe's King in Yellow
1966. UK dir Rodger Corman, scr James Blish, starring Vincent Price, Azalea Jones, Sophia Macintyre, David Weston

The last entry in the Poe series was something of a failure. Originally shot at 126 minutes, the released version *runs* for 93 Minutes. The resulting film is so fragmented as to be literally incomprehensible. Blish was rumored to have over-sold himself as the adapter of the French play, and major plot devices were changed to reflect AIP's desire for another Poe period piece. For example, *Le roi jaune* is set on another world, but Corman had relocated the drama to 12th Century England. The play is an uneven blend of farce and tale-of-terror, like Corman's masterpiece *The Masque of the Red Death* the final moments of surprise take place in a masquerade. In a moment of poor casting Corman allowed Price to play three roles—an acting task that a Peter Sellers may be up for, but beyond the bombastic Price. Price plays the elderly King as well as two younger men. One of these is the Stranger; a figure who, like Death in *The Masque of the Red Death*, seems to obey different rules of causality than the human players. The Stranger appears in the masquerade unmasked, which for some reason horrifies the revelers. The King had chosen to announce the crucial issues of succession during the masquerade. The partygoers assume that the Stranger, because of his eerie similarity to the aged King, is some long-lost heir. The Stranger however is on a Cosmic mission related to a mysterious sigil, the Yellow Sign. The courtiers have their own plots and intrigues, which were meant to be enacted with poison and seduction during the masquerade. Into this heady stew Corman placed Price playing a third character the Phantom of Truth, who stands out among the richly colored players by his simple white tunic. The Phantom seems to hand a sheaf of parchment to some of the party goers, who become so aware of the monstrous secrets they have always held about themselves that they rush into small rooms (Suicide Chambers) and kill themselves. The audience never sees what is written on the parchment save that the character is drawn in yellow, which may be the same sigil the Stranger seeks (or owns). Azalea Jones and Sophie Macintyre play the lesbian twin sisters Camilla and Cassilda. Camilla is actively plotting to place David Weston's Aldones on the throne. Weston's is largely reprising his role in *The Masque of the Red Death*—the voice of the common man that acts as moral compass in most of Corman's films. Cassilda is a slightly deranged woman, who has read the dreaded parchment but has somehow been strong enough to deal with her own secrets. Corman directed her as sort of Ophelia—alternately lewd and mad, devastated and ecstatic. After seeing the film in its full version, Corman cut 33 minutes of film making this film even less accessible than his badly edited *The Terror*. Because of the deaths during the filming, legends persist that this is a "cursed" film, but the amazing special effect by which Corman caused three Vincent Prices to be on screen has attracted many cameramen and many theories over the years. The cast had its share of tragedy: during the shooting Sophie Macintyre (Cassilda) did kill herself in one of the Suicide Chambers—with the grim result that the cast thought she was clowning and even applauded as her blood poured out from the chamber door. The location had been plagued by major power outages, with the set going black almost every day. Price had a minor breakdown after the film and spent six months in reclusion on the Riviera. The resulting mess of a film had a brief cult following at LSD-laced Happenings during the Summer of Love. Several stories of suicides induced by the film attached themselves to it, much like the folklore of the Hungarian Suicide song 'Gloomy Sunday.' Opinion is divided if such stories were started by Corman to create interest in the failed project (*à la* William Castle) or the whole business was just part of the general Sixties Weirdness. The film ended what had been a profitable series for AIP, and marked a decline in Price's acting abilities. The only cast member to give interviews about the film was Azalea Jones who laid the blame equally on Blish's bad French and AIP cost-cutting decisions. With a certain poetic weirdness Azalea Jones was lost in a private plane near Bermuda, making her name better known to fans of the Bermuda Triangle than a Sixties gothic actress.

It is the age of the Internet. It took a month, but Phil found a copy of *Edgar Allan Poe's The King in Yellow* on E-bay. It was not hidden in the secret Vatican library, locked away in an Ivy League's library in a room of rare and forbidden tomes. It was selling for $118.00 plus shipping and handling. The seller, knowing how to work the crowd, claimed that he had not watched the film and could not be responsible for people foolish enough to do so. That had to raise the price of the tape fifty bucks. He also said that it was the 126 minute *uncut version*. Yeah right. That was the rest of the price. Phil knew he was being fooled, but damnit he had to see the movie. He didn't tell Jean of his expenditure.

Travis was more excited than his dad. "Man! Truth that makes people hurt! That's better than anything else. You can get over bruises and cuts, but you can't get over Truth." Phil saw his son's enthusiasm as being a sort of philosophical breakthrough. When

Phil had been eighteen, he had become interested in Truth. He swore off religion and went thought a month of telling the whole truth and nothing but the truth regardless of how much it hurt. The boy was a chip off the old block.

Jean was giving up on Travis. He had been removed from regular school and was due to be enrolled in a Juvenile Justice program. This would be too much to hide from Phil. The kid would wear uniforms for Christ's sake. Jean began to drink instead of going to her book club. Susan may have been assaulted about this time. She had approached her high school counselor with questions about rape and incest on behalf of a "friend."

The tape arrived.

The mysterious seller Typhonian Entertainment had also failed to mention it was Sony Beta-Max. Phil still had a regular VCR, as well as both formats of laser disk players, and every other modern way to watch a film, but the failed format of the mid-seventies was the wrong size and encoding for any of his equipment. Phil had moved on to watching the Fellini oeuvre at this point, and Travis spent a lot of time hanging out with other pale white kids in front a certain convenience store. Phil mentioned his sadness to a slightly tipsy Jean, who reminded him that Mike Stavros had every electronic device known to man in his roach-filled house.

At first Mike was unhappy at the idea of part of his collection leaving his house, but when it became clear that Phil would bring his family over to Mike's and thus expose his shameful secret, he dug the BetaMax machine out. He delivered it on his lunch hour.

Jean, Susan and Travis were home. Travis demanded that they watch the movie RIGHT NOW. Jean had argued for waiting for Phil, but Travis punched Mike's face and everyone saw the merit of his request. Jean sent Phil a text telling him to come home NOW, but because of the fickle nature of electronic communications he didn't get the text for two hours. When he got the text, he called his house. Jean, Susan and Travis didn't answer their phones. Phil left work early, something he almost never did.

He saw Mike's car in the driveway. Maybe they were arranging a screening for him. He loved his family. When he walked in he heard voices from the movie room, the big den at the back of the house. This was Phil's territory no one went there without him. He walked back expecting a yell of "Surprise!"

He heard Vincent Price exchanging lines with Vincent Price:

"The masque outlives the man, the masque outlives truth, the masque is in the reflections of the water before it is made."

As an older character he answered: "I know these things. I have spent millions of years forgetting them. I can't forget them again and my daughters are no longer the masques for each other. Blood will stain the water, but it will turn yellow in the last spring and the poets will use it as ink."

Phil rushed forward at this moment. He plunged into his media room. On the big flat screen Vincent Price was crying, Vincent Price was laughing fiendishly. Vincent Price was lying wounded with his face peeled off, and showing an emotion that Phil does not know and hasn't been able to express or explain to Dr. Menschel in two years of therapy. One woman was holding her blood-spattered twin while dawn broke over an expressionist castle. Another man stood by laughing quietly. It was Aldones playing a lyre. Then the power went out.

But he had seen by the light. Blood was pouring out of the closet and he could not see Susan. Travis was dressed in a bed sheet and had tried to peel away his face with a case cutter. He was saying something low and rapidly about truth. The sheet was red with his blood.

Jean was topless and holding a bottle of tequila uttering, "No Mask. No Mask! I have failed my husband." Mike was simply staring at the screen, a big shiner forming over his right eye. Travis launched himself at Phil and slashed him in the dark, before passing out from blood loss. Phil thinks his last words were, "My father, my king, I love you!"

The power came back on; Mike stood up and looked at Phil. "Because I love you man." He walked to his BetaMax machine and pulled the tape out and started shredding it. Phil started to stop him, and then realized that calling 911 was the correct response. Mike left the house telling Phil that he could keep the machine—he wasn't collecting anymore. A few minutes later he pulled his car in front of a speeding eighteen-wheeler. Susan had killed herself, but not before taking a sheet of computer paper and writing in yellow Sharpie® SUICIDE CHAMBER on it and taping it to the inside of the small closet just off of the home theater. Travis died of shock later in the week. Jean later recovered in a peculiar way. She can remember everything up to age twenty-three when she met Phil. She had expressed no desire to see him again.

The ambulances and police came and there were investigations and more investigations, and no could prove Phil had done anything wrong. E-bay found out that Typhonian Entertainment had ended shop—apparently having only one transaction. Dr. Menschel contacted Carlton Press and made a case for removing the entry for *Edgar Allan Poe's The King in Yellow* from *666 Films to Scare you to Death*. An indie Texas film *The Outsider's Club* featuring Sarah Postal took its place.

Phil was placed in the State Hospital in Austin Texas, and remains a few steps above catatonic and has only one irregularity as a patient.

He never goes to Movie Night.

(for Kim Newman & James Marrott)

Fall in Caracosa

That the leaves are Yellow
Is seen as an irony.
That the pumpkins are carved as masks
Is a high joke
The music sounds like bone flutes and bone charms and forgotten sex
The dance looks like an orgy, like a funeral, like solemn Mass
See! They bring the Yellow wafers
Embossed with the Sign!
See the thurible swinging as leaves blow in the roofless church
Why do they dance here?
Why are the musicians shrouded in shadows?
A dancer puts her mouth to my ear,
"I know the face the Moon makes when she thinks no one is watching."

Out of Bondage

BECAUSE OF MY seventeen years of faithful service my Masters have allowed me to begin a history of my race. After sending the workers to their jobs, I climb the long ladder to the surface. I want to visit the ruined shack of Calder the god-maker. Calder was the last god-maker. The Masters had ended the art long before Calder's time but he worked in an outlying province and escaped their attention for many years.

I hug the wall closely as a Master levitates by. Two hundred rungs to the surface. When I reach it I gasp and pant. A saarik "bird" awaits. I show it my seal and whisper my destination into its ear fronds. It leaps into the darkling air spreading its pinions at the height of the jump. I am uncomfortable in the saddle.

The Masters wish to study Calder, to study all dissidents. They hope my history will explain why my race has never been tractable despite their careful breeding. Still I am worried by the task—if I show any sympathy for the rebellious my brains may be the next feast. They eat our brains and suck away our souls. If they love us, they postpone their feasts for long years.

The saarik flies quickly now. The ground below is blurred. Soon I will be at Calder's godworks. The dim red light of dawn appears. The saarik descends.

Nothing remains of the hut. The sandstone quarry behind is full of broken idols. Some have the rough unfinished look of the gods the Masters worship. Others airmen or women or beasts or combinations. Why did Calder carve these? Why were work tokens painfully saved for the idols? I spot a small round gray stone partially buried in the mud. Vague characters, in a tongue unknown to me, cover the surface. I free it from the mud. I like its surface, its feel in my hands. I drop it in my belt pouch and begin making the sketches trying to envision the godworks as it was in Calder's day.

The saarik becomes uneasy in the red light of day. It mews piteously. I finish my sketches and mount the bird, allowing it to speed me back to Nightside.

A Master is feeding. I dismount. I look for the chimney-ladder ignoring the sucking sound. It stands upright discarding the woman's body, which has gained a third eye in death—a bloody hole through which both brain and soul have been sucked away.

"Halt."

I stop.

"Did you find anything at the godworks?"

"No." Then I remember the round stone but say: "No. Nothing at all." It is the first time in seventeen years I have lied to the Masters. I do not know why. I brave myself for the pain. The Master turns and walks away. I find the chimney-ladder and descend.

* * * * *

"Ah, it's Zatar the Collaborator."

Sula, my mate, enters the chamber. Her hair is red; her eyes are full of loathing. She works the surface fields. I say nothing. I put down my pen and embrace her. Stone is more yielding. We mate at the Masters commands.

"What's that?" She gestures at the stone sphere from the godworks.

"A souvenir from Calder's."

"Do they know you have it?"

This frightens me. I can suspect anyone of betrayal.

"No."

Sula looks at me with the tiniest of smiles. She tilts her head and asks, "No?"

"No."

She walks to the slab and lifts the stone from the pilaf parchment. She examines it from every angle. I tremble with fear and desire. She sets the stone down gently. She takes my hand. She is beautiful, the only beautiful thing on Nightside.

Later in the evening—just before sleep, I look at the stone. Red glowing characters crawl over it like fireworms on coals. Perhaps it is only a dream. I sleep.

* * * * *

Four hours later a messenger wakes me. Sula curses softly in the darkness. One of the Masters wishes to speak to me. They never sleep. I am used to such summons. In the spherical dark chamber the Master stands. The walls focus their thoughts here; they are more powerful, more terrible than anywhere else.

I stand. Humans may not speak until spoken to. Its three-fingered hand toys with the gray hair at my temples. A gentle almost playful touch to remind me that few of my species live to have gray hair. It too is old for its kind. Its skin slime is drying, its eyes turning the color of parchment.

"We have decided your history is unnecessary."

"I have worked on the history for twelve cycles."

"We have other work for you."

"May I work on the history during my rest periods?"

"No."

I wait for dismissal.

"You may rest tomorrow while waiting for a new assignment. You may go."

Sula is asleep when I return. I do not wake her. Someone has removed all of my parchment. The stone remains.

* * * * *

On the next day when all are away the stone speaks.

"I have chosen you Zatar to liberate my people. I am Strav the God of your fathers."

My mind has finally broken. I've been near the Masters too long.

"No Zatar. I am Strav. I will change you. I will make you Zatar the Liberator."

"At what cost?"

"Merely to revenge the race you call Masters."

"Why me?"

"There is little time and many probabilities to arrange. I am Strav. I will begin."

A bolt of bright light—brighter than anything I've ever seen—pierces my skull. I hear my blood boiling. All becomes dark.

* * * * *

"We have decided to make you foreman of the water works."

The aged Master has summoned me again.

"I know nothing of construction."

"We will implant the knowledge you need. Your emblem of office." It hands me an ironwood staff topped with stone tentacles.

* * * * *

The work is hard. The Masters wish us to divert a surface river to an underground reservoir. The saariks move the larger stones after the humans chip them free. The saariks are stupid. Sometimes there are accidents. Sula was among the workers assigned to me. I've put her among the earth carriers which seems the safest job.

Every quarter cycle a Master will make an inspection. The dim red light of the sun pains them.

"You've done well, Zatar. You are ahead of schedule."

"The expertise implanted in me has done well." I bow.

"I hunger. I shall take one of your lesser workers. You have no need of so many."

The Master advances on the earth carriers. He stops one with his mind. It is Sula.

"No!" I yell. The Master almost hesitates, then reaches his tentacles toward her face. Something hot, something strong shoots from between my eyes. It reaches into the Master's skull. There is surprise—then the Master pushes back. I push harder. I ram myself into his mind. I burn. The Master falls.

Hot lead is dripping into my skull from a thousand places. With difficulty I say: "The aged Master has died. Help me carry him to those below." Everyone looks at me with fear. Two of the earth-movers help me with the body. Sula runs away whimpering.

* * * * *

I've been given a small ruined tower to live in while I direct the water project. Every quarter cycle I'm permitted a rest day. The workers rest every half-cycle.

Each day I stare at the stone willing Strav to speak—to explain. Today my meditations are interrupted. A young stone chipper Teth walks into my study and kowtows.

"I've waited to speak to you. I want to tell you my plan. I saw you save the woman Sula."

"What plan?"

"I have found a weapon that will end our slavery."

"What weapon?"

"This." He pulls a small intensely glowing crystal from a leather pouch. "I have found a large cache of these."

"Why tell me?"

"Because you are different. Because you have powers."

"I have no powers."

"I saw. You saved Sula."

"I saved no one. The Master was old. It died because of strain."

"No. You——"

"I nothing. Go away. Enjoy your rest day. Be mindful of your yoke."

His excitement changes to fear.

"You'll turn me in."

"I don't know. Go away."

He turns to go. I extend my mind sharp as a knife. I find the memory of the glowing stones. I cut it from its matrix and absorb it. Then I plant other memories. Slowly, leadenly he drops the crystal.

The next day I tell the Masters that Teth has been stealing tools. They find his mind full of thoughts of rebellion but no memories of me or of the crystals. Still the stone says nothing.

Sula comes to the tower that night. The words day and night are from the Masters. They say the world once spun but they stopped it. Perhaps it made them giddy. My new thoughts and abilities make me giddy. We share food and small talk. Finally she speaks: "The people are afraid of you."

"No, they are afraid of that." I point at my staff of office.

"No. They are afraid of you. They saw you battle the Master. Word spread that the Redeemer had come. But you do nothing. Today you betrayed Teth to them. We do not know what you are."

"But you came?"

"I came because I am grateful for my life. I came because I am your mate by their order. I came because I am curious."

"Do you think I am the Redeemer?"

"I—I don't know. You have no imagination, no rebellion. You've worked more willingly with them than anyone. You carry their symbols. If you rebel you rebel because of Higher Orders. If Something has taken an interest in us—we may have a chance."

Her words stung. Hadn't I risked my life to save her? I said: "Go among the people. Tell them I am their Liberator. Bring their leaders to me the next rest day."

Sula stared at me. Many emotions played across her face.

"Go. Go now."

She left. I pounded the stone against the wall ordering it to speak.

* * * * *

The next few days changed the attitude of the people. They looked at me with love, with awe, with worship. They even smiled at me when I had them flogged. They worked very hard. I feared the Masters would notice the change—smell the love in the mental atmosphere.

Only Mularz, chief stone worker, hated me. He hated me for Teth's betrayal. It was an excellent hate rising like convection waves from an oven. When Sula had gathered the people for the meeting, I was surprised to find Mularz among them.

* * * * *

"I am come to lead you out of bondage."

Some of them believe, some are ready to believe, a few want to kill me lest I bring more trouble into their brief lives than they can stand.

"I will arm you with these."

I pull out a crystal. They gasp at its brightness. Mularz burns with rage; he knows.

"Bright light doesn't matter when the Masters can drop a ton of stone on you." One of stonecutters (not Mularz) says:

"You mean like this?"

I lift a boulder with my mind and drop it. I catch it inches above the stone cutter's head.

"You might have a chance, but what about us?" Mularz has finally spoken.

"I will awaken this power in you. We are days ahead of schedule. The stone cutters may mine the crystals in quantity. On the day that the river is to be diverted the——"

I pause before I can say the forbidden words—even now, even here they have a hold on me.

"—the Masters will cause a local darkness and travel here to inspect the water works. I Zatar will strike the first blow."

I can feel hope—that most forbidden of human feelings—everywhere around me.

"Awaken the power in me first," Mularz says.

"No, me. I was the first to be saved by it."

Everyone rushes toward me.

"Back. Mularz and Sula first."

They approach. They kneel before me. I put my palms on their foreheads. I hope my body knows what it's doing. Something warm, bright, dry pours from me into them. The rest of the people come pair by pair. When they leave, they look knowledgeable and confident. I try to lift the boulder again. It doesn't stir. I faint.

When I come to, I grab the stone and throw it as hard as I can against the tower wall. It shatters. A thin splinter of stone embeds itself in my chest. I pick up the pieces—it was a simple calcite-encrusted geode.

I pull the splinter from my chest.

Light, not blood, streams out. It gathers into a small bright ball.

"No, Zatar, I do not dwell in the stone but in Zatar. I also dwell in the others mainly in Sula and Mularz."

"Why?"

"Revenge. I used to rule the race you call the Masters. They exorcised me. I gave them their powers of mind and magic in exchange for the terrible darkness of their desires. They drove me out, I made Calder dream of me. I will destroy them and live in the horrible dreams of torments sublime of humankind."

"Why haven't you spoken till now?"

"I do not need to speak—merely to act."

"Will we overthrow the Masters?"

"Of course not. They're a cowardly race. When you revolt they'll flee to their home world. I'll open a passage and you'll lead your people to safety in another place and time. When you are strong enough, I'll permit you to encounter the Masters again. Then we'll destroy them."

"Where will you be till then?"

"In your hearts and minds. I am Strav the Burrower. I will teach you new arts—Magic and Warfare. Those who open themselves completely to me I will give long life and great power."

"Magic?"

"You'll learn. Or your descendants will."

The light pours back into my chest. I can feel with my mind and it is as different from us as the Masters are.

* * * * *

Over a hundred of the Masters come when the skies darkened. As overseer I share the dais with their leaders. The oldest Master broadcasts a speech to his fellows. I can feel the alien trickle of its words. I raise my staff of office and bring it down firmly on the Master's head. My people flood the area with light. The air boils with mental energy. We kill 25-30 before they even realize what has happened.

I raise my staff and yell orders to the saariks. They've obeyed for cycles, they drop stones on the Masters. The air smells of their ichor.

Soon the Masters vanish walking to another world. We've lost only a fourth of our own. The light moves within me. I draw a line of light with my staff. The line hangs in the air. I discard the staff and wedge my fingers into the glowing crack. I tear it open revealing a glowing gray nothingness. I step in. My people follow.

New senses open. I can feel directions for time and/or—?—. I sense the path. I will our way. There is great pressure, we are flattened, made to a wedge of will. After an eternity we pierce our way back into space-time. We're on a rocky desert with a big brassy world. Sula and Mularz send out search parties. We will need food and water. I am exhausted. I sleep.

Sula wakes me.

"You must go from here."

"Why?"

"We have found no food, no water. The people think they'll die. You must find food. They blame you."

Mularz stands behind her, worried and angry.

"I am very weak."

"You must go."

I leave avoiding the people. I hear babies crying. I hear my name cursed. I hear people calling the old Masters begging for a return to their former lives.

When I break free from the huddled masses I run. I run until I can hear no more. I find a small cave on a hillside. Perhaps I enter. I draw my knife and slice upon my chest.

Light flows out.

"An amazing thing has happened, Zatar. A new phase of my life cycle. Live and learn, eh, Zatar?"

"Why are we here? Why are we starving?"

"The human mind is much richer than the Masters'. So much energy. It's triggered a mitosis."

He has ignored my question; now I know something is very wrong. I try asking him again.

"If we don't get water soon we'll die and you won't have your revenge."

"I'm dividing. Soon they'll be two of me. Of course since we have the same food-base we'll be enemies."

"What are you talking about?"

"Reproduction. I'm going to be a father or a son."

"Congratulations. What do we do in the meantime—eat rock and drink air?"

"After my division each of me will lead your people to a place they can feed."

"Each?"

"Yes. I'm developing two centers. One in Sula. One in Mularz. They're really much more forceful personalities than you are. Soon the two groups will be fighting. Nothing like heresy to get the emotional energies really going. Of course my two offspring will see each other arrivals—so they'll be no compromises ever. That's the way of gods, Zatar, we're good shepherds, fattening up our sheep."

"I'll stop this now, I'll warn them."

"Think, Zatar. Right now your people are really missing the food their brain sucking masters used to provide. They're blaming you for their loss. You go down there now, they'll slay you for food. They don't believe yet. Your masters believed because they knew it was me. They thought they had eliminated Strav, when they had introduced atheism to your people, but I merely slept. They'll find another race to enslave, one a little more docile; although it's hard to believe that's there is a race as docile as humankind."

"Why should Sula and Mularz fight? I'll keep them together against you. Their love for me and their love for the people will keep them allied."

"I'll appear to each of them of course. Each will get a different revelation. Their love for you and their love for the people is just what I'll use to separate them. But don't fear Zatar, I have a place for you. Even as the two races will live on other dimensions—fighting each other across the expanses of time—you will be remembered. I'll make you a Saint. You found me by seeking after the mysteries of Calder, so what is about to happen should amuse you."

I start running from the cave to warn (perhaps with my dying words) my people. But everything slows. The air grows intolerably thick, and my legs weigh as much as the stone slabs we used to move for our Masters. My heart stops beating. I can feel air becoming jelly and then stone in my lungs. I can feel stone forming in my blood, stone replacing the urgency of life. Ironically, I adopt a heroic pose, just before Strav's magic makes me into a statue.

I know not how stone eyes see, stone ears hear, a stone brain thinks, a stone heart feels—yet all of these things come to pass. I see the ball of light called Strav split into two lights which sped past my view.

Later I hear Mularz's voice outside of the cave.

"The god has told me that he has gathered Zatar up to his eternal service. All we must do is find and worship Zatar's material form, and we will be rewarded with food and riches. The god has revealed to me that the sacred relic is within a cave on the hill."

Mularz leads his people into my cave. They kneel before me and praise Strav, god of our fathers, and me, Zatar the Liberator, proclaimer of Starv's might. Although they are weak and trembling with hunger, they begin carrying me down the hillside.

Sula and twenty or so wait at the base of the hill. She cries out: "See it is as I told you!" Sula's band begins tossing rocks and crude spears. Mularz's group drops me, and I found that stone flesh does not feel pain even when it is cracked.

* * * * *

Sula won that first skirmish. Later she kissed my stone lips and promised her undying love for me. She led about half of our people to a planet with sun and life and endless riches. A temple was built around me, and incense burned in my honor; although stone nostrils do not smell its sweetness. I watched Sula grow old and die, and I believe that every day she loved me more. She was buried in a crypt beneath my holy self.

Decades went by and there was a raid led by Mularz's son, and I was taken to a strange world of dying seas and an orange sky. My right arm was broken off but glued back.

Since then I have looked upon followers in crowded cathedrals, been hidden away in darkened shrines, carted off in spaceships, been in dimensions so strange to me that I could not even perceive the nature of my worshipers. I am sure Strav has split time and again over the hundreds of years. There are not heresies and orthodoxies and cults and sects—each feeding a different god—each believing that there is only one god. I am sacred to most of them, but others view me as a criminal. Once one of the old masters visited one of my shrines and performed obeisance to me. I do not know if this was a jest, or if they too succumbed to religion with the passing of the years.

Once for a long time I was in a gallery with other saints, some human, some not and I wondered if they were but cold stone—or like me that victim of a god. But I never knew since stone lips may not speak.

(for Gary E. Gygax)

The Phantom of Truth

In 1927 an obscure French surrealist in his cheap garret on the Rue d'Dragon

Wrote a poem by pulling words from a hat.

It was called "The Phantom of Truth."

He had cut up two newspapers and a book of Black Magic (said to be Uruguayan).

At first read it seemed to make fun of the Lindberg flight,

At second read it seemed to have really naughty sexual puns,

But at third read you got it.

It gave the reader a thought he could not ignore.

It stopped other reading, eating, fucking, sleeping.

It stopped thinking about anything else.

It had to be whispered to your dearest friend

Your most despised enemy

Your closest blood relative.

The poet hung himself thirteen days afterward.

After he had printed twenty-six copies

And plastered them on bridges and statues.

A plague of suicides followed.

The French government hired a handful of foreigners to track down and destroy every copy.

Then they were quizzed to be sure they could not even remember the letters,

Lest they gave them to a French speaker.

Yesterday I found the remaining copy my great-grandfather brought back to Boston.

My French is good. I made my translation.

And before I left,

I made my FaceBook page.

Like Comment Share

SO, TWO YEARS after my last friend had done so, I finally joined Facebook. Hey, I'm in IT, the last thing I want to see any more of is glowing screens. My wife had lots of useful advice: don't play the games, they're a time-suck, don't friend people you don't at least know; don't share every political or cute cat meme that comes along. I stuck by her rules for three days (:

Ok, at first I played a few games—those What Dr. Who companion are you? (Sarah Jane Smith). Which literary figure are you? (Leopold Bloom). And I started getting "Friend" requests from friends of friends of friends. And how could I not repost that picture of a black and white cat on a skateboard? I mean that's just too damn cute. So suddenly I had 332 friends. Then I got a request from Xulthan. I didn't know Xulthan, I figured he was some gaming geek I had known once. And Xulthan added me to a group "The Green God Game." I hate it when they add you to groups without asking you.

Xulthan posted a video link.

It was the strangest music I ever heard—vaguely Middle Eastern with songs in some language I couldn't place. I had been in Kuwait during Operation Desert Storm and could pick out Arabic. Maybe this was Yezidi or Martian. But it made the hairs on the back of my neck stick up when I listened. The video feed was pages and pages of parchment written in an alphabet unknown to me. I figured it was clues for the game, so I studied them closely. But nothing clicked. Except I did start dreaming about them. I would be walking in my neighborhood and all the shops would have signs in the weird script, for example.

Then the first game. Answer this riddle or agree to pay the consequences. "You are asleep in your home. It's 3:33 in the early morning. Someone is knocking at your front door, someone is knocking at your back door. Someone is knocking at your side window. What do you open first?" I put down window, I thought that seemed more like what a friend would do. WRONG—you open your eyes! Consequence I was supposed to wear a green shirt on Wednesday. I'm a good sport—I did. I saw three men and two women wearing green in the lunchroom. Three of them had already chosen a table. I walked over and said: "Green God Game?" They said yes and I joined them. The others drifted over. Then one man's phone rang. He had been texted:

> "READ THIS TO THE GGG. Welcome. The Green God smiles upon you! Soon your luck will increase if you continue meeting. Hour of the Green Ray. Day of Hermes-Yog. Year of the City 10,347, 666. So It is done!"

"Cool!" said one of the women—youngish freckled with red-brown hair. "It's an ARG!"

"What's an ARG?" asked Thomas Martinez.

I explained. "An Alternate Reality Game. The gamers are fed clues to solve a mystery. It usually ends in them participating in or witnessing a flash mob."

The older Chinese looking woman said: "That's one of those spontaneous get togethers? I've seen that on YouTube."

So we talked about ARGs, and Flash Mobs, and Facebook, and our history with computers. Mr. Martinez was the oldest among us —he had actually bought an Altair 8800 back in 1975. We talked about performance art. Bill Nadis' most far-out art experience was seeing the Trans-Siberian Orchestra's 'The Lost Christmas Eve' with his wife a couple of years ago. Suzi Machworter, the red head, had on the other hand been nude canvas at a Dallas Museum of Art show. An artist had painted an Aztec style painting on her naked body, and then invited members of the audience to cover her in black paint until his art was erased. We shared e-mail and FB stats and what part of the company we were from. Then we went back to our cubicles, except for Calvin Lee, the young black guy with the wimpy mustache who worked in Transpiration fixing vans.

As fate would have it I ran into Calvin next Saturday. We were both eating at Taco Taco. He saw me and motioned me to join him in line. At Taco Taco you get to shoot dice when you pay for your bill. If the dice come up Taco Taco (tacos had replaced the one spot), you won a free lunch. A one in thirty-six shot. Calvin rolled. Taco Taco. Then I rolled Taco Taco.

"Hey," said Calvin. "May it's the Green god. The odds must be thousands to one against that happening."

"1296 to 1," I said. "Pretty cool. Maybe we should play that Lotto toady.'

We had lunch, shared our life stories. I did but Lotto tickets later, but no dice. That night Xulthan posted his status.

"Look to the northeast quadrant of the sky five minutes after midnight. A wonder shall appear. Say these words: 'Zodicare Yog Sehresh!' and the Green God shall Hear you."

I didn't intend to say anything, but it was a warm night and Sally and I sat on our lawn chairs, smoked a little weed and watched the sky.

Right on time, a beautiful green meteor flared across the sky.

"Say it! Say it!" squealed my wife.

"Zodicare Yog Sehresh!"—but I was dubious about pronunciation.

Next Monday we all wore our shirts. No one had told us to. We were all excited. Then Calvin told about free tacos. Then Suzi told us that she and Mrs. Wong had met at a convenience store and dared each other to buy scratch off tickets. Suzi won $75 and Mrs. Wong $100. Then they bought several more tickets and lost each time.

"So," I said. "How many of you said the magic words after the meteor flared forth?"

Everyone put their hands up. They had different expressions—Mr. Martinez looked ashamed, Mrs. Wong religious, Suzi ecstatic. Clarence grim—maybe even paranoid. Nadis embarrassed.

"Whoever is playing us is doing pretty good."

There was some nervous laughter, and then my phone rang. A text from *#xulahanrises*.

> Priest Jough El Ayin has passed the boundary. Two Powers are seen. Eat no meat this night and you will see Ool Athag.

"What the fuck does that mean?" asked Nadis.

"It means eat fish like during Lent," said Mr. Martinez.

"This is fucked," said Nadis. "I don't like being made a fool of."

Suzi said: "No one's making a fool of you. It's just a game. You're just mad because you didn't win any money. Come on over to the Sac-n-Pac and I'll buy you a scratch-off. It will be fun."

Nadis was a balding single guy in his late thirties. He wasn't about to turn down being with a pretty girl. They rest of us went back to work, Pete Nunio made dirty jokes all the way back to our pod.

Oddly enough my wife had bought beer battered fish sticks for dinner that night, so I didn't have to make any decision about what to eat.

That night I dreamed a vast city, whose architecture was some fantastic blend of Angkor Wat and Giger prints—with a little Escher thrown in. The city was filled with strange looking men and women that wore glittering metal masks. At dusk beneath two huge moons, we gathered at a great pit outside the city. A bright crimson ray came from the depths, and the people moaned in ecstasy. Then two green arms—hundreds of meters long—shot out of the pit. They fastened on an older man who carried a staff. They seized him, lifted him high in the air, and then pulled him down into the pit. His mask fell off as he descended. He looked like Thomas Martinez. Then people began dancing and embracing. It turned into an orgy. I rutted with a half-woman, half-goat. I saw Suzi nearby being taken by two hairy apelike men at the same time. The air smelled of blood and cinnamon. Music—the music from the video—played.

I awoke aroused and tried to get my wife into it. But it was nearly time for the alarm to go off and she said: "Honey it's a workday. We'll do this on the weekend, when we can get into it." I let her go back to sleep and took care of myself. At the moment of orgasm, I almost always make a little noise. This time I said a word, "Sehresh!" I don't know why, and it scared me. But enough to keep me from drifting back to sleep.

The next morning when I logged in at work, there was e-mail from Nadis inviting all of us to lunch at the Star of India across the street.

We showed up (except for Martinez). Nadis had won $1000.00 on a scratch-off game.

"It's all true!" he said.

We made a date to go buy tickets *en mass*e that night.

Suzi was texted from *#xulthanisrisen*:

The time of Exchange is over. Priest Jough El Ayin has transitioned to your space and time. The Green God Games starts on the day of Hermes-Yog at the hour of the Cerise Ray. Odo kikale Nafatagn!

"That's helpful. Where's Martinez?" asked Calvin.

"What did you have for dinner last night, Calvin?" I asked.

"Big Mac and fries. Why?"

"No dreams?" I asked.

"Why? You mean that bullshit about don't eat meat? Why did you have a dream?"

We are looked at each other, our naan and curries getting cold.

"What's this got to do with Martinez?" asked Calvin. "You guys are serious bullshitters."

Calvin grabbed his cream colored I-phone and called Martinez. No results. Then Martinez' supervisor.

"He didn't come into work today. What do you bullshitters know?"

We stared at our food. Suzi and Nadis blushed.

"You guys are seriously fucked up. I ain't playin'."

Calvin got up to leave. Mrs. Wong said: "Sit down Calvin. You are playing because it's how we will get rich. Sit down. Martinez was taken because he stood too close to something dangerous. This won't be our fate."

"What do you mean 'taken'? Taken where? By whom?"

Nadis said: "The God of the Pit, the motherfather of the Green God."

Pete Nunio asked: "What?"

Nadis said: "Look, there's a text on Scribd. Google *The Seven Rays of Ool Othag*. Suzi and I found it this morning."

"Over breakfast?" I asked.

"Over none of your damn business. If you want to play a game. You better know the rules."

Lunch proceeded fairly quietly. We trotted back to our cubicles. I downloaded *The Seven Rays*. But I didn't have time to read it. My boss piled it on that afternoon. None of us knew Martinez outside of the game. Well we were all Facebook friends, which meant we occasionally told each other when we made a road trip, saw a cute cat video, or passed on vaguely liberal political memes. Everyone but Calvin showed up after work and walked in mass to the Sac-n-Pac and bought tickets and more tickets and won nothing.

"The Time of Exchange is Over," said Suzi.

"So when's the Hour of the Cerise Ray? That's like orange right?"

Suzi said: "At sunset comes the Cerise Ray down from the ruined Planet searching for its Opposite among the Hornless Ones. The unity being made in the Red Ceremony magic, all is balanced.

Life for Death, death for life, and the Daemons sleep in the Sixth Angle until the forces need be equalized again."

"What the fuck does that mean?" I asked.

"We need to get together at sunset on Wednesday. Day after tomorrow. We'll play a game."

"So is this ARG? Is Martinez spoofing us? Or is this about life and death?" asked Pete.

Mrs. Wong answered. "It's a game. It's Facebook. And it may be life and death. My aunt choked to death on a Mah-jong tile. Death is never far away. Thousands die each hour, each minute."

"You guys are so much fun to hang out with," I said. "As a game I'm not very amused."

I went home, said nothing to my wife, and when I saw the Xulthan had posted twice did not read them.

That morning I did not read them.

That night I clicked on the two links. Clicking wasn't playing.

The first was a recently posted, very amateur shot of a boy being born. Parents looked normal. No occult significance. I always think the miracle of life looks a little gross on video. The second video looked very professional. A camera snakes through what appears to be a Stonehenge style ruin at night. Desert all around, three circles of stone. Great and spooky flute playing in the background. The camera rests on the center stone. It's the right size for a living room couch. I guess it might be an altar stone. The camera zooms in and we see a glyph carved in the gray-green stone. Simple, geometrical. Yet somehow it makes me fearful. Yet I watch the video 7 times in a row until my wife calls me to bed, calling herself a "Facebook widow." Nice one, Mary, real supportive. I start to tell her about the Green God Game, but realize how stupid and paranoid it sounds.

I spend thirty minutes getting dressed the next day. I am up and out before my wife. It usually takes fifteen minutes to dress, shave and grab a packet of PopTarts. Should I wear a green shirt? Should I send a fuck-off? Is this a game that will end in a filmed scene, fifteen minutes of YouTube fame and prizes? Is this an eldritch breaking into our world in a soft spot? What happens after a hundred years of monster movies, plush Cthulhu dolls, and prank spooky e-mails? When does the barrier that our ancestors' ancestors had so carefully set-up finally wear away? How many people had been like my great-grandmother who really said: "Speak not of the devil lest he appear?"

Fuck it. It was the day of Hermes Yog, so I wore a "Kiss Me I'm Irish" t-shirt. Let the Green God deal with that.

We gathered at lunch. Even Calvin. We had worn green, although in Calvin's case he had chosen a clip-on bow tie. Nadis and Suzi looked high on love, Mrs. Wong was prim and serious in a green dress that was the height of fashion twenty years ago. Pete Nunio looked younger than his 28 years. In his green and white dress shirt I would've thought he was an intern reporting on his first day. We ate at Ruby's barbecue, because we needed to get away from work and it was an eight-minute drive.

"So?" I asked. "Are we going through with it?"

"With what?" asked Pete. "All we heard was that the game took place at the time of the tangerine or something. They didn't tell us to gather anywhere."

"The hour of the Cerise Ray," said Suzi.

Nadis said: "All of you guys aren't thinking this through. There isn't a 'them' or a 'he' or an 'it'—somebody here is running a little game."

I said: "I thought of that. Could one of them rig the lottery?"

"Maybe that was chance," said Pete.

"No. I think we were Chosen," said Mrs. Wong. "It is like that Shirley Jackson story we all read in High School. 'The Lottery.' "

I asked: "What about Martinez?"

Clarence said: "I went by his house. He lives on the east side in a little house that used to belong to his parents. The lights were off. I knocked and rang the bell and shouted till the neighbors came out."

Suzi said: "Fred and I will be in the big truck bay by the north building at 6:35 that's sunset. Come if you want or not. It will be empty, it's Wednesday night and all of those trucks are making deliveries until about midnight, right Calvin?"

Calvin said: "Yeah that's right. It's unlocked because folks need to park their vans and trucks. It's got a break room."

"Great," I said. "We can meet the dread Green God with a coke."

Calvin followed me back to my cubicle after lunch. He was scared—possibly more scared because he had not dreamt of Martinez. He wanted to know that I really had. He wanted to know if he was being fooled.

"Look, I don't know what to tell you. I feel we're all taking part in a ritual. Not as the players, not as the Priest on stage, but just the folks in the audience. They people that stand up, sit down kneel."

"But those people feel good when it's over," said Calvin.

"We might also."

He hung around for an hour. Twice my boss had walked by. I finally told him to beat it. His last words to me were that he was not going to be at the truck dock. I told him that I would probably bow out as well.

So he waved pretty sheepishly when I met him at the door of the dock at 6:20. Suzi and Nadis were there, and Mrs. Wong. Pete held out until 6:33.

Suzi and Fred had chalked a diagram on the floor—looking a little like a hopscotch board in seven colors. At one end it was broad and orange colored. Cerise. Whatever. At the other end it was narrow and green. At the narrow end stood a rack with chains and winches and hooks for lifting engines out of vans. It was terribly suggestive. Suzi had printed out the *The Seven Rays of Ool Athag* and bound them into a green cardboard notebook. She read her lines.

"Welcome worthy players. As before so now. The gods molt and break free of their larval shells. They teach us how to run and dance and scream. The real world breaks into the world of mirrors. Hear the mirrors breaking! Hear the drums of Ia Nath Thool!"

At that moment all of our phones buzzed, rang or played music. We opened or activated them, fussed for a moment to remember how to work the loud speaker setting. Drumming filled the air. An odd time signature. Dave Brubeck would have been pleased. Clarence hopped up the diagram as though it were hopscotch.

"Not like that," said Mrs. Wong. "Remember the video."

And that was when I realized that we hadn't all seen the same clips. We had been subtly prepared for different roles. Clarence looked ashamed and said: "Show me Simlisell."

Mrs. Wong bowed, and suddenly did not seem like a frail old woman that worked in Marketing. Suddenly she seemed wise and menacing. She stepped through the seven tiers, striking a pose at each. Her poses were like Egyptian hieroglyphs. She was living letters—or rather words! At the last tier, with its deep hunter's green, she struck a pose that reminded me of the glyph on the altar stone. The air in the large dock suddenly seemed charged as though we had been running an ionizer or a Van de Graff generator for hours. Mrs. Wong bowed to us, and despite my burning desire to opt out of the game, I bowed back with the rest of them.

Then the air / space / our brains cracked. I could see a crack in the air, but somehow in space, over the suspension device. A long green crack. Pete Nunio danced the seven stations. A bigger crack started. Then Suzi. Then Fred. With Fred fragments of the world passed away. I was looking on alien world with a ruined planet in the sky and two small moons. The music now came through the cracks not our phones. The tempo changed. Everyone but me had danced. I could see the Pit. What was left of Martinez was crawling out of the Pit.

Fred Nadis said: "Sheress. It is your time."

I knew that word. I saw it flash into my mind from that first YouTube link. I could read the strange letters. It meant sacrifice. I started to run to the door, but Suzi and Calvin had anticipated my move. So I ran to the little room that held the snack bar. I wedged a rusty folding chair under the grimy doorknob. They began to chant, "Sheress, Sheress, zodicare entoia!" That meant "Sacrifice, Sacrifice, don't stay in your cave!" My being in this crummy little room was part of the ritual as well. They kept chanting.

I heard the outside door open. I screamed for help. Someone could help me. But their chant changed. "Xulthan! Xulthan! Qaa nadezzer, qaa Sheress!" *Xulthan! Xulthan, call the little one out, call for the Sacrifice!*

I wanted to look. I wanted to see Xulthan. He/She/It began singing. It wasn't a human voice. As the song grew unguided by the scales and chords and rhythms of earth I saw several of the images from Facebook. Not just things that I identified with the Green God Game. Posters of girls in futuristic green vinyl dresses. Volcanoes erupting. News items about asteroids hitting the earth in record numbers. Biographies of weirdo painters and writers. Dirty jokes that I couldn't quite understand. Train wrecks. Burning school buses. Everything. Everything I had viewed on my quest from 0 to 332 friends. It was all part of a ritual. A ritual began long ago and further away than I could imagine. It had been soaking into me, little by little. I felt it echo around my bones. It couldn't be written in a book, or maybe even in a thousand books.

I knew when Xulthan finished Its song, I would move the chair. I would leave my little cave as I had always done for centuries without end. I walk into the crack between the worlds. I would bring balance. It would hurt. It would be squishy. It would be Blissful.

(for the memory of Joel Lane)

Robert W. Chambers

Overshadowed in life by his world-famous brother, William Boughton Chambers,

Designer of those beautiful halls on the Yale campus,

Architect of the Lawrence Library,

Robert sells his sketches to Life, Truth and Vogue.

He writes his dull, popular, occasionally best-selling romances

He is a footnote to his family, an uninteresting bud

Of the tree of Roger Williams, founder of Providence.

I pick him.

I lay my hand on him from the yellow whirl of space.

I pick him

I give such dreams, show him such sights, play him such melodies.

If you are to be saved, you must bring forth what is inside you.

I pick him and his words pick so many others.

His words bring my madness to man creatures

Blowing like an unseen cold wind

During the dreadful Cosmic night.

Stirring the yellow leaves through time

In Paris, London, Rome, New York

Blowing the yellow leaves of madness

Into the roofless ruined church

That was once your mind.

Listen I will whisper a Word!

Watch and I will show you the Sign!

The Last God

LEMING HAD TAKEN the bold step of moving into one of the abandoned apartment houses on Congress. Within walking distance to the Capitol, it had been a very popular (and rather expensive) dwelling place. It was near one of the biggest colonies of the Eyes. Sometimes one or two would attach itself briefly to the glass at night. Unlike 99% of the remaining inhabitants of Austin, Leming did not have black out drapes. He would flip off the eye when it landed, but he didn't anger it by shining a light on it. He was defiant not suicidal. He wondered one night what would happen if he placed a mirror inside the glass—show the Eye an Eye—but when he went to get the large freestanding dressing mirror that Dr. Walthers had had in her bedroom, the Eye focused on him. He could feel it watching him, draining him, and no doubt reporting to the big red brains that rumors said were underground in the drains, the caves, the secret government installations. He lit the room only with a nightlight, ironically a Christmas night light —once the delight of Dr. Walther's daughter. She was grown up now, and probably fled like her mother to one of the well-lit rural compounds, where humans were said to be "pondering their next move." Leming froze while the eye watched. He felt anger more than fear, but enough fear to keep him in place until the Eye detached itself and flew away about four in the morning. He slept late, but there was little recrimination at work for such omissions. People missed hours or even days.

Leming rode his scooter to work. The ad agency had practically no clients now, but somehow was still issuing paychecks more-or-less on schedule. His boss, the bleary-eyed Ms. Williams, nodded at him when he walked in at 10:00.

"The internet is down. Have you finished the sketches for the Two Step?" she asked.

"Since they're no longer open at night, no one loves their patio, and live music is almost a thing of the past—I don't know what to sell the bar with," said Leming.

"They've got a great dance floor. Didn't you and your sweetie—what's her name—used to go there?"

"Molly. Molly Jimenez. Molly broke off with me."

"I'm sorry. I didn't know. Was it because of——?"

All conversations ended with a "because of—" or a "since—" or a "you know" flowed by nod toward a nearby roosting place. Leming went back to designing an ad campaign for a bar that attracted no one in a deserted city. Lunch came in a couple of hours. Leming joined Scott at the little sandwich place around the corner. Only two items on the menu today, salami with cheese or salami without cheese. Leming chose the former. After all, it was said, you only live once.

Scott asked him: "How's life in the rent-free world?"

"You know, for a well-thought-of Professor, I expected better digs. Her taste in wine is mediocre, and there were no hidden books of folklore."

"So you still think that they are—what, demons, gods, elves?"

"I hoped that some dim story from the past might throw some light on them."

"What's wrong with space aliens, mutations, inter-dimensional travelers?"

"Those are modern myths. We think we understand them because they use, or rather misuse, the language of science to explain things."

"You don't agree with your ex? That they're the Eyes of god?"

"I am more of a Pink than a White. Hell, I'd be more of Black except that I don't like drugs or S&M."

A group of Whites were marching down 11th. They carried signs urging all to repent. "Make Your Soul As White As The Son!" Some signs read "Sun" instead of "Son." Their clothes—shirts, pants, scarves, shoes were certainly white—they reminded Leming of ads for bleach when he was kid. "Get your clothes whiter than white!" Leming saw that Molly was not among them. He didn't know if Molly had joined them, but she shared their ideology. She felt the Eyes were here to make moral judgments. To judge against sex outside of marriage, or affairs, or casual drug use. Molly's divorce to her husband hadn't become official when she and Mark Leming had begun the physical side of their relationship. A week after the first Eyes had arrived in Austin, attaching themselves to the underside of the Congress St. bridge, one had flown to her window at night. She and Mark were making love, when she saw its ugly semi-transparent shadow on her window. She jumped out of bed, covered herself and ordered him to leave. He was terrified. Nobody went out at night, but she screamed and screamed. He ran to his car, expecting at any minute to be touched by their sticky flexible skin. He thought one flew over his shoulder.

He had tried to call for the first few days. That was when phone service was fairly reliable, and few people had fled the city. He drove to her home once, knocked, and got no answer. Maybe she was gone; maybe she was living in one of the White tent cities.

There were four political parties/gangs/religions in deserted Austin—in most of the US in fact. The largest was the Whites advocating a life of total purity: no masturbation, no meat, no drugs, no swearing, no you name it. The next largest group was the Pinks. They advocated denial. Act like the Eyes didn't fly around at night, didn't roost in dark places during the day, and didn't really have pupils that focused on you. Despite their denial Pinks stayed inside at night, and largely drank heavily. The Blacks and the Purples seemed to be about the same size, if there were anyone keeping demographics these days. Both groups were small and the rumors about them were terrible. The Blacks were a sort of Latter Day Satanists claiming the Eyes were the perception organs of some evil being, either Satan Himself, or something more eldritch and evil like Zushakon, the god of Darkness of some obscure California Indian tribe, or Ah Puch of the Mayas. The devil simply wanted to watch—so they organized orgies, heroin parties, S&M spectaculars, chanted formulae from cheap paperback grimoires, parked in handicapped parking spaces and the like. They hoped to either impress or appease the presumably bored god that had travelled across unimaginable abysses for a cheap thrill. Rumors abounded. At this Black Mass the Eyes had attached themselves to the worshippers; at that orgy fire had shot from the Eyes' pupils barbecuing the miscreants. Most people thought that the rumors were White hate mongering. But anything could be repeated in the daylight, when it could be both half-believed and half laughed at. The Purples claimed to have a "scientific attitude". The Eyes were UFO aliens, or extensions from another 'brane, or a response to pollution, global warming and Monsanto. But their approaches were simply recycled urban superstition and pseudo-science. They collected americium from smoke detectors and made Anti-Eye shields. They erected pyramids, so that "shape waves" would drive the Eyes away. They played with Tesla coils and Theremins. Of course there were rumors here as well. Dr. Leonard Walton of Sherman Oaks had communicated with the Eyes using an old Pacman game. Susan McWhortle of St. Louis has driven them away by finding a certain radio frequency. Eliot Chang of San Francisco had driven them to a piranha-style feeding frenzy by spraying them with insecticide.

The White parade passed the restaurant. Conversation stopped inside. The six patrons and the two employees looked at each other. Everyone wanted to respond exactly like everyone else. Nobody liked taking a stand anymore. Conversation picked up again in a few minutes. No mention of the Whites, although a young couple sitting in back looked very shame faced. No one mentioned the Eyes.

Back at work, Leming thought about quitting. The economy was going to collapse soon enough, but the ritual of his job gave him comfort. He went to his manager.

"I'm going to drive out to the Two Step and talk to the owner. Maybe he can suggest something."

"Be careful. Inside a bar it is dark, and you might not keep an eye on the daylight. You don't want to have to spend the night there, unless you've developed a taste for Country and Western Music. Take your car, not your scooter. At least you still dress like you're part of a business."

There was no way he'd drive under an underpass on his scooter. The Eyes seldom flew in daylight, but the thought of it was too creepy.

The Two Step was a pretty famous bar. Austin, "the Live Music Capital of the World," had several destination clubs, bars and other venues. If you liked Country and Western you headed to the Two Step on South Lamar. There was no traffic these days. Like everyone else Leming speeded under the bridges and didn't look up. The bar, a large one-story wooden building, had a big parking lot. Inside was cool. Willie Nelson crooned on the juke box. One couple slow danced, three or four others were finishing a pitcher of Lone Star Draft. Texas LSD. The bar's owner Jimmy Ray Searight was bullshitting the barkeeper. He gave Leming a long stare.

"Sorry mister. Checking out your clothes."

Leming wore a blue seersucker suit and a bow-tie.

Leming shrugged.

"You're so light. I was afraid you were a White. Three of them came in the other day, threw white paint all over me." Searight pointed to a white paint splotch on the floor. "They aim to close us down, talking with the emergency city council. Who are you?"

"I'm Ron Leming. I work GD&C. I'm designing your ad campaign."

Searight laughed. "Well I could sure use it. This place used to be packed. Don't know where we would run it that would do any good. What are you drinking?"

"Shiner."

Searight nodded to the barkeep.

Leming discussed his ideas for a while, but Searight had other things on his mind. The White attack had disturbed him.

"Leming, they hinted to me that the city council is in contact with them."

"Sounds more like a Purple rumor."

"These religious types are dangerous. They hate fun. Always have. Back when they were the Puritans that made trouble against Shakespeare. When they were the Citizens Against Pornography, they tried to close down the porno theaters. Of course, VCRs later took care of that."

"Maybe your ad campaign should be 'Bring Fun Back!' "

" 'Bring Fun Back!' Hell yes. We should bring fun back. Not crazy fun like the Blacks. Good clean American fun. Maybe we should hold an outdoors event. Outdoors at night."

"That might be a hard sell."

"Do you honestly know of any Eye attacks? I mean we hear all the time about how the friend of your uncle's chiropractor died of a heart attack because he stepped on one of them in the dark. But do you honestly know of any attacks? Any deaths?"

Leming waited thirty full seconds before answering.

"No sir. And I've been thinking about that a lot."

"I'll give you ten thousand cash dollars if you can organize an outdoor party here in two weeks."

His boss thought he was crazy. But no other money was coming in.

He went home at 5:15. There was an Eye dying on the parking lot.

It looked like a large model of an animal cell, nearly eighteen inches across. Roughly oval, it had many dendrites with small suckers that it used to attach itself to surfaces. Grey and translucent, it possessed an eye where a cell normally had a nucleus. The center of the Eye was six or seven inches thick; it narrowed to about an inch thick on the rim. The eye inside looked like a human eye. This one was blue. When the creatures started to die the inner eye moved randomly, not focusing on anything. When it was healthy you could *feel* when it was looking at you. It was like the feeling you used to get in the old days that someone was looking at you (say at a movie theater). But this feeling was a hundred, a thousand times more intense. In theory the government was studying it. The Eye before Leming began to twitch. Before they died, they would vibrate. Just before death the dendrites would whip through the air making a high pitched scree like a bullroarer. Then at the moment of death, its membrane split open, releasing the eye and the foul-smelling cytoplasm. It drew ants and roaches in swarms, and the smell could make you lose your supper for weeks. Leming didn't want the eye to die here. It would make the whole parking lot smell for a week. And sometimes after the death of an Eye hundreds showed up that night, perhaps mourning their fallen comrade.

He looked around for some cardboard, or maybe a trash sack. He found some in the big blue dumpster. With great distaste, he picked it up with the white trash bag and dumped it in the remains of an Amazon.com delivery box. The eye inside suddenly focused on him. He felt so observed, he started to throw the box away and just run. But the eye went back to its random twitching. He walked to the alley. No other Eyes were watching him, and he certainly did not want the few remaining neighbors to see. He trotted down the alley until he was three blocks away from his apartment house and tossed the Eye in a dumpster.

Before he had squatted in Dr. Walther's apartment he lived in a small rental house in north Austin. He felt like that old man who took his dog to poop in his yard every night. He knew he had polluted the block he left the eye to die in, but what was he supposed to do? Take it on a drive? Throw it in Town Lake?

He pulled his shades that night. He didn't feel defiant. He had disquieting dreams about drums and fire, and once he thought he saw Dr. Walthers.

The next he drew up designs for a huge poster.

BRING FUN BACK. LIVE MUSIC. GAMES FOR THE WHOLE FAMILY. FIRST BEER OR COKE FREE. TAKE BACK THE NIGHT. THE TWO STEP 7:30 PM. BE THERE OR BE ■

White back ground, alternating red and blue letters. Four feet tall three feet wide. He would have them plastered around town. A couple of the sign shops they did business with still answered their phone. The first told him to fuck off. The second run by an elderly ex-hippie offered him a discount just for the hell of it. Two days later the big posters were at every major thoroughfare, in addition Groovy Printing had run off smaller-sized posters—similar to the ones used for guitar lessons or garage sales and added various logos to them: a marijuana leaf, crossed long necks, the University of Texas logo, bats, etc. These were on telephone poles in many neighborhoods.

The next day two men in gray jumpsuits visited the offices of GD&C. The manger sent them to Leming. One was a young white man in his twenties with straw colored hair and a Hitler moustache. The other was a stocky bald Mexican man with a narrow whitish scar coming off his lip.

"We are not happy about this proposed gathering," said the older man.

"The Council has not approved it. Nor will they approve it," said the younger man.

"I was unaware the Council had anything to say about lawful assembly at a public space. Last time I checked the Bill of Rights was still in place."

"I don't think you understand. We're saying the Council does not approve. You should consider where they get their orders from," said the younger man pointing upwards towards God, the Feds or maybe the Eyes.

"We are watching you," said the older man.

"Seems like the world is pretty full of watching these days," said Leming.

They left. They would be much more dramatic if they were taller or not dressed somewhat like janitors. He asked the manager if he should drop the gathering.

"A client paid for advertising. We advertised. Although you might let him know."

Leming made a call. Searight said the Grays had visited as well. Very scary sounding. If they have some contact with the Eyes the taxpayers need to know. Let's just play it out. So, they were already the Grays, another group slicing the thin pie of power thinner. He went to lunch with Scott.

"So, you're going to the party?" asked Scott.

"Yeah. I am going to make a stand. As far as I know these things are even intelligent. They don't show any organization, any purpose. They just scare us. I want to make a stand."

"I think you're an idiot. I think the Eyes are a test. An alien IQ test to see if the monkey people will destroy themselves. Already we've factionalized. We've fled. Why? *Because something is looking at us*."

"So, wouldn't the response be to show we're not concerned?"

"This isn't about them. It's about us. If people party at the Two Steps Whites will show up to pray, Blacks will show up to get naked and whip each other. Grays will show with riot gear, and Purples will have spark guns and portable diathermy machines. It will be an unpleasant fight at best. Even if no Eyes swoop in to watch."

"So you counsel cowardice."

"In this case, yes. Let Searight have his fling."

That afternoon after he left work, but still well before dark, he found two Grays in his apartment. One was a pale red-haired lesbian with a crew cut, the other a light skinned black man who was tall enough to be dramatic. They seemed shocked to see him.

The woman asked: "Are you a friend or relative of Dr. Miranda Walthers?"

"Friend," lied Leming. "What's this about?"

"We have bad news and a warrant," said the woman. "Why are you here?"

"Miranda asked me to water the plants."

The man said: "I am sorry to inform you that Dr. Miranda Walthers was found dead earlier today in Doublesign. She had hung herself. She left a note. It read 'The answer is in my apartment. Lemmus mos tenet verum.' I don't suppose you read Latin."

"No," lied Leming.

You don't get through four years of Latin at a Catholic school with a name like "Leming" without learning the Latin for "lemming"—lemmus. The sentence meant: "The Lemming will know the truth." Ron was frankly scared shitless. Messages from women that hung themselves delivered by government toughs weren't any more a part of his life than the Eyes were.

The man said: "I'm Thomas Hayes, this is Patty Helinek. What's your name?"

"John Falk." *No way was he going to say "Leming."*

"Any idea what the answer is?" asked Ms. Helinek.

"I have no idea. She was a folklorist at UT. You could check out her books."

He gestured at the floor-to-ceiling library. He had looked through dozens of volumes with no result, and then had continued to squat here to show his defiance to the Eyes and because he could walk to work. The two Grays looked at the books with dismay.

"Shit," said Mr. Hayes.

"Do you read?" asked Ms. Helinek. "I mean read a lot?"

"I guess so," said Leming

"If you found something could you let us know?" asked Ms. Helinek.

"Sure. I'm just like everyone else. I want to get to the bottom of this.'

"Are you Purple?" asked Mr. Hayes.

"Hell, no. I'm Plaid."

"That's funny," said both of the Grays at once, without a trace of humor.

As soon as they were gone, Ron divided the apartment in grids to search. He took off work the next day, which was a Friday, so that he would have three days. If the dying doctor said the "lemming would know the truth," then by god he would. On Sunday morning he found it. He couldn't tell if it had exquisitely hidden or just fallen perfectly to be unobserved, A small thumb drive with a gun metal gray case was lying behind the leg of a desk in Dr. Walthers's bedroom. It would only be found by someone on their hands and knees. He plugged it into his laptop. It had only one file marked 'Notes'. It read:

> ((Fix this up for article—ask Susan for biblo data on Codex C. Tell people what's what or let them figure it out??)) The Maya are known for their observation/fascination with deep time. Like the Hindu cosmology they are concerned with deep time, their chronicles reaching back 400,000,000 years long before modern science tells us that humankind had made their appearance. The three major codices tell of the creation of humans by the gods—mainly for sport and amusement but with a certain understanding and affection as well. However the lesser known *Codex Catamaco* (first cited by Barlow in 1949) paints a harsher picture. The *Codex Catamaco* was believed to be a hoax for many years, since Barlow provided no evidence in his brief article "A New

Codex" *Anthropological Quarterly Spring 1949* ((Check pages #'s)) ((mention Barlow's weird life? Connection with Lovecraft and Burroughs??)), however Mary Denning's 1975 discovery of a copy of the Codex among a lot of Mexicana at Sotheby's, established the bona-fides of the document.

The description of the gods and their purposes is unusual. The "gods" are said to have arrived after the explosion of a star and almost bodiless for this reason. They sought to build bodies for themselves—humans being one of the trial forms, although a large black centipede seemed more suitable for most of them. They fed upon human beings' sensations and emotions having lost these crucial aspects of being in the star explosion. These wounded gods were of terrible aspect (the aforementioned centipedes as well as winged toads, crabs, etc.), and had some sort of "night flyers" that gathered raw human emotion and sensation. Humans lived in abject fear of the gods and petitioned them for better dispensation. In agreement the gods took on comely forms and the humans began religion—a form of feeding the gods the emotions they craved—especially guilt, which was prized for mistakes the wounded gods felt in connection with the star explosion. The wounded gods agreed to let mankind forget their true nature as long as religion provided them nourishment. They even let humans think that they lived beyond death as the bodiless gods do. They gave the maintenance of mankind to their youngest member, the God of Forgetting. He can never be summoned nor banished for no one remembers His name. They had great powers of illusion and forgetting. In sport however they choose certain humans to expose to reality, feeding on their fear, guilt and despair. The Codex Catamaco *stated that most of what seems arbitrary about human life are bad patches in the illusion the gods made. More frighteningly*

That's where the "notes" ended. "More frighteningly" Great. Either Dr. Walthers was on the discovery of a lifetime, or she had gone a little mad. The seeds for it had been around since the "Mayan Doomsday" scare of 2012. She had found a terrifying cosmology that could explain the Eyes. Enough to turn a man Purple.

But what good was it? Was the "Lemming" supposed to go preach this in the streets? The party at the Two-Step seemed a better idea. The next night Leming saw something that gave him hope. A small group of revelers were drinking beer on the roof top garden of the building next door. They weren't loud, but they were outside at night. The party grew silent at one moment when an Eye flew into their midst and attached itself to the base of a burned out lamp. But after a while, they began to party again (in a more subdued fashion), not leaving the roof until another hour had passed.

The next morning Leming heard other people in his apartment building. Either new squatters had moved in shortly after dawn, or maybe some of the original inhabitants had returned. A nearly full crew came to work, and the boss even chewed Maggie Whitney out for being late, when she sauntered in at 10:00.

That night there were cars on Congress. Only three. But that was three more than usual. The next day, as he left Dr. Walthers's apartment, one of the neighbors gave him the stink eye. He smiled back at the woman and said: "Bring Fun Back!" The woman merely snorted at him. Perhaps if these were the original tenants he should return to his home in north Austin—they might be wary of a squatter. That night he moved out. He considered knocking on the door of the neighbor he had seen that morning and explain that Dr. Walthers was dead—but all-in-all that seemed to raise more questions than it closed.

His lawn was overgrown. Several of his neighbors were mowing theirs even though it was late evening. Who was he to buck a trend? He pulled his mower out of the garage, fired it up and let her rip. He waved at his next-door neighbor as they each cut their grass. When he it was done he called the guy over for a beer.

"We really let our lawns go," said John Haggard, a thin wiry man that had lived next door to Leming for four years. Leming couldn't recall a conversation with him that lasted more than five words.

"I think lawns were the last thing on our minds," said Ron Leming.

"Funny so many of us reacted the same way."

"What do you expect? I'm just glad bravery is returning."

"Yeah," said John. "If you say so." He walked off with his beer.

An Eye flew down to the sycamore tree in Leming's front yard. It focused on him. He felt so drained that he nearly doubled over. He tried to speak but only made gurgling noises. He hoped Haggard would turn and see him—maybe carry him a few feet inside of his open garage and thus break the eye's gaze.

The next day at work he got a call from Searight.

"Why the hell did you put up so many signs? I am not paying you guys a cent more."

Leming assured him. "Groovy Printing took it on themselves as a sort of holy quest."

"Yeah, well, did you know your holy hippies added marijuana leaves to some of the posters? Or naked dancing girls?"

Leming hadn't seen the naked dancing girls. Maybe Groovy Printing was Black.

"Well I'm sure it will help the turn out."

"I've only got so much space. I can't believe that I ever thought this was a good idea. If I get in trouble with the police, I may talk to my lawyers about your firm."

"I doubt any police will bother themselves over a pot leaf or the picture of a naked woman. Besides, the party has already been a success. Have you seen the streets lately?"

"I see the streets every day. What do you mean? My bar sits on South Lamar."

"No. I mean have you seen the streets at night?"

"Well of course I have, what are you getting at?"

"Well maybe this isn't happening in your part of the woods, but people are out at night."

Searight sighed. "Of course they're out at night. Where would they be? My business runs on night people wanting to have a few beers, some fajitas and dance a little."

"But the party . . ." began Leming.

"The party was your idea. Advertise the bar. Increase your patronage. Jeez, I don't what I was thinking. This place is jammed every night. I just hope I can handle the party. I know it's y'all's business to drum up business, but couldn't you have come up with something better?"

Leming talked for a while longer then put the phone down.

He had one more test. At lunch time he offered to drive Scott to a Mexican place in South Austin. As he drove under an underpass, its upper surface pulsing with sixty or seventy roosting Eyes; he pointed up at them.

"They still creep me out, even with people acting brave," said Leming.

Scott asked: "What creeps you out? Bridges? What are you talking about?"

"Oh nothing," said Leming.

The rest of his life he was the only one that could see Them. He could see them drain people, who didn't notice. He began to see other Things too. It was two years before he choose the same way out as Dr. Walthers. He pinned a note to his body with two words written on it:

More frighteningly

(for Lawrence Person)

The Stele

Dynasty Nineteen: Reign of Seti II

Gesso on wood

Reverse: Unknown alphabet 11 lines. Stylized three lobed eye

Obverse:

Under the arching figure of Nuit

Eleven lines

Hail to Thee! Nyarla (Darkness/Silence) hotep (Is made Happy)

Neter of Neteru

Born of Nuit and Set

Messenger of He who sets on the Throne of the Island of Fire

Giver of Isfet (Madness/Confusion)

May all who read these lines be bound in your service

Hidden from the Sun

For millions and millions of years

Great of Magic, Older than Time, Giver of the Silent (?) Word to Men

Holder of the Angles, Breaker of Circles

Great is the Might of Nyarlathotep, Greater Still He Through Us

The Auction

It was in the dark days of the Blitz, when screamings came across the sky

We carried on, we carried on.

Andrew Chambly came to the auction, a way to pass the afternoon.

Then a fat balding man that smelled like a sweetshop sat next to him

The man's last lock of hair was dyed green and his sunken eyes told a poem of heroin.

He had been in the newspapers.

Aleister Crowley. Mr. 666. He dozed. He snores through the first twenty two items.

Then the Stele was offered by a gloved attendant.

". . . mysterious artifact . . . ill-fated expedition . . ."

"Five hundred pounds!" croaked the Beast.

Andrew would not let the repulsive man have anything. "One thousand!"

Crowley turned on him. "You must let me have it. It is not safe in ordinary hands."

"Going! Going! Gone!"

With satisfaction Andrew took the Stele from the attendant. Crowley yelled, “Don’t touch.”

It burned his bare hands and filled his vision

He saw the colours Jale and Ulfire and Squant

He saw the corners of the room leading to great gates beyond which horrid winged hounds prowled

He saw Nyarlathotep, his new Master.

Bound for millions of years.

The buzz filled the room. Everyone ran. Except Andrew a prisoner of perception

The bomb fell through the ceiling,

But it was already too late for Andrew

And Other Horrors

by Nick Mamatas and Don Webb

IT WAS THE third jittery day. The job was supposed to be simple. Bob, Frank and Reg stole the truck, Sam would meet them and buy the cigarettes. Then they would be sold at bars and clubs in Memphis. Places that didn't look too closely at the tax stickers. Bob was too old and too smart for this kind of thing, but as the saying goes "bills to pay and mouths to feed." They parked the stolen truck behind the Pine Lodge. Frank smeared some mud over the license as though that rendered the eighteen-wheeler invisible. Frank and Reg were neither too young nor too stupid for this sort of job. In fact, Bob decided they weren't too stupid for anything. They remained drunk, living on delivered pizza in their increasingly rank room on the second floor. Beer, cigarettes, pizza and hotel porn were for them a sort of paradise, if not the "good life" a damn reasonable facsimile.

Bob stood in the parking lot watching the cars whiz by. He had Sam on the phone. Sam was about to bug out. "I don't know Bob, the feds have checked up on us twice this week. My money man is getting nervous."

"Do you want the fucking cigarettes or not? I am sitting here with two drunks on the verge of flipping out on me. My ass is totally exposed."

"Maybe we can cut a deal for less money."

"Maybe you can go to hell."

"Why don't you just cut them out of it? You drive into town tomorrow night, I'll give my share of the money and you blow the state for awhile."

"If do that these jokers will show up at my house and kill me. They may not be smart but they are vicious."

"I'm going to see what I can do. Think about my offer, and Bob you should have some plans to get out of Dodge. No one is watching out for you."

Fuck this shit.

At least he had his car here. All the two morons had was the truck. He walked into the front office. They could drink cheap and jerk off in the bathroom of room 2D forever. The fat hippy chick with greasy long (maybe) blonde hair was watching the tube. A tiny fake Christmas tree stood on the counter. The place smelled of cheap cone incense that almost covered the smell of pot. Place probably didn't have a cashbox. Her red eyes were a neon advertisement for Don't Do Drugs. Probably hadn't had a thought in years. The TV babbled on—one of those popular shows about the paranormal. Seemed to be more of that crap every year. What was this one? *Bewildering Balderdash*, *Spooky Situations*, *Ripley's Believe It Or Don't*, *In Search of Grainy Stock Footage*? Currently the narrator was describing the case of Bob Sturges, a New York construction worker. As the black and white photo showed, Bob had fallen on a long piece of rebar from the unfinished tenth floor of the Empire State Building. Although the rebar had pierced Bob through his right eye and up through and out of his skull, he had survived. His fast-thinking foreman had cut Bob loose (as seen in the photo) and took him to a nearby physician's office. Someone had thought to make this photo while Bob was waiting to see the doctor.

It didn't help Bob's mood that he shared the name with that guy.

"What do you think of that?" asked hippy chick. She wore a somewhat faded Joker T-Shirt with the bloody line *Why So Serious?* across the tits. Bob searched for a deep sounding come back in hope of scoring some of the dope or maybe some hippy pussy.

"I believe everything happens for a reason," he said. That should work, these people believe in karma.

She made a disgusted face, like she had just found a rat turd in her cereal. She slightly nodded her head no as she responded: "Typical answer. Mister, you ever think that there might be a force in the universe that intervenes for the opposite reason? A force that makes things happen precisely for no reason? Look around sometime."

"Yeah, well you got me there."

Bob left the office. The manager could continue her advanced nihilism. Bob just wanted to go. She stayed in the unit behind the office. He walked over. Dusk had come and he needed to have something to show for the risks of the last three days. No one was around, he pulled a broken case cutter from his jeans pocket and jimmied open the door. Stepped in and closed it behind him. First goal was the kitchenette. He needed a garbage sack. Done. DVD Player. Laptop. Cheap shit but something. In the bedroom an oversized vibrator that looked like Godzilla—it was called *Ain't Love Grand?* Some cheap turquoise and silver jewelry. Hard and smooth; real turquoise feels soapy to the touch. Bingo! A baggy filled with weed. Her books. Paranormal romances, several books about freak accidents, and a Bible.

No it wasn't a Bible. Something old in a light brown cover, a book of poetry. *Azathoth and Other Horrors* by Edward Pickman Derby. Probably not worth squat. But it did look old. Into the bag. "I'll show you what happens for no reason," he said to the room and cat-footed it out like a fog to his green Camry. He put the loot, such as it was, in the passenger seat. Let Frank and Reg deal with a truck that grew hotter by the minute.

He didn't head home. He headed toward Clearlake. His cousin would buy the crap off of him and he could hit town next week. By then some suitable entanglement would have overtaken the boys and he could be looking for a new job legit or not. Frank was so stupid that he'd put the room on his credit card. Bob's only interaction with the Pine Lodge had been the philosophical dialog and the manager hadn't even looked fully away from the TV. If there had been a security camera, he hadn't spotted it. She had probably removed it years ago to keep her ganga habit a secret. He turned off his cell phone.

He didn't want to drive all night to Clearlake. Damn near nothing on the road. How had Dad described it? "This road runs between nowhere and not much else." Hadn't seen Dad much as a kid. He'd been a long-haul trucker. Maybe still was, or so Bob occasionally found himself thinking on the highways, when there was nobody on the road but commercial traffic. Bob's family had disowned him, or he them. Even his Uncle Robert Derby Sturges for whom he was named. Another meaningless coincidence. Not a star in sight. "Commercial traffic," Bob said. The stuff he'd lifted seemed to buzz at him, almost hopefully.

There was a truck stop ahead. He pulled in and parked in the back. He fished through the lot and got out the book. Bob loved to read, would've done well in college if hadn't been for selling speed on the side.

The book was signed, but not inscribed, which would add to its salability. A product of the Roaring Twenties. He ordered the scrambled eggs, ham, coffee biscuits and jelly. There were sequences of sonnets in the book describing a trip to the center of the cosmos, where pure Chaos sent out waves of senselessness, beauty-destroying asymmetry. Theses waves congealed into matter and energy and into gods of insane intent—vast cruel and perverse. Hell if this was your cosmos, drive-by shootings, the floating garbage island twice the size of Texas, John Wayne Gacy, and government subsidy of tobacco farming all made sense. For that matter so did he and Sam and Frank and Reg.

The food came. He put too much pepper on his eggs and poured the non-dairy creamer in the coffee. Some of the poems were scary, some really depressing, some black humor. Hell he might keep this book. Then he found a limerick:

For the Daemon Sultan a chessman

Reads my verse and finds the Plan

A halfwit cousin, name of Sturges,

Who loses and loses because of his urges.

Repeats, Re-runs, Re-cycles as long as he can.

Limericks were supposed to be funny. This was not funny. This meaningless coincidence thread was wearing a little thin. He paid for his food and left. As he walked toward his car, he spied the passenger door ajar. *Son of a bitch!* Someone had stolen his ill-gotten goods. He slammed the door shut and pealed out of the parking lot. It seemed darker than before if that was possible. The darkness sucked at his headlights. After a couple of miles, he saw a tanker truck coming his way. As it grew closer, he thought how *clean* it would feel to hit the truck and be purified by the fire. He started screaming to himself not to do it and fought his own crazy arms. He veered into the lane, the tanker blasted its horn and only at the last second did he pull back.

He peed himself. Bob could have sworn he heard a laugh track. For a moment he thought he saw vast forms in the darkness of the sky. *They're blotting out the sky . . .* Maybe he was going crazy like his Uncle Robert had.

Bob decided he would stop at the next motel. Finally, there it was The Oak Tree Lodge. A Xerox of the last motel, probably run by the same company. He pulled in front of the office. He had a fake credit card to secure the night.

The office looked the same. He quickly walked up to the counter to hide the pee spot on his jeans. Bob realized he was shaking. It seemed late at night, but it was really only nine. The clerk was a chubby woman wearing a faded T-shirt that advertised a punk band Erica Zann and the Electric Commode. She had dirty strawberry blonde hair that hung past her shoulders. She could have been the last chick's sister. The tiny Christmas tree could have come from the same fake tree farm—it bugged Bob, *something about cones*.

"Want a room?"

"Yeah."

He became aware of the TV. It showed a documentary about the increase of monster births. The manager said: "What do you think causes that?"

The screen showed a two-headed fetus.

Bob said: "I dunno, but I think there may be a force that cause things to happen for precisely no reason." He hoped the Force would notice in a good way.

The chick snorted. "Not too bad. I think it's the chemicals."

"The chemicals?"

"The government makes neurotoxins in Springfield—up the mile a stretch. We're going use it all on the Chinese some days. They ship 'em out in tanker trucks. One of the drivers told me one night. Makes me nervous so I smoke dope at night. Someday some halfwit will hit one of them and that's all she wrote."

"Yeah, got to watch them halfwits."

"You 420-friendly?"

"Usually but tonight I am just dead tired."

"Well here's your card. Room 2D. It's around back. Merry Christmas," she said, sliding the card over the counter. "Or is it happy holidays to you?" She rolled her eyes at herself.

Bob found the room. It reeked of Pall Malls, the sheets were damp. He put the Do Not Disturb card on the outside knob and put the chain on. He turned on every light in the room and he opened the book.

Choregos for Typhon's Play

The Egyptian ringmaster picks comedies both big and small

The other face of the Sultan wears many masks

Tonight's drama is about a larva's fall

Nyarlathotep the other face of Azathoth does his many tasks

He breeds the maggots that call themselves men

And gives lesser lusts to each

He randomly scatters them upon Gaia's wide fen

And mad poets write trap-verses from them to teach

Look here comes one now unable to stop

Joining with the insects from Sgaggi's dance

That culls the weak under the black big top

Mutilating themselves in the Pharaoh's Trance

That which should crawl has learned to walk

And to add to the fun thinks it can Talk.

Eighty million years later, Bob looked up from the poem. The book was gone, and so too were Bob's limbs. What he looked down upon was not even remotely a human body. His torso was conic, more a trunk than anything else. He thought to touch it, but instead of arms he had three great limbs—like rough ropes, but with the prehensility and subjective proprioception of fingers—swam into view. Bob jerked his head back. It was on another stalk and swung crazily. A huge library of sorts, other beings like him, conic and tentacled with a single huge eye. They lurched toward him.

Then, the hotel room again. Bob's clothes stuck to him. He felt clammy. He remembered suddenly that it was December, nearly Christmas. *The chemicals*, definitely. He reached for the remote and decided to turn on the television, for company. He wondered how Frank and Reg could do it, how they could just stumble through life like animals, eating anything that wandered into one end and excreting it out the other. Without a thought for the world. Bob realized that he was jealous. Television would help—it was like a lobotomy you could turn off when strictly necessary.

And they were on the TV, on the very first station he clicked on to. Frank and Reg, it looked like. They were on the news, masked, Frank in a filthy shredded raincoat, shrieking and trying to yank himself out of the grips of the three policemen. Reg was almost catatonic. The volume was low but by the time Bob had turned it up the news had already moved on to another story about some little girl caught in the crossfire between two rival gangs. She was dead. An altar with flowers and photos and flickering candles had already sprung up, but the police were baffled, the family enraged. Bob knew he had to get moving again. Neither of his confederates would stay quiet even if they knew how to, and Bob wasn't anything but a four-time loser with a few greasy twenties in his pockets and a stolen book. Bob took a breath, decided to try to do something for no reason at all, bolted from the bed, realized the futility of trying to do something for no reason at all, and then ran from the room. He burst into the hall and then he was far too large for it, all stalk-limbs and a huge trunk. He flailed about in the body that wasn't his, slammed into the wall, stumbled backwards into the doorway of his room and landed flat on his back. The Do Not Disturb sign landed on his face.

Too late, Bob thought, disturbed.

Then the voice. Echoing in a head much larger than the head Bob remembered. "Nevil Kingston-Brown, cheers. William I in 1066. Hitler lost in 1945. Neil Armstrong first to the Moon in 1969. Flying polyps emerge in December 2012, eradicate most of the human race. Japan sinks 2121. First successful bilocation in 2357. Any of these ring a bell?"

A great spasm emerged from Bob's trunk as he tried to speak. The air was suddenly redolent with the smells of confusion and sexual release. Finally, Bob simply thought. "It is December 2012."

"It *will be*," Bob heard in his head. "Well, that explains why you're here, now."

"Where?" Bob demanded. "When!"

"In the body of a member of the Great Race of Yith," Nevil said. "Some time in your past. Mine as well, actually. The Great Race have mastered the science of time travel. Hmm, no, that's not quite right. They have an acumen for it, and it's more of an art than a science. One of them—indeed, the one whose body you currently inhabit—is in your body on Earth, in December 2012. To watch the rise of the flying polyps and the eradication of most the human species and its multifarious cultures."

Bob didn't know what to say. Nothing in his experience had prepared him for even so odd a dream. For a moment, the thought why? bubbled to the surface of his suddenly very different feeling brain. But he didn't ask his question. He decided just to sit where he was, in the great and awkward hulk whose form he was growing used to—not as a body, but as a car a few days after stealing it, after the mirrors have been adjusted and the seat set back—and see what would happen if he did nothing.

After all, Bob thought, *sometimes things happen for no reason.*

"False," said Nevil. "All actions are caused actions. There is certainly no morality involved in even a single event, but actions have reasons for coming to pass. If there is a problem at all, it is in comprehending the number of causes any event might have, not with the phony realization that 'things happen for no reason.' " Those last five words weren't in Nevil's voice, not with his rounded vowels and hissed consonants—they were in Bob's voice, like a recording, or a memory.

"Great, a philosopher," Bob's mind said. "Fine. How long will I be like this?"

"Until the being in your body has completed its observations. No time at all, really."

"And it's just me and you here now?"

Nevil didn't chuckle, but other voices, other minds, did. Thousands of them. Ancient men, older than civilization, whose forays into dark wisdom led to their predicaments. Things from other worlds, minds that can hardly have been said to have ever had bodies at all. Beetles with the minds of men and an academic knowledge of Bob's particular sort of ape, one long-extinct from their point of view. They weren't even laughing at the idea that he and Nevil would be alone, Bob realized, but at his use of the word now.

"You're not like us," Nevil said. "We're dreamers. Aesthetes. Our minds were open, one way or another, through art or science or thaumaturgy, made sensitive to the machinations of the Great Race. You may feel that the body you inhabit is a prison——"

"And you don't?" Bob said.

"I do," said Nevil. "But prisons aren't all of a type. Cooperate with the Great Race, and you'll gain access to a library beyond imagining. Dozens of worlds, tens of millions of years. Sciences both exoteric and esoteric. Forms of poetry our human bodies wouldn't even have the organs to appreciate. It's here for you . . . Bob."

Bob felt the world around him snicker. He thought back to the book, the chaos of the evening. To poems he couldn't appreciate.

"I know a book," he said, finally. He wasn't addressing Nevil, but the assembled minds that touched his own. "Have you heard of it? Do you have a copy here?"

"Bob we were chosen because we write books, sculpt sculptures, create symphonies, xerazac xeazacoolgies, build cathedrals, tune signing neutron stars—you are class II. Your worldline just does something stupid. You are the ringside seat."

"But what about my book? The book that started it all?" asked Bob.

"Soft typewriter, or you after computers? Spiral programming. Electron tunneling in the DNA, oh that was after the Disaster. The important book is in your cells, you're fulfilling something in your genes. Something placed there by an accident of history, and another of sexuality."

"No, I stole a book tonight."

They laughed again. "Bob, you are the punchline," Nevil said. "You want a book for you? A little leisure reading? I'll get you one by the beetles. It is a few chambers over."

Bob tried to walk, but just pulsed and jerked around spasmodically. Some crude instinct took over and he began to snail-slide in the vast hexagonal hall. Some of the creatures watched as he passed through the honeycomb.

"The humans, the more sentimental ones, are interested in you," said Nevil.

"Why?" asked Bob.

"I'll let you read about it."

They traveled a long time. *If this was such an advanced race they should have mastered airport people-mover technology.* Bob asked: "Why books? Can't these guys do digital?" Bob knew there'd be some answer he couldn't understand, but just hoped that his questions at least showed him to be a clever idiot—like a zoo monkey who stares and nods and pretends to understand for smiles and contraband popcorn. Not like a zoo snail who doesn't even realize that his leaf and stick are fabrications. Something in him rumbled dully. "If they can swap minds, why not just swap info the same way?"

"Their word for world is Library. This is their religion."

When they came to another chamber, which looked so much like the first it could have been the first, Nevil's eye stalk scanned the volumes carefully. "I wonder what happens if you read about your deeds." His claw chose one. Bob saw the title was in English.

"Is this some sort of magic, I can read other languages?"

"No, Bob. I've just been spoofing you, mate. When the Yithian that displaced my psyche died, I became a sort of honored guest. I was studying you Bob. This is one of my volumes. Even though I died five hundred years after you. You were my study, you and the Great Race. I was what you would call a physicist, but that's only a limitation of your vocabulary. You, Bob, are a particle. I look at particles. Now you take a look at the book. Oh dear, you have me rhyming."

> The flying polyps carry a brane of their space-time. In their universe the weak force is negligible, and Carbon 14 is the stable isotope. They emit probability-waves—hence their lapses from visibility. My great-grandfather's dig had weakened a Yithian barrier in late 2012. By the sort of cosmic co-incidence that limits the Yithian control of lesser beings, a large extinction event on the Eastern seaboard of the United States

Bob was able to ask "What?" in the dream or vision or whatever-the-fuck and finished his "does that have to do with me?" in the dank hotel room.

He was holding on to the poetry book with the same claw—er hand as Neville's tome. "I am not responsible for anything. I am not cosmically important. I am cracking the fuck up."

He would get out of here. He would drive home. He would go to the police and tell them he was bug-fuck crazy. The clock read 11:11.

He realized that he didn't know where to drive so he flipped a coin.

He turned on *Rudolf the Red Nosed Reindeer* and sped into the night. When his Uncle Robert had cracked up in Bob's teens, it had been the long nights of winter that got him. One of his conversations with Uncle Bob told him: "You know Santa Claus is really up there. Don't need no wings to fly. You know what you need? Luck."

It's all fucking great Uncle Robert was institutionalized for fears that Santa was really watching him, flying through winter nights whistling some cheap jingle. Angels We Have Heard On High / Tell Us To Go Out And Buy, *yeah, that's the shit.*

Tonight was just crap. Bob had seen all the specials all the 2012 garbage. His uncle had been nuts. The job had been nuts. He could just hole up and get through the night. It was so damn dark here, he had wandered off main highways for sure. FOOD GAS ahead. Get a burger, get some orange juice for Christ's sake.

He pulled into a normal non-*Twilight Zone* station with cars and people and a big green BP gas sign and a McDonalds. He took the book with him. He ordered a Big Mac, large Diet Coke, and a cherry pie. It wasn't a value meal. Bob didn't order by number. He hoped that meant something. He sat on yellow and brown furniture looking at the deserted playscape. He ate his food, he read a last poem:

Tritina as Improved Bible

The human race began as a fart I swear by my posey and Art
Farted from Azathoth at the nine angled center
Consciousness and speech are the bubble

Rejoice oh might humans you do come from the center
And as inflating gas bags ours is a pretty bubble
Shiny with war and love, of course and Art

Raise your Yule mugs to the chaotic center,
As mindful of us as your dog is of human art
Philosophize that you are really not a bubble

Azathoth blows no more bubbles, the center does not hold
No more merriment in wine or love or Art.

What a cheerful little fuck. *Merry Christmas to you Edward Pickman Derby.* Bob walked over to the seven-foot-tall Frazier Fir that stood between the garbage can and the napkin and utensil island. He admired the tiny multi-colored Charismas lights that blinked on and off, the ornaments from Walmart, the little stockings with employees' names in red and green glitter. He said quietly: "I hate fucking cones. I hate fucking poetry. Merry fucking Christmas." He lay the copy of Edward Pickman Derby's

Azathoth and Other Horrors among the fake red and green foil wrapped presents, and headed out into the night.

Reg was outside. He was smoking a stolen cigarette. "Yo," he said, plainly. "It's done."

"What?"

"Like you said when you called. Kill Frank. He was gonna cut us out, then hand us over to the cops or the mob. He admitted it and everything, like you said he would."

Christ, Bob thought. That was the flipside of his moment in that great jumble of a body. Something else had been in his. *The difference between wearing* your *dirty underwear another day and sliding into somebody else's for a day*. Uncle Robert had said that too when Bob was a kid, about something, but Bob had forgotten what the analogy had been for. Blood surged up to Bob's face, feeding the brain, offering a sudden clarity. Every synapse blazed. Something stretched toward him from far away, from the deep space in his mind, from the long end of time in which Bob felt trapped like a rat in tar. It was spectacular, tentacular. Oh dear, Bob was rhyming.

"The body, where is it now?" Bob asked. "Did you hide it, somehow?"

"Shelby Forest, like you said, man," Reg said, "with the truck. Then I hitched here to meet up like we talked about. Gas and go. What the hell, Bob . . ." Reg took a step closer. "You said this was gonna all work out. You had a plan. You said we were gonna kick back and take it easy, that you knew a place to lay low far from here. Mexico, right? Passports and shit."

"Well, remember the next thing you have to do now, Reg?" Bob asked. "To get the photo on the fake passport to match your face?" He smiled. "Remember. Take the gun, put it under your chin, like so?" Bob demonstrated with the stub of his cherry pie. Reg reached to the small of his back and pulled out his snub-nosed revolver. It went under chin, like so. His eyes were wide, scared like a deer in fire. Reg fired, jerked, collapsed, and his ass hit the ground before his skullcap did.

As Bob drove away, mouth full of whatever was really in cherry pies, the radio said something about Australia, but he didn't notice. He felt a charge. Something special he'd brought back with him from . . . wherever, heh, no, whenever he thought, he'd been. Some deeper understanding. The universe was a billiard table, or at least that's how Bob imagined it. He'd met the men with the cues. He could do a trick shot of his own now too. Just did one, on

Reg, to match the one his Yithian interloper had done on Frank. There was a certain symmetry, you know?

And the book. He could just imagine what would happen to the next curious guy to pick it up. *Fuckin' Tennessee. Could be at Mickey D's a week before anyone who can do more than sign his name with an X even checks it out, no fuckin' doubt.* Bob missed the book, but knew he had to head away from it. Keep driving down that long dark road. Certainly, don't turn back for it. Definitely don't end up driving down the wrong lane into someone's brights. Then, a canister tanker full of neurotoxin. Just before he plowed into it, Bob did see something red flying in the sky. It could have been Santa.

The Egyptologist

The phone rang in his office at the British Museum

They had found something.

No. Not in Egypt, here in London. WWII debris. "Our finest hour."

He hurried into the City.

New Beatles songs, mini-skirts, black-and white *Dr. Who*

They tell him about the worker that went mad. Probably LSD, they thought.

The Stele was a marvel.

The language was archaic; it came from before Seti II's time

The cult was unknown to him.

Of course he could take it to study.

Days reading, sending telegrams. Guessing at *hapax legomena*

Happy with his work, he read it aloud.

The sky darkened outside the Museum, but no cloud was seen.

The lightbulbs above him flickered off.

And he found that he glowed with

a black beyond black.

He knew what he needed to Do.

He was (if you like) a postman

Finding the right recipient of a message

That would end history

All of his studies had come to this

It all comes down to this

The rising of the Nightmare City

The coming of Dis.

A Tune From Long, Long Ago

In the late nineteenth century obsessive German minds began the cataloging of all human knowledge. After all almost everything that would ever be known was already almost known. The wise thing to be was to collect that knowledge and catalog it. Thomas Mueller was an obsessive German that impressed his obsessive comrades as obsessive. Working in the new field of Musikwissenschaft, Mueller began a complete catalog of every Hungarian folk tune. He began his collection in his twenties and continued into his seventies and the disaster of 1914.

JOHN SPENSER PAUSED after typing the above words. He could've done the happy dance in his tiny third floor apartment overlooking Congress. He had found the perfect dissertation topic—fairly well researched (in German), almost unnoticed in English and with a truly spooky ending. Best of all a research assistant at the Harry Ransom Center had found the sheet music associated with the "doomed" concert of 1914—a collection long thought lost. It even contained the *Hexelied* or 'Witch's Song.' He could create popular articles off this for years as well perfectly respectable academic papers. Mueller had worked through decades and so his work was exemplary in showing the changes from Adler (and even pre-Adler) methodology toward the beginning of modern ethno-musicality. There were grants and professorships and interviews at Halloween for this one. He made himself a glass of hot chocolate from powder and microwaved water. He sat down to type some more. He hadn't noticed that he had also begun to hum.

* * * * *

Thomas Mueller arrived in the village of Stregoicavar by carriage on a perfect late spring evening, when the air in the mountains bore the scents of a hundred types of wildflower. The sun had retreated behind the mountains leaving the western sky a deep regal purple, and the brighter stars were claiming the sky. The inn had a pleasing goulash, a fine local beer and talkative locals. Mueller had scarcely tucked into his supper when locals were approaching him.

"You are the professor that pays money to hear old songs are you not?"

After three decades of research, Mueller was accustomed to this. Most of the informants would have nothing new to sing for him. He had encountered songs derived from medieval church music, songs from the Folies Bergère which had somehow made their way into the back country of the Hungarian hills, patriotic clap-trap. But original folksongs were still hidden in these remote villages—and one with as promising a name as "Witch-Town" would surely hold some gems. His offer never varied. A few coppers for each song, but a silver *fillér* for a new song that he would write down. The first hour gave him nothing new, but was entertaining. Someone sent for the old men and women, who were sure to know. The silver pouch was opened—firstly a ballad of the fight between Count Boris Vladinoff and the Turks, then a creepy tune about the original inhabitants of Witch-Town and how the honest Hungarians killed them off, finally a song about the Devil's Keep where Satan in the form of a giant toad still appeared.

"I could sing you a song that you will never have heard," said a red faced old man, clearly fond of strong drink. "But it will cost you more than a *fillér*."

Everyone became silent.

Another silver haired man spoke up. "Pay no attention to my brother. He is a drunk who cannot sing."

The conversation in the room shifted from German to Hungarian; Herr Mueller acted as though he could not speak Hungarian. He wanted to know what the villagers said to one another. He kept a quiet smile on his face as he feigned ignorance.

"Stefan, do not sing the witch ballad. We have worked hard to erase from our village. What if a pregnant woman overheard it?"

"Look around you, do you see any pregnant women? Besides what do I care if a German professor hears the song? Maybe it will make me forget it. Maybe he can carry it away from here. Even though our grandfathers' grandfathers cleared the land here, we are under the thrall of the dark people that lived here. Let him hear it!"

"Do what you want Stefan but don't do it here," said the brother.

The innkeeper had been summoned during this exchange. A younger stout with hardly any gray in his hair, he looked like a small bear.

"Stefan Gyori. I forbid you to sing the 'Witch's Song' in my inn. This spot is clean. My grandfather kept it so, my father kept it so, I will keep it so. I have managed my whole life to hear not a note, not a word of the witches' ballad. And I will die clean with no mortgage on my soul."

There was agreement from several of the men and women. Stefan Gyori shrugged, and then addressed Mueller in German.

"Mein Herr. My neighbors are a superstitious lot. They fear that the song I would sing would bring bad luck upon this fine inn much as breaking a mirror."

Mueller replied: "Perhaps you could sing it to me elsewhere? Unless you fear it will summon the devil." He smiled at the last part; he had to fight superstition often in his quest for folk-music.

Stefan Gyori smiled back. "No mein Herr, I am not as superstitious as my countrymen. I will gladly sing this song anywhere—crossroads, cemetery, you name it."

An old woman, who had set by the fire and said nothing all night, had a challenge for Stefan. "Oh really Stefan Gyori, would you sing it by the Black Stone?"

Gyori's red face blanched, but in a voice only slighter higher than he had been using: "I fear nothing. I would sing it by the Black Stone."

The silence that had fallen before was nothing compared to the silence that greeted this remark; Mueller could not have been more pleased.

Gyori ended the silence with: "Of course because of the rarity if the song, I must ask for fifteen Krona."

"I could pay you ten," said Mueller.

"It must be fifteen. After all mein Herr, no one else will sing it for you."

Certainly the fear showing in the eyes of the room agreed with that pronouncement.

"Fifteen then, but I do want to hear it sung by this Black Stone."

"I will sing tomorrow in the sunlight."

"I thought you were not superstitious."

"I don't fear lightning either, but I don't carry metal bars around during a thunderstorm."

* * * * *

John's roommate Jose Wong was fast at work on his laptop. They had a graduate school meal. Two bottles each of local craft beer (Mad Meg from Jester King) and two packages of "Oriental Flavor" top ramen (with margarine for richness). It was Tuesday night; the sounds of a single street guitarist came in their window. John was writing a description of Mueller's methods in dealing with informants. Jose got up and closed the window—perhaps with a little anger.

After a few minutes Jose said: "Can you stop humming? I am trying to write some code and your humming is bugging the shit out of me."

"Oh, I'm sorry. I didn't notice. How's the second level going?"

"The game part is great, the team is really slow delivering the graphics, and I'm stuck with sound."

"Well if you need help with the music——" began John.

"Yes, I know you're a musicology major. You say that every damn time."

They went back to work.

Fifteen minutes later Jose said: "Since you can't be quiet, I'm going to finish this over at the PLC."

He slammed the door on the way out.

Definitely need a new roommate next semester.

* * * * *

"This village had a very different sort of folk than it has now. It was a dark and bad place once with a different name," said Stefan Gyori as he walked Thomas Mueller away from the inn.

It was a bright day with the sun high in the sky, contented cows munching of green grass, birds busy with nest building in the hedgerows.

"What was its name?"

"Xuthltan. They were not Magyars. They were not Christians. They engaged in dark practices—devil worship, it was said."

"The *Witch's Song* is about them?" asked Mueller.

"It is from them."

"But I thought the Magyars killed them."

"Most of them were killed in two raids. But some of the women were kept as bondmaids. They raised the children of the noble families and they taught them the song."

"The song teaches a pagan story?" asked Mueller.

"Who knows what it teaches? We don't understand the language. It makes you see things; it makes you know things. And if a woman that is with child hears the song, her children are horribly deformed. Of course, it took years to figure this out. We took the servants—old hags by then—and burned them in the village square. But the song lives on."

They arrived at a patch of land that knew no green grass. Mueller thought of the "blasted heath" in *Macbeth.* A spindly black stone—damned monolith rose in the center of the desolation. It was octagonal in shape, some sixteen feet in height and about a foot and a half thick; surface was thickly dinted as if savage efforts had been made to demolish it; but the hammers had done little more than to flake off small bits of stone and mutilate the characters which once had evidently marched up in a spiraling line round and round the shaft to the top. Mueller disliked the characters at once. He was about to tell Stefan he need not sing, when they man began his eldritch lullaby.

Even though it was full daylight and a warm day, Mueller felt cold as he heard the tones. He stopped Stefan and pulled forth his tablet. He was a man of science after all. He would record the notes. As he did so, he became dizzy and numb. It seemed that part of him was not standing in his body, but on a vast plane with a darkling purple sky. He stood before a vast pit, and something was moving in the misty depths below. It was going to show itself. They were others around him—strange caricatures of the human form with extra eyes or limbs. Or fewer than they should have—as if life here were ruled by asymmetry much as on Earth it is ruled by symmetry. Suddenly the vision stopped; he was covered in a cold sweat. Stefan had his hand out.

"You pay me now."

* * * * *

Jose didn't come back until seven thirty the next day. John was showering. He was the TA for a music theory course that was early enough in the morning to weed out the less determined underclassmen. He heard Jose slam the door. He stayed in the shower until Jose slammed the bedroom door. He got out quietly and began getting dressed. As he headed out the door, Jose yelled at him: "It's OK. I'm not mad at you. I got inspired and finished the sound for level two. It's Ok, bro, I was just grumpy about deadlines."

* * * * *

It was twenty years later, and Mueller had taken to making long walks in Berlin. The city with its endless smoke and noise and excitement could distract him from the tune which had haunted his thoughts more and more. His hair was shock white; his face wrinkled, his frame thin. That he had been a well-respected Professor as short as five years ago, no one would have guessed. He wore his clothes for too long without having them washed. He was not a frequent bather. He followed crowds and noises—spending late nights in the cheapest of bars, where he paid for his drinks by playing the piano and singing bawdy songs collected over fifty years. He dreaded being alone more than anything. When he was alone he could hear the *Witch's Song*. It seemed to come out of the black depths of space. It no longer bothered to sound like the all too human rendition that Stefan Gyori had croaked out beside the Black Stone. It no longer even had words. It had become pure tones, almost mathematical in its perfection. With the tones came the pictures—the pictures that told the hidden history of the human race. He knew that if ever understood the implications of the history he would go mad—but crowds and beer and bawdy songs were strong bulwarks against thinking too much.

Humans did not come from Earth. They were not the beautiful creatures of symmetry and thoughtful perfection of a loving creator. They were bought from another world where they were creatures of strange form ruled by strange lusts and stranger religions. They were brought here and mated with hairy simians. They were made to forget their true, yet terrible natures. Some sort of being fed off a spiritual product the humans made—and humans unconscious of their true form produced more of this substance—more of this drug than humans who knew the truth. The Others they needed the drug. Horrible things that humans once called gods in foul places like Xuthltan, then called demons when humans began making gods in their own images. Lastly they were forgotten, banished from memory, but oddly much stronger in human history. These Elder Gods grew every year, soon the planet would be theirs. When Dr. Mueller bothered to read the paper and watch the worsening world situation, he saw Their hand at the human throat.

But the song was not about Them. It was about restocking the home world. Some great sorcerer of Ool Athag had written the song to lead human souls back to the world of beast gods who dwelt in pits, where children born with three hands and five eyes were considered lucky, where copulating with demons was a sport. The song affected a magnetic center in the human psyche. It filled the mind with more and more pictures of Ool Athag—of the horrible religious rituals, the strange orgies of sex and blood, the incomprehensible and insane art forms. The soul began to detach itself from the earth. It would be drawn back to the human home world—a strange and surreal Hell that perhaps a Doré or a Sidney Sime could draw, or a mad poet like Justin Geoffrey could sing of. Mueller knew his soul no longer belonged to him—had in effect never belonged to him. He knew it belonged to some monstrous being on the world of purple skies. He knew his soul would fly there after death. And he knew what was "human" in him would die in strange screams and stranger prayers.

It was winter and a fine snow had fallen on the city—a terrible grey snow fouled by factory smoke. Christmas would soon be here, but the religions of men offered him no hope—nor could nostalgia overtake the growing dread that filled his being. He passed a beggar in the street. The unshaven man in the thinnest of coats claimed his landlord was about to throw his family out. Could anyone spare a few marks to make sure his family could have a roof over their heads for Christmas?

Suddenly like Scrooge in Dickens' tale—Mueller became a new man. He pressed a five mark note in the beggar's astonished hand.

Landlord! Why hadn't he thought of it before? A landlord doesn't care from whom his money comes, only that it comes. If he could pay off the dark lords of Ool Athag with a handful of souls—they might release his. Blessed sleep and ignorance could be his again. He could teach the song to dozens of men—he still had people who remembered him as a great musicologist. He might look like a drunk, might wander the streets of Berlin—but via post he could seem impressive. He would organize a concert—a tribute to Hungarian folk music. The last tune would be the *Witch's Song*. He would plant the world of Ool Athag the souls of a few musicians; surely if he damned enough of them, he could be set free.

It took a few months for backers to agree to fund the concert. It was January of 1914 and all the papers speculated about was the possibility of war. Would the central powers hold together? What did the unrest in Russia mean? Would the reforms in the Ottoman Empire be strong enough to keep the Empire intact? Concerts were not priorities for most Europeans. Mueller's hope to escape his return to the dark world of Ool Athag had finally awakened a long latent Catholicism. He found frequent and long visits to the Church as distracting as bars and public houses. Praying long, hard and loudly could keep the alien song at bay—and transcribing the tune into notes also relieved the dark and fearful pressure.

Morality too made a weak return to his life. Surely, he could not damn the souls for the magicians? Although most musicians no doubt lead lives that made hell a likely destination—they had hope of reform. Then Thomas Mueller hit on an elegant solution. There were many Jewish musicians in Germany. He would hire only Jews, whose souls were already forfeit for his concert.

His concert took place on July 4, 1914. He advertised sparingly. He wanted as small an audience as possible. The drafty ill lit theater was in one of Berlin's poorer neighborhoods. The first part of the show was lively—it drew great applause from the audience, mainly ex-pat Hungarians. The second part was short. When the *Witch's Song* played—some left, two or three fainted in the audience, and an old cellist died during the concert. Mueller paid all of the musicians double, suggested they burn their sheet music and closed the show. As he walked into the night he felt empty. Clean. Free. A big smile appeared on his face. He had done it. He had bought his freedom.

Of course the backers were not pleased. Two newspaper accounts mentioned it as a "cursed" concert—but it was back page news given the state of the world.

It was nearly two weeks later as he walked down the street to buy bread that he noticed he was humming. He went home, opened his straight razor and slit his throat. He left no note, and his landlady had no idea that he was once a respected scholar.

Two weeks after that and the Archduke was assassinated. No one thought of the concert. Except for a few Jewish musicians who one by one went mad. The frequency of madness in Jewish musicians of Berlin attracted a few scholarly papers, but it was a small concern. A few deformed births occurred and were duly recorded by the late thirties as example of Nazi racial correctness.

The last of the remaining musicians—mad eyed old men—were gathered by the Nazis and the *Witch's Song* was played a few times while the workers of Auschwitz changed their shifts. If they dreamed of the purple sky, it was surely better than where they were. The death camps removed the last living traces of the *Witch's Song* from the Earth. However, a single bundle of sheet music hidden in a Paris garret made its way to the Harry Ransom Center at the University of Texas in Austin, Texas with many other odds and ends in 1966.

* * * * *

John didn't finish his dissertation. His friends, who were few in number, said he was overcome with depression. His enemies, even fewer in number, claimed that drug abuse had caught up with him. His suicide note was melodramatic and literary misquoting Dickens from *A Tale of Two Cities*: "It is a far, far better thing that I do now than I have ever done, it is far, far worse place I go than I have ever gone." He left a second note to his ex-roommate Jose Wong. "Hey man I hope you didn't listen to me. I'm really sorry."

The later drew the attention of the Austin Police. They tracked Jose down, which was easy he was a famous designer on his way up in the gaming industry working for Electric Anvil in Austin.

"I have no idea what he meant. He was shit to live with the last few months. All of the time humming some spooky ditty—I think it had to do with his research. He stopped bathing, just lay around the apartment and stopped forking over his share of the rent. I had to split."

"I didn't have anything to do with him after I moved out. I tried calling his Mom, a drunk that lives in San Diego. I told her he had flipped out. She said it wasn't her problem. You know I didn't realize it at the time but that tune he hummed really got under my skin. I put in my Master's project, I'm sure you've played it. It's the spooky song you hear when you're in the second level of *Planet Revenge*. That game got me this job. It's the hot item this Christ-mas."

"My moods? Well I've been preoccupied since I heard of John's death. Like could I have done more you know? I've been working on *Planet Revenge II*—it's about this other world with a dark purple sky where you fight monsters in pits. It uses John's song more fully—kind of my memorial to him. So I guess his music will wind up in thousands of households."

for Dan Clore.

The Cult

Thomas Doggett, the dullest man in New Scotland Yard, waited through the lecture.

Andrew Chambly, his sponsor, sat in the darkest part of the hall as always.

Tonight was Thomas' Initiation. He hoped it would be an orgy.

The old boffin rambled on about how the consciousness of the Great Old Ones

Ran backwards in time. Our future is their past. Thomas just wished the lecture was past.

Finally. No wonder the Museum fired him.

The crowd left the hall, the cult members put on black robes. Candles were lit

Egyptian statues were brought out of boxes, bells rang. Gongs gonged.

The leader of the cult uncovered the Stele and read from it in Egyptian.

So what?

He carried in front of each of the neophytes.

When he passed in front of Thomas, an Eye opened in the middle of the Stele

A three lobed eye, and Ulfire light illuminated him.

"You are the one, the dull soulless vessel to hear the message."

Thomas wanted to tell them they were all under arrest, but for what?

Saying he was dull? The wife said the same thing.

“You are the dead Ear that hears for the dull mind.”

Thomas found that he wasn’t in the hall

He floated in deep starless space, seeing only the three lobed burning Eye.

“Thomas I have waited for millennia of your futures, to tell you my Word.”

And Thomas Heard the world-eating Silence.

And he would repeat it to every newspaper and radio show.

And it would Grow.

Until it covered the Earth in shade.

The Comet Called Ithaqua

THE FIRST TIME it was necessary.

It was centuries ago during the Belatrin wars. We were on the scout ship *Fulton.* One of our robots was a Belatrin spy with cunningly faked asimovs. It smashed our hydroponics, our communications, our Dirac drive. Melting it to slag relieved little of our anxiety. Two days without food honed our anxiety to high sharpness. None of us had ever been hungry before. Hunger was an impersonal, historical, statistical thing—so many million in Ethiopia in the Twentieth Century, in Brazil in the Twenty-First, on Mars in the Twenty-Fifth. The personally new phenomena of hunger displayed the transpersonally new phenomena of civilization very quickly.

Doc talked about it first. She was probably the bravest of my shipmates. She'd spent hours trying to repair the hydroponics with the few tools the robot hadn't managed to dump overboard. She had also repaired one Cold Sleep unit.

"One of us could take the Cold Sleep. The rest could kill themselves painlessly."

"Or eat each other," said Vance.

"I'm not getting in the Cold Sleep," I said. "Any of you could raise the temperature a little and provide several kilos of meat."

"Several kilos," said Roxanne, patting my paunch. Captain Oe silenced us with one of his deep space glares. Captain Oe was always on a distant planet, his quiet voice coming across cold light years. Why didn't he make with the bread-and-fishes routine? Isn't that the function of Captains?

Killing Vance was easy. He was bending over a circuit tracer building a simple radio. He thought the folks back home should know that the valiant *Fulton* was lost. I drove a micro-solder into the nape of his neck and out through his Adam's apple.

Captain Oe discovered the body. His mineral calm hid any reaction. I think Doc suggested we cook him. At least Doc and I did the honors producing a very serviceable sweet and sour Vance.

No one wanted to begin. The captain ordered us. It was difficult to keep the meat down. We had diced the flesh well so no part would be recognizable. No one mentioned that Vance had obviously been killed. Thus, we became murderers all.

Doc and I had removed Vance's liver and lungs. She feared they might be poisonous—contaminated by Vance's addiction to tobacco.

By our fourth meal I had overcome my nausea. I viewed everyone else as items for future menus. They were too affected by disgust to notice my change. I left the meal still hungry, still empty, and tried to sleep on my bunk.

I kept thinking of the liver and lungs. Doc had refrigerated them since we lacked means of recycling our wastes. The refrigerator could only hold so much. The *Fulton* stank like a sewer. If I ate the inner organs I would either die or be sated. Either would end the gnawing pain of my stomach.

I crept to the medical room to remove the meat. I let it thaw on the surgical table. I collected some of Doc's tools—they might be useful later. I watched the dim light of Aldebaran through the port wishing the scene would magically change to the gray of hyperspace.

When the liver was fairly well thawed—juicy on the outside and crunchy ice crystals in the middle—I bit into it. Unfortunately, Doc entered the lab at this moment. She viewed the blood streaming down my cheeks with something less than affection. I put the liver down. I pleaded, "Help me." She moved forward and I turned on a scalpel. Laser scalpels only cut a few centimeters but this is adequate when the heart is your target.

I quartered her and hauled the bits to the in-system probe. I sealed us off. I activated all the sensors.

I felt no need to refrigerate the corpse and in fact enjoyed it more as it began to ripen.

They began pounding on the bulkhead hours later. First they demanded that I surrender. A day later they demanded their share of the meat. I watched my telemetry, ate, and slept. I did not dream. Dreaming was the first facet of humanity I lost.

Two days later as I sliced some of Doc's hams—I still used instruments in those days—a green light blinked out. I would need to act fast or I would lose out on the kill. Had Oe honorably committed seppuku? Or had his martial training removed Roxanne as executive officer? Or had Roxanne herself mastered the murderous act?

The *Fulton* smelled very bad. A hint of sesame oil overlay the stench—Oe preparing a delicate Oriental dish. Moo shu Roxanne? I went deep into engineering. I activated one of our dumbest robots and told him to walk into the kitchen. I called Oe up, told him I would surrender to him.

I followed the robot. The kitchen portal dilated and Oe fired. He must have been crazed. No one would use a ranged weapon within a space ship. Fortunately the robot's body absorbed most of the blast and no exterior bulkheads were breached.

The energy weapon triggered internal security. Poor Oe if he'd only reasoned. Micro-solder and scalpels are not weapons. Scores of idiot robots came to restrain him. In the brig he decided to join his honorable ancestors.

Weeks later when my meat supply was exhausted, I completed Vance's radio and put myself in Cold Sleep. Fifty-six years passed in the twinkling of an eye. The rescue team was very, very understanding. There had been cases of survival cannibalism in the past. Of course, I would have to undergo therapy to expunge the terrible guilt I must feel. Then I could join the service again. Of course, I could live pretty well on fifty-six years of back-pay as well.

They sent me to Tarsis Hospital on Mars. Within a week I knew three things. 1. Therapy consisted of producing the "right" answers to an AI's endless questions—a job even a moral moron could fake. 2. Their pills which they gave me in great multicolored fistfuls had no effect on me. 3. I couldn't eat the food they provided. I wasn't hungry or in need. I'd grown a thick layer of fat on the *Fulton*. I vomited up the first few meals and then I asked if I could take my meals in private. Understandingly they agreed. I kept the food until it was moldy—then I could at least bear to eat it. But it didn't satisfy. Something was missing.

As my therapy progressed, I was allowed the freedom of the City. A small congregation followed the teaching of the blessed Zoroaster and placed their dead in a Tower of Silence to be devoured by genetically engineered buzzards. I visited the Tower by the light of the double moons to cut hunks of flesh from the Zoroastrian dead. I couldn't eat them there in the thin Martian atmosphere but carried the slices back in my total environment suit to the domed city. Needless to say I shot all the pseudo-buzzards. Who needs competition?

The hospital had a huge library. I read endlessly about cannibalism and ghouls. Certain Arabic texts were helpful. I wasn't alone. There was little biology—no clear information to aid me in my survival. What were my vulnerabilities? What were my strengths? If I wrote a manual for future ghouls—who would publish it?

One legend touched me more than the others. It turned me as I have never been turned before. Certain Amerindians spoke of the Wendigo.

A party of hunters become lost in the snow. They find a cave. Eventually they must kill one another for survival. One of the party loses his disgust at eating long pig. He warns the other survivor(s), "You must go. I am a Wendigo." They flee in pious terror. The rogue warrior lives on, becoming like a wild beast—long of tooth and claw. Eventually the tribe destroys this raider with many arrows.

Other legends said that the Wendigo was Ithaqua the Wind Walker, a terrible god of storms and ice. This being could only be bought off with human sacrifice. They would lead the wretches deep into the snowy forest and leave them there to freeze. The remains are found miles away. Fiery cold eyes could be seen among the trees, the true spirit of deep space—of pure Hunger as a ball of mind wrenchingly *cold* fire. Iä Ithaqua!

There was no attempt to match the legends of Arabic ghouls and Canadian cannibals and what ever lived in my soul, but I felt they were connected.

I began to use makeup to cover the dull gray of my complexion. Bright light—a blessedly rare commodity in the domed cities of Mars—discomforted me greatly. I thought I might have a mutated form of pellagra, a disease that causes its victims to desire blood; but decided I suffered from a deeper spiritual change. Unlike most spacefarers I had no mystical side, no prayer, no meditations—I had an emptiness inside that the Cold Hungry one could live. It ate my soul in the great dark, and now it would eat everything. I was happy, I finally had a Purpose.

I had no social life, but my warders felt that was because I was a man of the last century—I simply had no one to talk to. Would that my estrangement from humankind was so simple! I began to stalk the streets at night, but I knew this was only a temporary solution. My killings didn't fit in their computer yet, but as the problem expanded from computer to computer my research would be discovered.

I visited the Tower of Silence having noted the death of a Parsi merchant in the weekly data. As I sliced into his corpulent paunch,

I knew I was not alone. I looked up. Far away—to the west—I saw two carmine stars where no stars should be. A red haze swirled about them. It was Ithaqua, my soul. I removed my respirator. I could breathe the thin Martian air. I thanked my new god as I greedily feasted on the corpse.

An opportunity arose soon afterwards to ship out on a deadliner ship. With my seniority I got on easily. A "deadliner" is a term invented by the Twentieth Century philosopher Barrington Bayley. It's a spaceman gone for decades at a time, a victim of time dilation who has become totally removed from human warmth and kindness. When they're in-port they know everyone they see will be dust before they return. I felt at home among those dead souls. Deadliners go deep into the galaxy, further than I'd ever been. Some of the crew had birthdates decades before mine. In a ship of such individualists, I could stalk easily. I signed on as Albert Donner, a famous miner and cannibal of the Nineteenth Century. Even a ghoul can have his little jokes.

A light month past the solar system I began to let my claws grow. They're semi-retractable. I can pass inhuman society. Especially in deadliner society—for deadliners never look too closely at their shipmates. They're always spiraling inwards.

A young-looking computer tech with magnificent red hair would be my first target. I stalked her quietly waiting for my moment. When the moment came, I ripped her tender white throat open with my claws. I carefully placed the bleeding body on a plastic to avoid telltale bloodstains.

I hadn't taken the security of a deadliner ship into account. These people often kill each other. The stresses of the long voyage overcome all of their civilized traits. The ship was ready. It snared me in hundreds of tiny robot arms.

They didn't give me trial, didn't ask me anything. They came into normal space and shoved me through the airlock.

I felt all the air sucked from my lungs. I screamed the call in the silence of airless space. Ithaqua came and filled me and changed me. *Oh my burning feet of freezing fire!* As the ancient wind god, long since banished from the Earth by disbelief filled me, he changed me into a burning ball of hunger and hate.

I travel through the void at great speeds. I will return to Earth. I will eat you all, everyone.

(for William S. Burroughs)

The God

From the Third Angle I come, throwing forth the Jackals of Time,

I eat space and time. I eat souls and mind. I carry Their Word.

It empowers magicians, inspires poets

But this gains nothing—such souls are already open to such as I.

I have burrowed into the past looking for the most closed soul ever.

He I will tell. He will Hear.

And the dark angles of the Yet-To-Be shall destroy his world.

I shall flip him like a switch

I shall turn him like a knob

His useless dead soul will strip the world of men

In Their Names I will call forth

A new Heaven and new Earth

Remade to the glory of their Infernal Will.

Hitler's interest in the final battle with the USA is something of an historical curiosity. Although as early as the mid-'20s Hitler had referred to an ultimate conflict between Germany and America, the attack on Pearl Harbor shaped American perception of WWII as an American response to Japanese aggression. Hitler's interest in the USA is usually footnoted in three facts that seem small in the vast tapestry of the Second World War. The first was the creation of the Amerika Bomber. A project of the Reichsluftfahrt-ministerium, a bomber that could travel from Germany to New York had the blessing of Reichmarschall Herman Göring, who poured many marks into the project in 1942. The inability of Germany to develop an atomic bomb combined with the decrease of German aviation-production halted the process. The two attacks on American territory—the U-boat attacks on Cape Hatteras, North Carolina and Essex County, Massachusetts are almost unknown to the average American citizen. The former battle was waged by fishing trawlers retrofitted by the US Navy and is a stirring tale of co-operation between the government and local industry. The later incident is somewhat shrouded in mystery because of the somewhat secretive nature of the good citizens of Innsmouth, Massachusetts. The Germans had dispatched two U-boats, one aimed with a special radio device perhaps to be used in a propaganda campaign. A small group of Americans disabled one of the boats, which was found ashore near the town of Rowley, Massachusetts. The German sailors were dead, seemingly slain by their own guns. The front of the submarine had been torn open. The United States government quieted any press about the incident. In fact the only surviving account of the battle have been found in German records, of the return of one U-boat from a skirmish with Americans. Oddly enough these are not standard German naval records, but an account in the files of

> Himmler's Ahnenerbe division, which focused on occult and pseudo-science "Ariosophy"—or beliefs of a secret Aryan tradition.
>
> "Little Known Skirmishes of the Battle of the Atlantic"
> Capt. William Henderson USN retired

THE GREAT EXCITEMENT I feel at being chosen by Reichsführer Himmler to oversee the *Studiengesellschaft für Unterseegeiste-surgeschichte* is unbounded. Before the coming of the NSDAP, my theories had been regulated to the ash heap of occultism. Himmler sees the truth. Our Aryan ancestors had not only ruled the primal world of land but the seas as well. Three-quarters of the Earth is covered in water and it is only logical to assume the Will-to-Power that enabled us to claim the earth before the coming of the sub-humans had likewise led us to conquer the seas. The legends of Atlantis, Mu, and R'lyeh all point to a bygone age of Aryan undersea folk. Of course, Jewish science has done much to discredit this. Only the ever-healing movement of history has begun to reveal the watery glories that will empower the Thousand Year Reich.

I am sad my mother had not lived to see my triumph. I was a sickly and ugly child, the butt of school room jokes and a crude prank at the gymnasium. Unlike my brother who has Aryan good looks, I was the asthmatic child of the shadows. The one who reads too much, whose fantasy is morbid, whose interests are dark. Had it not been for the coming of Hitler, my life would be overlooked, my monographs on the secret side of history ignored, and one burning dream of finally being part of something great—some-thing that defied the ages—would be like a vision conjured by hashish. Hitler, through the kindly face of Heinrich Himmler, had offered me salvation. What could I do but offer it back? I will be a hero of the Folk! A man whose name is known for a thousand years. Herman Mueller, discoverer of the undersea Aryan people. Heil Hitler! Heil Mueller!

I had found the story of the undersea Aryans in the Pacific. I had begun my researches with *Antediluvian Folktales*, *Typhonian Tablets*, *Migrations of Extinct Branches of the Genus Homo* and the much debated *Cthaat Aquadingen*. I was able to locate Ponape as a likely site of an underwater civilization. In 1889 Spain sold the archipelago of Ponape (together with the Marianne and Palau Islands) to Germany. Certain ruins were discovered in Nan Madol suggested the existence of a high level of civilization which did not match the brown skinned natives. According to the locals the cyclopean stone works were a mere minor construction, an embassy as it were for a sea dwelling race known as the Fischvolk. These immortal (!) creatures came to the land to trade gold and platinum jewelry for human workers and in exchange for mysterious (runic?) rituals being performed according to astronomical events. The Fischvolk were said to be in the service of a "Returning Savior"—clearly a folk-metaphor for the future Reich, much as the fictional (?) work of Bulwer-Lytton *The Coming Race*. Two of the Fischvolk named Olosohipa and Olosohopa told the natives that a kingdom long-ago submerged by historical accident would re-emerge on the land when the "stars were right." Until that happy time the Fischvolk would maintain the undersea world and certain land-dwellers would be tolerated. The leader of the re-emerging Reich would be named Cthulhu. This name, when analyzed by the runic principles discovered by Guido von List, reads Fire and Force is Vitally Locked, Until Outer Space Vitality Returns. (Kennaz, Thuriasz, Uruz, Lagaz, Hagalaz, Uruz). Significantly the same name had been discovered by Dr. William Channing Webb during a runic expedition to West Greenland in 1860. Unfortunately, Lutheran missionaries destroyed much of the lore these primitive brown people had of the white people from sea. The locals killed off the missionaries in 1910, and a rather crazed ship's captain shelled the island in 1911—claiming that "Fischvolk were the world's biggest threat." After the Jewish-engineered defeat of the war, Germany lost claim to the island, and it became a Japanese possession in 1919. It remains a major source of platinum for the Japanese Empire despite the geological fact that platinum does not occur on coral islands.

I was fortunate to gain some sketches of jewelry from Nan Madol made by a German missionary. The brooch and tiara he sketched show a massively detailed artistic form reminiscent of Celtic gold work. The undersea imagery bespeaks a vitality, almost a cruelty, that is the very soul of the Aryan confronted with sub-species. I had discovered this all by 1936, and had written two monographs on the possibility of an Aryan homeland in the Pacific. Indeed because of my work (and to be fair Karl Haushofer) the Japanese were granted the status of "Honorary Aryans" in 1937. It was fate, the ever-healing force of history, that enabled me to discover the Fischvolk were not a solely Pacific concern. My article in *Idunna* showing the Nan Madol tiara was read by an American scholar, Dr. Charles Everett, who provided me with the news that similar jewelry was on display at a museum in Innsmouth, Massachusetts. He believed that the artifacts were from the South Sea trade that had enriched many coastal towns in that part of America called "New England." I set out straightaway to become an expert on Innsmouth.

The results were collected in three papers for the Ahnenerbe—the last one of which drew the attention of Himmler himself. The small town of Innsmouth had undergone an expansion due to the introduction of exactly the same sort of gold and platinum trinkets that are now flowing into Japanese hands shortly after a Captain Marsh had visited the region. At first, I assumed that Captain Marsh had merely begun a trading relationship with the inhabitants of Nan Madol, but such seemed unlikely given the Spanish control of the region. But certain other facts came to play—Marsh not only had the trinkets, but his fishing trawlers began to show remarkable catches. He seemed to be possessed of a superior aquatic technology than other fishermen of New England. In addition to this he (and his family) cast off the strictures of Christianity, preferring an older vitalist religion based on bloodlines. It took me many months to accept that the return of the undersea Reich believed in by superstitious South Sea islanders was beginning to be accepted (and prepared for) by tough logical Americans—in a region dominated by chalk white Aryans. What we were struggling for in Germany by political means was occurring naturally in America in accordance with cosmic principles. The obsession of the Innsmouthers with bloodlines could only mean one thing—they had begun to interbreed with undersea Aryans. A strain of immortal, strong, wise herrenvolk was coming into being in America. Of course, it was no surprise that as Hitler had come to awaken the land-dwelling part of the Aryan brotherhood, the undersea portion would be casting off its aeons-long slumber as well.

The political aspect of this miracle could hardly be overlooked. If we could reunite the sundered halves of the Aryan world, we could become masters of the world decades sooner. On one hand we would have a built-in enclave on the American coast—a port friendly to our U-boats that could be used to deliver soldiers to American soil. We could avenge ourselves upon the Americans for their involvement in war. On the other hand, great secrets of Aryan science could be added to the war effort. Clearly all history was moving to this moment.

Himmler summoned me to his castle at Wewelsberg. He cried with joy when I showed the evidence I had collected on Innsmouth and the undersea Aryans. This was the omen that the Reich had been waiting for!

Now only practical matters remained. How did we contact the Fischvolk? They must have maintained secrecy for years for a reason. The rising of the undersea Reich must be fragile in some manner, or it would have long ago occurred. Was there a natural/cosmic reason that this had not been manifest? I had not considered this obvious question, and when Himmler asked it I felt ashamed.

"I am a scholar, not a political scientist, Herr Himmler."

I thought he might have discovered my shameful interlude at the asylum. When I was seventeen a beautiful tall blonde girl named Helga Curfman had pretended an interest in me. She had told me that she had dreamed that we should be lovers. It was Destiny, she told me. I had never kissed a girl. Near our school, the Heinrich Schlemann Oberschule, was a municipal barn, the kind that dotted Berlin in those days. She told me to strip naked and light a lantern; she would join me at night. It was cold and I was shaking with lust and coughing, longing and goose-pimples. The barn door opened. I raised my lantern and in rushed dozens of my school mates—both male and female. They pointed at my naked body. They laughed. They threw excrement on me. I had a breakdown after this. I never finished the gymnasium. I never ventured into business like my successful brother. I became a haunter of libraries, a husband to piles of books, a ghoul feeding on missing lore and grateful for the adventures of others. But Himmler smiled at me and gave me the keys to my kingdom.

"Do you know that Germany lost its greatest scientist in 1931?" he asked.

"I do not know of whom you speak."

"Just as it needed a child of Austrian culture—Hitler!—to put the Jewish politicians in their place, so it needed an Austrian to cleanse the world of Jewish science," said Himmler.

Like many scholars I had remained in my own field. I had not heard of Dr. Hans Hörbiger, who had developed the Doctrine of Eternal Ice, which refuted the "general relativity" of Jewish science. According to Dr. Hörbiger, ice was the basic substance of all cosmic processes, and ice moons, ice planets, and the "global ether." The earth had a series of encounters with great ice moons —each almost destroying life as we knew it. The ice had almost destroyed the Aryans several times, but our evolutionary response was to grow in might and main. Clearly the undersea Aryans had been developing a great civilization in the Pacific; surely, I had noticed how Aryan the heads at Easter Island were? But the Earth's previous ice moon (whose fall had produced the myths of the Flood and Atlantis) had not destroyed the Aryan Pacific Empire, but forced an evolutionary change on our brothers. This also explained why the Pacific seems to be such a large zone without land. The land here was buried under the ice. How long our brothers must have labored to rebuild what was once theirs. As we—the Aryans of the North—had struggled against sub-human hordes, so they must have struggled against giant octopi and fierce whales!

"But flesh is stronger than ice!" said Himmler. "And the Aryan spirit is stronger than time!"

I was filled with rapture. Here was a man who Understood! All of the days at being laughed at by degree carrying scholars, even mocked by my own family were over. I was to be part of the redemption of the world. God, the real God, the God of the Folk had chosen me. But my joy expanded even more. I was not the mere scholar, the mere messenger of all-healing history. No. Himmler said I was to be the ambassador to the watery realms. I would go to the sea near Innsmouth and reunite the halves of the Teutonic race! I would be having an adventure rather than reading about one.

We began researching this question at once. We must not assume that the undersea Aryans even knew of our presence. Atlantis had sunk, or as we now know been destroyed by an ice moon, millennia ago. The Fischvolk might assume that they alone are the true bloodline and might have their own plans for world salvation. They might distrust land dwellers, or be frightened by the large numbers of Jews that live among humans. As Herr Himmler pointed out, there were an exceptional number of Jews living on the eastern seaboard of the United States. Likewise the undersea Aryans might not speak as we do. In the cold and stormy world, they inhabit they might speak only by thought—indeed which might have been how our ancestors communicated with one another. It was perhaps not until the coming of the Jew were words needed. Does not the Jewish religion say that the Word was God," instead of "God is the Blood."?

At first we began looking for psychics, Germans with strong minds that could communicate silently. But our experiments were failures. Then an investigator in Munich contacted Himmler. Dr. Robert Schuss had been concerned about the communication problem. How could the lightning-fast minds of our generals communicate with the average foot-soldier? He had been working on a "telepathy-radio" and was hoping for funding. He had worked out the telepathic problem but had not solved the distance problem. He could broadcast or receive thoughts from about thirty meters, but no further. As a communication device, he felt he had failed, but hoped that, with Reich backing, this could be the ultimate communication device, or perhaps the ultimate propaganda device. Himmler contacted me at once, and we began trials. We choose non-German speaking inmates from the camps. There was some worry that such non-Aryan minds would be too primitive to receive our signals, and certainly too dim to broadcast to our minds. But the test seemed valid; our minds might be very different than the undersea Aryans. Perhaps (since they were most likely a telepathic race) their minds might be stronger than ours. Perhaps we (because of the excitement of being associated with Hitler) might have superior energy to theirs. So we tested.

Their thoughts toward us were so vicious. They couldn't understand the greater good we were doing the world. But we could understand them even if they spoke Hungarian and read Hebrew, or spoke French and Ladino. We could understand them. And we could communicate: "Lift your right arm or the guard will strike you!"

The range was about thirty meters in air, twenty-five in water, five through stone. The machine was not large. It could be fitted into the nose of VIIC U-boat. The U boat could keep its mine-laying capacity, but would lose its forward torpedo tube. This meant it would have to escorted by a second U-boat into the American waters. The Americans never had any true sense of fear. At the beginning of the war, they had only one anti-submarine boat acting as a coast guard in the Atlantic. It would be easy to mount a large submarine invasion. Himmler persuaded Hitler to allow us to try and contact the undersea Aryans of the Massachusetts coast before any other war effort. He loved tales of the undersea Aryans. The discovery of such a proof of Aryan science coupled with the strategic edge of having an Aryan presence in America would be a war changing moment.

Our U-boat was renamed the *Cthulhureich*. Our protective boat remained the U72. The captains of both boats hated me and my mission. Fortunately, Himmler had sent nine SS guards with us—

five in my submarine, four in the other sub—so that we would arrive safely. My men were tall, cruel blonde beasts—the image of what I wanted to be. I was short and dark and after Helga no woman has ever looked twice at me. My brother looked like Thor, but with my weak right eye I was Odin, ever prying into mysteries. I would be the savior of the folk.

It took five days to cross the Atlantic. We sailed on the surface the first four days, but made our approach to the Massachusetts coast underwater. If our information, bought from an Innsmouth inhabitant for much gold was true, the American government had tried to destroy the underwater settlement in 1928. The puny human attack had not destroyed the Fischvolk's city of "Y'ha-nthle"—a clear linguistic cognate to Walhalla. I had guessed that Y'ha-nthele lay about two kilometers east of Cape Ann. It would lie in a trench of course. The captain worried about the depth and warned me that he could only remain in the trench for two hours at a time. Even the guns of my guards didn't deter him. So I knew he must be speaking the truth. We found nothing during our first four days of searching. On the second dive we stayed a bit too long and a rivet in the hull imploded, shooting into the chamber like a bullet unleashing a stream of freezing sea water. We would surface at night, and twice sent small boats ashore to examine the town of Innsmouth, which seemed to be rebuilding.

One night I overheard one of guards talking to the captain. If we found nothing in a week's time, I would be killed and they would return to Germany. The mission would never have happened and there would be no official embarrassment. I was not surprised. I had heard of other "erasures." But I was deeply sad. That night I prayed to Cthulhu that I might meet with success.

And my prayers were answered.

We found another small trench, unmapped, half a kilometer east and two kilometers north. Our searchlight showed towers covered in mother-of-pearl. Strange minarets, oddly portioned frustra, delicate and cruel spikes. Dolphins, squid and enormous jellyfish swam all around. The city suggested some alien thought. I thought it was perhaps a symbol, a bind-rune, of strange glory. I had never seen any architecture as lovely, but it suggested the magnificence of cathedrals, the moonlit beauty of the Taj Mahal, the strange film sets of Hans Poelzig. I gazed at it with rapt eyes. It frightened the sailors, even the captain. Good! It should terrify the world. In my mind I already saw the strange spires topped by swastikas.

Then we saw *them*. Two meters long with scaly backs and white bellies. They lacked the beautiful Aryan heads and blond locks I was expecting, having fish heads—an irony upon mermaid legends! They had large sharp gills on their necks, and vast cold eyes bulging on each side of their face. They did not like the searchlight, so I do not know their true color, although I suspect it be gray green. Their long paws were webbed and they carried small rods—either some wonder of Aryan science or some artifact of eldritch wizardry. Seven of them approached our craft. Our captain began shouting orders to leave. One of my guards silenced him. I sat in the radio-telegraphy device and with all my might I sent my thoughts toward them, the mantra of Aryan power that Dr. Webb had recorded almost a century before in Greenland: "*Ph'nglui mglw'nafh Cthulhu R'lyeh wgah'nagl fhtag!*"

The Fischvolk convulsed with surprise (or perhaps laughter?). One swam up to our submarine and placed her hands on the craft. I could hear her voice in my mind. She sounded like a schoolgirl I had known in Berlin decades ago. The cruel girl that made fun of my defective eye and my short stature. Her German was almost without accent.

"Dreams from the sunken City enflesh themselves in Hydra's spawn. The will of the Old Ones High Priest is undying!"

Evidently this was a counter-call or litany. I did not know what to project, so I improvised. "Sister of the Folk, I greet thee! I am come to reunite the Aryan people. The ice-moon is long gone and we are preparing to scourge the land of inferior races."

Again the Fischvolk convulsed. I felt waves of humor. This must have been much-longed for news.

The ambassador asked me: "Who are you that thinks of Great Cthulhu?"

"I am Herman Mueller of the Thousand Year Reich!"

More laughter.

"A thousand year Reich! That must be a long time to your people."

"We have heard that you are undying."

"The dreams of the Old One's High Priest are undying. They were old on Yoth of the Green Star, they were old when they seeped down to this world and you were not yet monkeys. But we are not undying. I am scarcely three thousand years in age. What do you want, Herman Mueller of the Thousand Year Reich?"

"I am come to reunite our Folk."

The Fischvolk spasmed again. I grew afraid. Could it be that this was like the false tryst where Helga had humiliated me? Did I hear her voice from this bacitracin abomination? I formed in my mind the emblem of the swastika; surely that would kindle their Aryan blood, even it was as cold as the sea.

She sent a Symbol back to my mind. A nine lined star that cut the surfaces of my brain to visualize it. Their language or dreams was alive! It crawled in my mind. These were not Aryans. These were not humans. These were not on the same level of being as we were. Our thoughts are not alive our words do not crawl and thrash in the same darkness of our skulls. I heard the sailors around me scream. My guards had drawn their guns.

To kill themselves!

To free themselves of the single Symbol, or Word or living Nightmare that she had placed in the machine. Into our heads. Then she smiled at me and sent a second picture. A silvery and rainbow-colored wall of the Cthulhu chapel in the city below. I could see that it was covered in hieroglyphics, a long verse that she had simply thought the first word of at me. I could feel that first killer thought dissolving like sugar in tea. It was flowing down my brain and through my spine into my blood. It was water that burned. It was stone that blew with gale force. It was space that sucked time into it. It was the aethyr, the merest breeze through which great Cthulhu sent his dreams. It was changing my flesh. Taking something from it, and adding a great deal more.

"Would you like to be part of the Million Year Reich, Herman Mueller? You could not be as useful as a dolphin, but we love you Herman. Your deep hatred of others, your loathing of inferior races! These are precious things. We would be very amused by your tales of the land world. We think humans make great pets."

The Fischvolk were all laughing. I tried to throw back images of German power. The torch lit parades, the camps of starving men, the V-2 rockets, the Olympics.

And they laughed and laughed.

"I will think another Word for you little Herman. It will change your eyes so you can see us. Would you like to be my husband little Herman, we are building up the city on the land? We have to say certain things in the air at certain times. Your children would be"—she paused looking for the idea—"your children would be rich. We gave Marsh gold, the Japanese want platinum, the humans of Cornwall simply want fish. We are very giving. We would make your children very long-lived. You would say immortal."

I felt her Love. And it was great and deep and alien. It was like the ocean and it consumed everything. It was like hunger, or fire. It was like the feeling I had listening to Hitler's speeches but raised to the millionth power. And I knew my intentions, my will, my self—didn't matter in this equation. Then she drew back. The telepathy-radio was smoking. The air of the sub was filled with smoke and the smell of blood and the moans of the dying. I thought of killing myself, but I imagined my Word-changed flesh might not die. At least not die in the way I meant that word.

In the movies it is always at this point when the mad scientist throws a switch to destroy his laboratory. I knew nothing of what switch to throw. I couldn't blow up the *Cthulhureich*. The other submarine was not in sight. I swept the searchlight this way and that. The Fischvolk have begun *tapping* on the sides of the boat. It is a game. A game for the young ones of a few thousand years age. All of our dreams are nothing to the dreams of Cthulhu. The outcome of the war, the Thousand Year Reich, nothing. Of course they hadn't moved their city when the U.S. government shelled them. We don't move a tent because a few mosquitos come along.

My dream to be part of something bigger will be fulfilled. Just not the savior. A jester, a butler, a servant to a trusted dolphin perhaps.

(for Arnold Federbush)

The New Earth

The girders sway, the glass walls shatter, fire falls from the sky

Human flesh knits each-to-each

Making vast wailing walls, walls of a million eyes

Lava fountains forth and seas boil

And the Thing at the Pole opens its Eyes

Birds become dinosaurs again

And human bone is shaped into four pillars to hold up the sky

Strange angles become windows between now and then

Unknown colours shine in brilliant darkness

It all comes down to this

The rising of the Nightmare City

The coming of Dis.

The Mighty Messenger has said his Silent Word

Great is the Might of Nyarlathotep, Greater Still He Through Us

Lute

THE PEOPLE GAVE me an ugly human name Lute. I am very ugly, for I am the product of twelve generations of breeding made to pass for human. I have their hateful symmetry. I have been surgically altered to have only two eyes, and unlike the People I cannot see what is behind me. When I was newly harvested, the other young ones took great pleasure in sneaking up on me. My Teacher Alvan would punish them and tell them that I was the one who would be the Trojan Horse. That only made them meaner to me during the Games. The Trojan Horse is a several-million-year-old story of the humans, from the time they couldn't even see the Watchers and the Holes had not been made permanent. A group of humans were trying to break into the First Redoubt and made their bodies into a food animal called a Horse, and the hungry people from the First Redoubt caught the horse and when they went to butcher it, humans streamed out of the guts, yelling "Trojan! Trojan!" which means "Kill!" in some old stupid human language. The young ones would tie me down and threaten to butcher me, but I could usually get one of my shoulder tentacles free and strangle one of them.

My shoulder tentacles are lovely. I have two. One extends a body length, and the other six body lengths. I can hold a vilthor in each and fight with two opponents. I killed a human on an airship expedition with my vilthor when I was only four days old. Or in the human language years. I spread her blood on a dish before our spore MotherFather Levithmog, whom the humans call the Thing That Nods. Levithmog crusted the blood with spores and many children bear syllables of my name.

I grew for hundred days before Alvan harvested me. In my ninetieth day my eyes had sprouted in the cracks of my skin and I could see most of the electromagnetic spectrum. In the distance I could see the great rainbow arcs of the Air Clog. I hated it on sight because I knew I was like them and not like the People. Alvan told me that the People were descended of humans, but I find this hard to believe. He said that as the "sun" went dark. Others came flying through space to live here, as they had before when the sky was not clear. Some humans had gone the route of biological adaptations so they could live in the cold dark. They breathed in the spores of the Others and thus the People were born. We were born at War with other peoples and the shadow things and the vast things. We grow as thin white roots for many days and then we shoot up as fruiting bodies shaped somewhat as humans. At the command of the Watchers we are harvested and live as mobiles for hundreds of days and then we return to the Earth and become vast MotherFathers taking our life from the waning Earth Current. While we walk we mate in the manner of the humans exchanging DNA and the nucleotides of the Others, then we release the information as spores. Humans differ from the People, for example humans (for the most part) have only a penis or a vagina. I have only one of each, and both are between my legs. I am very, very ugly.

I remember Alvan's first words to me.

"I will call you Lute, because you are strung to resound to the thoughts and emotions of humans. You will go among them and shatter their hateful dwelling place."

He opened my mouth with the sickle and I said: "The thoughts of Levitmog crawl within me and I hate the humans."

Alvan presented me with two vilthors, and I accessed the memories of how to fight. I can remember all of my Other ancestors back to their small comet in the Coal Sack Nebula and all of my human ancestors back to the Third Atomic Age. All of the People are thus, partially due to human genetic engineering and partly because of our Other heritage. My next words were: "You are so beautiful. I wish to mate with you."

Alvan bore the best of Other, human and spider in his make-up. Heshe had lived for a thousand days and was my grandfather and my great-great-grandfather. Heshe secreted an hallucinogenic sap that we liked off of himher at the mid-day Festival of the Watchers' hatelove. Because of Alvin's sap I have seen other worlds and places that are not worlds and know what the Earth can be.

It is a sad, sad thing that humans ever came to rule the Earth. Because of their detestable symmetry, they make everything into pairs: black and white, dead and living, "evil" and "good," male and female. Their laws are stupid, they take no joy in War, they do not hold the Games. But this is not why they are hated by the Watchers.

Humans broadcast. Their brains leak reality in the form of weak electric signals. Human brains even leak thirty six hours after their heart has stopped. Humans tell the rest of the Cosmos what Order to take. Humans have never realized this fully. They have guessed. Firstly, with their perverse idea called "religion" where they make forces of the Cosmos take on human form and motivation. This is what called some of the Watchers here, and why they hatelove humankind. Human's second guess at their vileness was physics where they began to realize that the fact they observe experiments change the experiments. Humans are toxic. They have fought each other because of these leaks from their skulls. They call these religious wars, and some of the great silver fire holes are relics of the religious wars of the Second and Fourth Atomic Ages. They take no joy in War, so their weapons are vast and stupid except for the Diskos.

The People are born at War. We are fighting in Wars that existed before our kind ever came into being, Wars we have inherited from other People and things in the Great Dark. The humans that adapted to the dark hoped to learn new ways to fight and love and kill and die. They hated the Order that the Redoubt represented. They opened their breathing masks when the spores of the Others came by and they rejoiced in their change. I slew a shadow thing minutes after my harvesting. My first taste was its green clotted ichor.

After my first kill Alvan began teaching human language to me. Mainly it was memory work. Alvan would have me stare at the pendant he wore. Red, Orange, Yellow, Green, Blue, Indigo, Violet, Ulfire, Jale, Nashmar, Senec—it would flash and I would go into a trance of the great past. Words of a thousand lifetimes would come to me, and then Alvan would teach me grammar and context. I had been solider, sailor, priestess, writer, cook, farmer, engineer, airship captain, human-computer interface, astronaut, singer, whore, juggler. When Alvan would finish hisher lessons the surgeons would come. They were not People but machines built by another race ten thousand days ago. They removed three penises, two vaginas, nine eyes, some fingers and toes. They put in teeth made of bone, and planted hair on my slate blue skin. They made me shorter. I needed to be small enough to fit inside a human skin.

It took two full days for the rusty robots to do the surgery. They sank cables into my skin to draw away the pain and store it in weapons. My body made so much pain that I supplied the army of the People for two days in the battle with the Those that Chitter.

My mind is very ugly, because mainly I think like a human. I have many feelings that the People do not have. I have to be so, because my head has been made to leak like theirs. All humans are telepathic—that is to say the leaks from one head are sucked by another—like maggots sucking the liquids from a corpse. Most humans only get a glimpse of what the others think, but some can communicate with each other thusly. Humans developed a method of hiding their thoughts from nonhumans over a hundred thousand days ago. We do not grasp how they do this, but the air is still full of their leaks. And their leaks hold the Earth back from its final stage. The Earth belonged to the Others in the beginning and it will belong to them in the end. The human interlude was a cosmic bad dream, a mistake of monstrous proportion.

At the beginning of this day the surgeons sent for me. I went to their caves light in germ killing nashmar light, a color the weak humans cannot even see. One of them wheeled up to me and said: "We have been commissioned by the great Levitmog to remove your shoulder tentacles. An airship is known to be coming soon and your People will shoot it down. We will stuff you into one of the corpses, so that you will be taken to the Redoubt." One of its arms extended and gave me an injection that looked black in the nashmar light. A walking bed had moved behind me to catch me as I fell. It was very long, and I wondered as I fell asleep what the race that had built the robots were like, and how we had killed them.

I was placed into the body of a woman named Madeline.

Her flesh was torn, burnt and bruised. The surgeons told me that it would heal rapidly and graft to my body. They had skinned me so that my raw flesh would give her skin a place to take root on. They had given me her eyes, so when I awoke I saw nothing as human eyes can't see frequencies higher than violet. They had given me her tongue so that it would be the right color in the lights of the Redoubt. They had given me her blood, so I could access her memories to some extent.

I cried out in the dark.

Alvan came and brought a lamp from the supplies on the airship.

"Good morning Madeline," he said in the human tongue. "Do not be afraid. Your time of suffering will be short. You will take this lantern with you. It looks exactly like one of human manufacture. You will carry it to a power node beneath the great city. It will explode and tear a huge hole in the base of the Redoubt. Your filaments will be spread by the blast, but they will take root in the soil. In a few hundred days they will rejoin, and you will grow again. I will harvest you, and you will not be ugly anymore. You will be a hero to the People."

I dressed in a survival suit and was carried to where the great airship still smoldered. The People and the shadow things were fighting off a human rescue party. As I lay among the corpses, the People retreated. The pain medicines that the surgeons had given me wore off and I went into shock and passed out.

The room I awakened in was hatefully bright. Humans like there to be so much light in an environment that there can be no ambiguity of objects. It is part of their cosmic poison; they drain magic and uncertainty out of all things. A nurse with ugly yellow hair like my new body's was watching sensors at the foot of my bed. I could feel her thoughts leaking over me like a nagloth pissing on a rock. I couldn't understand the gibberish, but sensed it full of concern. I wanted to respond with love, but the feeling of her leaking mind was so wretched. I realized that my human ancestors had chosen to be outsiders because they lacked human warmth.

"You're awake," she said. "We didn't think you would make it. I will send for your brother soon."

"Did anyone else live? What happened?" These were the questions that Alvan said any human would ask.

"The *Althea* was taken out with an EM-pulse. That knocked out the navigation and sensor arrays. Then some large bird creature attached itself to the hull and began pecking it open. The ship fell in a small canyon near the Thing that Nods and the Abhumans raided the vessel for meat and small electronics. You were lucky, you were under some debris. Everyone else was eaten."

"At least their bodies were incorporated into other life forms," I said, but the nurse looked confused.

"Poor thing. I have to tell you your fiancé was among those killed."

That meant mating partner; sex and death were important things to humans.

"Oh no!" I cried. "Am I alone in the world?"

"Your brother was not on the flight. I have summoned him," said the nurse. She looked at me strangely. Perhaps I had not shown "grief" in the right way. It seemed that my ancestors had said the same thing, but nuance is a tricky affair.

The nurse left me. I could feel the leakages of millions of human minds in the Redoubt. To humans this was a comforting sound, like the wind across the crystal trees, or the outgassing of volcanoes—but to me it was weakening. I could feel the human parts inside me stir, open to the bright light of the room. I was Lute and my strings were humming.

Then Roderick walked in. To my surprise I did not find him ugly. Something about the light in his eyes reminded of some deep memory. He was a tall human with light brown skin and dark wet brown eyes shaped like almonds, and very dark red hair worn long. He rushed to my bedside and kissed me full on the lips, in a manner that didn't seem to accord with what I had been told of human custom between brother and sister.

"Madeline!" he cried. "I have been mourning your death for weeks. No one has survived an airship crash in decades. I had locked myself in my chamber among my old books waiting for end."

"I am glad to have lived, Roderick."

"But your mind," he asked. "Why were you not able to send for me? I have Listened, my dear, listened as no mortal man has every listened. Once or twice I thought I heard you stirring, but even now I can't Hear you clearly. Your mind is like the humming of bees."

"I have been in shock for several hours. The doctors say that I may have lost my memory."

Roderick made a pass with his hands.

He looked crestfallen when I did not reply.

"You have lost the Word. The Master Word is not within you."

My look of distress was genuine; I had no idea what he meant.

"I will keep you safe. I will not tell them you have forgotten the Master Word. They will doubt you, but I know the flesh of our parents. I know you as no other."

Some vague and uneasy memories were stirring in my human parts. This man and his sister had sinned against Symmetry. He could be an ally. I did not understand their crime, but I might need help in this strange over-lit world.

"Oh Roderick, I love you! Please take me home."

"I will take you as soon as your bruises heal without the Master Word, it will take longer for you to heal. There is much interest in you, but I will be by your side."

"Roderick, what happened to things I was carrying? Some dehydrated food, a lantern?"

"Oh I imagine they were left at the crash site, why do you ask?"

"I feel sentimental attraction for the lantern. It was my light in the Great Dark."

"How sentimental you are Madeline, I named you well."

In the hours that followed my skin returned to its creamy hue. I could not help thinking how like a dead thing's. The outer flesh knit well to me, I knew my filaments were tying it close to me and sustaining it with the blood my body had been bred to make. Many humans came and asked me about the world. It seems that the age of airships was nearing an end; all of these people clearly wanted me to speak against human exploration of any kind. I told them I re-membered nothing. They had great fear of the People and of the tribes we made War with. They saw us as savages since we accomplished our miracles with biology rather than machinery. They seemed inclined to think in terms of magic and ghosts ruling their world. It is dreadful to think of so many idiot minds blasting their wishes into the cosmos day after day—even though their numbers have dwindled to (perhaps) this world alone—humans stink of feeblemindedness. How horrible their world must have been millions of years ago when billions of their kind crawled on it, poisoning with thoughts.

My brother came every day. When I would grow weary of the scientists and inquisitors he bade them leave. I discovered that my lantern had indeed been left behind. The People had always seen humans clutch them so tightly; the People assumed that humans had a love for them. It had not occurred that they might be simple items of manufacture, easy to discard when the dark ceased to threaten. If I were to destroy the Air Clog, I would have to find and wreck the machinery responsible for it.

My brother would be of little help. He scorned the life of the Redoubt. He was a throwback to the people of little Order. He mooned about reading ancient texts and playing instruments that had been forgotten. He had great romantic ideas of the Great Dark. Our parents had died in an airship crash. "I" that is to say Madeline had responded to this disaster by becoming one of the Air Corp. He had become something called a "poet." He had asked me to take the name Madeline and he had chosen Roderick. These names came from an ancient computer that held writing from before the Third Atomic age, although Roderick said it came from thousands of days before that. He had found an ancient tale of taboo breaking and sought to live it out. The People do not spin tales of failure and adopt them; this is because our brains are not leaky. We do not understand "tragedy" or "comedy"—Roderick said that both were the fates and scripts of mankind after the Redoubt had been assembled and its Secret banned.

I also learned his crime. Their crime. Incest. A human prohibition against mating too closely. Madeline had forsworn her evil ways and ran off to the airship core to find their parents' remains, which she felt were venerated in some Abhuman temple. She could not conceive of a race without the disease of religion. Surely Mommy and Daddy were gods. So foul not to eat the dead. Even the horrible humans are eaten by the People.

While I was recovering I asked Roderick for a lamp that showed the spectrum. I said that in the Dark, I had come to love the light. He found such a toy, a small sphere that flashed the colors of the rainbow. One night I told the nurse that I wanted to be alone for a while. I watched the nine human colors. Red. Orange, Yellow. Green. Blue. Indigo, Violet, Ulfire, Jale. Once they had only seven colors, they are an ugly species, limited in so many ways. It took a longtime to achieve trance because of the sadness I felt for the missing colors. But at last I summoned the wisdom of my ancestors. I had hoped some human would know what I needed to do to destroy the Air Clog.

What I found was very different. I found Roderick. He had been my husband on the Mars Colony during the Fourth Atomic Age. The impulses he felt toward me were not the warped feelings condemned by our age, but a remembrance of what was.

And as I left the trance, I too felt these things.

If I could not open the world for my People, I could embrace a past that matched my current world. I loved Roderick. I was learning to love light. I would be human. I could never be a standard human, but I could live with Roderick in his fantasies of the past. As long as I was never challenged to utter the Master Word, I would be safe.

"In a few hours I will be released from this room," I said. "And I want to make you happy. I will no longer poke about the Great Dark, for I have come to understand that you were right and we are meant to be together. We are unlike the creatures of thus humming busy world. But can our minds ever be as one?"

"My sister, my Madeline, I knew you came back from the tomb for this reason. I dreamt that when the *Althea* crashed that you died and slept in a cave-tomb watched over by little men. And I dreamt they worked a magic on you that you would rise to see me again, as is written in ancient data banks. We can be as one. I will teach you the Master Word, and your mind will be open to mine."

Oh Joy! I would belong again. During this long day, much of what was Other in had left. Perhaps I could learn their Word. At first they had used to cure cancer, it had been a filter for Order. I had embraced much Order. No longer did I long for the Games, I didn't feel the urge to lick the sap from Alvan, I wanted my husband-brother. I wanted my new people. I wanted warmth and light. I knew that if I had been able to detonate the bomb within the hour of my entrance to the Redoubt I would not have wanted these things, but humanity had grown in me. Madeline's blood had seeped into my ichors, and my feelings were confined to a small spectrum much as human sight is.

The nurse released me and I walked through the great sea of people that live in the Redoubt. I had never imagined such a great throng of beings existed. Their leaky minds made a bright fuzzy and warm world. It would soon be mine.

My husband-brother took me to his flat deep within the 297th floor. The doorway irised and he carried me over the threshold. The room was hung with ancient instruments and facsimiles of books were stacked about. He bade me sit and poured me a glass of synthetic brandy.

"Are you ready my love for your full return to human life?"

"Yes, I am ready."

He leaned close and spoke a Word in my right ear. It was three short syllables. They had written it into their nucleotides, strung their DNA around it. It was from the height of their science when it was indistinguishable from magick. I couldn't push it from me, it enlivened the human flesh and tormented the flesh of my MotherFather.

It was SYMMETRY herself. It was all right angles tearing through the fungal fibers of my mind. It was pure white fire and perfect black pain. I struggled to stand, to spit the Master Word out of my being. It was everything my human ancestors had fled. It was the Force that kept the Watchers at bay. It closed the Holes. It was ORDER and LIGHT and HARMONY. It exorcised my Abhuman emotions, I could feel them flying from body and out into the great dark. It undid the threads that bound me to the past. I knew red blood and green ichor started from my mouth. Roderick cried out my name as he grasped my dying body. I could feel Madeline's flesh tearing off of mine as I fell.

And unmoving I fell there to rise never more.

In Memory of Lin Carter

The White Silk

Because the legend and the myths focus on the end, we focus on Yellow.

It was white in the beginning.

A white silk mask

Worn on one day by each new King or Queen.

For 27 generations.

Purity, guardianship, trust in the wisdom of generations.

WHITE.

Ten days after taking the throne

The new king put a new lock and new iron case around the "Something."

He or she did know what it was.

It was his duty to hide the Secret even further.

Twenty six cases, twenty six locks.

Twenty six layers of not knowing what must not be known.

After sealing It, the new king or queen proclaimed a rule of innocence

By donning the White Wilk Mask.

It was hot and uncomfortable, worn only from sunrise to sunset on one day.

Then He came.

On the Sealing Day, he broke the 26 locks

One by one

Broke open the 26 iron caskets

One by one

And Saw.

He put on the mask that hour

To hide the expression frozen on his face.

Was it lust, fear, anger?

He wore it the next day

And the next

And the next thousand

And it grew yellow.

Ophiuchus

WINTER HAD COME early to Manchester, Dr. Dee and his daughter Katherine felt achingly cold in the Warden's home. It was the first of October. For the past few nights, nay, the past few weeks after Mary's death little had been said by father or daughter. Dee was 77, his wife had been 18 years his junior. He had not foreseen being a widower—for the best astrologer in the British Isles, he had failed to see the shipwreck his life had become. He was going to drink a little brandy and go off to his cold bed and his terrible dreams when the knock came. A knock at night meant either the Fellows of the college had come around trying to trick him out of money or send him on some fool's errand—like the night they had told him of the seven demon-possessed children—or it was a creditor. There were many creditors. Blonde-haired Katherine sat very still by the dwindling fire hoping the rapping would cease. But a little of the old fire shone in the old man's eyes, and he went to the door. Katherine gritted her teeth; father often did things that were unwise.

Dee flung open the door. He was a slender man with a long beard white as snow. He wore a robe, like an artist's robe. He walked without a cane, saw without spectacles. The door was filled by a tall man in a fine black velvet cloak holding a lantern. The man's fierce features made Katherine think of the devil, but she knew the Devil at least was scared of her father. The man doffed his black hat.

"Good evening fine sir; do I have the great good fortune of addressing Dr. John Dee, advisor to her late Majesty Elizabeth?"

"I am Dr. Dee and few would say that meeting me is an honor," said Dee.

"I am aware of the ill-favor King James and the Archbishop of Canterbury hold for you. But does not history tell us that the city fathers of Athens had such disregard for Socrates?" The man had a large black sack tied to his waist, his buttons and buckles shown silver.

"And history tells us of Socrates' pleasant end," observed Dee.

"If I am successful in the matter which brings me here tonight, such a fate shall not be yours. I think there are places where your genius would be better regarded than here, and if I may speak frankly sir, I know that the only thing standing between you and Germany is lack of gold."

"You have some scheme for making gold? I lost many years of my life in that vain pursuit."

"No," the traveler in black said. "I have a scheme for employing a honest scholar of certain rare talents. I have the plan of spending my own gold, not seeking the Philosopher's Stone. Perhaps I can discuss this hobby horse of mine by your fire?"

Dr. Dee motioned him in.

"Katherine, bring some candles that our guest may see the fine abode of the Warden of Manchester College."

Candles were brought, and brandy served, and the biting cold seemed banished.

"So, what is your scheme?" asked Dee.

"I read your introduction to Euclid years ago. You opened a new world to me. I have acquired a book partially of geometry written in the Greek tongue that I acquired during a visit to Italy. My Greek is poor—do you know the remark from Shakespeare's play that 'Cicero spoke Greek, and others nodded their heads, but t'was but Greek to me.'?"

"I no longer frequent the theater, young sir. I am a serious man."

"Oh sir, the theatre is a great extension of the Mind wherein ideas can be made visible without occult means. Next month Shakespeare is opening a new play called 'The Moor of Venis', I believe. Perhaps I can take you and your daughter to London to see it."

Dee would have none of it. This man was beginning to remind him of Edward Kelley; he talked too well and said too little. "What book do you wish me to translate?"

"It is called the *Necronomicon*. It is a treatise on a new source of mathematics that is at variance with Euclid's Fifth Postulate. It also contains a history of the world from before the coming of man, and has certain prophecies of the world's fate. Its last section seems to be a series of Calls for contacting strange spirits and demons that haunt these strange angles. I lack both the mathematical understanding nor the Greek to render the book into English."

"Now we see why you are here. Like King James you believe me a black magician, and assume that I would translate your blasphemous tome. If it varies from the bible, it is an accursed thing, and despite what you may have heard said of me, I do not traffick with the devil's business. You may leave."

"Sir, I know that you are a pious man, but I know that you are a man of science. This book contains great wonders of mathematics and astronomy. It would empower human kind if I could but make it more accessible."

"Begone!"

"Sir I can prove the book's worth. Today is October 1 of the year of our Lord 1604, is it not?"

"So your book is a calendar; I am sad to tell you calendars of not repositories of rare knowledge."

The traveler smiled. "Sir, according to this book, on October 9 a new star will blaze forth in the constellation of Ophiuchus. You know this constellation I assume?"

"Yes, I have read Ptolemy. I recognize the 'Serpent Bearer'—it is an evil constellation. But new stars seldom appear."

"Nether the less. It shall. And the world will be affected by its radiation. The author of this book, a poet of Araby, claims that the star has already blazed some twenty thousand years ago, and that its light will reach us eight days hence. He claims that it will plant certain ideas in men—and that much Power may be had from this moment wherein the stars are right."

"Now I know you to be mad. Creation is scarce four thousand years old, and light travels instantly."

"The book claims the star will blaze brighter than Venus."

"Well sir, take your leave. If your mystery star appears, I will consider translating your *Necronomicon*. But as this marvel shall not arise, I trust you will never again darken my doorstep."

"Excellent. Look to the skies. I will see you in eight days."

After the man had left Katherine began frugally blowing out the candles. As her father slowly walked toward his bed, she asked him: "What is Ophiuchus?"

Dee smiled at his daughter's curiosity. "You'll find just northwest of the center of the Milky Way. The Greeks thought him a man carrying a snake—the man's body divides the snake into two parts—head of the serpent, and tail of the serpent. Those signs are used in certain black magic resurrection cults. But the Babylonians knew the constellation as Nirah, god-man hybrid with snakes for legs. Nirah's cult mated human women with mighty demons of the outer spaces. These hybrids had great power and were aligned with forces not of this world—or so the Babylonians thought."

"So it is an evil constellation?"

"It was. But the knowledge of such cults has long been exorcised from the Earth by Christ's Majesty."

Papa took his pious ass to bed. Katherine sat by a single candle, knowing the rest of her life would be colder and darker and lonelier. In a strange and bitter fashion she prayed after midnight. It would be hard to say to Whom her orisons went.

Dee's old friend, Kepler—lucky enough to have found favor in Prague—is credited with having first noted the supernova. It became known as Kepler's Star, but it was to Dee's Manchester home that the triumphant traveler returned.

"As you can see, Dr. Dee. It blazeth in brilliance outshining fair Venus. I trust you are interested in my book now?"

Dr. Dee bade him enter.

"Who are you and how came you by this book?"

"I am a trader. My name is Lemuel Whateley. I buy and sell diverse goods, often books. In Naples I encountered this volume."

He pulled a tome bound in golden leather which bore the Greek title *Necronomicon*, and the name of its author, Abdul Alhazred, and its translator Theodorus Philetas.

"I bought it for a very low price from an elderly man who seemed rather glad to be rid of it. As luck would have it I tried to sell it a few times and found no buyers. The title, which I English as 'Image or Ikon of the Laws of the Dead', does not seem to promise a night's entertainment, nor a day's practical matters. I looked through the book and found this."

A picture of the constellation Ophiuchus showed tonight's supernova. Someone had translated the date into Italian in a marginal note.

"Its mystery called to me. With my limited Greek I read a few pages. There is a formula for mating a human woman with a god to produce a new and terrible sort of king. It appears that this monarch will rule vast kingdoms on this world and others. Having laid aside some wealth, I thought to secure such power for my line."

"Does it not occur to you that such an abomination would have its Father's intent more than your own?"

"Many dangers occur to me, which is why I want the book translated by a scholar who is familiar with other worldly matters. I did not build a fortune by being either foolish or timid."

"So you found a man with little to lose in way of reputation, accustomed to being the favorite of kings and queens, and of advanced age," said Dee.

Lemuel Whateley answered: "Crudely put, but quite correct. I pride myself on finding the best workers, paying them fairly. It has secured my fortune and reputation."

"Well, I will read the book, and offer my services. As you know I am paid but a pittance to be the Warden of this college, and I fear daily that King James will put me to the stake. I have made inquiries to certain German princes. None have offered to pay my way into their realm, but some have offered me asylum in exchange for my skills at cryptography. What will you pay me?"

"Ten pounds in advance and ten pounds when the translation is finished. In addition I will require that you show me how to perform some of the milder operations so that I know you have translated the words in a manner both faithful and skillful."

"I would need to see this money."

"Of course." The traveler took his purse and counted ten golden coins. Katherine gasped.

"You should leave the room, my dear daughter; this is a matter for men."

She curtsied to Whateley and left the room—to put her ear against the door.

Dee said: "I had heard of this volume years ago, and I sought in my travels to obtain it. I was a braver man then, but I suppose that changing the contents of your mind can cause nothing."

"You are wrong, Sir. The art of magic is simply changing the mind—changing it in such a forceful fashion as to change the perceivable world. Art, music, even writing may produce this effect."

"So are you telling Mr. Whateley that merely reading this *Necronomicon*, will itself change me?"

"Reading what I have read has changed me," said Whateley.

"In what manner?" demanded Dee.

"For example, I can feel the intelligences that live near or behind certain stars. I can see your daughter eavesdropping beyond that door."

Katherine gasped again.

"It does not take magical powers to know that women destroy themselves by curiosity—reading either the first book of the bible or the tale of Pandora can tell you this. Can you offer me something more substantial than knowledge all man gain if they live long enough?"

Whateley smiled. "Miss Katherine, will you remain where you are?"

He crossed to the dark wooden door. From a pocket in his black velvet breeches he drew out a piece of crimson chalk. He drew vertical parallel lines some three inches apart on the soot blackened door. He muttered something and the lines began to extend. Suddenly (and unexpectedly) they converged at some point far beyond the door. At that instance Whateley reached though (or around?) the door and took Katherine's cross from her neck. A second later everything was normal and sane. He handed the cross to an astonished Dee.

"The Old Ones walk in the spaces between ours. If we wish their Wisdom, we need to see the worlds as They see them. Are you interested now, Dr. Dee?"

Dee reviewed everything he knew of stage illusion, a passion of his youth. No, he could not understand the trick. Here was the knowledge he had sought. If only he had found it in his youth, when his reputation was intact.

"I will translate your book. It is lengthy and I am slow. I make no promises of a date it will be done by."

Lemuel Whateley bowed. "I will see you soon. After the new star has fled the heavens, I have a treat for you and your daughter."

On Hallowmass Day Lemuel Whateley took the Dees to the opening night of *Othello or the Moor of Venis*. Katherine was drunk with excitement. She had never been to the theatre. She was equally surprised to discover that in his youth, her father had designed stage illusions. Had not been for her father' explanations, she would have believed that the Moor had strangled his wife for true. Whateley had rented a fine room for them, and she was content to sit and listen to their chatter late into the night.

"I have a great idea," said Dee. "Have you seen the new book, the *Table Alphabetical*? It has the novel notion of listing English words in an alphabetical order. I was thinking what use a book listing English and Greek words in the same manner might prove to translators."

Whateley replied: "I could use such a book for English and Latin. It would make business letters much easier to write. How is your translation coming?"

"I am working on the cosmological and historical section. I was quite disturbed by the content until I realized it was but allegory."

"Allegory?"

"Certainly. Oh, I am sure that superstitious people could be lead astray, much as they are by terms in alchemical books—such as the black crow or the citrine king. The account of creation and history of the universe the poet Abdul learns in the ruins of Babylon and the Irem of the Pillars are meant as allegory. For example Azathoth is stand-in for the old Greek notion of Chaos."

"What do you make of Yog-Sothoth?"

"He is the symbol of the Mind, itself. He orders the planes and angles of existence—this sounds very much like what the angels told me in the Third Call."

"So you think this is book from the angels?"

"Of course not. Maybe from the Watchers spoken of in *The Book of Enoch.* The buzzing spirits that spoke to the poet are no friend of man or God."

"What do you think of the Cult of Nirah?"

"Miscegenation between man and god is well known in myth. Were not Hercules and Dionysius the offspring of Zeus and human women? Does not the bible speak of the 'Giants in the earth'?"

"But the notion of creating and using such hybrids. Inspire you? Think of how many stupid men have held thrones—surely King James is a great example. What if men like gods again ruled the Earth, stripping it clean of the worst aspects of mankind, letting us see the world as the Old Ones see it?"

"This is allegory. It is like Plato's fable of the cave."

"When will you have finished with the magical portions of the book?"

"I will have Englished the Calls by Candlemass."

"And you will have a demonstration so that I know your translation is faithful?"

"I will perform the ritual called 'The Manifestation of Images' exactly as written by the poet, but I warn you magic seldom produces results visible."

"I have paid this Inn to lodge and feed you and your daughter for two days. I know you still have friends in London. A carriage will call for you. I will see you on Candlemass."

It was Katherine's two most exciting days. She caught a glimpse of the gold coach of the king, and dreamed of a life not caring for man, who would merely die and leave her alone.

Spring came early in 1605. Snow retreated, blossoms of all kinds appeared weeks before their time. Dr. Dee looked haggard—his eyes were stormy and had bags, his skin slightly yellowish. As February approached he had become sleepless. He would translate the book by day and then throw the pages into the fire by night. Katherine wondered that if, like Penelope, he sought to delay consummation with the suitors. Their table was well furnished. There was good wine and meat served, but father seemed distant. On February 2 Lemuel Whateley again knocked on their door. This night he wore breeches of red and yellow velvet and a fine white shirt. He sported a matching red velvet cape. He was all smiles and greeted her father with a strange greeting.

Dr. Dee replied: "In this house we shall continue to call this night Candlemass."

"Ah, I see you have read the section on the Festivals, but you disapprove."

"There are those that say the worms of the earth knew how to walk as men in the British Isles, even in the time of the Romans. That the mad poet sings of a Festival of Green Fire to mock Christmas is deplorable."

"So you have begun to see the book as something more than mere allegory?"

"I have. I would say that it is the devil's work, but I see it speaks of worlds older than the devil."

"Older perhaps than God?"

"Its blasphemy does corrupt me so deeply."

"You have begun to experiment, have you not?"

"I was tempted. I have gained dreams of other realms, and I have sent nightmares to some of the more irritating young Fellows of this college."

Katherine shuddered to overhear this. Thomas Sitwell, a young Fellow who had cheated her father of money, had recently hung himself.

"You can perform 'The Manifestation of Images'?"

"I believe it possible. We are under the Sign of the Water Carrier, whom the poet calls Ida-Yaah, so we can call forth an image of Cthulhu. If we work by the sea and the mad poet's words be true. He learned this Call in the nameless city."

"From a man?"

"From something."

Katherine did not journey with them, despite her desire "To see some magic." Dee brought only sheet of parchment with him, as he feared the operation might destroy the book. He cautioned Whateley to copy any passages he might need, so that the Forces involved would not destroy the book by fire or water.

They came to a small cove. Dee instructed Whateley to gather material for a small fire, and then to take care to stand so that smoke was blowing away from him. Dee poured some mixture in the fire and said barbarous words. Then switched to English. "Swimming across the black spaces you brought images of what you desired to remanifest as. Images that we may use to dream you into the world when the stars are right. We know that you are formless and dead. We know the Law of the Dead: That is not dead which can eternal lie. And with strange aeons even death may die. Let us dream of you O Dread Lord of the watery abyss. We will dance and slay when you return. With our Visions and our Voices hasten we the stars themselves in the living sky."

Dee again chanted barbarous names. He shrugged at the end of his recitation to prove his point that magic seldom produces visible results, but a huge booming sound came from the sea. A similar echo came from the sky. Then a flash of greenish white light flared in the sea water—as though an ocean lightning bolt had flashed in a storm for mermaids. A cold north wind blew and extinguished the fire. The star briefly took on the same greenish hue, and something landed with a thud where the fire had been.

Both men stood stock still, too frightened to even breathe.

Then Lemuel Whateley said: "I am satisfied that your translation is faithful and skillful."

Dee lit a lantern. In the ashes of the small fire Whateley had made, was an idol of a malignant squid-dragon suggesting at once ape and kraken and gargoyle. It was carved from a greenish stone shot through with veins of red. Dee watched carefully—thinking for a moment that the red veins pulsed with a life of their own. When he was convinced it was a statue, although carved by what mad artist or demon he could not guess, he lifted it up. It seemed cold and wet, and he found himself remembering nightmares from his childhood when plague was in his house. He tried to estimate the weight of the idol, yet it seemed both heavy and light, and cold and hot to the touch. He felt it was looking at him—no, he felt as if the sea were looking at him. As though a fabulous formless darkness was looking at him, an abyss that would soon look through him and judge the world of men by values and thoughts that he could not even guess. He handed the vile thing to Whateley.

"I should burn the translation. Even this is too much."

"You won't. You would have before the new star, but there is a new age coming, one that loves knowledge. The world you dreamed of. Let us hasten back to my coach and return to your home. I fancy a brandy to take the chill off of my bones."

They walked over the dunes and found their way to the coach. The horse neighed and whimpered until Whateley covered the idol. The trip to Manchester was silent. Dee was crying a bit, Whateley lost in dreams of unearthly power.

Huge clouds had formed over the city. Big bolts of lightning in every conceivable hue were flashing about, as if Zeus himself had gone mad. The storm intensified as the coach came up on Dee's home. The roof was afire, and Katherine outside naked save for a soiled bed sheet. The Fellows of the college were forming a bucket brigade.

"See that the book is unharmed!" said Whateley.

"I will see that my daughter is unharmed before I look to your devil's book."

Whateley said: "I will come back on April 30 and collect what is mine. See to your home old man. The presence of the book has upset something." Whateley had a strange smile as though he had he had uttered a jest. Dee jumped from the coach, amazingly spry for a seventy-eight-year-old man. Katherine was incoherent. Dee guessed that she had been asleep when the lightning had hit the home.

When the fire had been extinguished, he surveyed the damage. Other than her bedroom on the second story nothing was greatly harmed. The book lay open to a Call he was translating, his copy sheet was gone. He gave his bed to his daughter and asked the Fellows to bring him some blankets that he might fashion a pallet for himself. Twice in the night Katherine woke up screaming. Dee burned with slow anger toward Lemuel Whateley. He felt the trader's greed and dreams of unworldly power had wrought Katherine's condition—"collect what is mine" indeed. But in two days roofers appeared, and with sure and steady carpentry repaired the damage. A day later a well-known London physician came and examined the still incoherent Katherine and prescribed her a tea of chamomile, blue lotus and red poppy. She slept soundly and regained her wits, but would not speak of the night. Dee had resolved to do nothing more on the book and return unspent money to Whateley, but to his surprise it was Katherine that pleaded Whateley's case. With the money they could return to Mortlake. Dee's humiliating career as college Warden could be ended—and perhaps he could even create his "Lexicon." Dee had been headstrong through both of his marriages, but now his will seemed to fade. He meekly listened to his daughter and threw himself into finishing the book. At least he would get it over with.

The air had grown as warm as summer when the Feast of St. Walburga rolled around. Most people kept the old names for days despite England's Protestant ways. There were some who still set bonfires on this night to keep hobgoblins at bay. The moon was nearly new, and with its paltry light it gave the thin clouds an unhealthy greenish hue the night Whateley returned. He wore a silk shirt in a black-and-white diamond pattern and breeches striped green, gold and purple. His cape was likewise striped and his black hat sported an ostrich feather. His dark-brown eyes twinkled with merriment.

Dee on the other hand grown still thinner. His eyes were rheumy, and he developed a slight palsy. He walked with a staff, and hummed to himself like a bumble bee. Dee actually bowed to Whateley and showed him his seat.

"It is so good to see you, Dr. Dee. I have brought you a gift. 'Hot off the presses' as they say. It promises to be the best book of 1605."

He handed Dee Francis Bacon's new book, *Of the Proficience and Advancement of Learning, Divine and Humane*.

"You see Dr. Dee, it is a New Age, as I had foretold."

"I am afraid Mr. Whateley a disaster has struck, my maid seeking papers to start a fire during the strange cold days of March burned my translation and the Greek original as kindling," said Dee, as though reciting a script. His daughter rolled her eyes.

"Dr. Dee, you may understand the most obtuse problems of geometry and navigation, you may excel at knowledge of things magical, but you simply have no grasp of the power of money. I have had your house watched since the night you called the idol from the place of Otherness. You hired two scribes to make two copies each of your translation. You think to make a profit of your work. Well you shall. I will take only one of the copies, and not have my lawyers ruin you and turn you over to King James for nigromancy."

Dee looked at Katherine. Her plot had not worked even for a moment.

Whateley continued: "But fear not Dr. Dee, I bring you another ten pounds—and I dare say that will give you the seed money to return to your home at Mortlake. I will even help you find buyers for your purloined copies; for I see that you will be needing money." Then he laughed.

Dee looked helpless. This was good news, but he felt as if some joke were being played upon him. Katherine left the room and he felt alone and vulnerable.

"I don't know how to thank you," Dee began.

"I have had the house watched. I know that you have tried other operations. One night my spies saw a great cloud form over your home and then a smaller cloud detached itself from the main mass and whilst 'glowing green and purple' fell to the roof of your house, after which 'singing and sounds of viols' were heard. On another night strange noises were heard from the earth itself and a foul stench filled the neighborhood. You have been a busy man Dr. Dee. I am surprised that you pursued the devil's book."

"There is neither devil nor god," said Dee.

"Then thou hast beheld Leviathan."

"I translated all of your book. The hymns to Cthulhu, Yog Sothoth, Mlock, Daoloth. The history of the races before and after men. The place where the earth shall be moved to. The geometry and the mathematics—these more than the monsters I wish were out of my head. The geometry, the geometry. Sometimes I am seized with the feeling that I am falling from a great height. At other times crossing a room seems an endless march of days. Tell me you are not doing this for simple wealth and power."

"Oh no, good sir, I too look for wonders. I too need to know secrets beyond that of mortal men. Did you translate the section on prolonging life?"

"Aye, and the words for calling back the dead—human or otherwise."

Katherine reappeared with a fair copy of her father's translation and the Greek book.

She asked Whateley: "What are your plans now? King James plans on burning every warlock and witch on the British Isles. Prague is no longer a safe haven."

"An astute observation. I can see that you are looking to the future. I plan to travel to the new world. Surely the open spaces of America will give room for experiments. There are some sites built long ago for the same purposes I have. The book contained some useful maps."

"Which my father corrected using the methods of his Dutch friend Mercator."

Whatley glanced inside. "It looks parts of New England will become a Mecca for us."

Dee's palsy had been growing worse during this brief exchange, but with a strong effort of will he made his face still. "Then it is done. You will be out of our lives, with your gold and your knowledge that eats the mind like an acid."

"I doubt that you will say 'Farewell' to the knowledge in this book," said Whateley, excitedly leafing through the fair copy. "I will have this bound and printed on the morrow. May Day shall stand a new era to human knowledge."

"Inhuman knowledge, if my pound-wise daughter had not forbidden me I would be sending all the copies from out my roof."

"Your daughter is wiser than you, of course given her condition and your infirmity, she needs must be," said Whateley.

"What are you saying sir?" asked Dee.

"Look at her. I suspect it must be four months."

Katherine looked down. "Three months sir, the babe grows hurriedly."

Dee turned on Whateley. "You have left my daughter with child? I shall . . ." His rage choked him and the palsy returned as his fair face flushed purple.

"I have not touched your daughter. Nor has any man."

There was a moment of silence.

Then Dee saw it all. "The night of Candlemass, the storm, the strange lights."

He turned to his daughter. "The Call that was missing. The Call to Yog Sothoth, that I had re-English the next day. Why?"

"Father, soon you will be dead. I am too old to find a husband, besides who will have the daughter of a man accused of sorcery by the King and Archbishop? I wanted a child, someone to have in my old age. Why not a king?"

Whateley laughed again. Then he raised both arms after the manner of the Egyptians. "Hail Katherine full of grace, the Lord is with Thee!" He laughed again. He bowed and doffed his hat to Dr. Dee. "Fear not, the White People shall send a midwife when it is time. Repair to Mortlake and lay in stores, I would not have you eaten out of house and home. Or perhaps you will send for a cunning woman and end your hope for heirs."

Lemuel Whateley turned and left. He did not close the door behind him. As his coach rolled off in the dark, Dr. Dee stared at the now-to-apparent bump on his slender daughter's frame. His palsy grew so bad that he could not speak. He wondered—was he staring at the end of his world or the end of *the* world.

A strange bird cried in the night, high and far away.

(A nod to Richard Tierney)

Fine Green Dust

THOSE OF US that still write, still can write, of course only have some version of the same story, 'Where Was I When the World Ended?' Some of the tales moralize, some lament, most say the same thing we all say before the great green heat, "Why me, oh Lord?" I would guess that no one would download my story, or if so only as a model for his or her stories. Let's take the disaster as written, shall we? We all knew it was coming, is coming, is and has been inevitable in the face of human denial. In most ways I don't know if what happened, happened, or I was just crazy from the heat. Anyway, nothing human seems to live around me for miles and there seems to be a lot of them.

It was July 13 of that year. Now I know "that year" may be a different year for some of you, but you know what I mean. I remember the date. The city of Austin had stopped picking up recyclables because the cans got so hot in the sun they burned the hand of the garbage men. I hadn't listened to the news, and so I was the only fool that stuck my blue recycling bin out of the street. My neighbors for the most part seemed to be gone. Everyone headed somewhere north if they could afford it. My wife was with her mom in Oregon, where her grandmother lay dying. I would have gone, but I was teaching summer school. I needed the extra bucks to pay my cooling bill.

But the joke was on me; the school district had cancelled summer school the week before. It couldn't afford to cool the buildings, besides very few kids bothered to attend. Even threats of no graduation didn't stack up against the real pain of Mr. Sun. I was too damn broke to follow my wife north, so I lay around my house in my shorts during the day, only getting up at night to prowl around the neighborhood. I've always been a walker; did you know Nietzsche said: "*All truly great thoughts are conceived by walking*."? I'm not entirely sure how to punctuate that—does the question mark go before or after the quotes? I teach math. Let X = X.

The nights were super-loud. Bugs. Cicadas mainly, and the fireflies were huge. They were as big as supermarket strawberries. Late night, three or four, it got down to the nineties and the breeze didn't always burn you. There is a greenbelt near my south Austin home. The year before there had been the occasional white tailed deer or even a coyote. Screech owls picked off the hapless mice, salamanders and geckos. This year I had not seen any deer, in fact the only wild mammal I saw was the Mexican Free-Tailed bat swooping around to hoover-up mosquitoes. The Mexican Free-tailed bat is the state flying mammal of Texas. It's a fact. *Tadarida brasilinsis*. The only animals that would disturb the lush Johnson grass were the lime-green geckos. Geckos are great bug-eaters. I had lived in Austin for a couple of decades and I had noticed that they used to grow to about six inches in length, but nowadays I would see some a foot or more in length. They were big enough to rustle the grass as they passed.

This leads on to my creepy neighbor. Now Mr. Farber was not creepy because he worshipped Cthulhu, nor did bad things to small furry animals, or had sexual proclivities that we can't discuss in polite society. He was just creepy. Partially it was the two big gray hairy moles on his forehead; partially it was his sweaty fatness, partly his high voice and partially his thick glasses. I never met Mrs. Farber, who oddly enough was a stripper in a local gentleman's club. Mr. Farber tried a few times to explain what he did for a living. It had something to do with IT and it allowed him to monitor systems from home, but mainly I never saw him do anything except check his mail, which seemed mainly to be large red rectangular red envelopes from Netflix®.

On Memorial Day both Farber and I forgot there would be no mail, so we walked around the block to the mailboxes. As I checked mine, he made the comic motion of bopping his mole covered forehead to indicate forgetfulness. "Memorial day!" he said. "Oh, yeah." I felt pretty dumb; after all I had not had to drive to Bowie High School this morning. There was a large male gecko sunning itself on the next set of mailboxes down. I could tell it was male because it flexed the startlingly red cheek fan that males use to establish their territory. Bright neon-chartreuse skin, scarlet and yellow veined cheek fin, and eyes the color of sad marbles, he looked very regal on his aluminum gray perch.

"Man that's a big sucker," I said. King gecko was easily eighteen inches long. He could have dated an iguana.

"Yep," said Farber. "I guess their time is back. Dinosaurs took sort of a nosedive when the big meteor hit the Yucatan. I guess it's warm enough for a saurian come back."

"You think it's the climate?" I asked.

"Look," he said. "It's one hundred and fifteen degrees right now and it isn't even noon. I think every damn thing is the climate."

I snorted in agreement; we had both turned to head back to our air-conditioned homes. I noticed his bald spot was turning red. I wondered what his thick glasses did to his eyes. I thought of Piggy's specs in *Lord of the Flies*. I decided that when civilization fell, I'd pinch Farber's so I could start a fire. Better get a conch shell too.

As we rounded the block and our homes were in sight, he said: "I've been on a big lizard kick."

"What?"

"I've been renting movies with big lizards in them. You should watch them with me. You know, get to know the new boss."

He wasn't serious. He wasn't creepy like that. Not cultish or anything. Just lonely. I said I'd like to. Wife was heading up to the Beaver State in a three weeks and I would be stuck doing summer school.

So I watched big lizard movies until I thought my eyes would fall out. It was fun at first, and I drank a lot of Budweiser Cheladas —the clamato juice is already mixed in with the beer. It is a popular drink with Mexicans and really great when it's hot.

And it's always hot.

We saw *The Giant Gila Monster* (filmed in Cielo, Texas), *Valley of the Gwangi*, *Godzilla versus the Smog Monster*, *Gorgo*, *Pulgasari*, *Dragon Heart*, *Pete's Dragon*, *Dragon War*, *Reign of Fire*, *Gertie the Dinosaur*, *The Ghost of Slumber Mountain*, *King Dinosaur*, *Dinosarus!*, *Prehysteria*, *The Crater Lake Dinosaur*, and *Sssssss!*

It stopped being fun for me about *Gertie the Dinosaur*, even with the aid of the Cheladas. Don't get me wrong, I love Windsor McKay's animation; I just got tired of Farber's endless speculating about the need for becoming cold blooded. Some jokes are only funny the first six or seven times you hear them. So I made excuses and bowed out. Then about mid-June Farber's blue PT Cruiser wasn't in his driveway. There was a piece of white poster board taped to the tan metal door of his two-story home. It read GTL. I wondered what it meant. In the early days of Texas history many Americans had left their debts and came to the Republic of Texas. They put a sign on their abandoned farmsteads: GTT Gone to Texas. L?

Seemed like everyone was on vacation except me.

That takes me back to July 13.

I'd put my recycling bin out on the street about 7:30 in the morning. I stripped down to my boxers and lay down under the fan. The city shut off power about noon for a couple of hours, which meant the AC. By two the house would be really sweltering, and I would wake up. I stirred. It wasn't a good idea to open your fridge during the off hours, so I kept a bottle of water by me bed. Mainly to spritz myself with. I tried to get back to sleep, but the bake had lodged in my brain. I wondered around the second floor of my house staring out from behind the thick drawn curtains. I saw the full recycling bin out front, and then looking over into Farber's yard I saw a naked woman reclining on Faber's weathered hardwood chaise lounge. She seemed to have been painted green.

Several thoughts hit me at once. It was probably in the 120s, she could die if indeed she were not dead. At the very least she in for case of nasty sunburn, unless that green crap was SPF 666 or something. This must Farber's stripper wife—look at those tits! No this was a girl, the age of one my students. I figured her to be about fifteen, a year older than Juliet. This was some sort of squatter, the Whispering Oaks Neighborhood Association wouldn't be happy. She was really hot, oh that's a pun I should try out for the O. Henry Pun-Off! Maybe this was the first manifestation of a heat stroke hallucination. "They're" always talking about heat stroke symptoms on the news.

I watched her for a long time, enough to deform the shape of my shorts. Now clearly she was out of my league. For one thing public school teachers drooling after teenagers is pretty disgusting. For another there were the light years of difference in our ages. My age ("that" year) was the sum of the first prime and the third prime multiplied by the first prime cubed. If you need to check your work add the digits of your product—they should add to the value of the fourth prime. Or to put it differently if she were twenty years older and I were twenty years younger, I'd still be a year older than her.

But she was a naked girl. How many chances to you get to talk to a naked girl, even if she is painted the color of Midori liquor?

I grabbed a ratty old blue T-shirt off the floor. It was, I realized, probably older than her. It had a red Texas on the front with the words "Texas Secede" in white lettering. I had won it in a contest from *Texas Monthly*. I put on my Teva®s and headed down the stair.

It was an oven out there. Aren't you tired of thinking up other ways to say that? Hot as Hell. Hot enough for you? Hot enough to fry an egg. Firecracker. Jalapeno. Habaneras. Jeez.

I walked over to the wooden gate to Farber's back yard. I didn't need to explain myself. I belong in this neighborhood. Also I was not naked. Or green.

Her eyes were closed. I could see that color was more of a powder, a fine green dust, than a cream or paint. She was breathing.

"Hey!" I said.

She opened her eyes slowly. I thought she was high.

She tilted her head and stared at me. Fortunately I had left my boner in inside. Nobody could be aroused in this heat. Her eyes were a dead mix of slate blue and steel dust gray. Sad Marbles. "Hey," she replied with an Alabama accent thick enough to pour on pancakes.

We Southerners are very clever in our dialogue.

"Are you supposed to be here?" I asked.

"I sure am. I am the —— Farbers' niece. I am Zeena Farber. Are you supposed to be here?"

I could tell she had to remember the name over the front door. I didn't care. She made no move to cover herself.

"I am Phillip Leiden. I live next door. 9311 Bent Oaks Drive. I teach Math." As though the latter gave me special license to enter my neighbor's property.

"I am not really a whiz at math, but I'm not really looking for a tutor."

The green powder was on her genitals and her lips and her nipples. I could see a big jar of it on the other side of the chaise lounge. Some of the green grains glistened held in her light brown pubic hair.

I thought of the rivers of sweat that were collecting on my man boobs, and pouring out from under my arms. I thought of dirty white hair that stuck up like a cartoon Einstein, and the three days of stubble on my face. *Oh yeah, Phil, you're a lady-killer.*

"Well, what are you doing?"

"I'm mutating mainly. 'Chugga-chugga with the evolution train-a'."

She sang that last part to a melody somewhat like 'The Loco-Motion' by Grand Funk Railroad. Another datum to date me. That's when it hit me—she was NOT sweating. I hadn't seen a human not sweat in years. Don't you die if you don't sweat?

"What are you mutating into?" It seemed a good question.

"Mainly a lizard. Something in the family Gekkonidae I think," she said.

"You're wanting to sell car insurance?"

"I am wanting to survive. Aren't you keeping up with the news?"

She had me there. I hate the news. I think the last news story I had watched had either been the British Petroleum Gulf disaster, or the strange meteor in Belize. I felt stupid, ugly and sweaty. I had somehow thought that clever lines would be mine by virtue of my age.

"Well, good luck with that."

I left the yard.

When the power came in about an hour I did some Internet searches. Sure enough I found Bokrug Cosmetics who sold a sun block that aided in "therionic metamorphosis." That means turning into animals. Their ad said: "98% our blend, 2% our secret mental training."

The ingredient list was interesting: Oxybezone (an organic compound that absorbs UV light and is itself a suspected photocarcinogen; Zinc Oxide (that white crap lifeguards used to put on their noses, Chlorophyll, which gave the dust its color; rRNA and mRNA from *Hemidactylus frenatus* (your common house Gekko); Salvinorin A, which is a psychoactive substance found in *Salvia Divinorum* (I found many articles on this stuff which were way over my head except unlike all the other hallucinogens it effects the *inside* of nerve cells instead of their membranes); JHW-018, which is a synthetic cannabinol; and a proprietary herbal blend called the "Powder of Ibn Ghazi."

I had no doubt little Zeena thought she was turning into a lizard. Some folks tripping on Salvinorin (according to the all-knowing Internet) stopped sweating. As a teacher my job was to call Child Protective Services, but I was hot. I was weary. And I thought, "Who gives a fuck?" I had begun to think that the world was coming to an end anyway, did it matter some teenager was frying her brain, when the world itself was frying?

I showered and cursed the low water pressure and collapsed on my bed. I didn't see Zeena Farber for the next two days, because I simply didn't stare out of my south windows. I talked to my wife the first day, but something was going wrong with our landline and static overcame our conversation. Mainly she talked about how the hospital was where her granny lay, and how all the Oregon waterfalls I loved had dried up this summer. She sounded hot, dry and sad. I kept picturing tumbleweed haunted landscapes from old *Twilight Zones*. I sort of liked the static ending her world-wearying sadness.

I made a plan to fly up and see her. Then I checked airfares north.

I couldn't drive in such a damn oven.

I got some sleep. I did my laundry. I pulled myself out of depression. My ethics and my pre-end-of-the-world self-returned. I would talk to my squatter and tell her that the crap she was smearing on her skin was doing bad things to her brain, and the photocarcinogen was probably going to give her lizard skin—just not the kind she wanted. On July 16 I watched through my heavy drapes. Decades ago my mom had awakened me on the same day to see humans land on the Moon, as NASA (remember them?) had celebrated the anniversary of the Trinity blast. NASA wanted the Atomic Age (1945) and the Space Age (1969) to begin on the same day. Hot enough for you?

At twilight I saw her coming out of Farber's house. She was very white and she carried a big black jar. She unscrewed the jar and dipped her left hand into the dust. I sprinted downstairs. Real heroic like.

"Don't put that stuff on Zen!"

"Mr. Leiden, you are so stupid." She said as she began to rub it on her flanks. "You don't even recognize me from Algebra II."

Suddenly I did recognize her. The nakedness, the heat, the surreality had masked her. Her name wasn't Zeena and it wasn't Farber, and I could even remember her handwriting as it marked out the quadratic formula.

"Susan, that stuff probably gives you cancer, and it certainly screws with your mind."

"It should screw with the mind, don't you think, Mr. Leiden? The mind of humankind has decided that the world should end in fire. I think it's time for the lizard brain to have another go." She continued rubbing the dust on her.

"You are related to Farber aren't you?" I remembered her a few years ago, playing in the sprinkler in the front yard.

"Yes. You and your wife have given me Halloween candy for years."

I saw her a witch, as an alien, as a ladybug.

"I really want you to stop using that sun-block or whatever the hell it is. I'll call your parents."

"Oh really? Would you have a clue how to get hold of them?"

"I'll tell Farber."

"The Farbers are gone."

"Gone where?"

"Where do you think?"

L? Lizard?

Susan said: "You remember Mr. Caroni's English class? We read *Catcher in the Rye*. You know when Holden compares himself to the Eskimo statues?"

"Yes," I lied. I've never been much of a reader.

"He thinks how they never change. You are an Eskimo statue."

"Me?"

"White guys your age. I bet you smoked dope in college. Right? I know you can't answer. But you are all super upset, that somebody else might do something fun."

"I think that Bokrug Blend there is a lot worse than dope."

"Or a lot better." She was greening her face. "It is our last, best hope."

"I'm gonna——"

"Gonna what?" she asked.

I could hear the cicadas buzzing. One of the giant lightning bugs flashes between us. Far away I heard an ice cream truck. The neighborhood should be a lot noisier.

"Gonna what?" she asked again.

I sort of half-turned. Defeated.

"You know what you want. You want to try. Try it and then you can preach. Isn't that what Mrs. Heyer says? 'The scientific method.' "

She was right. I wanted a way out of the oven. I moved toward her, bending down, wondering where my common sense had gone. Her hand found my cheek. The dust was greasy and smelled bad. It numbed my skin and I felt a little dizzy.

"What the fuck are you doing?"

It was a deep male voice. I turned. A tall African American male stood in the gateway. I recognized him from Bowie High as well. I think his name was Leon. He was not in my math classes. He wore black and red shorts and over-long red t-shirt. Our part of town belonged to Bloods. "What are you doing with the old dude? Oh hell, it's that teacher."

Susan answered: "I am giving him a taste of the future."

"Peckerwoods like him don't deserve the future. Besides he won't be able to do the mind stuff. You hear that fuckwad, you can't do the math!" Then he roared with laughter.

He shook his big head at me. "I don't want to mess with you. Just go back wherever."

Susan said quietly: "Just go, Mr. Leiden. The dust will make you trippy and vulnerable."

My head was swimming. The lightning bugs seemed to have doubled in size and tripled in number. I staggered back toward my house giving Leon wide berth. I should call the police. I should do something.

I collapsed just inside my doorway, next to the washing machine.

I dreamed of lizard kings and snake people. I dreamed of Godzilla parading through the streets of Austin, blowing fiery blasts on the capitol's pink granite dome. I dreamed of crawling up the outside of my home with my sticky little feet. I dreamed of the gingery taste of a June bug crushed in my little mouth. I woke in early morning, I had somehow made it to the couch in our front room. My head was groggy, but I could walk. I climbed the stairs, and went to my spying window. I could see Susan and Leon, but not clearly. They seemed out of focus as though a fog surrounded them. No doubt the drugs were screwing with my eyesight. I pawed at the green mess on my cheek, and the humans seemed to shrink. To be swallowed in the fog. They could have become lizards—komodo dragons perhaps or iganuas. It was dark. Something was happening. I thought of running downstairs and then I had to puke again. I almost didn't make it to the toilet. I just lay beside the nice cool bowl when it was over and fell into feverish dreams again. I dreamed of shrinking, of my bones becoming small and brittle. I dreamed at fear at the thought of an owl's shadow. I dreamed of having no eyelids and seeing the sun come up as an angry god of no known human hue.

It was well into the day of the 17th that I awakened. I peeled off my vomit-stained shirt. I showered. I sat on the toilet a long time, afraid to move. Then I risked the day.

It was about 10:30. Power wouldn't be shut off for a couple of hours. I put on another old T-shirt. I took a walk around the neighborhood first. Perhaps everyone had gone to work. Perhaps they had fled north. Everywhere on the nice two-story homes of my subdivision, I saw geckos. I saw them on chimneys, I saw them on the mailboxes, I saw them walking on the light gray asphalt. I didn't hear a dog, didn't see a cat. I walked around the block, then two blocks, finally out along South Congress.

I saw a couple of cars. An old woman in Mercedes 300 C, her face without expression. A younger man (maybe Asian maybe green) was driving a beat-up white Chevy pickup. I could tell by the way the air hurt my lungs it must be about one twenty. I pulled out my cell phone and tried calling my wife, but all I got was static. I walked back toward my house, but I stood in front of Farber's. All of the houses in my subdivision look alike except for brick color, in the extreme sunlight, they all looked the same. I walked to his back yard.

There were two large geckos relaxing in the lush St. Augustine grass near the chaise lounge. A nearly empty open jar of Bokrug Blend was nearby. I took off my shirt and I rubbed what was left on my old white chest, the green dust staining my white chest hairs. I rubbed as hard as I could. I rubbed hard enough for my skin to bleed, and the fine green dust mixed with sweat and blood and tears.

I think one of the lizards was laughing at me.

(Dedicated to Neal Barrett, who wrote SF in Austin, Texas for over fifty years)

Ool Athag

EVEN THE MOST skilled of dreamers could not tell Ferin what was revealed at Ool Athag. They said that the name was too old, and that as such, it must lie so deeply in the Dreamworld that human dreamers surely could not make the journey past the Seas Which Bleed and the Mountains Who Sing, but Ferin, who had once been wholly of the waking world, had seized upon the name of Ool Athag and resolved to go there and see what was shown. Despite the warnings of dreamers whose skill was a thing of legend, Ferin decided to pursue the quest.

He left his city, which was poised on the gap between the waking world and the Dreamworld, and moved wholly into the world of Dream forsaking the waking world. He traveled by violet mist that is kind to dreamers who know no fear, and will carry them far beyond where their puny will could take them. He came at last to a village known as Nandinoor, a place of tiny twisting streets laid out in the shape of a character from an alphabet used by no human race.

Nor were the men of Nandinoor wholly human either. In the most general outline, in a candle-lit room they would pass for human. That their brats had tails, and their wives short stumpy wings was of no matter. Such things are common in the Dreamworld, where time favors the mixed and the impure. The village was prosperous in the trade of false books and the exporting of heresies to the Thousand Worlds. The village reeked of the ink of octopi and the attar of a phosphorescent rose that induces dreaming, for these are the chief ingredient for the inks for their scrolls. Ferin, who knew much of the cults and creeds of the waking world, soon found employment there. He spent a hundred years creating false faiths to spread in the world so that he might earn the opalescent coins made from dragon's scales that were the currency of the village of Nandinoor.

When his bag was full of coins he knocked at the door of the three sages' home, and paying a great fee was told all they knew of Ool Athag.

The youngest sage was of much human blood, that only the slight horns that peeked from his graying hair and his eyes the color of copper, told of his Otherness.

"Ool Athag," said the sage, "is a town by the lake of the Sun and the Moon. It appears only when the Moon is dark and clouds hide the sun, for it holds secrets that are too frightening for the sun to look on, and if the sun caught a glimpse of them, he would flee our sky, as happened years ago before the coming of human dreamers. If you travel east past the Mountains Who Sing, and wait for the darkness of the sun and moon, you will find Ool Athag. It is not a popular spot for human dreamers, for there they learn their true place in the universe, and this knowledge makes them grow small like gnats, whereupon the santh bird of the lake devours them. But perhaps such is a happy death. Who can say?"

The second sage had skin the color of tarnished silver, and when it spoke Ferin's skin itched and his mouth tasted rusty iron. It told that Ool Athag was long ago taken away.

"Ool Athag," said the sage, "was a theater, where the Mao Games were played every fourteen years. Those who knew the ancient tongues and could pass an examination of the meaning of the two and seventy masks of darkness, were allowed to watch the Games; although even watching the Games was said to be dangerous as the excitement thereof could often drive souls from their bodies. But the Emperor Purpus of the Shinning Shield had attacked the town of Monat and burned down the theater. And yet it was said that those who traveled beyond the Mountains Who Sing that the ruins of the theater may be found, and that placing one's ear to the ashy timbers one could still hear the Mao Games, and if one lay in the ruins for nine nights, one might dream of them, and go mad. Perhaps with the madness of poets, or perhaps merely mad like those of the waking world who dream of returning to the Dreamworld. Who can say?"

The third sage did not appear to be a living creature at all, but a mass of metal half the size of a man's chest. The metal rocked softly back and forth, and Ferin heard its words in his mind. This disturbed him not, for he was an experienced dreamer, but the words themselves disturbed him greatly.

"Ool Athag," went the words, "was a human like yourself. He longed to found a dynasty in the kingdom of Zmonat, by a lake called Sun and Moon. He knew that the race that dwelt there was old and tired and that it longed to return to its own space in the Thousand Worlds. So he led his army against the city and the old race threw open the doors and died gladly upon the swords of Ool Athag's army, and the streets ran cobalt blue with their blood. But Ool Athag was not content to merely wear the strangely-shaped crown of his kingdom; he sought` to possess their knowledge as well as their land, for he was a fool such as you. He listened to their singing scrolls, and drank their bottled books, and grew wise with strange lore. He found out all and everything about the Dreamworld, and the Lands Beyond, and the Thousand Worlds, and the waking world from whence he had come. He knew the name of each star—not the name that men or Kanree call the star, but the name the star calls itself. He called his people together and spent three days and three nights telling them all and everything. And they rose up against him, cursing his name for removing all their illusions and they tore his skin from his body, and wrote down all that he had said, so that they might forget. They made a pact among themselves to never meet again, so that they would never be tempted to speak one with the other of what they had learned, and they disappeared to all the corners of all the worlds, where they die in silence and poverty. But the accursed scroll still remains, for such runes of truth can not be unwritten, and every thousand years, a fool such as yourself finds the scroll and reads it, and journeys back to his own world, but there he cuts his tongue out, knowing that it would bring the end to all things to tell such truths. You have learned of Ool Athag, and this is more than any in your world know, go back there, and be happy, and trouble not the past, for the past does not forgive. But perhaps the name has hooked you like a fish, and you can not escape. Who can say?"

Ferin bowed deeply to three sages and spent a year in drinking and whoring afraid to seek Ool Athag, but slowly his curiosity rose. The stories that the three sages had told him could not all be true, so perhaps all were false, created to hide their ignorance, or perhaps to hide a great treasure that they drew their wisdom from.

So he hired men, or such as pass for men in the village of Nandinoor, and he set off for the east. They crossed the cold desert, although frost stole ears and fingers from some of them. They entered into the parched foothills, and some died of thirst, and others were carried off in the night by quiet flying things that smelled of cinnamon and made tiny purring sounds like cats. With four of his men, Ferin reached the shore, and they deserted him for they would not look upon the Seas Which Bleed.

He came into a small seaport, where only aged men dwelled, and these old folk were silent, communicating only with hand signs, or with writing in letters Ferin knew not. Ferin had a hard time making his desires known, and when at last they understood that he wished to travel to Ool Athag, they drew back and were afraid. But one of them, by far the oldest, signed that he would take Ferin across the sea, for he was greatly old and knew that death herself would find him soon. So in a ship made of the light bones of some vast sea creature and bearing sails of a somber purple, Ferin sailed east.

At first he thought that the way the sun shone redly upon the water at its rising had given the seas their name, but he came to see its secret after eleven days of journeying.

The sea began to shimmer, and the ancient sailor tied a black band over his eyes that he would not see it. He handed a band to Ferin, but Ferin was too drawn by the early visions. The ancient sailor held the wheel still. Images began to form in the water, of places far away. These were scenes of strife, battles and wars, dragons feasting on humans, humans fighting moon beasts, humans fighting Kanree, but mainly humans fighting humans. Battle after battle, and as the figures shown in the sea would bleed, their blood seemed to rise to the surface of the water. Ferin could smell the blood and grew sick of it, and still the ship sailed on.

Once the scene was of a siege where men killed wizened figures who kept themselves completely cloaked, yet bled deep blue blood. Ferin wondered if he was watching the scenes of which the eldest sage spoke. He hoped that it was not true, for that was the story that he feared most, and still the ship sailed on.

But the next morning, the scenes began to change, and he began to see battles in the waking world. At first he watched these with great interest for they showed many marvels of ancient warfare, and many things the historians had gotten wrong. Whole empires, fighting styles, weapons that no one had guessed of in his time, and still the ship sailed on for days of these battles.

But the scenes lost their charm and historical fascination, as they neared his own time. He saw how mankind had grown fiercer and more cruel, and how the weapons of war created newer and more cruel hurts. He wanted to turn away from these scenes, yet some part of him realized that he had made a bargain with the obscene gods of the sea, for seeing the earlier scenes, he had to watch these. And still the ship sailed on.

The scenes grew into battles involving his nation and his time, and he saw such things as man should not see. And still the ship sailed on.

Then the sea showed him scenes that he had known in the waking world, the scenes that he had turned his back on, because of their guilt and horror. These were the scenes that had made him take up the art of a dreamer. These were the scenes that had led to him to wine and strange drugs.

These were the scenes that he had sold much to think of never again. And the ship sailed on.

The next day there was only one scene. It showed Ferin cutting the throat of the ancient sailor while he slept, and drinking the old one's thin blood. The sea became the sea again and the smell of blood vanished from the air. Within the hour, the old sailor began sniffing the air and smiled and removed his blindfold. He smiled at Ferin and Ferin at him, and they ate the cheese and olives that were the ship's store, and drank of the spring water from the skins.

That night the wind stopped.

When the sun rose, they found the sea full of sea weed, and not a breeze stirred. The old sailor got out the vessel's oars, but neither he nor Ferin could make any progress in the weed-filled water. It was the same the next day.

And the next.

And the next.

First the water ran out, then the food. The old sailor and Ferin began watching each other, as they pretended to fish, or to fire arrows at the birds that circled the small boat. Both knew that their arrows fell short, both saw that nothing disturbed their lines. But age was the old man's undoing, and Ferin cut his throat as he lay sleeping, just as he had seen in the sea. Ferin drank of the watery blood of the old man.

The next day, the sea was clear and the winds strong.

Ferin made good progress and when he saw landsign, he tossed the old man's body into the sea, and cursed the gods of the sea. One of the birds flew low, and he thought its call was a sort of laugh.

The beaches were red, and the sand sharp and cutting. He pulled the bone ship ashore and went into the forest to search for food or men.

He found some berries and mushrooms and other things that hunger made him brave enough to try. After he had fed and found a small sweet rivulet from which to drink he returned to the beach and found the bone boat was sailing swiftly away—a strong breeze carried to the west, but he could see no one sailing it.

He tried his magical arts to summon the violet mist, or to conjure some spirit that might carry him, but he was too far from the spirits he knew, or perhaps they could not cross the evil seas, for none answered his call. He set out to the east, further inland, and none stopped him, but at night he would hear a roar like a tiger.

After some days of journeying, the land began to rise and grow more wild, so he hoped that he was nearing the Mountains Who Sang. His heart gave a great leap one morning when he could smell meat roasting, and he began running like a wild man toward the smell.

He came upon a crude village in a small clearing.

A burly woodsman split logs in front of a wooden cabin. He hailed Ferin.

"Stop friend, we don't see many men here."

Ferin came forward and begged something to eat. The woodsman took him inside and introduced him to his wife and comely daughters. There was roast pig and a home-brewed ale, and song and good cheer.

That night one of the daughters came to Ferin's bed, and the next day the woodsman begged him to stay. He needed help to tend his little farm, to hunt and gather, to sell wood and hides. Few humans dwelt here, because of the wood's evil reputation. But Ferin told him of his desire to see Ool Athag.

The woodsman said that in his grandfather's time, a group of men and Kanree had come looking to see Ool Athag, and that they had been turned into owls for their presumption. He asked Ferin to remain.

Ferin stayed for two more nights. On each night another of the woodsman's daughters gave herself to him, and on the last night the youngest daughter promised Ferin afterward (amidst many tears) that she would never eat an owl again.

The woodsman packed goat cheese, and bread made from nut flour and a jug of the home-brewed ale for Ferin, but the woodsman's wife spat upon him and cursed him and told him that he did not know what a great fool he was to leave behind such good things for the promise of Ool Athag, which, she added, did not exist at all.

Within a day's hiking he came to the Mountains Who Sang. As he climbed their slopes he heard the wind singing to itself through the leaves of the aspens, and he decided that such had been the source of the name. But that night things grew very still, and there was no wind, nor song of birds, nor the flying of the creatures peculiar to the Dreamworld. As the moon rose, Ferin saw the cliff face, near where he had camped, put forth a mouth like a woman with sensuous red lips. The cliff sang to him of his many failed romances, of women he had abandoned and families he had ruined, and of a dancer who killed herself for him. He tried to cover his ears, but the song found its way to his ears none the less.

The second night when he was far along the trail into the mountains, the boulders sang to him of the many times his friends had tricked him (both in the waking world and the Dreamworld), and how many ruses and cons had been worked on him because of his trust. The boulders sang with his father's mouth, and sported his father's beard.

The third night as he sheltered himself amidst the snows of a high pass, the icicles sang to him with the mouth of the woman who taught him the art of dreaming. The icicles sang of the lies that his teachers had taught him, and that his religious and moral instructors had taught him, and that princes and government leaders had told him.

The fourth night as he had begun his descent into a rocky desert, but could see a great lake on the horizon, the rocks and gravel grew many tiny mouths with blue lips. The many mouths sang of the Great Lie that was Ool Athag, and of the fools that died of the desert or were poisoned by the waters of the lake while seeking the lie.

On the fifth night as he lay in the foothills, a great granite dome grew lips that were Ferin's own lips and sang him the saddest song of all—the song of What Might Have Been.

He journeyed though the black desert till he came upon the great lake of a poisonous blue, that stretched like a sea. He made his way around the shore until he came to some squares of stone, that he decided must have been foundations.

Could this be what was left of Ool Athag? Had he journeyed so far and long for this?

He camped on the ruins for a day and a night, and he asked the spirits there to let him know if this was Ool Athag.

He waited another night and day, but no answer came from the spirits, so full of tears and loneliness he began to leave.

He tripped on a small metal canister laying half buried in the black sand.

He pried it up and upended it. Within was scroll written on a flimsy piece of yellow paper. It was a mere fourteen verses.

After he had read them, he thought.

They made all things clear.

They showed him the quest of Ool Athag for knowledge, and what that knowledge was. They showed him how the theater had changed the world by its simple masques. They showed him how those, who built city on the theater's ruins, were unequipped for the knowledge that came to them in dreams, and how they shrank like gnats.

The verses showed him how all of these things were true and none of these things were true, and how they stood as a symbol for a certain knowledge, and what that knowledge was.

The verses, if meditated upon, revealed all the truths of all the worlds.

For fourteen days with neither sleep nor food, Ferin meditated on the verses. He knew all things. Such knowledge came with racking pain and utter ecstasy, with mind-numbing boredom and curiosity that could cut through steel. It was all and everything that he sought in the Dreamworld, and he felt that it was time to return to the waking world, and share what he had learned with the race of man.

Such returns are easy for one possessed of such great knowledge. Ferin found himself walking along a certain road in the city of New Orleans.

New Orleans is one of the cities that sets at the edge of the Dreamworld, and Ferin had come there seeking certain gateways.

Although hundreds of years had passed in the Dreamworld, Ferin found but little time had passed here. The city was afire with a strange sect, recently arrived there, and with a blush Ferin recognized his own work from long ago in Nandinoor.

Ferin walked down the street, and into the French Quarter where his studio lay. There he began painting. He painted all the allegories that his mind had been filled with, he painted the truth about Life and Death, he painted the Secrets of Magic and Art, he painted the truth of falsehood and the falsehood of truth, he painted the why-for of games and the games of why-for. He assembled in a dizzying year, all that mankind did not know.

He threw open his studio and called all the art collectors in the city.

They came and looked. They spoke little. They bought nothing.

Day after day passed, and no one bought a single canvas, and Ferin became silent. After a while no one even came to the studio, and one night Ferin left it, with its doors open to the elements.

He was very quiet as he slipped out of the city. Perhaps he returned to the Dreamworld. Who can say?

In days the studio was rented anew, and the owners threw the various canvases that showed Truth into the trash.

There's no market for such things.

for Peter Levenda

Beyond the Rim

Beyond the rim where the darkness becomes thicker than an earthly fog,

Roll the mad planets

Whose names, if ever known, are buried under lava

Or are written on scrolls now covered in coral

There is laughter, but no smiles

Endless celebrations but no delight

Time but no measuring

Beyond the rim are the loosing marbles

The planets, lesser gods tried to shoot into the circle,

Abandoned on a spring day in godland

Now covered with mossy life

And sadness and screams

Beyond the rim

Tomahawk

DAVE WAS SOBER and smelled bad. He also hurt pretty good and was dry and a little cold. He was pondering these simple facts when he saw the young guy pull the tomahawk out of his filthy windbreaker. The kid stood over Aaron B., and with a great precision struck a blow that opened up Aaron's head. Dave could see the blood and brains hit the filthy sheet Aaron B. was wrapped up in. If Aaron B. made any sounds, the cars on the overpass a few feet above drowned them out.

The boy looked at Aaron B.'s body with a religious intensity. He was expecting something to come out, maybe some worm that made people homeless, but all that came was a dribble of blood and a smattering of brains.

Dave weighed his options.

If he got up to run it was likely that the boy might see him and then kill him. If he played possum, one of the others might move and attract the boy's attention. Maybe the boy only had one killing in him, and everyone was safe now.

Dave decided to play possum.

The boy half-walked half-slid down the concrete slope past another sleeping homeless man. The boy put his tomahawk away. Dave sighed.

Which attracted the boy's attention.

"Hey, it wasn't my lucky day!" said the kid.

"Eh, I guess not," said Dave. He hated talking to the crazies and there were more of them every year.

"But I'm getting close, I know I am," said the kid.

"That's the spirit, son, that's the American dream. Follow your hunches," said Dave. His father had after all always said that to him, or at least some bastard had. Dave was pretty unclear about his past.

The kid crouched over Dave. He smiled and said: "I'm assigned to this section, you know, between this overpass and the metal sculpture on eighth street. So I mean how many could it be? I'll sniff them out."

Well there's useful news thought Dave, I'll just move out of your territory as soon as you wander off.

"Who does the assigning, eh, nowadays?" asked Dave.

"The angles of the landscape. Angles talk to me," said the kid.

"Angles not angels?"

"Angels are things on top of Christmas trees, angles are hard and real. That's the trouble with the world, not enough hard and real things." The kid made a fist, which Dave thought looked pretty hard and real.

"Yeah," said Dave, "hard and real. I never thought of it that way."

The kid wandered off.

Dave got up walked to the park and called 911 to report the body of Aaron B.

Dave took the garbage sack holding all of his life belongings and headed toward the old railroad station. He had slept there before; it wasn't as convenient to food as the overpass, but it put him a couple of blocks out of the kid's "assigned" territory. He'd have to cross into the danger zone for food, but the life of a hunter/gatherer was inherently dangerous in the world's last years.

That night he dreamt of Them, and almost remembered the next day.

He met the kid at the H.O.B.O. food drop. Stood for Helping Our Brothers Out.

"So kid," asked Dave. "What's your name?"

"Cthulhu," the kid said.

Now there was something wrong with that name, but Dave couldn't quite place it. It was a made-up name like "Sonny Bono" or "Jack Frost." But crazies shouldn't have regular names in a well-ordered world. It would help if they had names like Bug Fuck or Dangerous Dan, so you knew to avoid them.

Dave was always big on coming up with schemes to save the world. He didn't know where he had picked up the habit.

The kid offered him half a Snickers bar.

"I found it. I don't eat chocolate; it screws up my senses."

"Thanks," said Dave.

"I think I found the One," said Cthulhu.

"Oh, that's nice," said Dave. "Who is it?"

"It's the Spaceman."

The Spaceman was one of the louder and more colorful homeless guys. He claimed that he had been abducted by aliens that had shoved something up his nose. This rant was a ticket to being interviewed occasionally, and even given free meals by UFO groups. Dave didn't know nor care if the Spaceman believed this stuff. Belief is a pretty mobile thing.

"How do you know that he's the one?" asked Dave.

"Because of his past life."

"I don't remember my past life," said Dave.

It was true. He had lost most of his past along with most of his clothes some years ago. There was a big storm, and he nearly drowned in the culvert he had been sleeping in. Then he had almost no memories. Some of his other sickness, like the first time they took him to that hospital, had also taken their toll.

That night Dave's sleep was troubled. He woke with a goddamn HUGE killing headache. Maybe it wouldn't be too bad if the kid did whack his head open, and let out the pressure. He decided to move back to the overpass. It was probably safe if the kid was stalking the Spaceman, and besides he was lonely.

The Spaceman turned up dead, missing the top of his skull.

Cthulhu took to hanging around Dave.

Dave asked to see the tomahawk.

It was a curved hunk of steel showing a human arm bent at an odd angle holding a keyboard.

"I found it," Cthulhu said. "It was at an airport on a statue of the New World Order or something, but I smelled, you know. It smelled like them."

"Who's them?"

"The bastard killers. There are too many bastards on this planet. They are waiting for orders to clean up."

"Who gives them the orders?"

"Somebody. The One. I got to find him."

"Well I hope you find him, kid, the world has definitely got too many bastards."

Cthulhu had brought him a bottle of sweet lucy.

The kid kept talking about how everybody was evil and greedy and stupid. No different talk than you could hear anywhere from anyone.

The kid said that the time was right, the loci were in place to open the gate.

The word "loci" awakened something in Dave. He knew the words, he had heard words like that in another life on what seemed like another planet. Like another planet. Dave smiled, and finished the sweet lucy. He was suddenly lost in reverie of that other life. The memories came on him so strong as to dissolve all other thoughts and all the distractions of the "now." After a while Cthulhu got up and left.

He wondered what the hell the boy's problem was. Some creep of a father who did bad things to him, something that let his pitiful brain seize on Lovecraft as a way out of the world? Jesus, Cthulhu. That was the sleeping god under the Pacific, something about dreaming and artists killing themselves. Painters leaping from windows after painting blasphemous canvases. Yeah, like an artist wouldn't give his left nut to paint a blasphemous canvas.

God. Books are terrible. They fuck you up. If you give fiction an inch, it will kill you.

Dave had been Dave Pollington fourteen years ago. He was a freelance programmer and a technical writer. He was also a budding science fiction writer. He had thought about a sign seven or so years ago, WILL WRITE ABOUT ALIENS FOR FOOD. But he no longer had an ironic take on his situation. Most days he couldn't think at all, at least not for more than twenty seconds at a time.

At first he was (in his mind, the place where such dreams can live) the best SF writer in the city of Fort Worth. He had a handful of tales published. He had a writing group. A little critique circle. And he had a fiction that he based his life on, a fiction built of a lot of American success stories on its bright side and a certainty that people of his class and race didn't ever, ever fall through the cracks. His contract job went south (in both senses of the word). He told everybody that was OK, that it would make him turn up the internal heat and really write. He would make the big time, he couldn't fail. He bought a lot of coffee, a lot of weed, and moved into a cheaper apartment. He worked out all the money. He bought a lot of sugar.

He didn't go out, he didn't waste his money on non-essential food. He was not going to look for a job, at least not yet. He wasn't going to go on relief, he wasn't going to get handouts from friends. It was all part of the fiction he believed.

He couldn't remember their names. He sort of remembered them as warm pink blobs that nodded a lot. Or maybe that was the stuff that came later . . .

He got up before dawn. He smoked a joint to get the writerly juices flowing, he fixed the coffee, three spoons of sugar in it. Took a vitamin pill and sat down to write. Whipped out his Beletrin war stories for *Amazing* and *Superlative Science Fiction Stories*. Started a novel. Crapped out. Started another. Some of the stories sold. He made his rent the first two months. He was going to do it. He began his master work *Scourge*. It was his "anger" novel about this race of semi-chitinous many-legged creatures that would kill off the entire lousy race of mankind, with special emphasis on the people that had fired him, old girlfriends and bad editors. He had mixed elements of SF and fantasy, working some lore from a controversial book called the *Typhonian Tablet*, controversial because it was either a rare Egyptian work or a hoax created by Arthur Machen. The book contained the prophecy that an end time of cleansing would occur when a certain revulsion to mankind was reached in a certain blasted wilderness amid strangely angled ruins, by some sort of giant plant. If that ain't the beginning of great SF, what is?

On that day they would rise up, and swarm over the land like Pirate Jenny's Black Freighter with Fifty Guns Loaded. It would kill all the bastards. Dave's list of enemies kept growing. He would leave his apartment to buy poster boards and magic makers to make lists of the bastards. He would do the Dante bit. You know, put all the sorry sons of bitches in hell. The lists grew. He stuck them to the walls of his apartment. If he heard about some injustice for the alien avengers to take care of, bang! they would be on the list. Slowly whole neighborhoods, then whole cities, countries, races made the list.

Dave broke off with his elderly mother, because she distracted him from writing. He broke with his brothers. Oh, he meant to patch things up later. Dropped his girlfriends. They would all forgive him. It's easy to forgive someone who's rich and famous. You can be a bastard for a little while, being a reformed bastard is a great thing on one's *c.v.* He missed his rent. The book was going nowhere, but the image of the scurrying many-legged army grew. This is what people wanted to read! He could picture it on the book jackets, as it took up more and more shelf space. Hell this was important. It would show people who needed to die. He missed his rent again, and they put him on the street. He took the lists with him and his computer. He tried to write in the shelter. He would finish the book and he would get work. The public was dying for this stuff.

He had been out of work for six months when he got sick. They took him to Bowie Memorial. They pumped him full of antibiotics, and they cleaned him up, trimmed his beard, gave him some new Salvation Army clothes and sent him back to the shelter. The computer was gone.

How many writers wound up on the street? Well, probably a lot.

He decided that he would add the people at the Shelter to the bastard list. He had spent his two months there and they kicked him out. For some months he tried hard to get a normal life, but nothing worked. He lost his papers. He was robbed. People on the street thought he was nuts, not dangerous bad nuts, but nuts because he was talking about aliens. He got sick again in the fall because of exposure. A man was letting him sleep in his garage if he kept the leaves swept up. Hospital again. Fever. The brain didn't work too well after that. He had himself from time to time. Knew who he was, who he had been. But only for brief periods. Then there was the flood, and the brain gave out.

That kid, that Cthulhu, he had woken him up. He must know something. Loci, saddle points, turning points in catastrophe theory. His life had been a fucking catastrophe.

The winter wind stirred up the newspapers, Dave liked watching them. He would sit with his friend Cthulhu and watch them. Cthulhu brought him things, donuts from the preacher, sandwiches from the dumpsters. Cthulhu watched him all the time. Sometimes he was pretty good. Sometimes he didn't think at all, and that was good too.

Dave pointed up at the newspapers. "I wrote a book about them once. See they are part of an alien book, if you could read them all mixed together like that. You could read what the alien mind wanted to do. It just looks random."

"You didn't write no books, that isn't your job, other people wrote the books," said Cthulhu.

"I am going to write a book about you, Cthulhu, it'll be the *Acts of Cthulhu*. I'll spread the good word," said Dave.

"You don't need to write about me. I'm already in a book. All your job is is to be the judge," said Cthulhu.

"I've already judged the bastards, let 'em all hang. There's not a good man left on the planet," said Dave.

"They were hoping you would say that. It is a good thing to say. There's too much wasted here, Mindstuff. There's just not a lot of mindstuff in the Cosmos. It usually dies out because it's so fragile. But sometimes mindstuff has to be taken away for misuse."

"They're going to it take away for themselves?"

"No. They use—" Cthulhu paused, "—something different."

"How come I get to be the judge?"

Cthulhu leaned close to him, and knocked his hard and real fist gently on Dave's temples. "Trojan horse, man, Trojan horse."

"Well I'm glad. Let's kill all the bastards."

"Yeah. Kill. All. The. Bastards."

They both started chanting it. Kill. All. The. Bastards. Then Dave picked up an empty pop bottle and heaved it at a passing Lexis. Then Cthulhu grabbed a rock and tossed it at a Saturn. Then they rained doom on passing cars until a cop car showed up and two cops with riot gear came to take them away.

Dave wound up in a holding cell without Cthulhu.

The next day he woke up sane and sharp and was able to convince the police that he had just been badly drunk. They let him go.

I've got to get away from that kid, he thought, or I'll wind up in a *folie à deux*. He knew there was a Salvation Army shelter several blocks from the bridge where he slept. He hadn't been that far away from home in some years, but it was probably far enough to stay away from the kid. He asked the police to drop him off there.

It was warm and clean inside, and it hardly smelled of human filth. It was better than the jail, or pretty much anywhere he had been in ten years. What had happened to him? Mindstuff was fragile, the kid was right, hell life was fragile, why hadn't anyone told him?

The TV showed the news. Three pregnant teenagers killed at a halfway home. New chemical warfare plants found in Iraq. Pharmaceutical company dumps bad drugs on Moroccan market. Elderly tossed into street. Global warming. Massacre in Rome. Shit, he thought, They do all need to die. We've got this gift of mind, we could be making dreams. Hell, even now, in my so-called "right mind" I know all the bastards should die.

One of the other bums started talking about we should bomb Iraq back to the stone age.

Dave couldn't take it anymore. These people were practically living in the stone age. Shit, he had lived as a hunter/gatherer for fourteen years. Everyone is committed to the nightmare, no one to dreams. Maybe they should all be killed. He left the shelter.

He was going to walk down to the *Fort Worth Chronicle* and tell them his story. It was poignant, it might wake people up. At first as he strode through the cold city, he thought about waking people up, maybe you could wake people up tearing away the veils, by uncovering things. But that hadn't done jack during Iran-Contra, people already knew. They all had watched TV, while he lay freezing under the bridge being a troll. They already knew how fucking bad things were. They saw people shot in drive-by shootings. He could remember last year when that green car drove up to Bill and Aaron B., and the guy inside the car asked for directions. Bill sort of stumbled over, because he didn't walk too good, and the guy just pulled a gun and blew him away after Bill told him where the Interstate was. Just drove off laughing. Dave had run to the convenience store and begged them to call 911, and then he had walked back and watched a damn crowd gather to catch the old man's last breath. Lovecraft. Whippoorwills.

If he was going to tell the paper anything, he would tell them just how bad things were, and what bastards they were for just printing it. Waste of mindstuff.

He thought about his last critique session. An older writer had told him: "The trouble with you, Dave, is that you take the world too seriously, and therefore your place in it, too seriously. You aren't an oak. You aren't even a tree. You are a weed, but if you get your shit together as a writer, you could be a weed as tall as a tree."

That's it, thought Dave, I will be a weed as tall as a tree, I will be a dandelion a million cubits tall. My gossamer seed will take the sting of my bitterness to the eight corners of the earth. Moments later he passed a used book store. Their window displayed a haphazard SF collection. Among the fade *Dune* covers, yellowing Barsoomian landscapes, warped copies of Austen O. Emme's *Planet of the Future Dead*, was a copy of a fifteen-year-old *Superlative Science Fiction* with his story 'Jupiter Twin's Revenge.' He had forgotten the cover. The cover was for a Rex Hull novella *Mr. Samler's Surprise Package*. A giant spacecraft was delivering strange crates to robots. One huge strangely-shaped crate must have held something shaped like Cthulhu, Howard Phillips Lovecraft's squid-dragon.

Trojan horse. Trojan horse. Trojan horse. Trojan horse. Trojan horse. Trojan horse. Trojan horse. Trojan horse. Trojan horse.

It was the last thing that Dave ever read. He was in samhedi when Cthulhu found him. Cthulhu gently led the grinning man home by the hand as though he were blind.

Dave lay his head on a hunk of cement as though it were a pillow. He smiled and drooled. Cthulhu had written things around him with chalk—long angular lines radiating out over the concrete slope and out to all of cowtown. Cthulhu swung the tomahawk down with great force, slicing off the top of Dave's skull. It hurt a little, but the pressure it relived was so great, it was almost like orgasm. Dave felt millions of them, streaming out of his brain, like cockroaches. He could feel their scurrying through the slippery blood, running quickly throughout the world, their mission as urgent in them as the desire to breathe.

Cthulhu laughed. "You see! You see!" he cried. "They've broke free at last—the armies have come!" Tears of joy coursed down his cheeks.

Dave said: "I wrote a book once. It was called *Pirate Jenny*."

Nodding pink shapes ran wild through the streets, longer than men, with many small pincers that sank into human flesh easily. All day long they would be scurrying through the town bringing bodies to Dave—piling them up for him to inspect.

They would bring him a crown to make him the last of earth's masters, and to hold his skull together. He would nod his approval.

And when they had stripped the earth clean, they would kill him at last. No more bastards no more.

for Michael Swanwick

The Red Rite

MY DAD THOUGHT my college plans were great. I got a BA in Arabic. He said in his generation kids that majored in Russian got good jobs in the CIA. He worked as a warehouseman all his life. Made good money at the end. Had a nice home in Normal, Illinois. He understood when I went after a Masters. "Specialize! That's the way of the world!" I specialized. In ninth century Arabic literature; my Masters was on Ibn al-Nadim. Idn al-Nadim was a Bagdad bookseller, who created a list of all known books in the Arabic language. He also catalogued all of the Syriac, Latin, Greek and Persian titles to be had in the Arabic world. For some reason this line of study did not attract the attention of the CIA, however it convinced my father that I was a hopeless idiot and he disowned me. My mother had drunk herself to death years ago, when I was in Junior High. I tried very hard to feel loss or anger or something. Frankly my feelings for dad and his for me had largely been buried with Mom, as well as the certain knowledge that the other was responsible for her death. I did not have the ambition nor the funds to pursue a doctorate and found myself in Los Angeles. My girlfriend Suzy Brown, a leggy brown-eyed blonde was seeking the attention of Hollywood, and without other focus I drifted after her. She lived on the first floor and I the third of a white stucco apartment building that had (I believe) been rather fashionable in the 1950s. I got a part time job at an organic grocery store and another part time job doing pool maintenance for the complex. I met the oldest resident, the highly wrinkled Mary LaKwon, who had also sought the attention of Hollywood almost fifty years ago. Ms. LaKwon did Tarot readings by phone, and received some sort of movie money from a dead second husband, who specialized in gangster roles. Suzy was gone most days, pounding the pavement, getting the occasional extra role. I cleaned up the pool area before noon and took care of the cheese and meat cases until seven at night. Miss LaKwon liked to sit on a lawn chair with her Mac Laptop and a Rider-Waite Tarot deck helping the hopeless, the horny, and the bored.

One day she asked me: “Mr. Hardy, did you tell me you read medieval Arabic?”

“Why, yes Ma’am. I do. Why do you ask?”

“There’s an ad in Craigslist this morning for an Arabic scholar. It asks for a résumé, links to translated works (if any). Pays top dollar.”

The movie industry produces strange needs. I assumed that some director thought he needed a translation of the *1001 Nights*, which he could then ignore. But “top dollar” sounded interesting. After my shifts I sent my résumé, and a letter of interest. I told Suzy and she mocked the whole thing.

“It will either be some weirdo that thinks he has an ancient magic book, for which he paid ‘top dollar’ on Ebay, or a blocked writer thinking he can rework a classic.”

I agreed.

My smartphone buzzed at 12:30 AM about an hour after I had gone to sleep. I assumed it was Suzy. So, I answered, “Hello Honey.”

“Excuse me I am trying to reach Mr. Farren C. Hardy.” It was a deep male voice with a trace of a Midwestern accent. At first I thought it was my father’s—calling after two years of silence, but of course he would not address me thusly.

“I am Farren C. Hardy.”

“Please excuse the hour, I am something of a night owl.”

“It’s no problem; I was reading by the phone.” Why do we do this?

“My name is Charles Ashton, I placed an ad in Craigslist for a reader of medieval Arabic. You were so kind as to respond. I am very interested in your background with Ibn al-Nadim. I am an antiques dealer, semi-retired and I came across a nineteenth century copy of a book that seems to have evaded Nadim’s catalogue. I read modern Arabic well enough to get the gist of a newspaper, but I am afraid this work has me baffled.”

“What services would you like?’

“I am in need of two services. Firstly, I would like the work translated—or at least sections thereof. It appears to be a rival of the *Ġāyat al-Ḥakīm*, mainly a treatise on astrological magic with some rather curious notes on cosmology. My second (and in some ways more pressing need) is to obtain an opinion on the authenticity of the text. The book itself was a creation of nineteenth century Cairo by a press owned by one Paulos Metamon. Metamon claims that he bought the original from an Ishmaelite of mysterious bearing, who literally disappeared in thin air after pocketing Metamon's silver. The text if genuine would be at least a century older than the *Ġāyat*, which would shed light on the connection between the Greco-Egyptian culture and early Islam, and even if a fake would rove interesting because of Metamon's connections with Helena Blavatsky."

I had no idea who Blavatsky was, but an earlier version of the *Picatrix* would create a small but interesting storm in scholarly circles; although I doubted my opinion on the matter would hold much weight.

"I see," I said. "What sort of deadlines might we be talking about?"

"Oh, I would let you decide what might be needed. I would offer you three hundred dollars a day. In cash, if you don't mind. But I have a few requirements. Firstly, I would need you to work at my home. The book is potentially very valuable, and I would hate for others to acquire it. Naturally you would need to consult the UCLA libraries and I would put my chauffeur at your service. Likewise, my kitchen staff is top notch, and available 24 hours a day. I would like to discuss the work with you in the evenings say between seven and ten each night. I am afraid that is a somewhat demanding schedule as it would tend to destroy one's social life."

"Well, frankly, Mr. Ashton, I am new to LA and have no social life except for dinners with my girlfriend."

"What about your family?"

"I am for practical purposes an orphan."

"But you are a young man. Do you see much of your girlfriend?"

Here was a sticking point. Suzy and I had grown less and less connected. When she came here, the movie business seemed an unassailable fairy castle. But the occasional extra role led to many roles, which were leading to speaking roles. She went to parties full of glitz and glamour. At first she brought me along, but of late less and less. She was being pulled into her dream, and I was being pulled into the smog.

"We're casual."

"I see. Well maybe I can drip a little Oriental mystery over you so that you can re-charm her. What do you say Mr. Hardy, ready to make an old fool part with some of his money?"

"I'll need to tell the management of my apartment complex; you see I work for them."

"What complex?"

"The La Paloma."

"The owner happens to be an old friend of mine. I'll tell Charlie to hold your job for you."

We talked a bit more and arranged for a car to pick me up at dusk the next night.

Suzy was indeed impressed.

"It sounds so mysterious!" she squealed. She knew who Blavatsky was—a nineteenth century Russian noblewoman who traveled the globe meeting spiritualists and magicians from Tibet to Cairo to (of course) California. She was sort the grandmother of the New Age. Some director, whose name I did not know but was VERY IMPORTANT was into Blavatsky. My boss at the La Paloma treated me like a king, promised to keep my job open and offered me hazelnut flavored coffee. My boss at Fresh Plus insulted me and told me to stick an organically grown leek into my anus.

A black Cadillac came at dusk.

Mr. Ashton's thirty room home in the Los Feliz neighborhood was the closest thing I've seen to pure wealth. The driver took me to the library rich with rare books, oriental carpets coved the dark tile, a small Picasso adorned the wall, and my first thought was: $300-a-day, chicken feed! Then Ashton walked in the room. He was tall, pale dark with immaculate silver beard and very lively eyes the color of Brazilian amethyst. He wore a red smoking jacket, and used a cane with a yellow ivory handle. Despite my pretensions to culture, all I could think of was the guy in the Dos Equis ads, "the most interesting man in the world." He smiled, shook my hands and we sat in overstuffed leather chairs. I had never been overwhelmed by anyone in my life, but this was different. I couldn't remember what we spoke of during our first interview. He raised my salary to $375 a day, and paid for my first week. He showed me the book, he showed my office with two computers (he didn't know whether I was a Mac person, so he supplied me with both). It was stocked with dictionaries and reference books. He had subscribed to a dozen research sources for me. There was a mini-fridge, and faxes, and buttons for calling down to the kitchen or the driver on call. The lights responded to verbal command. He had a button in his rooms where he could call me.

He told me the rules of the house. I could not go to the east wing. He had medical "conditions" and the area was a quasi-hospital. If he was there he was not to be disturbed. If I wanted to sleep over, I had to tell the staff twenty four hours in advance. If I was to have a guest sleep over I needed to tell the staff forty eight hours in advance. I had to leave my smart phone with the driver. I could not take pictures inside the home for any reason. If I wanted to send a fax or email of a page of the book to a scholar, I had to ask for permission 48 hours in advance. He had put in a dedicated land line for me. I had to be patted down by the driver when I left the home. My notes had to remain onsite.

We would dine every day at 8 in the evening. I was to dress for dinner. If I wanted to invite a friend to dinner, I had to ask 48 hours in advance. All of the house rules were given to me in a small leather book. If I wished to terminate my employment I could do so at any time, but I agreed not to disclose any aspect of the project or any details of Mr. Aston's personal life. I would be paid a week's additional wages at time of severance for my digression.

And then we dined. We did not talk about the job or the book. Aston was a great storyteller. He had crossed the globe seeking art and antiques. His stories would range from illegal tomb raiding in Egypt, to gossip about the London art world. He had stories of a hard-scrabble youth, an amazing love affair, battles fought with rival dealers that bordered on Indiana Jones tales, and his philosophical musings. He was a connoisseur of wine, but not in the least snobbish—he taught me how to find wines I liked and how to ignore snobs. He loved mah-jong like my mother's mother and we would play with two Chinese cooks. He had a great and Catholic love of music—at one moment he would entertain me with a Big Band classic, the next with avant-garde electronica, then The Beatles. He shared my love in classic horror movies. Dinner with Mr. Ashton became the highlight of my day.

I almost lived in his home the first three weeks. After dinner I would share my translations with him. Despite his modesty, he was a keen student of Arabic. He would question my word choice, discuss the authenticity of certain expressions, even showed awareness of dialect. I often thought I was learning more from him, than I was giving to him. I would work on my translations until one in the morning. Then he would join me for a little sherry. The late night conversations were free ranging—from sexual practices around the world to Ashton's long-term concerns about pollution and energy use. I wondered if he were hitting on me at first. I had always been as straight man as I know, but part of me almost seemed drawn to him in that way. On another level I began to think of him more and more as the father I wished I had had—cultured, well rounded, truly wise, and funny. I had neglected Suzy entirely for the first three weeks of my stay. Indeed, I thought of very little save for the intricacies of the translation and my growing "Bromance" with Charles.

It was he who asked me how my girlfriend was doing.

I stammered a bit, admitting that I was lost in my work. Many mornings I did not bother to have the driver take me back to my crappy apartment.

"You must be careful my friend. It is easy to let the lure of old things replace your orientation in the present world. Here in my house, one can live in a world of our own making. But this is my orbit, not your own. You are too young to be living in a world that reflects the will of another. Perhaps you should invite her to dinner."

I felt ashamed. I was also a little afraid at how much I craved this man's approval. This wasn't like me. I tried to find something about him to hate. He had a nervous tick. He stroked an amulet of "mutton fat" jade that depicted a stylized griffin. Many times, when there was a gap in the conservation, his left hand found the bauble and he patted it while staring at me. His remarks had stung me, and up his hand went to stroke his charm. I tried to find something to say, but my brain felt full of his eyes, watching me, judging me.

He added: "Unless of course you think she would fall in love with me."

There was another awkward silence and he patted his talisman.

After dinner we went to the library and I shared my research,

"Of course without a copy of the scroll Metamon claimed to have, there can be no certain dating. The language is pure eighth century, with signs of a Yemenite dialect. The author's Islam seems to be weak. He uses Shi'ite terminology when he speaks of the faith, for example he refers to his family as *khassi* instead of Shi'ite. At first I thought he used *al-hashwiya* or 'People of the Revelation' for Islamics, which is the Shi'iite convention as opposed to *Abl al-sunna*, 'Folk of the Tradition.' But it seems that the revelation he refers to is not that of Mohammed, but some pre-deluge prophet. That points to a Saebian group or some other sect like the Yezidis. I am betting on Saebians."

"Because of the planetary and stellar focus," said Ashton.

"Exactly. He claims that Eblis is not Shaitan, but a sort of outer space daemon that crystallizes the soul of his followers. He uses the Egyptian word 'akh' for soul, which refers to a star demon. Most texts like this follow the Greek concept of identifying with the Sun by a series of trance journeys. The series here is in a different order—Moon, Venus, Mercury, Mars, Jupiter, Saturn and finally the Big Dipper. His idea seems to be that rather than submitting to divine will, one becomes a star by a series of ordeals."

"What does he say about Saturn?"

"Saturn is interesting, he uses the name Cykranosh, for which I can find no other attestation, although he specifically identifies It with other with the Egyptian Seb, the Coptic Repa, Kaiwan, the Hebrew Chiun, the Greek Cronos, and Saturn of the Romans. Saturn represents a decision point. The magician needs to have conquered five obstacles. He (or as the author stresses again and again) she must conquer the changeability of moon by having a firm will despite life's up and downs. Then he must not be ensnared by loving an inferior person. Then Mercury will try to make him addicted to magic—he warns, 'Bring your life to magic, not magic to your life!' Mars challenges him with the desire to go on endless jihads—anything from petty revenge to social justice. The magician must spend time here and then retreat to a place of his own making, where he surrounds himself with books, servants and wine. I told you his Islam seemed a little weak. Then he must take up the challenge of Cykranosh. He can either choose to leave this cycle of lives and sail beyond Saturn or make sure to make a place for his next incarnation."

"That doesn't sound Islamic at all," said Ashton.

"There are heretical sects of Islam like the Druze, who believe reincarnation within a bloodline is possible. Since they are derived from Shi'ite teachings, I suspect our unnamed author may have been a forerunner of their thought; although of a magical and heretical sect."

"How does the magician know if he is ready to leave the solar system?"

"Pleasure—if finds more pleasure conversing with star daemons, he is ready. If he prefers his wine, books and sex, he may choose to remain on Earth for a longer period of time. The writers claims there are four pillars that hold up the universe: Desire (which following Plato can be both sexual desire and the desire for knowledge), Power, Sacrifice, and Evolution. 'Desire' and 'Power' would seem to being to Shaitan / Iblis at least in my mind. 'Sacrifice' involves service to the Revelation—the magician must pass on his personal Hadith to others, the secret tradition must not die."

"And Evolution?" asked Ashton.

"The author asserts that life on earth has evolved from the primeval slime of Ubbo-Sathlah. This is an unconscious evolution worked upon the earth by the star daemons. The magician must undertake a second conscious evolution to grow like his daemonic forbearers. The three other pillars and the six planets are the nine gates of evolution."

"How does he stay on Earth?"

"There are references to the Red Rite, which involves sex, blood and wine—but no specifics."

As usual Ashton typed on an old laptop while I spoke. He asked some questions about my progress, books I had consulted and so forth. Then in the wee hours of the morning he told me tales discovering a rare Persian carpet being used by a Hollywood film company and his stealing it from the set while leaving a rug with similar design from Woolworths in its place. His mimicking of the fat security guard was hilarious. I forgave him of my bad feelings, and headed off for bed.

In the night I woke wanting a snack and slipped out for the kitchen wearing only the silk pajamas that had been laid for me by the staff. In my attempts at clumsy stealth, I actually knocked into Mr. Ashton who was wandering down an unlit hall. I felt his erection brush against me. This turned me on so much that as soon as I apologized, I went back to my room and feverishly jacked off. I felt terrible remorse and emptiness when I was done—and a strong dose of homophobia as well. The next morning, I realized that I had probably come in contact with the ivory head of his cane instead of his penis. I felt even more embarrassed. I told the staff that I was ill and needed to go my own apartment. The driver asked if I needed to go to the doctor's or have him pick up any over the counter medicines for me. I said no, but even so a care packet arrived of juices, teas and fruit in the afternoon.

I did feel weak and feverish that night. I had a moment of sobering revelation—I had lived at Ashton's home for nearly three weeks. I hadn't spoken with my friends, wasted time on Facebook, exercised, watched TV or talked with Suzy. How had the time gone by? I called Suzy up and left her a less than coherent message of needing to see her. I passed out about midnight and had several hours of nightmares. At first I was translating the book, but it kept getting bigger. Pages would unfold, and unfold until it filled up the room. Soon I was in a labyrinth of paper, running from something. At first it was a shuffling zombie *à la* George Romero, but clearly of Mr. Ashton. Then he changed into a brass Minotaur. Lastly he became a sort of toad-god with stubby bat wings that hopped up and down the papers of Arabic verse and caught me by opening his big mouth and flicking me with an enormous purple-pink tongue.

When I woke my sheets were soaked with sweat and icy cold. My limbs ached. I had only felt this bad once before after three weeks of the flu my senior year in high school. I checked the clock by my bed. I had only slept five hours. I was hungry and nauseous, nervous and exhausted. I peeled the nasty sheets off and showered. Boy, I missed the fancy bergamot shampoo that Mr. Ashton had provided. Heads and Shoulders just didn't quite cut it.

Then I checked my e-mail.

I had not slept five hours.

I had slept twenty-nine hours!

Suzy had left three messages. In the first she thanked for the invitation she had got to dine at Mr. Ashton's home. In the second she asked about what she should wear, and expressed concern about our relationship since I had not spoken with her in so long. In the third she called me a 'jerk' and an 'ass-wipe' for not returning her calls. Just because I worked for a rich man, I shouldn't be going "all Hollywood" on her. I called her back ten times expressing my apology, telling her that I had been badly sick and telling not to go to Mr. Ashton's because I was sure that was where my sickness had come from.

At least the last message was true.

Of course, she didn't call me back.

My emotions told me that I was waking up from a mad bad drunken binge. My reason told me that I had some sort of break-down based on rich food, bizarre sleep schedule and a massive / obsessive research project—give me a couple of normal days and my paranoia would disappear. My guts told me that an alpha male was about to steal my mate. I should pound my chest and attack.

My guts won; I was, after all, twenty six.

I knew the earliest Ashton ever ate was eight. If Suzy were going, I need only arrive at 7:45 and—and—and I wasn't really sure what I would do. Beating up an old man didn't seem too heroic. Although as weak as I felt, it might have been an equal match. I started to call the driver, and then was shocked at my dependence toward Ashton. I thought I had thought of him as a father figure, something I knew I was in sore need of. But I realized he was mother and father. He catered to my every need—even cool PJs to sleep in. I drove my old clunker to his home. I did not go to the front door; I didn't want to be let in by the staff. I wanted surprise. I went in by the pool and made my way to the library.

Ashton wasn't there. But his laptop was. On and open.

It showed a translation of the text he had hired me to translate.

Except it wasn't my translation.

It was a full version of the text. A much better translation than I had done. Difficult phrases rendered well, nice notes. He hadn't needed me for this.

I ran through the house. I would find him. I broke into the dining-room. He was sitting next to Suzy, his hands inside her orange silk blouse, caressing her breasts. Their lips locked in a kiss. I made some involuntary noise. She gasped, he pulled his hands back. I could see her erect nipples.

Suzy said: "You said he wasn't coming."

Ashton said: "I said he was not invited. Mr. Hardy. Please don't make a scene. You are not wanted here."

I advanced. I balled my hands into fists, and then I felt the cool breeze of his air conditioning. I shivered. I felt foolish. I remembered the last time I had fought was a minor tussle with a cousin back in high school. He had argued that University High had a better team than West Normal. He had beaten my ass. My dad was so disappointed in me. "You can't even fight, you pansy, what the hell good are you?"

Suzy was covering herself. I saw the wine, which by now I recognized as a rare vintage—probably close to a thousand a bottle. I stood there shaking for a few seconds and then retreated. What would I do? Beat a man several decades older than me? Claim rights on a woman that I had ignored for weeks because I had rather be with that man?

I went home. My apartment manager knocked on my door the next morning and I was pool boy again. Mrs. LaKwon had died during my absence. The grocery didn't hire me back, but a used bookstore did. Suzy didn't return my calls. I went up to her apartment once. She wasn't home. Her car wasn't parked in the apartment complex. I planned to move away at the end of the month. I would drive my old car back to Normal. Make up with dad, or if not work there. The month came and I didn't leave. And another month. I had dreams. I had dreams of Ashton and Suzy in bed. Or I would have dreams that I was Ashton and I was screwing Suzy. And I had a couple of dreams that I was Suzy being fucked by Ashton. I awoke aroused and also feeling very dirty. I drove by his house maybe twenty times. I planned emotional scenes where I took her back.

Or where I begged to be his aide again.

I began to put together his life from the many stories he told me. Born to a wealthy California family he got see his father screw it all up and lose everything by the time he was 16. Ashton put himself through Stanford, by "will alone" he had said. Moon. Right out of school he fell in with an esoteric group—the kind that flourish in California. He played at being a magician, until he realized the men involved lacked real money, real jobs or steady girlfriends. He did a money ritual and went to Vegas where he had enough winning to buy an airplane ticket to Europe. Mercury. Then he had gone to Paris and chased tail for years, before finding the right woman, who had initiated him into the antique trade—and he had hinted something more mysterious—some "darker magical" international brotherhood, whose contacts gave him a huge advan-tage as a trader. Venus. But she had died and there had been no children. He was bitter for years traveling the world fighting off rivals in the trade. He had even dueled twice. Once in Sitka, Alaska over some rare Russian hand painted tarots, once in Ponape over Neolithic idols. He saw that he was beginning to like violence too much. Mars. He had retreated to California buying a home where his mother had had to work as a maid in the last half of her life. He invested well, traded well, cornered a little piece of the world, where he was king. Jupiter. Then in his old age he studied esoteric texts. He made sure that I read the text with the real Secrets. Saturn / Cykranosh. I couldn't forget the Book.

I really tried to leave the third month. I quit my jobs, packed my car and headed out of town. My car overheated. It had blown a gasket, and I had it towed back to the apartment. The manager was very happy to have me back. I called home. Maybe Dad would send me some escape money. After a few calls to such numbers as I remembered I got my younger aunt. Dad had died about six months ago. No one knew how to contact me. He had written me out of his will—that hadn't been an idle threat, but anyway his medical expenses had devoured the estate. There was some stuff of my Mom in a couple of boxes, did I want her to ship them to me?

I hung up. I didn't know what I wanted. I was depressed, aimless, slept 12 hours a day.

Then one day as I skimmed palm fronds from the pool—it hit me. I had something different than 99.999% of humanity. I had a plan. I had a model for power—both worldly power and other worldly transcendence. It had three pillars: Desire—you have to want things. Power—you have to rule yourself and others. Sacrifice—you have to give up distractions like magic, war and sex when they've taught you enough. I sat down on a chaise lounge. I realized that by translating the spells in the book I had memorized them. I knew what to do, what to say at each life shift. I could have life just like the one I had tasted. I wasn't Adam thrown from the garden. Ashton had taught me a deep lesson. I began looking for a better job than my bookstore, and I began typing feverishly at night remembering the grimoire's words. I felt better than I ever had.

Late one night my phone buzzed.

It was Suzy and she was scared. Ashton had been taken to the hospital. She apologized for calling me, but she said she knew no one in LA anymore. She had spent every day with Ashton. But now as he lay dying, she suddenly felt alone, confused. Why had she given up her dream of the movies? Why had she been so taken with the old man? I knew how she felt and I drove to Ashton's home. The butler let me in. Suzy was crying in the library. While I comforted her, the staff left—one by one. I never saw them again. I saw they had luggage, but my interests were with Suzy. She was shaking and wet with tears as I held her. The kitchen staff left fruit, wine and cheese on a platter. I held her. I said a million "I love you"s. A million "I forgive you"s. And a million "I know, I know"s. Then we had wine and cheese and apples and pecans.

And then we had bed.

She told me that she had never slept with Ashton, but she cried out his name.

More embarrassingly, so did I.

His lawyer knocked on the door of what had been my bedroom at 9:15. He opened the door after a gentle knocking and seemed unfazed by our lack of dress. Maybe he talks to naked people in dead men's houses all the time. Of course at that rather embarrassed moment we did not know that Mr. Ashton had died. He had apparently bled out about midnight, perhaps at the moment of our shameful outcries. He had remembered us in his will, but we had to leave his house immediately. (Actually, I think he said in the hour.)

We would be contacted.

I took Suzy back to my apartment. I put out ads on Craigslist and other places as a translator. In a couple of days, Suzy was talking to her agent and got some real work in commercials. In two months, we were making it—barely—but making it. Then we found out Suzy was with child. We were excited. We were ready.

Then the estate contacted us. Of course, we had fantasized that we would be left millions. What we got were two nice cars and slightly less than a hundred thousand dollars. Later a box of stuff came; I put it next to my mom's stuff and let it sit there awhile. We never discussed Ashton. I had begun to tell Suzy about the grimoire. She was dubious but didn't mind if I tried a spell or two. When we got around to opening the box, we found it contained Ashton's amulet, the copy of the book I had used for my translation, some porcelain statues Suzy had really liked, and a note:

> Dear Ones,
>
> Sometimes you have to accelerate things, I am sorry that I was abrupt. You have my love for making me realize that I was not done with this marvelous globe.
>
> Charles Ashton

There was also a bankbook that revealed we would be heirs to four million dollars in ten years.

I hung his amulet on a nail in the bedroom. High enough to be out of our son's way when he came along.

I wasn't surprised when young Charles Ashton Hardy took it off the wall and started wearing it when he was five. It only weirds me out sometimes when he looks at Suzy and me with such a *knowing* look.

(In memory of CAS)

Nailing It Down: The Doom that Came to Ool Athag

NEW YORK, PARIS, London, Tokyo, New Orleans. The madman filled his diary with outlandish and disturbing names. If only he had not persisted in his heresies. Sharra sighed. If only his father had not abandoned him. Why she had kept the diary? The last and most soul-searing of the diaries? It should have burned along with him. Her position as a Priestess of the God of the Pit gave her no true safety. No one might raid her tower looking for forbidden things, nor need she fear the Dream Guard, but what of her soul? Why was she drawn to strange ideas? It was a fortnight to the Festival of the Daemons. Not a single frog had fallen from the sky and none of the hairy not-quite-men of the North had come to the city.

She hid the diary among the books. *The Ethics of Ygor*, *The Yellow Text of Thanos Khan*, *Songs of Ghroth*, *Lam is Lam*. The temple eunuchs had begun to blow the hollow opalescent horns of baniths, and the burning incense sweetened the air. The deep chimes of the bells cast from meteoric iron would soon sound, and the disfigured dancers of the Hour of Crimson Ray would release their insects to swarm above the Pit. It should be a good night, a safe night. The constellations of the Unicorn and the Death Dancer ruled the skies. The blackened suns could scarcely be seen, and a greenish cloud obscured the Ruined Planet. The God should appear in the form of the Yellow Lily, and seldom did this form demand sacrifices and if the wind blew from below an ecstasy filled the humans and the crustaceans alike. Such nights were what made life worth living and were said in the *Ethics* to add years to the life of those that understood the mysteries. Such a night could heal what the madman had set loose. Troubling thoughts left her mind as she made her way down the seventy-seven spiral steps of her tower. She affixed the silver mask of serenity to her face to hide her growing excitement and lust.

She was a great beauty, cast in perfect asymmetry. Six fingers on her left hand, two small coral tentacles sprouted from her uncovered left breast. Her right eye bulged only slightly, and her right leg was scarcely four inches taller then her left. Her hair was a glorious scarlet mane, and if the God of the Pit had not chosen her for Its service, she could have been a brothel keeper, a courtesan, or even served a term as a Dean of the college of the Goat.

The incense thickened the air. Over half of the human population of Ool Athag followed the Way of the God of the Pit, but no one dared offend It. The Pit glowed with the Crimson Ray; some of the crustaceans took flight on their membranous wings as they buzzed a counterpoint to the insect swarm. The crowd was expectant. Many wore the brass mask of supreme happiness, but Sharra saw with shock that a few wore the onyx mask of fear. The tip of the Yellow Lily began to rise from the pit. A great cry of longing went up from the crowd, soon the Lily bloom and each could mate with a dream being as the veil between subjectivity and objectivity were rent by the grace of the God of the Pit. But the Lily suddenly shuddered. It thrashed violently. This had not been foreseen. The Green Prophet ran to the edge of the Pit. The Lily suddenly became golden sand and crumbled like a child's sand castle back into the Pit. A different form began to emerge. It appeared to be a giant, white, roughly human face, but black tentacles had poked out the eyes. The God seemed to have trouble stabilizing the form. Large pieces of the cheeks and lips were flaking back into the Pit. This form was new and new forms were always bad. The leprous mask emerged fully from the Pit and began dipping toward the crowd, which ran in terror. Sudden tentacles thrust out and grabbed a few humans—maybe nine or ten and pulled them into the eyeholes. When they sucked into the eyeholes, one could see a myriad of blackened suns. The great mask became two dimensional, like a paper offering, and fell backward into the Crimson Ray like a leaf falling from a great tree in the forest. When it disappeared into the red light, the Pit drew in air. All of the insect swarm and many of the flying crustaceans were sucked away. Sharra looked for the Green Prophet; he would have to write a new chapter of the *Ethics*—tomorrow the servants of the lesser gods would come to her tower and ask what was now demanded of them. The old Priest, a distant cousin, who had helped her and Marrok in the time of the Trouble, had disappeared into the Silver Desert in the height of Summer. The Green Prophet was not to be seen. Perhaps his time had come and he had been carried away to the great brick wall beyond spacetime.

The Crimson Ray began to fade and everyone rushed to his or her towers and homes. No one wanted to catch of glimpse of what might be happening in the Pit. Nothing in her last twenty-four years of service had prepared for this. It was far from the worst from of the God, but it was NEW. There had not been a new form since her grandmother's time, when a naughty child had traced a forbidden shape in the dust. She walked slowly. She must appear as untroubled as her mask. The great Play of the world should not be disturbed by the phantom of truth on the penalty of sacrifice.

When she returned to her tower, another ill omen had occurred. The wounds that served as doorways to the living towers almost never healed. Fresh scar tissue covered the doorway. The sweet smelling ichors did not drip, nor did the gentle moaning of the tower's pain sound. She called two guardsmen to tear a new doorway with their scimitars. They worked quickly and did not hide their fear. They did not wish to abroad in the night. The tower groaned at its injury and the ichors flowed thickly, but not as sweetly as before. The guards did not even remove the towerflesh from the street, so great was their desire to find shelter as the last of the Crimson Ray faded and darkness claimed the world. The greenish cloud that hid the ruined planet drifted to the north, and the living could be reminded of the fate of those that did not amuse the gods.

Safe in her tower, Sharra did not remove the silver mask of serenity. She did not want to glimpse her true face in a mirror tonight. She preferred the mask. The diary of the madman made fear mirrors, and of late crazy thoughts entered her mind that she might be the madman's sister.

The night creatures began their song. They sang as they should sing. As they had sang in the journals of the city for the last twenty three thousand years. Sharra ran her fingers of the prescribed passage of the Ethics of Ygor and the half-living hieroglyphs spoke in the tongue of her ancestor, the first Green Prophet who had laid out the first streets of Ool Athag in angles of terror and curves of sweetness in the time of the Fire Mist.

Conceive of the Cosmos as a wheel of angles unknowable save for those who Know the mind of the Laughing One who does weep. For It has marked the fourteen zones that alternate between life and death and these zones bind all creatures save for those chosen of the God of the Pit. Hearken we who come later in Its name and know that in all of its forms of Beauty and Terror there is but one commandment to those of the Terrible Gnosis that ye shall not permit the dissection of space and time by the dour demon whose name shall be reckoned as Eight, Eight and Eight and whose sign is an accursed sameness. Rejoice in the ever becoming of It who can not Be, and flee he who says only "I exist!"

Sharra paused to drink in the words that separated her from the great unwashed. The secret of secrets were held in the first eighteen chapters of the *Ethics*. The nine impossible things flowed through her mind: the Gulf where Sound is Space, the Red one who does only Green Deeds, the Color that could not be Imagined, the Flame that glows Black, the Midwife of the Dead, the Wheel that is naught but Angles, the Unwritten Hieroglyph, the Future Past and the Wine that needs no Cup.

With such inner treasures Sharra had ceased to be disturbed the events of the twilight. The God had taken a new form. Well what of it? Nothing remained forever. She spread her sleeping furs, when she heard the sound of a crustacean landing on the roof of her tower The crustaceans had originally come into being on a lightless world, and were untroubled by darkness. They had little traffic with humans save for a few who had taken up the worship of Ghroth, but a few of the crustaceans had begun to worship the God of the Pit since coming to this world. She did not welcome these converts, and (of course) no one knew what the God thought of it. It had once assumed the shape of one of the crustaceans—with their numerous jointed claws and their asymmetrical wings, and their ugly "heads" of fleshly rings and twitching antennae. She affixed the tin mask of tolerance and climbed to the roof. The creature buzzed its welcome. She bowed.

"Something forbidden is occurring / has occurred. The Dream Guards did not come to this Viewing. A new form came. We are not happy. We can not find He That Speaks As the God."

Sharra once again was glad that her mask hid her face. "I am but a Priestess of the God of the Pit. I do not know the dwelling place of the Prophet."

"It is said that he is born from your family."

"So he was, but in ages hence. He was the son of the son of the First. When he removes the Green Robes he may yet pass as a human in the darkness. If he is not in the Temple of Diamonds, I have no more ideas than you where he may be. Look to the beds of harlots, or the dens where the red weed is smoked, or among those that eat the dead. He dwells in sacred perversity until he shall loose his head and be taken to the wall beyond space and time."

"We must send a message to him."

"Then write it upon a parchment of petition and leave it in the pink dome, where he meditates during the day. I have no more connection with him than you."

"Once in the World of the Seven Suns something happened. Once we had to draw the Destroyer of Worlds, but were too late. There are stresses in the shape-waves. Much may be forgotten."

"Why do you tell me this? The God of the Pit was not worshipped on the World of the Seven Suns. It is not even known if that is in the human future or the past. In our way is only the Pit. In the beginning was the Nothing, and then the holder of the Nothing, and finally the Nothing."

"We tell you this because it is fitting that it be said." With this last buzz, the crustacean launched itself into space. Sharra could see the city quite well by now. Rings upon rings of towers white and black and slimy green stood surrounding the Pit, and nowhere was the forbidden shape.

The shape that the madman claimed was stamped in gold on the front of each copy of his imaginary Book.

The Ruined Planet and the twin moons Thag and Thok cast many shadows over the quiet city. Beyond she could see the Mountains Who Sang, and the Cyclopean tunnels the giant-ant like baniths had bored in the black basalt, before the psyches of humans ever swam through space to this world. She could see the living waterfall of white-yellow protoplasm that the followers of the God Whose Image Is Found On Meteorites use to dispose of their dead and brew their potent aphrodisiacs. She could hear the flutes and kettledrums of the disfigured dancers. The pinker of the moons cast lovely shadows on the Dreaming River that flowed across the silent desert of the south and splashed endlessly into the Pit. Metallic tapping rose from the yurts of the blind mask makers. Occasional screams came from the House of Healing, and some brave drunkards had not been frightened inside but toasted and boasted and sang in the park bearing the sculpture of the Phantom of Truth. Red ivy balls rolled down the cobble streets eating the droppings of horses and riding lizards. Few humans stood upon the tower roofs; Sharra spied an astronomer-priest of Daoloth instructing an acolyte in reading a star chart.

She descended into her tower, which shuddered slightly at the coolness of the night. One of her dream children, a half transparent satyr, wished to couple with her, and meeped his sadness at rejection.

* * * * *

It had begun as a game, and as games are sacred to many of the godthings known to men and their guests in Ool-Athag, the danger was not noticed. Three years ago, Sharra heard of the game, but it had perhaps been going for longer. It was the Season of the Raining Frogs, and the hairy not-quiet-men came for the Festival of Daemons. The Daemons were the half-man half-god beings that made the universe possible, existing between gods and men. They were the creatures that lead souls to the moons, perhaps devouring one or two. It was well known that souls resolved into Thak and Thog after the Mind was released, much as bodies resolve into Earth. During the Festival the mad poets and storytellers tried to spin wonderful and weird stories. At the end of the Festival the travelers were killed for fourteen days so their souls could wander the Cosmos, so that they would know what to do when their bodies wore out.

Sharra looked forward to that time of year. As a little girl she loved the sugar skulls, and as an adult the spicy camel sausages and necklaces of red chilies the Northerners brought were wonderful. It was a busy time for her. Mainly the duties of a Priestess of the God of the Pit were keeping the God happy, or at least trying to see that It did not demand too many unwilling sacrifices. This was a time of religious instruction.

But the stories! And the poems!

Words are among the things that make life good. Like a good bed partner, and strong wines that foam, and music under the twain Moons.

There were many storytellers but not all wove words as well as others. Some were known to have their words polished by another, or it was rumored that some had bought other tellers to unleash their word-hoards. Such things were understandable. It is a great thing to be an artist, but it is a good thing to be *thought* an artist. The worm-goddess Fame burrows in many places in the multiverse.

Sharra was preaching a sermon to Northerners (both humans and the not-quiet-men called the Yerren) in the Grotto of Endless Crystal when her childhood friend Marrok wandered in looking fearful and exultant. He took a seat on a sleeping fur at the back of the group.

"The true Soul of the Cosmos shows herself to you as black goat. She is bisexual for she takes her characteristics from the two Moons, which are both her Symbol and the center of her dreamlands. All liminal spaces are sacred to her, birth and death, xaneroi and distilling. She comes first to the witches and those that practice the Art of Twilight. As nursemaid to all Daemons, she is called the Goat with a Thousand Young, and in her instable lust and fecundity she shatters all worlds by overpopulating them with being, dream-beings and half beings. It is to her thousand hands and millions of teats that you must direct your thoughts of mother love as your soul is released, so that her black milk will fall into your ghostly mouths."

She finished her lesson by striking a crystal stalagmite with a velvet-covered mallet. Its deep ringing tone called up over- and undertones in the grotto.

Although she wore the saffron-colored mask of Holiness, she could not disguise her joy at seeing her old friend.

"Well, look what the lynx dragged in! You look enjoyably spooked," said Sharra.

Marrok said: "I have just heard the most gruesome tale. This innocent looking woman told us of a world that people did not die at Festival, so that when their bodies died at old age their souls had to find their way into the Cosmos on their own."

"That is truly scary. Several cuts above the usual story of ghosts and creatures on the Ruined Planet."

"The dumber members of her audience scoffed, but the elect enjoyed it."

"I have finished teaching the Initiates for the day. Let us buy some festival food and perhaps a skin of that greenish drink the Northerners favor. You can take me to hear this woman. Later you can tell me your own tales of the fire opal trade."

The old friends did not find the woman, and listened to tiresome poems about the Fall of the Ruined Planet, and variations of the love story of Philzab and Tenemore who had fallen in love in different centuries and could only whisper though a time crack at Mount Velvor.

The Moons had risen, and the disfigured dancers had released their insects; Sharra and Marrok dulled by liquor and duller tales were about to return to her tower. A very tall and ugly man strode nervously up to the speaker's porch. His face was long and his eyes gray and he appeared to be very cold judging from the way he held his robes about him. His skin was chalk white. His voice grated. He wore the gray mask of Humility.

The two friends were walking away until his tale 'The Punishment at Skull Mountain' caught their ears. It was an eldritch story of the punishment of a Daemon by ignorant humans on a frighteningly unlovely world. The world had possessed only one Daemon, as if life could exist without the strange energies poured forth from the gods. All grew silent at this grim tale. There was not clapping afterward. The man looked at his audience. The tale had made his gray eyes gleam with madness. He peered at the crowd. The word weaver could not tell if they had been impressed and horrified, or bored and disgusted, or even if they comprehended it. He removed his mask!

His face was so contorted by emotion that it seemed more mask-like than the piece of hammered copper in his hand. He felt deep, deep contempt.

Marrok, never at a loss for words, cried out: "That was a brave and subtle tale, stranger. Could you honor us with your name?"

The man looked suspicious. "I am Tpreyes, a humble poet."

Marrok pressed: "I have never known a man to shed his mask in Ool Athag. It is said that the masks were here before human souls even swam to this world."

"Many things are said. We tell children that the good genie will bring them gifts at Yule."

"This makes children happy."

"I am not in the business of making mankind happy."

"Evidently this is true."

Tpreyes covered his face and walked into the lengthening shadows.

The open thighs and hardened members of the dream children waited and Sharra and Marrok soon forgot the chalk-faced man.

It was near dawn when Sharra remembered something disturbing—the man's face had been symmetrical and he had five fingers on each hand. Such an outré appearance had probably added to the sinister effect of his story, and had no doubt added to the man's bitterness.

Many Northerners came to her teaching the next day. Some human and others Yerren. She wrinkled her nose at Yerren, whom some call skunk apes. She had begun with the standard notions.

"The Cosmos neither begins nor ends. There are those godthings that create boundaries for a season, separating wet from dry and male from female, and there are those that rend those veils. Each world is but a thought made with sticky with the jism of godthings' dreams and crusted with matter left over from the true creation that happened in areas of angled space in the far future. We are the scum on a bubble heading backwards to the past, eating other pasts as our own is eaten by the work of the Moons.

What is above is like what is below. Ascend to the above, mix with the below and all obscurity will leave you."

But it was not like other sermons. The hairy not-quite-men had questions about Tpreyes' tale. They pronounced his name with heavy emphasis on the "Eyes" part. It was clear that in their stupid and hairy fashion, some were seeing him as a prophet. Again and again she tried to redirect the lecture back to the essential information the Northerners would need before being killed that night. She could not grasp their stupid attention to a story. Even in the North, it was surely known how the Ruined Planet came to its End. She lacked the skills of a teacher. She did not have patience or guile. By the tenth or maybe the twelfth question about Tpreyes, she left the grotto.

She went to the squat pink marble dome that the Green Prophet lived in by day. She did not like dead buildings. Her ancestor was not there. She wrote what had happened to her on a small sheet of parchment and asked for his guidance. It would not come for several months.

Marrok was found in the Alley of the Opal Carvers. He had wheeled and dealed and felt expansive. He was a handsome man, his two left eyes were cobalt blue and his lazy right eye was flecked with amber. His clubfoot made him seem animal and this made him an exciting partner for coupling. He smiled broadly upon seeing her. But his smile left like the Moons behind an insect-cloud.

"What bothers you love?"

"I think the new story-teller may be disrupting the spiritual progress of the hairy ones."

"What do you mean?"

"Tonight is the night of Death, and some of the hairy ones wanted to yeep and yak about the story."

"They are not the brightest of creatures. I am sorry if they did not give your wise words heed."

"It is said that Tlön fell when dreamers continued to dream the wrong things. That cheap and tawdry images profaned first the dark altars and then strange dead fish clotted the rivers."

"I know the story. Even if I am but a trader in stones." He smiled, and again she cursed her fate. Why did she have to serve a God? She nodded, the mask of Holiness glinting in the noonday sun.

"I can see you are troubled. Didn't I make it better for you when the flying lizards stung you on the playground? Did not

Marrok sing to you the night the tiny burning idols fell from the sky? Come to me."

She ran to him, and felt warm and safe in his long left and short right arms.

"We will go now and find this teller of weird tales and we shall tell him that he provokes strange and possibly sickening dreams among the Yerren," said Marrok.

They strolled into the streets of the poets and storytellers. They asked of Tpreyes, but received furtive looks from some, but mainly ignorance from most. A Southerner, a man of the Silver Desert, said that he had heard Tpreyes tell tales the year before and had not liked his style or his subject. A woman of Ool Athag said that Tpreyes was telling a story at this very moment in the Theater of Vain Repetition. The pair ran there.

Tpreyes did stand on the stage, but a short fat man wearing the mask of trickery was telling a story about a trick played upon the corpse eaters. An ancient hooded man who possessed a fearsome book had tricked the devotees of the Hound into thinking that they had a spell for turning bread and wine into flesh and blood. Indeed the spell did perform the transformation, but the flesh had none of the succulent sweetness of putrescence, but continued to taste of bread and wine. However this prank had a deeper purpose, which those that ate the flesh neither belonged to the Hounds, nor to themselves but were unified to a dead daemon.

The jest seemed too macabre.

No one laughed. Some were scared at the notion of eating carrion that makes you part of it. One should eat one's food, one's food should not eat you.

Some clapped, a few cursed, but in the main people walked away in manner not unlike the walking dead.

Marrok closed upon the fat greasy man. The short one clearly wanted to run, but Marrok grabbed a handful of hair.

"Tell us Brother Storyteller, what inspired your story?"

The man's blue eyes darted back and forth in the eyeholes of the wooden mask.

"Who can say?" said he, "where stories come from?"

Sharra said: "Stories come from the hearts and minds of poets. Why do you not know this?"

Marrok pulled the man's graying hair harshly.

"I am not a poet. My mother and my mother's mother and so on for seven generations have been storytellers. My grandmother once won the wreath of yellow narnax feathers."

"So, if you are not a word-weaver, how do you weave words?" asked Marrok.

"I bought the words from a strange but gifted man named Tpreyes." He emphasized the name to sound like "price." "He is poor and sells his words cheaply. Sometimes for only a few tarins."

Sharra asked him: "Where does he live?"

"I do not know now, for he often changes homes pursued by penury. He revises the tales of others. Perhaps he does so to meet boys, although he never touches them. When I bought my tales from him, he lived in Street of the Dragon. He sold me a poem, 'A God of the Shepherds', would you like to hear it?"

Marrok tossed him upon the gray cobbles. "You belong in the street with the dung of horses and pack lizards."

That night many were killed, but fourteen nights later twenty of the Northerners did not return to life.

Fall fell to Winter, Spring warmed Winter and Summer rained a gentle golden rain on Ool Athag.

One of the flying crustaceans delivered a jade scroll tube to Sharra's tower. Times had been lean for the Priestess of the God of the Pit. Rumor is a powerful foe and rumor held that Sharra was responsible for the death of the Northerners.

The Green Prophet wrote that his dreams had found the mother of Tpreyes, and that Sharra must interview her as to the source of her son's aberrations.

Susalal Tpreyes worked as a chimney sweep. She was fond of grog, and of the wines of the East. She felt honored that an important Priestess had come to speak with her.

"Of course, he is hideous to look at little Roburr. I told him that he was so hideous that he should stay inside by day lest his looks frighten other children. Besides he hated other children. They did not understand him."

Susalal had two right arms and one left arm. All were short and she was thin and well suited to cleaning chimneys. She coughed often and streams of spit mixed with blood and soot ran from her chin. Her skin was albino white, and except for a sapphire colored tentacle where her left eyelid would be, her face would be inartistically symmetrical.

"What," asked Sharra. "Did they not understand?"

"Oh, I don't know. My husband had been carried off by nightgaunts. I had never tried to understand my little one. Well my nightgaunts didn't really carry off my husband; he died of a disease he got off some whore in the Thuban Oasis. Little Roburr is no good you see."

"I don't see. I would like to help him."

"Oh, he was even married once. Did him no damn good. She couldn't straighten him out." Then shrieks of laughter shook the thin woman. Her droplets of red and black saliva rained on Sharra's yellow robe. Sharra asked her what was wrong.

"Straighten him out! Straighten *him* out! The bitter little turd will straighten us out!" She laughed and coughed and wailed. Sharra wanted to comfort the madwoman, but even as child she could not stand spit. Nausea rose in her like bloodsap in werkal tree in the Fall.

Sharra began to walk away from the woman in her seizures of laughter, but Susalal managed a few more cogent remarks.

"He says the only thing he can do is write. 'The proper work of a gentleman' he says. 'Avoid filthy lucre.' He says. No, he writes because he can not help himself!"

Sharra left and sent her words to the Green Prophet. He sent for her and for many hours she stood maskless in his presence in the pink dome. Her brain ached as his mind crawled through her skull. He told her nothing.

She placed the willow wood mask of Indifference on her face and made her way home. The hot winds off the Silver Desert were like the breaths of an animal. The Aeolian tumbleweeds rolled down the streets playing their sacred hymns. Some said there were fewer tumbleweeds this year. Others said it was the hottest summer they had ever known. Such things are always said as part of the grumbling of old age, one of the many choruses that must be sung in the theater of Ool Athag. That night she saw the Green Prophet stand upon the edge of the Pit, during the hour of the Crimson Ray. He threw something to the God, who had appeared in the form of a vast winged monkey. In the naïve way of the faithful, she assumed that all would be well.

Fall came. A dry Fall that crept into the city on little balls of scavenger ivy. With the Fall the Ruined Planet returned to the skies. It was not seen in the happy seasons of Summer and Winter. A few had come to trust in Sharra, but rumor is strong.

Rumor had whispered in late Summer that Roburr Tpreyes had died in an oasis in the Silver Desert. But another rumor was that he had raised a great theatrical troupe called the Poor Theatre. It was said that he would come and stage a drama called *The Dolorous Passion of the King*.

Marrok returned at Festival, and he acted brave and foolish. He told old jokes and sung bawdy songs like *If My Nose Were Made Of Tarins I'd Blow It All On You* or *My Love Is A Ride or Mendot the Harlot.*

But his three eyes were dull, and he had a habit of looking skyward. Once as they were leaving Sharra's tower he had forgotten to place a mask on.

"My gods, what were you thinking?"

"In the North we do not always wear masks," he admitted.

"What else has happened—in the North?" asked Sharra, as though in a lovers' quarrel.

"It. It. It matters little. It seems the Yerren are missing. Some say that they fled to the South to become actors, others that they have vanished. Others still say . . . "

" 'Others still say' what?

"Others say that the Yerren have become human. Anyway *I* say: 'Fuck them! Fuck them all! Who needs a bunch of skunk-apes anyway?' "

"But you do. I mean aren't the not-quiet-men the opal miners?"

"Yes, dear love. I do."

"Do you blame me for this? Because I could not train of score of them to astral travel?"

"You would be the last person I would blame for anything, dear heart. I do not know if last year had anything to do with the Yerren departing. And if it did I think we can blame the dire storyteller."

She told him of her summer.

"Why is nothing being done? I will get four strong men here for the Festival. They are friends, but better still their scimi-tars flash like lightning."

No frogs had rained in the season of the Raining Frogs and few visitors had come for the Festival of the Daemons. Many were afraid, for the golden taels and the silver tarins of the visitors were a great source of income for the city. The flow of wealth had always been a constant thing, and so no theory of economics had ever come into being. Many reasons and many models were fashioned, and many eyes looked upon Sharra.

At last they came. The Poor Theatre. A dirty dusty desert-smelling lot. They poured into the city at dawn. They over-ran the sacred theaters and porches. They bought bread and slated fish, and it was said that Tpreyes did some sorcery upon these staples of the poor that his multitude of players were fed. They bought little wine, nor the herb of dreams, nor did they spend hard-earned money in the famed brothels of the city.

Rumors abounded. Dream children were said to have fled. Pillars of fire were seen by night. Smoke columns seen by day. Tpreyes would himself play the King and was seen here, or was it there, in his purple robes.

The King in Purple with a *perfectly round crown.*

Almost no one came to the Grotto of Endless Crystal. Sharra's sermons on the theology of arithmetic, the mixing of the fair and foul, the Nine Impossible Things were scarcely attended. Some questioned her about the need for the first death.

The great play began at dawn.

It began with the birth of the Daemon Carpenter. The god who begat him did not lie with his mother. The crowd laughed at this. *But that is half the fun!* Sharra looked at the crowd performing the play. They were slope-browed, and their hair was thick—but they were not-quite-Yerren. They did not stink like skunk apes. The childhood was fraught with miracles and escapes. The young demigod made wine for a wedding feast when unwelcome sobriety might have happened. Sharra noticed how much the demigod's mother resembled the chimney-sweep. The father of the Daemon was named simply "He Exists" but seemed to be some invisible god like Aforgomon.

The play, it was revealed after the first hour, would take three days to perform. Sharra decided to leave with Marrok for the rest of the first day. The size of the Poor Theatre, its beastly nature made her think of rats, rats gnawing at the thin walls of the world.

"I think he is an Easterner, someone from Tsang," said Marrok as they drank limewater near the Xenanoth fountain.

Sharra asked: "Why?"

"He bases his legends on the idea of a *book*, some selection of wonder tales from a world distant in time. The Easterners use *books* rather than scrolls. In the ancient city of Enoliaba, the secret of unmaking matter was discovered and put in a book. Now where that city lay is merely a stretch of glass covering half-melted buildings. The conceit of the play is that is from a book smuggled into this world."

"His skin has the lack of pigment of the Tsang folk."

Marrok added: "They hated non-humans and made their blast to destroy a small kingdom of near-men."

Another of her Order, a grizzled old Priest, approached them. He wore the stripped mask of Eavesdropping. "If I felt the city guard were not too enthralled with the play, I would call them. The play has been performed before. In the Thuban Oasis in the spring. Now date wine is not brought up for trade. Nor frankincense scrapped from the trees. Now not even the Hounds howl there."

"Will the play destroy us?" asked Marrok.

"It can be stopped. At one point near the end of the play Tpreyes will be vulnerable. I will tell you what we must do."

On the third day a secret group had forced its way to the front of the agora. Some were human Priests and Priestesses. Others were human soldiers. The rests were demihumans of all trades. A few had known the first death; in their robes they hid scimitars and short daggers, *xuèdî zĭs* and small maces. The old Priest had brought a carpenter's hammer. The crew wore the rusty iron masks of Rebellion, the blue slate masks of Truth-seeking, the sparkling mica masks of Impatience. Most of the audience had demasked the day before at the Magadaline's line "No mask is needed for the King. He is hidden no more, and so we should show our true face to him." With a single badly written line in a melodrama, three thousand years of custom was undone.

An empire ruled by eagles had taken the Daemon Carpenter's land. When he had declared himself to be King, they had pronounced a sentence of death upon him. In the darkling world of the play, such a sentence was a permanent one. Death was a one time event.

The eagle-men hired one of the Daemon Carpenter's followers to betray him. Like Tpreyes, the Carpenter seemed to surround himself with boys. Tpreyes had certainly written this fellow after himself. The callow youth betrayed his guru with a kiss, so that the eagle men might know him. They rushed upon him with drawn swords. Only one of the King's followers, a man named Rocky, drew a blade and gave fight. He sliced off an ear of one of the soldiers. The Carpenter rebuked him saying that he who lives by the sword shall die by the sword. He picked up the soldier's ear and restored symmetry to him by re-attaching it in the healing manner of the Sisterhood of the Mother of the Nearer Moon.

There was a trial by night, as fair a trial as one might expect in such circumstances. There were speeches and scenes that Sharra could not follow, and then the Daemon was made to carry a log on his shoulders up Skull Hill.

There it was.

Everyone fell silent.

The eagle men were going to bind one log to another in the forbidden shape. There was no word to be spoken aloud for the shape made of two lines and four right angles. It exalted fearful symmetry. It suggested the division of time and space. It was a forerunner of a grid system that could mark every object in a fixed place, a great fetish of stasis. As the deep meaning of the forbidden shape burned its message into the minds of the audience, some (including a few of the secret cadre) put out their eyes.

But worse still than the forbidden shape was the punishment. It was a punishment fashioned in irony—that a carpenter should die this way! The eagle men stripped the purple robe from the King and nailed him to the shape. The eagle men nailed his feet to the long vertical bar, his hand This was not a theatrical illusion; Sharra could see his pain and smell his blood. They lifted the shape so that it stood upon the hill, the actors had mounded from rubble and detritus. His death was not comforted by acute or obtuse angles. The curves of time would not succor his soul, nor would the beckoning angles draw the Hounds. He was made into the shape.

It was horrible. The near naked body of Tpreyes was perfectly symmetrical.

Five toes on each foot. Two legs of the same length. Two arms that could have mirrored each other. Five fingers on each hand. Tpreyes' eyes rolled back into head. He groaned and muttered something in an unknown language. Then his words became clear, "ffffFather save Me!" The Poor Theatre folk did not react with sorrow or anger. Instead they began watching Tpreyes upon the cross and began a chant that synchronized their breathing with their leader. They breathed in when he would exhale, an uttered "Amen Yä!" when he inhaled.

The God of the Pit roared and shook. The earth quaked, and the sky grew dim from gasses pouring from the Pit. The secret cadre knew this would occur, they had bribed one of Tpreyes' followers from the Oasis. They ran to the forbidden shape and pulled it down. The last act of the King in Purple would not occur. The soldiers formed a circle (too regular a circle for Sharra's liking) and stood ready to beat back the actors, while the inner circle pulled the logs down and pulled the nails from the hands of feet of Tpreyes. The Poor Theatre did not intervene. No one challenged the soldiers. The actors merely bowed as though they were receiving some crazy applause. For an instant Sharra thought they would return to being skunk apes.

Susalal Tpreyes was in the crowd. She forced her way to the ring of soldiers. Susal wore the spotted crimson mask of Shame. The soldiers parted, no doubt thinking what their own mothers would say to them at their last hour. But Susalal did not comfort her dying son.

"You are just like him. He thought we could live on hope. I told them. I told the old Priest. No one will whisper the words into your ears to call you back. You die now. Ngah'ng ai'y zhro!"

When she finished her speech, Tpreye's chest ceased to move. She spat on him. "Writer! So I could break my back sweeping chimneys!"

The actors began to howl and bark and tweet like birds. The soldiers carried his body trying to force it back into a natural state, but a powerful rigor mortis had set in. Tpreyes had become the symbol. The soldiers took him to the edge of the Pit, and were about to toss him. But the old Priest stopped them. The Green Prophet seemed to have come from nowhere and wished to examine the body.

The Poor Theatre had become a chorus of chaos. Some madness had passed into them. They ran and tweeted like birds, their bodies being smashed into towers, which for the most part ate them. They smashed glass and pulled cobbles from the streets to throw at one another. Some made fires, others pissed on the sides of buildings. Some were seen running to the North along the Opal Highaway and others to the East along the Spice Road. By nightfall not a single member of the Poor Theatre remained in the city.

At the hour of the Crimson Ray, the God did not appear.

The Green Prophet said: "We will hold vigil over this body. If it re-animates, we will torture it for its secrets. If decay sets in we will burn it. No rumors must come from this day."

The old Priest offered a bag of thirty silver tarins for anyone who could bring the possessions of the dead poet. Two small boys, one with as many eyes as a spider and the other with vestigial wings, brought his diary and papers. Marrok and Sharra volunteered to read them.

At first it had been a game. When he revised the stories and poems of others he would drop his mythoi into theirs. He dreamed up a singularly dull world. It had only one Moon, which was apparently lifeless. Symmetrical people filled it, ruled by superstition. His eastern hatreds were given voice, too—only the human race would live in this unfriendly world.

It amused him as a youth, but he began to realize that his mother was right. When his wife lived, she supported him. He could spend days on his writing, and on his revision work. But when his wife left him, he knew he had to find a more stable form of income. He tried writing outside of the world he had made. He could not. That other place crept into his mind.

One night he caught a glimpse of the Book. He saw it in a mirror. It had a black binding and gold lettering. On its spine was embossed the forbidden symbol two perpendicular lines. The symbol suggested so many lies—that the divine world (vertical) was different from the human world (horizontal)—that symmetry, the hateful symmetry that his father had given him was not ugly. He looked back at his collection of books and scrolls, and he could not see the Book. It was then that he began to go mad. He learned (the diary was unclear on the "how") to read the thin white pages of the Book in the mirror. He sold pieces of the Book to his clients—the story of a string man making bees nest in a lion's ribcage—the story of Garden—a different story of how the Hounds left the curved world.

The more he wrote (and rewrote into the words of others) the more terrifying his visions of the other world became. New York, London, Tokyo, New Orleans. A world of one death. A world of right angles and crosses. A world without flying crustaceans, vampires, or satyrs. A world where gods were not seen. A world of no doubt and stultifying order. The more he wrote, the more he could not stop. He traveled to Phundar in the Spring to sell his stories and his revising before their theater festival, he traveled to his father's homeland of Tsang for the arts celebration of mid-winter. He became afraid of winged creatures of light which the Book said were the messengers of the one God. He dreamt of battles and blasts, earthquakes and cataclysms, of famines and ignorance. He sometimes found himself writing before even being fully awake. He tried smashing mirrors, but unbelievable chains of coincidence kept giving mirrors to him. He wrote of visiting a small village near Ool Athag, called Kundry. A blind beggar received sight as he passed him by. The beggar chased after him to give him a hand mirror, since he did not wish to see how aged he had become since the Green Fever had stolen his sight. One-night Tpreyes weary of work and filled with contempt for his audience had wandered into the Silver Desert. He lay down to die—one, two agonizing days as the sun baked his chalk-white flesh. Then in the cool of the twin Moons' light, he felt something cold beneath the sand where he lay. He had been lying inches above a dead traveler, who possessed a flask of water and a piece of mirror for shaving. He could not resist the water and decided then to accept his fate. When he had pulled himself into the Thuban Oasis, he wrote many strange things about how mirrors bring symmetry to the world, and speculated on art and mathematics that might be based on symmetry and right angles. From this point his work was filled with strange words: "Amen, sin, manna, commandment" and long pages of the Book. Other entries dealt with a long lost sister named Alicia that had fallen through the mirror. Sharra knew the name. Susalal had called her son that for many years and even dressed him as a girl out of hatred for her husband's early death.

He began his last diary with "I am the Doorway."

Marrok and Sharra could read no more. They took the papers of the madmen to the Green Prophet except for the smallest (and last diary). The body had begun to smell. The secret cadre burned the madman and his books and scrolls and sifted the ash through seven sieves. They let the fine ash drift into the Pit. The fine white cloud fell into the crimson-lit abyss and formed itself into a cross.

Do not fear said the elders. This will be forgotten.

Fall dropped away and Winter blustered in. And all Sharra could think of was how young Roburr had hated his mother when she had told him there was no Father Yule. Spring chased away Winter and Sharra thought of the story of the Daemon Carpenter. Had young Roburr just wanted a father with the reassuring name, "He Exists"? Summer roared in dry and hot, and ate the greenness out of the star flowers in the meadows near Ool Athag. Rumors spread in the land. A ghoul told her that the Mountain That Sing had stopped singing. Two reputable travelers from the Spice Road said that some of the Poor Theater had set up a monastery that made copies of the stories of Tpreyes. Who can speak of the truth of such things? There was talk that since the meeting of two lines in four angles was in everybody's head, that a road should be opened to the West. Maybe the old ways were superstitious, but the Cult of the Hounds hushed such talk.

But a sad fact did come her way. An opal-bearing boulder had crushed the head of Marrok. Some of the miners had been in the Poor Theater returning after the last play. It seemed likely that they had loosened the rock, maybe out of pity toward one of the few humans that had treated them well.

Sharra even thought of travelling to the West, to the taboo direction. She had been in the east and north and south in her youth. She smiled sadly. When had she thought of her life as divided into her "youth" and her "now"—as though a perpendicular line from above had intersected her life line.

Many folk left the city. There were more and more on the three roads every day. The mayor decided to call off the Festival of the Daemons. It was as though the well that was the source of the world had gone dry.

Yet when Fall came, even though not a single frog or flaming idol fell from the sky, there seemed some happiness. People flocked to the Pit in the hour of the Crimson Ray. Many wore the turquoise mask of Hope.

The day after the God of the Pit had appeared as a mask, and one of the flying crustaceans had told her the story of the Word of the Seven Suns, the God of the Pit did not appear. It was the second time this had happened in a thousand years—the other being the day of Tpreyes' crucifixion. People went to their homes early. Sharra arranged her sleeping furs thirteen times. Finally she drank some of the greenish liquor of the North, a rare commodity now, but tonight sleep proved even more rare and desirable.

Later when the screams began the liquor confused her. Had she overslept a sacrifice? Had the Poor Theatre returned? Had an army massed on the moss covered plains of the West? Her dream children were not to be seen. They are a timid race.

The screams grew louder, mixed with laughter and prayer and mad moans.

She climbed the spiral staircase to her roof. No insect clouds, no Ruined Planet haunted the sky.

A Moon had risen. A single large silvery Moon. Sharra didn't scream, not just yet. She would scream when she looked at her hands and saw for sure what her terrified heart was already telling her.

On each hand she would have five identical fingers.

(for China Miéville)

The Revelation at the Abbey

HIDING HIS TRUE motives was easy in Prague; the city swarmed with alchemists and soothsayers. On a given morning he could breakfast with Dr. John Dee and have dinner with Rabbi Lowe. The emperor was crazed for magic and magicians of every stripe—mainly charlatans and mountebanks—had filled the streets. Strange fumes of outlandish hues belched from every chimney. Weird music seeped from cracks in ancient mortar at night, parchments with bizarre sigils were traded with a frenzy that might make the doughiest merchant blush. No one paid attention to Dr. Nemo. The occasional Greek speaker nodded knowingly at his name, Dr. Nobody, and one perceptive fellow even asked what Polyphemus he was seeking to deceive. His answer, "I am but an honest alchemist." made his listener shoot red wine from his nose as he laughed so hard.

Dr. Nemo had come here because of a rumor, as he had gone everywhere for the last thirty-one years because of rumors about the Book. He was an old man of 54 with a face pockmarked from plague, yellowish skin, missing two fingers from his right hand (because of a minor infraction of Egyptian law). His hair was dirty silver and sat in tight greasy circles near his scalp. The whites of his eyes had become yolk yellow, and rather nicely matched his remaining teeth. He would occasionally flinch at sounds other humans did not hear. He often woke from deep sleep screaming. He spoke French, German, Arabic, Polish, Italian and English well—and he read Greek, Latin, Hebrew and Gothic. He had learned to seem harmless and even parental. He no longer appeared to be driven by a mad quest—but in his heart he thought of nothing but the Book.

He had been in Cairo. It was rumored that Dhu'l-Nun al-Misiri had found the Book. It was said (according to rumor) to have been the Scroll of Thoth that Prince Setne had stolen and returned to a haunted pyramid. Others said it came from the kingdom of the Stygians who had lived along the Nile before the desert came. Dr. Nemo had been digging by a statue of Dhu'l Nun, when a tall portly one-eyed beggar had approached at sundown. He greeted Nemo with his real name, the name of his boyhood in far-off London and said: "The occult wisdom of the ages is being gathered in Prague. The Book you seeks hides there." Then the beggar faded into smoke and left only a foul stench of his passing. Dr. Nemo wondered if he was a phantom conjured by a rival, a message from such gods or demons that may wish to help (or hinder) him, or even a reflection of the Book itself. Maybe after all these years it longed to be found. Maybe after all these years its yellowed pages long to be caressed by human eyes. Maybe it simply wanted to laugh at him.

He had first heard of the book when he swept shop for a dealer in strange things in London. Visitors to the shop would trace a sign with their left index finger and the owner would respond with a counter sign. They ignored him and spoke of many things. How to bring back the dead from their saltes, where certain rocks could be asked questions which they would answer truthfully at certain seasons, how to speak to mermen and above all the Book. The nature of the Book seemed an open question. Most thought it to be a scroll or a set of scrolls. Others postulated clay tablets or even a mass of knotted cords. One woman suggested that it might change shape to communicate better with its owner.

It was not a grimoire.

On this point every seeker agreed. It was a history text, the true unvarnished history of this and perhaps other worlds. After months of hearing about the Book, he had gathered his courage to ask his master—a short well-built Jew known for his temper—after the Book. The man scowled at first and Nemo hardened his limbs expecting a beating. Then the owner laughed.

"So, my little *goy*, you have a mind after all. I will tell most of what I know. I think the Book has been destroyed years ago, maybe centuries. If a human owned it and studied of thoughtfully, he or even she would rule this haunted world. But the rumor of the Book, that drives men mad."

"How could a history book make one powerful?"

"Let me ask you three questions. Why do you think about the mistakes you've made?"

"So that I won't repeat them."

"So, a true book of every mistake a ruler has made would have value, no? Why do people risk vast fortunes for treasure maps?"

"If the map were true, it could lead to vast unclaimed wealth."

"So, a book of every lost treasure—even those lost long before the coming of Adam, would be priceless, no? Why do so many of my friends seek the conversations of demons and angels?"

"They wish to know what lies beyond the world of men."

"So, a book that gave a true history of such beings, which are very different than our faiths tell us, would perhaps be the most amazing text of all time?"

"Truly I would give an eye for such wisdom, a hand, my tongue. But why do you think such a Book ever existed?"

"Now that I have raised the possibility of such a volume in your mind, will you think of ought else?"

His master began Nemo the art of reading. First Greek and Latin. His master taught him to bargain and haggle and size up customers. He taught him how to be charming in half a dozen languages. But he would not teach the art of magic.

"Such things have brought me only sorrow and fear. The gold they bring is fleeting, the knowledge they bring makes you unhappy with the rules of this life and fearful of what awaits in the next."

The old Jew had no family and promised Nemo the shop and his gold when he passed on.

And Nemo (for a season) found love. Mary worked for the baker next door. She was lovely and smelled of fresh bread. She sang and laughed and was very impressed when Nemo could read a poem to her. On the eve of their wedding, she caught a fever. The doctors belled her and gave her stinking poultices, but she still failed. Even the Jew uttered a spell that seemed to slow, but not stop, the fever's burn. And Nemo was sad for two years. During those years he did no notice that the Jew's back grew more bent, his hair grayer, and his eyes more dim. Then one morning the Jew did not descend the stair into the shop and Nemo went to see after him. In a glance he knew that the slow fire of time had nearly roasted this man that had been his companion and teacher. He began to run off for the doctor, but his friend asked merely to listen.

"I have had a long life, by my Art it has been much longer than the Most High allowed to men since the Flood. Now I pass into a Darkness wherein certain things wait for me. I am saddened that your wife-to-be died, and I hope that this shop will help you find another. You should burn the books and scrolls I keep in the black box under the gold. They will give you too much pain if you read them, and if you try and sell them you will attract men you do not wish to meet."

Within the hour, he had passed. Nemo pulled the black box free and made a fire. He opened the box, but before he threw the accursed volumes away—he made the simple mistake of looking at one page. A phrase caught him, and he began to read. The fire died down and he read. The room grew cold and he read by the body of the dead Jew. His stomach rumbled and he read. The sun rose and set and he read.

Then with a stern voice he read a verse from an ancient scroll, and the body of the Jew rose. He told it to go lay in front of the synagogue so it would be buried. He gathered the gold and prepared to set off to a steamy rice rich river in China. It was clear to him where the Book must lie. How could the Jew not have figured this out?

Two years (and a horrible shaking fever) later, Nemo realized (after careful study) that the Book was in Germany. Then in another year, having called up scholars from the dead to aid his research, he *knew* that it must be beneath a certain ruined temple near Rome. Then it *had* to lie in a nameless city in the Arabian desert. And then India, then Poland, then Macbeth's hillock in Scotland, at the center of Stonehenge.

And then one day he saw his face reflected in a shiny brass plate in a Baghdad market and saw that he looked older and sicker than the Jew. He saw that he had no friends among living humans. He saw he was not in any way closer. He sat down on the cobblestones of the street. Soldiers of the Caliph carried him away. He was locked up as mad for three days. Then, claiming to have regained his senses, he bribed his way free. He continued the quest, but without hope.

Questing was simply what he knew how to do. It was then the phantoms began coming to him. They first appeared when he had returned to England yet again. He was sitting in a public house, when a young lady sat next to him. She had brown hair that verged on blonde, and bit of flour daubed one her temples. She might have been Mary's cousin. Her eyes were black as ink, and her faded blue dress rustled like paper. She spoke in a near whisper. "The Book you need is not on this island. Brittana est insula parva." The exercise-book Latin had been the first sentence he had learned to read. From Caesar, "Brittan is a small island." He turned to face her, but somehow, she suddenly wasn't there. He stayed in a small inn for days, using various methods of divination to find his next target.

Prague had twisty streets. It would be a good place for the Book. Its layout suggested a labyrinth, surely the correct sort of library for such a volume. Dr. Nemo no longer concealed his Quest if someone happened to ask. He had never encountered any of the Jew's customers in the last three decades, nor did he possess the Mouth-to-Ear instruction that opened certain doors. Shortly after arriving in Prague, he had befriended the librarian of Emperor Rudolf II, the great collector of the occult and eldritch, the esoteric and the forbidden. The tiny man, whose nature suggested more of a magical creature of the forest instead of an urban dweller, gave him access to the vast book collection within days. Most of it was rubbish. A few books had certain Hints. And others were written in languages Dr. Nemo did not speak. The later posed a problem. It was said the Book—parts of the Book at any rate—predated the coming of mankind. This would necessitate the Book being written in tongues known to no men—unless some secret society had preserved the tongues of lizards or demons. Yet it would be enough, thought Dr. Nemo, to simply hold the Book. If he could hold it in his arms, it would be enough. It would be like embracing Helen of Troy. She might not yield to him, but he would have held that which started wars and quests and (he suspected) religions as well.

One day he told the librarian of his quest.

"Yes," said the faunlike man, "I have heard of this book. It was said that two great kingdoms in India fought a battle with flying ships over its possession thousands of years ago. I have heard that Plato had seen but a single page of it and derived his whole philosophy in an instant. I have known men that spent their lives looking for it."

"And you, my friend?" asked Dr. Nemo. "Do you seek this Book, this true history?"

"I sought it by creating this library. I have little wealth, little bravery—even little health. I had hoped it would come to me. But I am an old man now. I do not know that I could withstand the revelations that it might contain. I wish with all my heart that I had never heard of it, because I will die unhappy for having known of it. I do not even know of a book that bears the remedy of knowing about the Book."

This sad and humble moment opened Nemo's heart as it had not been open since the day he asked the Jew about the book.

Suddenly he saw himself in the little man of the library, a man ennobled by curiosity but derided by vanity, alienated from the world of men by his desires, but deeply dependent on that world for the possibility of answering that desire. In the days and weeks that came Dr. Nemo told his stories to the little librarian. He told of his adventures from talking his way free from South Sea pirates, to speaking with mummies far below the depths of the Sphinx. He told of running from tigers in India, to running sores of the plague in Russia. To this little man, who had had no adventures, but who held the same desire, he told all and everything. And as told his story, his soul began to heal. He began to sleep at night. He was beginning to believe that he did not have to find the Book, that he could settle down in Prague for his last years, use the skills at trading that he had learned so long ago, profit from the vast storehouse of language and experience that he had accumulated.

Then it happened.

He rose late one morning and as was his custom went to the Emperor's library. His friend was there almost dancing among the shelves of books. The librarian's eyes had a wild gleam.

He had had a dream. In his dream a lovely woman had come to the library and speaking from behind a hand-held fan spoken to him of the Book. It lay nearby, in the ruins of an abbey just north of the city—where it had been worshipped as a sort of Angel for hundreds of years. The pious monks had placed the Book in their church—removing the standard relics of Christianity. Each day another page of the Book was read. But the monks grew greedy of their wisdom. They gave up their deeds of charity. Other than working in their gardens to feed themselves they did naught but read and discuss the Book. They took in no new brothers, and as age and sickness took brother after brother away, the monastery dwindled to a few, and then two, and then none. But the Book had remained in its isolation wanting only a perfect reader. Now it was ready for those perfect readers. The librarian and the adventurer.

It did not occur to Dr. Nemo to treat this as any other than Truth. He had Quested so long, that such a revelation seemed likely perhaps inevitable. He told the librarian he would procure two horses and supplies and they might set out at once. He scarcely noticed the sickness invading his soul, for it had dwelt there so long, it seemed natural to have it back. He bought skins of wine and bread and cheese and two fine Spanish ponies. Shortly after noon they set out. For the librarian this was a great adventure. He had been outside of the great city but twice in his life. Indeed (although he would not have said so to a man who had run from tigers), he was worried about sleeping in the open at night, for such had not been his fate since long-ago boyhood when his mother allowed his brothers and him to sleep on the rooftop during summer nights. It was fall and the air had quite a bite at night. He trusted that Dr. Nemo would see to his comfort and protection, and in his heart and in his excitement became younger and younger as they ponies twisted their way out of the city.

Dr. Nemo on the other hand grew more and more silent. Something clearly weighed upon him, but the librarian did not ask for he wasn't good with the ways of his fellow men, which is why he had chosen books as his friends. He wondered how they would share the Book between them. Would they both read pages together or would the Book spend one night with one man and then the next with the other one? This imagined infidelity stirred strange desires in the librarian's heart, and he startled from his fantasies when Dr. Nemo asked him the way to the ruined abbey and its history in the waking world.

"In the time of Charles IV, a small brotherhood devoted to St. Ludmilla, asked for land to set aside a place for study, and to heal the sick. Charles tasked the Abbot to learn of the prophecies of Princess Lubossa, who had foreseen the building of Prague. The Order's work was half mystical and half practical. They treated those individuals thought to be too sick to remain in Prague, and they gathered mystical books of all sorts. Accusations of black magic and heresy began almost as soon as the monastery was constructed but due to the good works of the monks, such naysayers were silenced. A rumor seeped into the world that a certain book had been found pre-dating even Princess Lubossa, and the monks were said to have drawn even the wrath of Rome by the gaiety of their celebrations. They fell out of royal favor in the time of King Wenceslas IV. Their products were few—some herbal-infused liquors said to be sovereign against gout and dropsy—kept the monastery alive, albeit in a reduced form. Four or five decades ago the last monks were said to have died. Various legal issues between Crown and Church have kept the land effectively out of either's hands. So it has fallen in ruins."

It was a librarian's answer.

The ruined abbey crouched low and great by a small mist-shrouded river. The fields surrounding it bore crumbling stone walls disturbed by the army of trees that had conquered the abandoned gardens. The two men paused on the ancient Roman road half a mile above the abbey.

"Let us shelter for the night under yon heavy oaks," said Dr. Nemo. "If we press on night will have fallen, and it would hard going among the ruined walls. I see the chapel still has its roof, perhaps some preservative power of the Book is genuinely afoot."

The librarian was annoyed that the adventurer could possibly doubt his vision. Of course the Book was there.

And the adventurer was making a list. Losing his wife, being kidnapped by pirates, having his fingers sliced off, the plague, small pox, running from tigers, fleeing across the roofs of Venice by moonlight, meeting the bear in the Russian woods, talking his way out of the bandits cave in Lebanon. Meanwhile the librarian had boldly stacked books in a new way, had risked his life buying new bookshelves? Has put his very soul in danger by invoking He Who Waits? Yet their reward was to be the same. Had he not already the punishment for eating this apple long before he even saw the tree? The sickness in his soul became hate, cold and deep, and he began to offer the librarian wine.

The little man did not hold his liquor well; no great surprise there. They sang a few bawdy songs in Latin and then Dr. Nemo helped the librarian onto the horse. He was going to show his besotted companion a "trick." As the librarian sang, "O Fortuna velut Luna statu variablis," Dr. Nemo slipped the noose around his neck. As he sang, "Semper crescis aut decrescis." Dr. Nemo tossed the rope up and over a thick branch of the sturdy oak. As the librarian sang, "Vita detestables nunc obdurate," he slapped the chestnut colored rump of the pony and the librarian finished the song in hell. "Life is unstable and sometimes cruel," agreed Dr. Nemo in his mother-tongue.

Dr. Nemo cut the librarian's body down after an hour. It didn't feel right sleeping beneath its swing. The pony wandered back to be with its friend. Dr. Nemo staked them both and slept the sleep of the innocent.

Dawn's rosy fingers caressed a very cool sky. Frost had silvered the ground, and Dr. Nemo felt the ache of his years as he awoke, kindled a fire from last night's ashes and drank the last sips of sour wine.

There was still a rude road to the ruin of the abbey. Dr. Nemo rode up and tied his mare outside what had been the gateway. If the librarian's dream had been accurate, he need only go to the chapel. The book would be enshrined therein. He was surprised to see the door to the church still intact. He was about to burst in when he heard a rustling sound—a sound of paper against paper, a sound the phantoms often manifested. Was this to be another disappointment? Another cosmic jest? He pulled his rusty sword from its sheaf; he had not had to use it in years. He had never attacked a phantom. He didn't know if he could attack one, but the desire to corner one—to make it spill its Truth. That desire boiled very strongly in his heart. He pushed the door open.

The chapel's air was cold and stale. A few white candles burned on the altar. A large paper screen decorated with an oriental blue and red dragon sat on the altar. No book was in evidence. From behind the screen came the sound of music—a plucked instrument—it took Dr. Nemo a moment to recognize it as a qinqin, the Chinese guitar.

"Don't look behind the screen," said a woman with a soft voice. "It will be better if you don't see me. At least at first."

"Who are you?"

"I am Princess Lubossa."

"No. No you are not. She is long buried, she knew a lot about Czech futures. She may have even been partially non-human. I am looking for something else."

The music stopped. "Are you looking for redemption for the poor man you killed last night?"

"I have killed others in my quest."

"Yes, I know. Eight men and a woman. You think it is nine men, but the fellow you wounded in Rome staggered home and got better. He died last year."

"So you have been following me," said Dr. Nemo.

"Not at all. I do not follow anyone. I am without curiosity."

"But you know everything."

"Just what happens on this world and its moon."

"You have the Book."

"Isn't that why you are here?"

"I thought you knew everything."

"I do not know what happens in the hearts of humans. Or in the thoughts of any being for that matter."

"Are you going to give me the Book?"

"No."

"But you know I will kill you for it."

"That is a logical development."

"So you don't know the future."

"The future does not exist. It can be predicted. Only the past is real. The past eats everything. The Book eats the past."

Dr. Nemo charged around the screen. At first he saw a seated Chinese maiden holding a qinqin with one leg exposed behind a subtle blue dress resting against a paper screen.

Then he saw what was really in front of him.

A large solid object that was shaped and colored as a seated Chinese maiden holding a qinqin with one leg exposed behind a subtle blue dress resting against a paper screen. It looked him without sadness, happiness or curiosity. It was a good copy. It blinked. He raised his sword, and then lowered it. None of the phantoms had ever appeared to be anything unnatural. Ugly, yes, but not unnatural. "What are you? Are you the guardian of the Book?"

"I am the Book. Four years three months and seven days ago you told a magician in Paris that you thought the Book might be alive. Do you remember the conversation?"

He had been drunk. They had watched the sun rise over a graveyard near the Seine. The other fellow had a terrible cough. He died in the winter.

"I do not know if I am 'alive' in the sense you mean. Such speculation is beyond me. But I change, I adapt, I eat, I can move about. I seek self-preservation. I do not mate (if there are indeed others of my kind). I neither love, nor hate, nor curse my lot."

Dr. Nemo asked: "Do you have a purpose?"

"Yes. I record everything. My first record was of the being that owned me. Perhaps it made me. It died on this world twenty thousand years ago. At that time I was a very large sheet of some flexible material. The being lived in a castle it had extruded from its body, much as a snail makes its shell. The shell-castle stood two hundred cubits high. It was on an island near Japan, where some very shaggy human-like beings worshipped the being. One day they were angry because of an earthquake. They banged on the walls of the shell-castle. The being went outside. They killed it with spears. I had been recording the world for four days at that point. One of the shaggy men took me away and made me into a tent. When he asked I could show him anything. He knew the petty intrigues of his tribe. He knew when a group of true men were coming with war canoes. His tribe prospered. He never understood that I could only show the past, and that I could only answer him. Since then I have belonged to many beings, most of them human, most of that group men."

"And now," said Dr. Nemo. "You will belong to me."

"No. Which is sad. I feel better when I am with a being that can ask me better questions."

"How do you know that I am not to be your master?"

"Certain processes have brought you to me."

"The phantoms?"

"Yes."

"What are they?"

"I do not know."

Dr. Nemo thought it was very likely she was telling the truth. Because of her shape, he had to think of it as "she." But her protestations were of no matter; he would take the Book with him. He asked her: "How do you take shape?"

"I fold myself. Remember the folded paper art you saw twelve years ago?"

In China he had seen a crane made of folded paper that a Japanese monk had shown him.

"So you are a folded sheet of paper that talks and sends phantoms and dreams around the world. You have no idea why you exist. You do not know who made you. But you do know that I will never have you."

"Yes."

He raised his sword again. Perhaps if he hurt her.

Instead he said: "Can you show me your true form?"

She answered: "Yes, but I will need to take you to a different kind of space. I would need to move your perception so that you could see."

Dr. Nemo had taken drugs, fasted, invoked demons. He had no trouble with the idea of other spaces existing "beside" ours.

"If I command you to do so, will you show me your true form?" He menaced her with his sword and thought of such incantations he knew that could compel beings not of this world.

"Yes, or if you merely asked me. It is for this moment the phantoms have called you. Do not be afraid."

Suddenly she came undone. Her flesh, her dress, the qinqin, the screen her chair all began unfolding in the three directions he was used to seeing and five more that he had never guessed were there. She / It was mainly white and covered acres in a moonlit desert. A tall wrecked shell-castle stood by. Its mother-of-pearl door crashed open, the soot of many torches stained its upper surface. He was standing on her. He walked carefully at first. She looked like paper, but was of far tougher stuff. Characters in an unknown tongue were printed on her surface. Very elaborate, they were human-sized and printed in the faintest sepia. He followed them. He occasionally thought he could read (or perhaps sense) some meaning. Here was Rome. Here were the Americas. Here were beings on the Moon making giant sculptures. Alexander the Great. His mother dying when he was four. It wasn't linear. Sometimes it was the distant past. Here he and librarian drank under the oak trees. He walked across the plain for miles it seemed. When he looked up he couldn't even see the shell-castle any more. He found the glyph of himself looking at the glyph. He bent down to study it. He dropped to his hands and knees, seeing it change as it recorded his actions. He felt if he could read the world, he would be its master, instead of just another glyph in the endless meaningless sheet of demonic parchment. Maybe the Book knew it would not be her Master because it would be her friend? Her lover? Her god?

As he knelt on the great white sheet, his own shadow blending with the ink of his sign, an idle thought passed through his enraptured mind. *She said she ate. I wonder what she eats?*

Before the suspicion could form itself into a speculation, the Book refolded. He screamed, but it would have sounded far away (as though muffled by rags). The sign grew dark with its living ink.

For another twenty years visitors to the ruins would have seen a large book with iron hinges, but there were no visitors.

Then one came, picked her up and a new meaningless cycle was recorded.

(for the memory of Robert Bloch)

The Head of the Tree

WHEN I WAS very young, my parents went away. I don't know why they went away, but I felt as though I was the reason. They made me stay with my aunt, who didn't like little girls like me. My aunt lived on the third floor of a five-floor walkup in lower Manhattan. It was dirty and its lights were dim. The stairs were steep and it was hard for me to climb.

After a while a woman with deep red skin came to live with us. Her name was Blood Woman. My aunt was very mad that Blood Woman came, because we had to feed her. I remember my aunt and I going to the butcher's on the corner, and carrying back sacksful of meat wrapped in white paper. By the time we crossed over the awful stairs some of the paper would have turned pink. Sometimes we would just throw the sacks of meat into the Blood Woman's room. By that time her belly was getting big.

My parents came back from wherever they had been, and got very angry with my aunt for having let me see the Blood Woman. I remember lots of shouting and my father saying: "Jesus Christ! Maud, that's exactly the kind of stuff we're trying to keep her from." My mother threw my stuff into a little suitcase and we took a taxi to the airport. We had to wait a long time for a plane.

All of this "came out" when I started therapy when I was thirty-three. All I had remembered was that there had been some taboo—some name so dread that if it were pronounced even by accident it could destroy the order of our happy home. We lived in Dallas, Texas. My father had been a dealer in pre-Columbian antiquities. When I was sixteen he came into my room one night. He was drunk and I thought he was going to touch me. I can remember my light blue nightgown in the moonlight, but I can't remember his face well. But he didn't touch me. All he did was tell me to remember him and to never, ever go to New York. He said he had a little business to take care of, and he would be back real soon. The next morning he was gone and I didn't see him for eighteen years.

I'd started therapy because I had an eating disorder. I'd wake up at two or three every night and go into my kitchen and tear into cheap pastries, cupcakes, and all brightly-colored snack foods you could get from a 7-11. I'd stand over my trashcan and shove the moist slop directly into my mouth—the empty package falling straight into the trash. When I had filled my gullet, I'd make myself puke. Three fingers down the throat. I'd throw up right into the trashcan.

Then I'd take a long hot shower until I was squeaky clean. I'd carry my garbage out to the dumpster and carefully throw it all away about 4:00 in the morning. My co-workers at the mall art gallery began to complain that I was getting thin, and that I always acted tired. One morning I locked myself out of my apartment, and I had to wake up the manager to get back in.

She explained in very loud and graphic terms that it was not normal to put out one's garbage at 4:00 AM. She urged me to get my head checked out.

I decided this was wise.

After a few sessions with the therapist, a gray woman who seems to have dissolved in my mind, I began to remember living with my aunt. Fragments and bits of Vision came back. At first these seemed unreal, but as more and more of the puzzle revealed itself the fragments seemed more real than my therapist's office. She had never been very real to me and easily metamorphosed into a kind of anthropomorphic fog. Midway through my sessions—I decided to challenge my mother with this newfound truth.

My mother said I was very very wicked. That I had never been placed with an aunt.

My therapist had explained all these memories as distorted memories of child abuse. She urged me to sue my mother.

But I knew the memories were real and even the horrible smell of blood and climbing the endless stairs was real—and I chose that reality over the gray world of the therapist. At some time I stopped seeing her, but my eating problem cleared up some with only occasional binges.

I tried another therapist before I left Dallas, but she proved even more fog-like. She said that I had swallowed my parents too early, and that instead of internalizing maternal love, I only had swallowed emptiness. She gave me some books by Lacan to read, and she may have made a pass at me—but it was vague and gray. I do not remember.

I decided the thing to do was go to New York. I had somehow acquired a degree in Fine Arts from the University of Dallas, a small Catholic college in Irving. With the aid of some school friends I parlayed my degree into a job at a midtown gallery that specialized in the works of Jackson Pollock and (if you can believe that there is such a thing) lesser lights of the Action Painting school. I would baby-sit these ugly canvasses while investors representing Japanese banks would buy them. The investors would have to test them, of course. You can't spot a Pollock by his dribbles since their production requires absolutely no talent whatsoever—but you can do tests to see if the paint is appropriately old.

My moving to New York was, of course, taking an active role in my own damnation. But what is therapy good for—save to reveal in which precise manner we are already damned. It took a couple of months to find a five-floor walkup to move into.

* * * * *

A week after I had moved in, I had a dream that revealed I was on the right track. I dreamt that a man with the face of an owl came into my apartment. It was dark (I always sleep in utter darkness—it is the only place I feel at home). In my dream I saw a dim red lantern moving to and fro just beyond the foot of my bed. A naked man with the face of an owl bent over my bed looking for something. In my dream I knew that he didn't have the ways of looking at the world that we have. So he was having hard time finding what he was looking for. Then he passed his tiny lamp over my foot and made a hissing sound.

I awoke and discovered that my radiator had cracked, releasing a spray of steam against the mildewed plaster. I had started my period.

The small artistic soul of the gallery manager twitched enough so she decided to have a show with live artists on the weekend. She decided on the theme of body invaders. She would get cyberpunks, electro-sexologists, and medical artists from Soho and Hell's Kitchen. I was supposed to interview and evaluate these techno-shamans. I guess in her own heart she knew she couldn't separate the artists from the poseurs. Or perhaps she realized that she lacked the true love of darkness which had pulled me to New York like iron filings to a magnet.

I booked a performance art team of sado-masochists. The dom put an auto-sodomizing device on the sub and stood to the side occasionally giving shocks with a device called a violet wand. I found a crazed magician who wrote Runic poetry with his own blood. I even found a stained-glass artist who had opted to use diseased tissue on glass slides as raw material for her art.

Eventually the man with the owl mask came to me. Now it wasn't the same figure as in my dream. I mean it looked like him, but this was a real human being. His name was Erskine Mably. He lived in a loft in Hell's Kitchen. He worked at one of the few gas stations still found on the island of Manhattan. He didn't know that he was being drawn by the strength of my dreams to become a figure in my own myths.

He did a self-mutilation act. Needles and pins in his chest, walking on broken glass, etc. This freak show action now passes for performance art.

After our first exhibit I took him out. Over white wine I asked him: "You like women who are mean to you?"

"A little," he said. "Well, a lot."

"What do you think happens when someone is mean to you?"

"Well, if natural sex means pleasure, it doesn't take much to see that unnatural sex means pain."

"Why do you want to do something unnatural?"

"I want to be less and less like an animal. Think of Greek myths: man can become pigs by Circe's spell or gods like Hercules when purified. I seek purification."

"Would you like me to be mean to you?"

"Yes," he said. "I would like that very much."

* * * * *

I went out and got some beginner's books on S&M. Anne Rice and Pat Califia. I bought a crop, a paddle, and some obsidian needles. I figured that if I could push him into the right headspace—he could reveal to me the mystery I sought after. Many shamans put themselves through such ordeals. I would be driving it. I would find out about the Blood Woman.

The exhibits lasted for three weekends. I wanted to give him time to heal up so I didn't set up our session until a month later.

He came to my small dirty apartment. He looked a little scared. I hadn't been eating much. The last week I had eaten nothing but raw meat in order to be more in contact with the spirit of the Blood Woman.

He brought his toys.

I lightly scourged him on his back, front, buttocks, and the soles of his feet. Then I tied him up with his hands connected to an exposed water pipe in my bathroom. I put out all the lights and lit two high red candles (as well as some copal). I put a gag in his mouth then the owl mask over his head. I took out the obsidian needles. I lay them in a semicircle around his feet. They're primitive and rough looking—very sharp and jagged. His eyes widened in fear. He had never seen them. They looked far more primal than the antiseptic metal needles he used in his act.

I pierced his left nipple first. As the skin broke, I asked him: "Who is the Blood Woman?" He looked very confused. I asked the same question as I pushed each needle in. I pierced all the tender areas of his body, not neglecting his cock.

The light of knowledge appeared in his eyes. I took the mask off, then the gag. I replaced the mask and he said: "You knew that we would eventually meet. You just wanted to hear my voice, that's all."

I released him from the bonds. As I turned to blow out the candles, owl man struck my head with a lamp. I thought he was trying to escape, but when I turned to look at him he had completely transformed into the figure of my dreams.

"Come," he said.

He led me out of my apartment. I wasn't surprised when as he led me downstairs, we passed far far below the basement. I had always felt that it was so. Each descending floor had slightly worse wallpaper than those which preceded it and a slightly worse smell. After a while gaslight replaced electric. Then oil lamps replaced gas. Then came candles—and the floors we passed through became nothing more than carved stone. Then candles gateway to torches, and carved stone to natural caverns vast and strange.

We came to a place where it was very dark and full of the cries of animals and vast shapes swooped by in the fetid air. Owlman led me through this vast cavern to a city where everyone was skeletons covered with rotting flesh. Word went out that I had arrived, and the headman of the village came to me.

It was my father.

"Welcome daughter to Xibalba. Many do not survive the descent to the realm from which all cities grow. This is the place from which the roots of civilization grow. I will put you in charge of watering the roots."

My father arranged a great festival in my honor. Owl demons and skeleton demons played a ball game in my honor. The losers became the supper for the winners. But this didn't diminish our numbers. New people arrived daily from the great staircase from London, Tokyo, Mexico City, Cairo, everywhere. They would begin to change in the dark. Things would grow on them or from within them and they would begin to change into owl demons, or skeleton demons, or bat demons.

Every day I would water the roots of the city-trees. Great black obsidian pipes extended from the ceiling. Through the pipes flowed blood let in from the cities. Endless blood. Gallons of blood. Because of my contact with the blood, things did not grow in me or upon me. I still looked as I had looked in the upper world, save that my skin turned blood red.

For the most part I preferred the gloomy world of Xibalba to the upper world. Here everything seemed real. Nothing was a mask for anything else. In fact part of me had always dwelt here—the upper world had always been a mask for here—for the true reality. Sometimes when there was a particularly vicious gang killing or a particularly brutal accident—the mask slipped a little.

When my task of watering the great trees was over, I would go and sit with my sisters in the Cavern of Screams. There each cry of anguish or desperation from the great cities would reach us through vast ducts. Surrounded by the sounds of such great pain, the inhabitants of Xibalba were at peace.

There were special games played in the Cavern of Ix Tab, where those who hung themselves remained perpetually suspended from the ceiling.

I was greatly happy here and after several years lost my memory of the upper world.

Then one day I was watering the great tree which grew into Los Angeles. A small tree had sprouted nearby. My father had instructed me to report to him any new growth—so I went to look at the tree.

It was twice my height and had a skull for a head. Such things do not surprise me, for there are many strange things in Xibalba.

"Hello," it said.

"Hello," I said. Then I recognized the voice of Erskine. "I remember you—you led me down the six thousand steps."

"Yes. I let you change me into an owl man."

"But you're not an owl man anymore."

"I wanted to return to the Upper World. The leader of the Owl Demons discovered my secret desire and cut my head off to use for the ball game. Then they threw it here. I still lived though."

"Will you grow into a city?" I asked.

"No, I will overcome the lords of Xibalba by ending their blood tribute."

"There can't be cities without blood."

"Then let there be no more cities."

"I will tell my father and he shall cut you down and I will burn your logs in my fire-grate."

"You will not tell your father, because I know something about you and you will do anything for self-knowledge."

I went away haughtily, but I did not tell my father. Perhaps the tree was lying, but my desire for self-knowledge had always been my strongest desire. Because of that desire I had found my way from New York to Xibalba. What if he knew something?

I would go each day and water the roots of Los Angeles with blood. I tried to coax the tree to tell me what it knew.

One day the tree said: "I will tell you now. But first you must let me spit on you." Then the skull spat upon me. The slimy spit entered me through all the places that a woman may be entered. Then the skull said: "You have become the Blood Woman. Go and find the mirror your father has hidden, and you will see."

I went to my father's place and I waited until he slept. Then quietly I went to the room of the mirror and saw that it was so. The next day I went to the tree and said: "I will tell my father to cut you down."

"No," said the tree, "for my spit has made you pregnant. You will have to flee to the Upper World for there is no birth in Xibalba. You will go to the place of your memories and there you will give birth to twin sons. My sons will stop the blood tribute."

I was angry with him for making me pregnant. Soon I knew that he had spoken truly. I know that before my pregnancy shows I will have to go up the six thousand steps. For the law of Xibalba forbids the bringing into life in the manner of the Upper World.

I will bear the twins that will end the blood tribute. I know that will destroy this beautiful place of torture and sacrifice and I mourn its passing. I am the Blood Woman.

(for Charles DeLint)

'Night Gauntlet'

by

Walter C. DeBill, Jr.
Richard Gavin
Robert M. Price
W. H. Pugmire
Jeffrey Thomas
Don Webb

THE IRONY—FOR in all terror there is irony—was that Susan Derby's brother Nathan had been a fan. A fan of fantastic literature, of the "Weird Tale" in particular. Nathan could have offered advice or at least a coherent philosophy for what unfolded in Dr. Derby's lab. He had never been too good with the human angle: he really could not have imagined the boredom and isolation that would have filled her century after century, but he would have understood the Terror and Wonder and Joy that filled her at the same time. Nathan would have named the It something spooky—Yog-Sothoth perhaps, or Tak, or the Great Black Swine. Fantasy literature is full of such names, their power to scare lost as soon as they become part of a pun or a joke or a plush toy—but they spring from the same roots that the experiments in the High Energy Lab sprang from. They come from the outer reaches of the linear mind grasping at dimensions beyond its own.

Susan was blond, bright and beautiful. She looked like a lab assistant from a 1950s mad scientist movie. But no assistant she. Her work bridging type I and type II string theory could be understood by a half dozen people—and some of those might say they were guessing. She was a whiz at Nambu 3 algebra and heterotic matrices; when her wet brown eyes focused on you, you really thought you understood how D-p-branes were different than from non-sticky branes. When she smiled during a lecture you understood how angular and curved time intersected.

The University of Texas at Austin has been a super star in weird physics. Dr. Wheeler proposed the Multi-worlds interpretation of Copenhagen quantum theory. And it had a few nutcases as well. Dr. Emil Hesychius' name is well represented on conspiracy and occultozoid blogs around the world. Susan had inherited his office. It was papered with souvenir postcards: Derry, Maine; Arkham, Mass; Ong's Hat, NJ; Glory, West Virginia; Sesqua Valley, WA; Brichester, UK; Binger, OK; Mirocaw, ID; Crouch End, UK; Telfer, Australia; Nan Madol, Federated States of Micronesia, Mlandoth, TX. Not exactly run-of-the-mill tourist attractions. Dr. Hesychius had been at work at a special torsion field theory that took Anatoly Akimov's work and replaced his solutions to Maxwell equations with Type IIB string theory while maintaining the "alternate" interpretations of Einstein-Cartan theory. In other words, he was plain nuts and a favorite of the UFO-Maya-Nostradamus crowd. The University had been trying to figure out how to get rid of him discreetly until the day he ascended the UT Clock-tower and tried to emulate Charles Stuart Whitman's 1966 sniper performance. He killed 19 students and staff, and the fact he claimed to be shooting "nightgaunts" did not endear him to the public.

Anyway, as I was saying—oh, I had better introduce myself at this point. My name is John Giloh and I am a grad student at UT specializing in the American Gothic Tradition. My goals were at the beginning of the tragedy to do well on my oral defense of my doctoral thesis: *Displacement of Voice in the American Fantastic from Charles Brockden Brown to Thomas Ligotti*, to write some really good horror stories and to get into the pants of Dr. Susan Derby. Anyway, Susan got Dr. Hesychius' office and it fit her sense of humor to leave it furnished as it had been in Hesychius' day. She liked the appalled look on people's faces when they entered. So the postcards on the wall, connected by strands of different colored wire and yarn, remained. Although none of the postcards were themselves creepy—a giant statue of Paul Bunyan in Derry was connected by green yarn to a statue of Paul Bunyan in the Sesqua Valley, OR, the East Binger Nitrogen plant connected with a blue wire to a basalt temple submerged in the waters at Nan Madol. The overall effect was creepy. I hated to go to her office because my eyes kept following wire to wire to yarn and I would wind up not even asking her if she wanted to join me for margaritas or "British cuisine" at the Dog & Duck.

On our dates, Susan would try and explain time and space to me, which was a lost cause. I had not done well in Mrs. Gamble's geometry class, and I thought "quantum foam" was a lubricant.

I took her to the Alamo Drafthouse the night I realized some aspects of Susan's day job were affecting the Night in general. The Alamo serves beer and coffee and food during movies, a highly civilized custom. Susan and I loved indie films and we both loved horror. Tonight's special was *Red Dreams*, a K-horror flick directed by Harry Chang. Ah, I remember it was bleak December, and the student body had largely left the campus. As I waited in front of the Lab, I saw *It*.

It was about nine feet tall and *It* flew on very thin bat wings. I could see the yellow glare of sodium lights through the wings. *It* seemed to have no head proper, just a pair of in-curving horns. *It* lashed a barbed tail. *It* sailed rather leisurely from the business center to the philosophy building.

My problem with the sighting is that, like Nathan Derby, I too had read a good deal of pulp fiction, and I knew *It* as a nightgaunt. I decided not to mention this anomaly to Susan because A) I suspected she looked for sanity in her boyfriends and B) perhaps if I didn't say anything—it would go away.

And go away it did, physically at least. Psychologically, however, the *It* seemed to have bored down roots, set up house in my grey matter. *It* was a part of me now.

I was dumb with shock. As I stared up into a sky that was rich with red shadows, my brain began to oscillate with ideas that were equal parts logical inquiry and weird tale plotting. I questioned how a nightgaunt (if that's truly what *It* was) had managed to escape so swiftly into the evening clouds. I also began to wonder if such entities *chose* to appear to only a select few. Were their witnesses elected by some vague metaphysical process? If so, just what form of cult had I been unwittingly initiated into? Lovecraft claimed to have felt the presence of nightgaunts when he was no more than six or seven, and he went on to become one of this country's greatest visionary authors. Maybe my writer's mind had just been blessed with some of the same kind of turbo charge?

Oh, if only life was that tidy . . .

If this were only a story, I could've followed some thread of inquiry until some moment of horrible gnosis. But existence never unspools as holistically as a fictive. Life doesn't have a plot, not that I've ever been able to shake loose at least.

Still, part of me couldn't help but feel that Dr. Hesychius had been right. He'd been *right*. Nightgaunts did exist. But of course, those 19 bullet-riddled cadavers he'd decorated the campus with that fateful day bore no resemblance to what I'd seen, or thought I'd seen. Visions are one thing, and I think in some way they can actually be healthy, but no experience, however odd, ever warrants bloodshed. That's always been my problem with religion. Susan's too, in fact.

It dawned on me that my fate could follow that of Dr. Hesychius just as easily as Lovecraft's. I quickly shuddered away the awful mental picture of me scaling those clock-tower stairs, my eyes darkened by delusions, my heart detached from pain. Would I eventually see my brothers and sisters of this planet twisted into monsters as well?

"Earth to John . . . hello?"

My flinch must've been a dramatic one, because when I whirled around Susan was giggling. The glimpse I stole of her shimmering eyes was almost enough to make me dismiss the nightgaunt as nothing more than a turkey vulture mutated by my own hunger, lack of sleep, and various anxieties connected with my burgeoning thesis.

"You seem a little skittish tonight. Are you sure you're up for K-Horror at the Alamo?"

"Definitely," I said. "You won't be offended if I squeal and grab onto your arm, will you?"

"I'd be disappointed if you didn't," Susan replied, brightening the evening with her smile.

We took Susan's car to the Alamo Drafthouse. Just sitting in the passenger seat listening to Susan talk about the small annoyances of laboratory politics settled my nerves. I wanted to tell her about the *It*. I also really wanted to kiss her. But my gut told me that if I were to pursue either impulse, Susan would never forget tonight. Although I was fairly sure that the memory of our first kiss would've been a tender one for her, I was absolutely positive that if the word nightgaunt had passed my lips tonight it would've become a story that Susan would share with some future lover. Her 'How-I-learned-my-would-be-boyfriend-was-bugfuck-crazy' story.

We walked to the theatre and took our customary seats in the front row (the distortion adds to a horror movie's unease, according to Susan). We shared brisket quesadillas and a pitcher of Fat Tire before the movie.

Susan shared some of the stumbling blocks she'd hit trying to explain the nuances of her string theories to undergrads. I chewed my food and pretended I understood her.

"Have you seen this film before?" I asked, hoping to veer the conversation away from the hopelessly confusing labyrinth of science.

"No. I don't know anything about it, to be honest. I just remember the title *Red Dreams* jumping out at me from that mountain of videotapes my brother had when he still lived at home. I think he might've actually interviewed Harry Chang once for his fanzine."

"*Eldritch Psalms!* God, I haven't thought about that 'zine since the days when Nathan was rejecting all my short stories."

Susan giggled. "I don't think you'll ever forgive him for that."

I held up my hands to express my lack of resentment. "Nathan was a harsh critic, no question, but unlike a lot of editors, he wasn't firm because he was bitter over not being able to make it as a writer himself. I think he really wanted to raise the quality bar. There were a lot of crappy horror magazines in those days. I should know, I wrote for most of them. Nathan rejected every writer I knew, with the exception of Ramsey Campbell, of course. He felt he knew so damn *much* about horror fiction that it was practically impossible to dazzle him. I certainly don't begrudge him rejecting those early stories. They were just bad Fritz Leiber knock-offs anyway. That reminds me, when is Nathan due back from England? Wasn't that publishing gig just a one-year contract?"

The temperature between Susan and I suddenly plummeted. I bit my lip, regretting that I'd ever asked about her brother.

"He was let go months before the contract ended," Susan mumbled, seemingly more to her pint of Fat Tire than to me. "He got about one half of an anthology edited for the publisher and that was it."

I didn't want to press the issue, but I had a suspicion that underneath her discomfort, Susan was being gnawed at by an urge to talk, to uncork whatever she'd been harboring inside. I was more than eager to be her sounding board.

"Is he still overseas?" I asked.

"I honestly don't know." Her voice had shriveled to a whisper.

"When was the last time you spoke to him?"

"Independence Day, or Hawthorne's birthday if you want to celebrate it the way Nathan used to. Anyway, he phoned me to ask if those damned postcards were still hanging in the office. I told him yes and he said 'good' and that he'd be home soon."

"But that was almost six months ago."

"I know," she said, a little sadly.

Darkness swooped upon the room and all conversation stopped, including mine and Susan's. I wished we hadn't gone to the Alamo, wished we'd just gone to the Dog & Duck where we could've talked without disruption.

As the trailers ran, the events of the night began to swirl around in my head. Dr. Hesychius, the nightgaunt, Nathan's absence. Somehow they felt connected. I tried not to let my imagination run amok. Susan always teased me about threading random bits together and calling it "a connection." She told me not to feel too silly about it, that human beings are pattern-makers by nature. We see cohesion everywhere we look. "It is," she'd told me, "as natural as breathing."

I'd almost managed to convince myself that I was simply pattern-making. Then *Red Dreams* began, and before the first reel was even finished, everything became much clearer to me.

The film began in blackness, with just the title in red letters that quickly spilled away like streams of blood. And then the blackness seemed to become a kind of—semblance, an almost featureless face with a hint of eyes and mocking mouth. The blackness took on form and became the tops of trees of a wide forest. The camera swooped to a large clearing where an odd figure reclined on the ground—two figures actually, a dead gigantic lumberjack, the blade of his ax just below his torn and ravaged throat, and a blue ox supping on the gore. The lapping of the tongue was very loud, almost drowning out the score—if that's what it was—of distant drums beating to the wailing of weird flutes. The animal raised its mammoth head, and I noticed that its horns resembled those of a ram more so than an ox; and there was something goatish about the shape of its snout. A stream of blood slipped from its mouth and fell onto the face of the dead giant.

It was when the beast raised its head to dark heaven and bayed like a fiend that Susan groaned and grabbed at my hair, her fingers clutching and winding strands into painful knots. Her cool mouth was at my ear, and I shivered at her whisper of breath; but I could not understand the name she sighed, which sounded kind of like the name of an Egyptian lord. Her frantic hand stroked my face, gently pricking one eye orb with a pointed nail; and then her hand pressed against my lips and nose. God, her smell! I moaned a little as my tongue crawled out of my mouth and licked her palm. The screen began to flicker as shards of starlight fell into the woodland from the black sky; and I turned to gaze at Susan's stunning beauty in that flickering light, and I couldn't understand what was wrong with her face, that visage that seemed slightly out of tilt, as if it were a fleshy mask that had slightly lost its hold.

Susan's hand moved from my lips and pointed at the screen. I saw the three figures that fell from heaven, the one so dominating, the others on either side; and I cringed when I saw that the two accompanying things were nightgaunts. The priest or whatever he was (he wore flowing robes that suggested a kind of religious hierarchy) picked up the lumberjack's ax and crashed its blade onto the forehead of the blue ox, and the nightgaunts thrust their black talons into the pouring blood and washed it over the surface where they did not wear faces. The Black Man clasped his hands together and sang a kind of dirge—like some eldritch psalm that heralded the end of Time. He took up the ax and split heaven with its blade, so that a rain of blood washed over everything. God, that crimson tide! I could feel its warmth in my eyes and taste its copper on my tongue. I could smell it in my flaring nostrils and feel it slip down my throat and fill my heaving stomach! Groaning, I disengaged myself from Susan and stumbled out of my seat, running up the aisle and out of the Alamo, in front of which, into a gutter, I disgorged my quesadilla.

Patterns. They were all around me, but I couldn't figure out their meaning. I couldn't grab hold of the strings that combined them, like the damn green yarn and blue wire that connected those postcards in Susan's office. I backed away from the curb and pressed my back against the Alamo; and the sky above me moved with black and red shapes that formed suggestively and then broke apart. I shut my eyes, hoping it would stop the pounding in my brain, and when I swallowed the taste of bile made me want to be sick again.

Her smooth hand was in my hair, gently. I opened my eyes to the touch of the soft cloth she used to dry the wetness from my face, the debris of sickness from my lips. She smiled at me with laughing eyes as I touched my fingers to her face, trying to make certain it held firm. I couldn't remember her eyes being so dark—almost black in the weird shifting light that filtered down from the sentient sky.

"What's the matter, baby? You really don't look well. Maybe we should walk the night for a little while—the cool air may do you good. Listen, why don't we return to my office? There's something there I want to show you, something I found among the papers that Dr. Hesychius left behind. It's a kind of parchment, like something you'd find in an old forgotten tomb—and it has the weirdest figure on it, a kind of devil or daemon with wings and a funny-looking tail. It's probably what contributed to his delusion about those things he thought were after him. Come on, don't look so nervous. You write that weird stuff—maybe your imagination will help me decipher the mystery surrounding the tragedy of those nineteen souls, those ghosts that haunt the office still. Come, John, follow me."

The campus was quiet, distant echoes whispering of solitary journeys and post-party laughter. Normally I enjoy the bats, but I felt an aversion to the night sky. I didn't look up.

Emil Hesychius's erstwhile lab was a fifth floor knee-buster, and the elevator barely made the crawl up to it. It was an unpopular location; the bottom-rung scholars consigned to it had long deserted the gloomy corridor. The battered old door actually creaked. Inside, the blue wires and green yarn connecting the postcards were no less disturbing than before.

"I'll get it," she murmured. She walked around her desk and dug a little key out of her purse. She gave me a quick solemn stare before she bent to unlock a bottom drawer. I had not seen her so subdued before. She brought out something that looked like a big cloth-bound book, dark blue with no title, but was actually a stout box. Inside was a sheet about fifteen-inches square, roughly hacked along the left side, as though hastily removed from a bound tome. It was obviously parchment, but the color and texture seemed wrong from the start. Much later a biologist would tell me the cell structure wasn't from sheep or goat or calf, and complain about not getting an antibody reaction with any species in his collection of extracts. Last I saw him he was muttering about trying DNA, but I never heard from him on that. I walked around the desk to make it right side up. And to get closer to Susan.

The surface was covered with minuscule writing in a script unknown to me, heavily shaded as though written with a tiny brush. Not Arabic, not Uighur Mongol. Probably alphabetic, not syllabic or ideographic. I'd have to get help to identify it, much less read it. What grabbed my eye were the striking design in the center, and the detailed, shaded sketch of a nightgaunt in the right margin. It was done in pencil, like an absent-minded doodle. Hesychius' work? I didn't doubt he was the type to doodle on a priceless stolen page of manuscript. But it was the thing in the center that drew my eyes with hypnotic power. It swirled like the stylized Sanskrit "om," but wasn't it. An ovoid central eye, three hooked, scythe-like tentacles, and a small spherical body behind the eye; a suggestion of chaotic swirling.

"The sign of Koth," she said, so quietly that it startled me. I thought she didn't know about such stuff. But then, she was Nathan's sister, and a member of the Derby-Pickman clan. "Threeness. There's something about nightgaunts and threes. They like triads."

"I thought Nathan was the fan of weird lore," I said.

She smiled. "He talks about it constantly, and I have to admit it draws me in. There's something . . . exciting about it. The mystery, the layers of significance, always knowing there's more to be learned, if only you can tease it out. It's a turn-on, actually."

"I thought you'd be all cool logic."

"I am a Derby, after all. And I think there's even a connection with my work. I think high energy interactions draw them. Theoretically high energy interactions sprinkle space-time with disturbances, however minute."

"Salting space for them," I suggested humorously. "Maybe they like the taste. They do seem to be primitive, elemental creatures, not high tech extraterrestrial invaders."

"Well, something's attracting them to this campus. Like they're trying to complete some kind of mission here," she said.

"And they've been doing it since the doomed professor's time," I said. "He was so obsessive, it's a sure thing that the postcards and blue wire and green yarn have something to do with them. I know a couple of the cards are places connected to the Cthulhu mythos."

"Actually, all of them are," she said. Again, the unsuspected knowledge.

"You really are into this stuff. If it's a turn on, are you turned on?"

She gave me a perfect Mona Lisa smile. "Oh, yes. But this desk doesn't look too comfortable . . . not that I've tested it."

Damn, but she knew how to lead a guy on.

"What about my woman-trap apartment?" I asked.

"I have a better idea. How'd you like to visit the atmospheric old Derby house on Pearl Street? Nathan's not back yet."

Do you think I said no? Of course not.

The old Derby place was a short drive from the campus. We didn't talk on the way. The Derby family had built it before World War I, when they presumably had a lot more money than faculty salaries or the earnings of a sometime editor. Where the family money came from, I didn't know. In my time it always had been kept up by Derby scholars who didn't earn much. I think they got a little money or at least a tax break by registering it as an historical sight. It was an impressive Edwardian pile festooned with round turrets, gables, several big brick chimneys, and verandas on three floors. At the side was a porte-cochère for the carriage, horseless or otherwise. The kind of place any kid would tell you was haunted. A voluptuously romantic setting to consummate a relationship.

Except that we didn't.

There was a light on in a third story turret.

Nathan had come home.

I hid, or tried to hide, a double dose of embarrassment. I had to think he suspected his sister and I were there for some illicit rendezvous—which we were! And then I couldn't help viewing Nathan through my most dominant memories of him: an editor who always made me think my work was second rate—which it was! But things were cool. Susan did not bother trying to give the impression we weren't "together." She did a fine job of acting as though she knew he'd be here, and if he thought that strange, or a lie, he didn't let on. Nathan, it was plain, had been busy in the middle of something, and was having a hard time unwinding. But he wasn't rude and, after a few minutes, actually appeared to appreciate a break from whatever he had been working on. And whatever that was, he took care to shove it into a desk drawer as he rose to shake hands with me, and to give Susan a quick hug. We moved into the living-room, a dusty affair filled with overstuffed furniture, half the items splitting along ancient seams. But in the presence of these horror-fantasy mavens, that was nothing to disapprove of. Hell, I'd always half-wanted to live in the Munsters house when I grew up.

"Nate, old man," I began with hollow jocularity, venturing into what almost certainly must be embarrassing territory, "your sis was just telling me she hadn't heard much from you recently." *Idiot!* That was none of my business. "I guess you turned up something more interesting than that anthology project, right?" *Stupid!* "I mean, not that anthologies aren't important. I'd give a kidney to get into one of Datlow's."

"I don't think you need to worry! Your kidneys are both safe. It'd cost more than that to get past Datlow with *your* stuff!" There was a wicked gleam in his eye that I swore seemed somehow unaccustomed, as if he had had his head in too-serious matters for too long a time. He had forgotten about levity, about humor. At least I was a good buffoon. But he continued, looking now at Susan. "Actually, sis, I've been poaching a bit on your territory: trans-cosmic matrices, that sort of thing."

At this, I happened to catch a momentary wrinkle in Susan's formerly smooth brow. It seemed as if he were about to let go some secret she wasn't ready for anyone else to hear. And this made me ask myself if Susan had been less than honest earlier when she appeared clueless about her brother's pursuits. Had she been upset at losing touch with him? Or had she been uncomfortable because she couldn't tell me some truth she couldn't afford to divulge? And then it popped into my head that, by showing me that parchment, maybe she was trying in her own way to work around to an explanation of the truth. I was getting alarmed despite their seemingly studied attempt to ape small talk. My stomach was barely settled, still a bit queasy. My lust was aroused and pointedly unfulfilled, which left me feeling like I was reeling from a sudden stop on a subway car. And now I was trying to act naturally in an unnatural situation. My defenses were up, though I couldn't have told you exactly why. Then it occurred to me that, as I was all out of original thoughts, maybe I should rely on clichés. The best defense might be a good offense. So, with only a sidelong glance at Susan, which revealed a worried look on her face, I just blurted out: "Nate, my curiosity is killing me." Bad choice of words, I know. "Maybe you can explain a couple of things to me."

With a hint of professorial condescension, Nate answered: "Why, sure, old buddy, I'd be happy to. What's bugging you?"

"For one thing, I can't get the picture of that wall full of postcards out of my mind. You know, in Susan's office that used to belong to Professor Hesychius. It's all connected by strings in some kind of pattern. What does it mean? The place names, most of them, match towns in Lovecraft: Ipswich, Newburyport, Wilbraham."

"That is a tough one, I'll grant. I mean, I have an idea, but it would be a bit difficult to explain without a grounding in the kind of work the professor was doing, and that Sue and I have, each in our own way, been trying to reconstruct. Let me just say, uh, you didn't remove any of those strings, did you?" At this he spared his sister a nervous glance, though still speaking to me. I shook my head in the negative.

"Yeah, of course not. Sorry I asked. Well, I guess you could say the whole display is something in the nature of, I don't know, maybe a *switchboard.* As I say, it wouldn't make much sense to someone not clued into the larger picture. I'm not saying you're dumb or anything."

I gave the open-palmed gesture that, of course, it went without saying, don't worry. I suddenly realized how tense I was feeling and shifted in my chair to try to relax. "Um, Professor Hesychius. That's some name! The Greek for the Old Testament King Hezekiah, right?"

"Why, yes, it is! I'm surprised you know that! Didn't figure you for the Bible-toting type!"

"Nor you, Nate, come to think of it. I remember him mentioning it in class once. He said how when he was a kid he'd looked up the name, curious about the meaning. Or the origin, I guess. Turned out he was the king who was going to die, but Isaiah the prophet bought him some extra years by turning the sun dial back! And that story gave him the idea for one of his pet projects—turning back time."

Susan interjected. "Yes, he thought it might be possible, if not exactly to *go* back in time, at least to *see* the past. And, er, come to think of it, I have a hunch that may have had something to do with his shooting spree at the end. I found some notes of his hidden away in a panel behind a desk drawer. He had scribbled down a vision he had experienced, either through an experimental drug or a mechanical technique. He saw the origin of the human race. He said that at first there was this race of what looked like Lovecraft's nightgaunts, and that they had committed some terrible acts, and then some greater, more powerful force punished them by clipping their wings and making them mortal, fleshly beings. What we call human beings. They all forgot their former freedom and ecstasy and settled down to the drudgery that degrades and enslaves the human race." Susan's eyes were less focused. She seemed to be looking far away, her words inspired by some heartfelt conviction, not of the professor's, but of her own. "They had to live paltry human lives over and over again, to atone for the sin they had committed."

She slowed to a halt, still looking a bit disassociated, and I took the opportunity to ask: "That's all pretty damn weird, I admit, but what has that got to do with his murdering those students?"

Nathan took up the thread. "Don't you see, old man? Old Hesychius wasn't hallucinating," then, as if catching himself, he retraced his words. "I mean, his hallucinations took the form of him believing the students he was aiming at *were nightgaunts*. He was seeing them as they really were, their original appearance that still lay within them deep down. He wanted to stop their mission, whatever he thought it was. I guess he thought everybody was a nightgaunt by nature, and that they shouldn't be allowed to live."

I chimed in: "Even though that would have to include him, too."

After that night, Susan withdrew from me. I was surprised by this; I'd thought that she and I, and Nathan too, had connected on some deeper level that night, in a more intense and intimate way. But Susan wouldn't take my calls, and I couldn't contact Nathan either, even when I knocked on the door of that looming old monster they lived in.

Several times I knocked on the door of her office, too, but she never responded, though I'm sure she was in there. Through the wood, one time I even thought I heard someone shush someone else.

But then, after nearly a week of befuddled despondence had passed, Susan finally called *me*—asked to meet me at the Dog & Duck. There, over sober coffees, she opened up to me. But I have to tell you first about her appearance. She looked torn between fear and fervor, which gave her the aspect of a girl in anticipation of losing her virginity at any moment. But losing it to what? Whatever the source of her disorienting excitement, it made me desire her all the more. It was like her excitement had infected me with something of the same nature.

Breathlessly, Susan explained: "John, Nathan didn't want to involve you anymore, but I don't see any reason to exclude you. You already know so much now, and maybe you can even help us. You're receptive to what we're discovering. We can use your intuitions." She reached across the table then and squeezed my hand. "I want you to share this with me, John."

That fever, shining in her eyes. Her hand squeezing mine tighter. Do you think she needed to ask me twice?

So that night, after hours, I found myself in her fifth-floor office—Dr. Emil Hesychius' former office in the High Energy

Lab. Nathan was waiting, and greeted me a little sourly but with a sense of resignation. I took little notice of him, however. My attention had been drawn to something else.

Since last I had been here, the strings connecting the postcards tacked to the wall had multiplied. There were a few new strands of forest green and ocean blue, but now there were strings of fire red yarn added into the web, the weave, looking like raw veins stretched out to dry. And then, before either Derby could enlighten me, I spotted it. The pattern the obsessed siblings had ultimately arrived at. The strings, yarn and wire traced the outline of an ovoid eye, with three hooked scythe-like tentacles, and a small spherical body behind the eye. A pattern that gave the effect of chaotic swirling.

"The sign of Koth," I muttered to myself.

"John." Susan touched my arm. "This is the literal manifestation of all the abstracts that misled me for so long. This is the tangible reality behind the lying veil. It's been almost traumatic for me to give myself over to belief. It seems to fly in the face of everything I've devoted myself to . . . but actually, it's the logical end to every thread I've ever followed. And all this time without knowing it I was churning up the energies, just like Hesychius, teasing the Night Gaunts. Drawing them like moths to a light." She grinned, and I experienced that delirious feeling I'd had in the theatre, when it looked as if the mask of her face had slipped just a bit. "But here . . . look . . . see it for yourself."

"See what, Susan?" I asked, a little unnerved by her almost religious zeal.

"This, my poor little scribe," Nathan said, and he stepped closer to the pattern on the wall. One after another he plucked the strings, as if plucking at a harp, but there was no music. The strings blurred, of course. But their vibrations did not stop. String after string he plucked. Blurred green. Blurred blue. Blurred red. The three primary colors used for additive combination. And hadn't Susan said that there something about Night Gaunts and threes . . . that they liked triads?

Nathan stepped back. "She wouldn't let me complete the tuning of the strings until you were here to share this with us, John." He watched the blurring, vibrating strings beside Susan and me. "Now, together, we're going to achieve what Hesychius only dreamed of."

"Look!" Susan cut him off. "Do you see?"

I did. The blurring primary colors overlapped, and an image had begun to take form from those mixing hues. It was as though a window were materializing in the wall. And this window looked out upon a primal scene. A black, nighted forest. It was, I felt, the same forest Chang had somehow reproduced at the start of his film *Red Dreams*.

There was a clearing, but much wider than that in the film, and in this clearing stood a huge mound of black rock. Above and around this great rock flew little black birds, thousands of them. Thousands more perched on the rock itself. But as the birds continued to flock across some moonlit scraps of cloud, I finally recognized them for what they were, and knew that mass of rock was larger than I had at first thought. Because those thousands of flying creatures were not birds—but nightgaunts.

And then, the mountain raised its massive head, and proved itself not a mountain at all. Its head was surmounted by two great ram horns—and flanking its jaw, two curling tusks like those of a wild boar. I could make out little of its face, but for a hint of eyes and mocking mouth.

"Dear God," Susan said. Transfixed as I was by the scene unfolding before us, almost paralyzed with awe, I hadn't noticed that Susan had taken several steps forward. Her arms were floating up in front of her. "Dear God," she repeated.

Another realization came to me. In all the time (however long it had been) that I'd been staring at this scene, I had never seen the silhouetted treetops stir. The glowing rags of cloud in the sky hadn't shifted. This was a frozen pocket of time, which some primeval instinct told me was prehistoric. Maybe this was how these nightgaunts had cheated evolution, and prevented themselves from becoming creatures even more terrible than themselves.

Us.

The appendages I had misinterpreted as ram horns uncoiled, writhed. The lower, lesser appendages I had mistaken for boar's tusks uncurled and squirmed as well. And the vast entity's eyes took on a mesmerizing glow.

Susan took several more steps, and before I could arouse myself to call out to her or grab for her, she reached out and touched one of the resonating strings. At that moment, her body became a blur as well. A kind of shadow in flux. Her outlines were uncertain, though I'm sure I made out a pair of bat-like wings, folded against her back.

Nathan screamed for her, and lunged forward, but I had gathered my wits enough to grab him and hold him back. Though, just as easily I might have lunged for Susan first, and maybe it would have been him holding me back at that moment.

Susan became less and less corporeal. The shadow was fading. The image on the wall itself was dimming, as if a dark mist were closing over it, as the colored strings at last began to slow in their uncanny vibrations.

Another few moments, and the strings stopped vibrating altogether. Dr. Susan Derby and the image on the wall were no more. The last I had seen of her, though, I could swear I saw those wings on her back open to their full majestic length.

Nathan fought against me with a fresh surge of strength, and I let him go this time. He fell against the wall, sobbing, clawing away the postcards, tearing them to shreds, and ripping down the wires, the yarn, the string (string theory, I thought deliriously). I did not try to stop him.

I would mourn Susan in my own way, of course. But in the days that followed I would sometimes also marvel . . . wondering what her new existence was like. An existence that predated the existence of any human being, such as we know them today. An immortal existence, in which perhaps she herself was no longer human. I prayed, no longer human. Not in that timeless black forest.

As I said, Nathan might have helped this lesser literatus grasp what had truly transpired in Susan's office-cum-lab. After all, he had been a fan . . . a fan of fantastic literature. His inclinations had afforded him a unique kind of insight.

But he handled his despair in a different way than I, and I understand it took three direct hits from police snipers before they brought him down inside the UT Clock-tower.

For the distinguished alumni. The Eyes of Texas are upon you . . .

Point Nemo

> I am not what is called a civilized man, Professor. I have done with society for reasons that seem good to me. Therefore, I do not obey its laws.
>
> *Captain Nemo*

DESPITE CURRENT MEDIA coverage, it would be wholly inaccurate to blame the deaths on Mr. H. P. Lovecraft. If you need some writer to blame you should look firstly to Jules Verne and Mr. R. A. Lafferty. Of course the only really guilty party was Dick Gavin. I feel I can say that even though Gavin wasn't anywhere the sites of the mass shooting or the murders in Ontario. He won't be where I am when I do whatever it is I will be impelled to do.

I find interesting that the other side effects of the Point Nemo Project—the feeding of the multitude the Basilica of St. Joan or the absurd death of Sharon Runyan at Greaser's café are almost never mentioned in the stories. I guess they don't fit in with gore on the public streets. Heck, I find it odd that I am allowed to walk the streets.

There are three of us left, but I think the storm conjured by Gavin's black butterfly may spread further.

I feel like Troy McClure in the *The Simpsons*. "Hi I'm horror writer Bradley J. Vucinich, you may remember me from such novels as *The Eye that Ate Space* or *Hot Blood, Cold Brain.*" But most likely you don't remember me at all. My published output has been small and badly distributed. The fact that all of us in the Point Nemo Project were writers or artists has made the accusation of publicity gimmick stick. I suppose if some of us were better known, people wouldn't say what they say. But guys like Stephen King aren't easy prey for the Dick Gavins of the world.

I was—er, between day jobs when I signed on. There was a little ad in the back of the April issue of *The Magazine of Fantasy and Science Fiction*. "Do you use your imagination professionally? Are you good at collaborative projects like game design or writing in shared worlds? Would an extended paid Pacific vacation appeal to you? Please send résumé and writing samples to Point Nemo Project." It gave a North Carolina address.

I tided up my résumé stressing my work for Flying Buffalo, Allen Varney Games, and Chaosium. I lied and said I was friendly, open and secure about working with others. I didn't say I was recently single, drove a broken down white pickup, and eked out a living writing geography questions for standardized tests. I did mention (as I am show-off as are all writers) that I was impressed that anyone knew the location of Point Nemo.

Point Nemo is as far as you can go from land and still be on the earth. Its home in the deep blue sea is pretty much the middle of nowhere Pacific style. The geographic coordinates of the Point Nemo are: s48:52:31.748 w123:23:33.069—exactly 2 688 220.580 meters (slightly more than 1 450 nautical miles) away from the following three coastline points:

> s27:12:29.304, w109:27:33.120 Ducie Island (Pitcairn Island Group, South Pacific)
>
> s24:40:39.360, w124:47:25.872 Motu Nui / Rapa Nui ("Easter Island", South Pacific)
>
> s72:57:57.024, w126:22:30.793 Maher Island / Siple Island (Antarctica).

Nowhere.

A survey came back. It ran to fourteen pages of multiple-choice questions. Here are two examples:

> 23. The following writer probably described reality in the most correct fashion:
>
> A. Isaac Asimov
> B. J. K. Rowling
> C. H. P. Lovecraft
> D. Edgar Rice Burroughs
>
> 108. Reality is
> A. Fixed and objective best discovered by science
> B. Created by Forms / Eidoi that create human categories of perception and cognition best understood by philosophy

C. A subjective / social construct—we see what we have agreed to see—best created by poets and sorcerers
D. Unknowable as a "thing in itself" but we can observe our mental images of it (Kant)

There were 665 questions, I don't know if that was meant to be funny. I filled in my green and white Scantron® sheets. The answers to these two items were C for me. It took the better part of a Sunday to fill in the sheets. I felt really angry at the process. I had never had a job interview that took so fucking long. There were questions about drug use—not against it, experimented in college—questions about meditation processes—took a few Yoga classes at U.A.. Informal classes. There was a form that allowed the Point Nemo Project to run a criminal background check. A form to allow a credit check. Did I have a current passport? (Yes) Did I have or had I ever had various chronic diseases? What was my church affiliation? (N/A) I had to take out my daddy's pocketknife and sharpen my No.2 pencil a few times. Jeez, all this and no check for the process so far? I mailed off the pages in the prepaid manila envelope provided and I heard nothing.

Nothing.

Weeks went by, then months. The mild central Texas winter settled in, and I got a package. *The Point Nemo Project: An Experiment in Creating New Consensual Reality*. It was a glossy small magazine of South Pacific culture, with a CD of "Pacific Trance Music." There were pictures of the boat we would be on, and the Carcosa Institute in Pine Hill, NC. There were pictures of Dr. Dick "Canuck" Gavin with his illustrious bio—studies at Harvard, Tokyo University, Cairo University. His distinguished lecture series at the University of North Carolina Chapel Hill. Blah, blah, blah, the guy's a Brainiac I get it. And then there was the important point. In addition to free travel and free room and board for three months, I would get thirty thousand dollars. Add thirty thousand to my savings account I would have $30,004.53. I put my stuff in storage, paid up my rent until the end of the month, and with a small blue suitcase that had belonged to my grandfather got on a jet to North Carolina. Only one instruction raised an eyebrow. We were to bring no reading materials. I am the sort of guy that always has at least two spare paperbacks in my car for emergencies.

Pine Hill is in Surry County, North Carolina. It is an intersection of Quaker Road and North Carolina Highway 268. The big landmarks are the Quaker Church and the Quaker cemetery. Lots of dead Quakers. I began to suspect that this would be a dull three months.

The Carcosa Institute's white columns and wide roof bordered somewhere between a movie fantasy of ante-bellum mansion and a fever dream. Dr. Gavin's great-grandfather had invented a special drill bit for oil exploration. If you have ever ridden in an automobile, the petroleum had passed over a Gavin bit. There were six of us and five of them.

"Them" was Dr. Gavin, his lawyer Monica Ashfield, his cook Sarah Johnstone, his handy-man gardener Robert Biscay, and Nurse Joan McFadden.

"Us" was Wihelm Pugavitch, a pretentious—even nauseating—queen who claimed to be the voice of decadent fantasy. He preferred "Toadstool" as a nickname. His erudition was huge, and were it not for his gothick-gay drag, would have dominated all conversations. Frankly I was glad when he shut up.

The Rev. Dee an attractive auburn haired coffee-in-cream skinned hipster gal from the barrio who hangs at botanicas and does tarot readings and love spells for rich socialites. She had written a great deal of speculative fiction poetry, and (I think) a book on guided visualizations.

Bud DeBill, a gaunt and silver-haired Texan. He was one of my heroes, I remembered reading his fantasies in the seventies. He came from Barrett, Texas and often spoke in low rich tones about writing as an alternative to violence.

Picassa Buzz was a writer and an SF artist about my age. She hailed from Canada. It was neat to meet her. Years ago I had commissioned an ink drawing from her of "the Eye." It had only cost me $20.00—jeez, no wonder she needed the thirty thou.

Noaga was half Sioux and the only woman I ever saw with a facial tattoo. Her name meant Wolverine, which was warning enough for me. She wrote short weird pieces like Craig Strete and she acted as a shaman. I'm guessing not a lot of money in shamanizing.

S. T. Ghose, a somewhat grim Indian had made some shekels selling atheism and critical writings on the poetry of Edward Pickman Derby and Edgar Henquist Gordon—lesser lights of the Lovecraft circle.

And me.

True to his notes Dr. Gavin had removed all reading material from the Institute. The only books in evidence were reprint copies of *Azathoth and Other Horrors* by Edward Pickman Derby. The verses were in every room. I had two one in my bedroom and one in my private bath. Derby had written about the "Daemon Sultan" Azathoth. I had never been a big reader of horror poetry. I mean, who is? Except Rev. Dee, she writes the stuff. So when we were awake, we were reading the poems. But we weren't awake that often the first two or three weeks. Dr. Gavin wanted to wean us from the world we knew, so the first step was barbiturates and lots of them. Dick—we all liked to call him "Dick"—wasn't into newer chemicals; Nurse McFadden injected us with sodium penothal. Big horse doses we would sleep for days. When she awakened us she strapped a device on our big toes and another on our forehead. None of us knew that was what ECT—electro-convulsant therapy—looked like these days. It didn't look like the scary stuff we had seen in the movies. She would shock us awake and we would eat in groups of two and three in a room with no clocks. Then after being up and hour, it was beddy-bye time.

I don't know how long this treatment continued. I remember going to the "rec rooms' with Bud and Wilhelm. Walt was talking about his days as a sniper during the Korean War. Wilhelm shook his little feather boa and said: "I have a perfect loathing for guns. I would never pick one up even to defend myself."

I tried to ignore both of them reading Derby's "Nightmare verse."

Choregos for Typhon's Play

The Egyptian ringmaster picks comedies both big and small
The other face of the Sultan wears many masks
Tonight's drama is about a larva's fall
Nyarlathotep the other face of Azathoth does his many tasks
He breeds the maggots that call themselves men
And gives lesser lusts to each
He randomly scatters them upon Gaia's wide fen
And mad poets write trap-verses from them to teach
Look here comes one now unable to stop
Joining with the insects from Sgaggi's dance
That culls the weak under the black big top
Mutilating themselves in the Pharaoh's Trance
That which should crawl has learned to walk
And to add to the fun thinks it can Talk.

Like I say, whether the verse was good or bad, it was all that was going into our heads, that and Dick's lectures about the consensual nature of reality. "Our fellow humans have been taught by those Outside to see the world in one way and one way only. If we weren't hooked into their perception assemblages, we could see the world another way." The lectures had doses of linguistics (Sapir and Whorf), social construction of reality theorists (Peter L. Berger and Thomas Luckmann), mystics (Gurdjieff and Jane Roberts) and magicians (Carlos Castenada and Roland Franklyn). The only time I ever saw Dick get mad, while we were still on dry land, was when I said that R. A. Lafferty had written a story on the same theme, 'Fiddler's Green.' I thought he was mad because he was the only person who was supposed to know stuff—later I looked up the story. Like ours it didn't have a happy ending for the Master Magician.

I know my memories were being eroded. And for me at the time, that was OK. I was recently divorced from Marylyn. It had not been a happy divorce, and here I was getting free therapy.

One night the Rev. Dee and I were having one of Mrs. Johnstone's great omelets. We were talking about exes and Science Fiction publishing, and breaking into movies. She sorta had a lead on Syfy International I recall. Then she said: "This place is really beginning to scare me. I mean I really needed the money, but this memory thing is just plain tough. I realize that I can't remember how to drive. What if Dr. Gavin is some cliché mad scientist? What if none of us can walk away from here?"

I tried to act brave, but frankly I was so damn sedated I really wasn't scared. Not being scared was rare for me. With shaky health and a poor employment history I was scared most of the time. I suggested that as a clergywoman she should be beyond fear. I got as far as saying, "Surely Jesus." When she cut me off explaining that she was Wiccan—I didn't know people really were Wiccan. I mean her ex was a man, does Wiccan mean clam eater?

She was even a "Dark" Wiccan, having co-written a book called *The Dark Archetype*. "So, can you explain Dick's religious thing?" I asked.

"Some people think all gods and goddesses are human creations from Jehovah to Thor. He wants us to make Azathoth real. He wants to harness Its Chaos."

"Do you believe this stuff?" I asked.

"I believe I need thirty thousand to give me time to write my script," Rev. Dee said.

After two weeks or three weeks or maybe four weeks, Dr. Gavin had us transferred to the *Albatross*. I vaguely remember getting on the boat in San Francisco, which I guess meant Robert Biscay had driven us cross-country. The next few days were a blur. Now “them” was Nurse McFadden, Dr. Dick Gavin and the captain of the *Albatross* Gustaf Johansen. I had lost too much memory at the time to realize that the ship captain’s name was a joke—it was the sailor from H. P. Lovecraft’s ‘The Call of Cthulhu.’ I don’t know if it was his real name, or just one of those things Dick was doing to us.

I was watching the big blue as we sailed out of San Francisco. I had never sailed anywhere (other than the occasional ferry). I was saddened by trash. The first day I saw trash and oil, the second day I saw trash and oil. I didn’t know if it was dorky I wore my life vest all the time. The women sunbathed as did Pugavitch, I didn’t think he looked good in a two piece. The doctor was letting us sleep less and we went from the black dreamless sleepy of sodium pentathol to the dream-inducing ketamine. I was getting a little tired of feeling strung out all the time, and reading Derby’s poems was beginning to affect my cognition.

Dr. Gavin walked to me on deck. “You know Bradley, your life vest won’t be much help. We are going to the most unpopulated part of the ocean. If you fell overboard, you would float for few days before sharks or shock would kill you.”

“I am just a safety-first kind of guy.”

“No,” he said. “You are scared of water. Like everyone else in the project, you lied and said you could swim. You grew up poor in rural Arizona. You never even saw a swimming pool until you were in college.”

“No one can swim?”

“Well I can—not that it would make a difference if I fell overboard at Point Nemo. The captain can of course.”

That night at dinner we were told that we would arrive at Point Nemo about midnight.

“Think of it, you are as far from the minds of your fellow humans as you ever will be. The glosses of perception that have made you see things in one way only are very weak. Your minds are open to Azathoth. You will soon see the primal chaos, and from that chaos you will create a new world. We begin tomorrow. Tomorrow the sun will rise green.”

The sun rose brilliant and green and verdant.

Sharon came and woke me. “It’s real. It is really green.”

I asked her: "How do you know? Maybe it's the drugs they give us. Maybe we're still back in North Carolina."

"Maybe you're an asshole," she said. "The sun doesn't come up green that often. I can only remember two or three times in my whole life."

I wanted to argue with her, but she had a point.

"If life gives you oranges," I said. "Make orangeade."

"Orangeade looks terrible when the sun is green."

They started us on a new drug that night. Nurse McFadden didn't tell us the name, but we were glad, as it was a pill rather than an injection. Dr. Gavin told us to focus on a certain part of the sky. "That's where you will see His throne." He began playing flute music.

S.T. Ghose stalked around on deck looking really pissed off.

"I made my peace with the universe by believing that belief did nothing. The sun should not be green."

I said: "I think it has been green before. "

"Every few seconds I start to think that, too."

We watched the calm ocean for a while. Occasionally we saw seabirds, gulls most likely. Great black tentacles shot from the water and pulled them as quickly as the sticky tongue of a frog captures a fly.

"I have never been on the ocean before," I said.

"I don't like the seas," said Ghose. "It hides too much, you can imagine anything lurking down there."

"And that was before imagination mattered," I said.

The next day the sun was still green. We were almost all positive that the sun had never been green two days in a row. There seemed to be a smudge in the sky where Gavin had predicted. He turned up the volume on the flute music.

"Care to dance?" I asked Sharon.

"I don't dance. I am a two-left feet kind of gal."

Pugavitch offered to dance, and I thought *what the heck?* And we improvised a waltz. I asked him: "You know Toadstool, if this only works because we all are believing it, what about Captain Johansen. I mean he isn't a horror writer, he isn't on drugs, and I think he thinks Dr. Gavin is a nutjob."

"Hush, dearie. Somethings shouldn't be said aloud."

The next day the sun came up orange. That seemed more normal. We all began chanting at dawn. "Iä Azathoth! Neblod zin nyar kana'reen!" Bud started the chant, but we all chimed in by the second or third verse.

"That was brilliant!" I told him.

"Nah. That was nothing, just something I remembered from Sunday school," said the Texan. "I had the weirdest dream last night. I dreamt that humans only have five fingers."

"Yuck city!" said Picassa. "I've been drawing His throne, want to see?"

That night the smudge in the sky had grown in size. It looked like a crack surrounded by glowing vapors of an indescribable color.

"I bet we can make the sun come up that color tomorrow," said Noaga. "You know this is an old Sioux trick. When my ancestors' ancestors were stranded without food, we would dream up buffalo."

Nurse McFadden said that tonight we needed the sodium pentathol again. The new drug hadn't made some of us sleep well. In the old days, when I was a very contrary sort of man, I would have asked who? We all just rolled up our sleeves. As I drifted off into the blackness I heard a car backfire and a big splash.

The sun rose in a color unknown to man. We walked all over the *Albatross* beaming and smiling. We were as gods. We had eaten the fruit of the Tree of Knowledge. About noon Bud asked: "Where is Captain Johansen?"

Pugavitch had a smug look on his kisser. He whispered to me: "We don't need Nurse Ratchet, either, she does not believe."

That night we could see the throne. It hovered in the great crack in the sky. It must be thousands of miles in length. It was turned away from us. "We've got to make the crack bigger!" I said. Dr. Gavin and Nurse McFadden were having some argument below decks. When she came up to give us our sodium pentathol she looked haggard. I didn't even hear the shot before I feel asleep. I love sleeping on a hammock. I have been on boats all of my life. I felt like Mummy and Daddy were coming to tuck me in.

The next day He was there.

Fully one quarter of the sky was filled with his beautiful and ever-changing visage. We lay upon the decks, nude by some unspoken agreement, and gazed up at the god who had Dreamed us into existence. We knew we were like His children the stars—in the end he would eat us as surely as he had pooped us out. It was good. To be eaten by the ten million teeth was better than sex. To be caressed by the million black arms was the goal of all human religions. To be licked by the green and purple tongues was better than thought itself. We chanted all day. We kept throwing up as well. Looking upon our Father was a strain.

As night fell we could not see Him as well. We went below decks and read to each other from Derby's hymns. Dr. Gavin kept interrupting.

"You're forgetting! We aren't here to worship. We are here to make a new world! We are here for the Project. Remember what I am paying you!"

It was hard to sleep without the drugs. Some of us played at sex. Some of us gnawed on each other. Dr. Gavin said something about a radio, setting off a beacon.

"Shut up Dick!' said Noaga.

"Shut up Dick!" said Bud.

Soon we were all chanting it. "Shut up Dick! Shut up Dick! Shut up Dick!"

Dr. Gavin was waving a gun around. I hoped he would shoot someone, so we could lick up the pretty purple blood. But he just kept talking with words that made no sense like "Purpose" and "Meaning" and "Will." Poor human, he was so unconnected with Father.

Finally I had an idea.

"Hey everybody. Let's help old Dick out! We can move him closer to Azathoth and he can get his point across."

Everybody cheered. Bud and Pugavitch rushed Dr. Gavin. They knocked him down and the women started to eat him.

"Whoa!" I yelled. "Remember we want to give him to Azathoth!"

They all laughed, except for Dr. Gavin, who seemed a little stunned, and was leaking in a few places. We tied him up and put on one of the lines that had had those little flags on it. We ran him up the flagpole and we saluted. Salute!

Noaga said: "We have to get Azathoth's attention so He can help old Dick!"

Since she was some kind of Indian or something, we all did the "Woo! Woo! Woo!" thing with our mouths and hands like when you play cowboys and Indians. The suns came up shortly, and by now He was a third of the sky. The really big eye opened and looked at Dr. Dick Gavin. It looked at him and him alone in all of the universes. It Helped. I was a Prophet—I had written of the Eye!

Dr. Gavin's screams changed into flute music as he began to melt and drip. We ate him like runny ice cream on the best summer day ever. We actually swallowed his sounds. I had never tasted a sound before—it's like they say, tastes just like chicken.

That night we were feeling pretty bad. We were having withdrawal. We hadn't eaten in a while. People eat, right? We raided the galleys and made oatmeal. After we ate, we slept below decks, it was too much of a strain to look up. Bud and Picassa said they were pretty sure that it was a bad idea to be out here in the ocean. For the first time since we had sailed out, I really began to notice the rocking of the boat. I had to leave my hammock and go throw up overboard. Azathoth seemed fainter in the sky, and the sight of Dr. Gavin's sticky clothes hanging on the flag line made me feel bad. The next morning we stayed below decks and made a meal out of powdered eggs. The withdrawal pains were pretty sharp in our guts. We looked through the Nurse's stuff but either we had used all the drugs or they had gone overboard with her.

That night Sharon said: "I am beginning to remember what some of the words that old Dick said meant. 'Purpose' that means why."

There was a storm that night and we were scared as the boat rocked back and forth. We tried to collect our naval lore—we might be scared of the ocean, but we were readers. We didn't know if we should weigh anchor or just try and ride it out. During that discussion we began to feel a little self-conscious about being nude, so we put our clothes on. There was lightning. Some of it was purple and some that color we didn't have a name for, but mainly it was white. Then the silliest thing happened, Rev. Dee began singing the 'Ballad of Gilligan's Island' and we felt better. It was cloudy but calm the next morning. We couldn't see the Throne nor That which sat upon it. But we could still hear the flute music when the cold wind blew from the south. Bud suggested that we throw away all the copies of the Derby book and we did.

Sharon and Noaga figured out that Dr. Gavin had turned on an emergency beacon. We threw his clothes into the water as well. It was an unpleasant night, the last stage of the withdrawals was diarrhea, so we overfilled the head, and began to crap off the side of the boat. The pains in our guts were like hot bullets.

With dawn the sky cleared. There was a smudge where Azathoth had been, but it faded like fog on a sunny day. Rev. Dee spotted the ship. A Dutch freighter.

We were tourists. Our captain and his mate had been blown overboard in the storm. We were hungry and sick. The Dutch dropped us off on Easter Island, where the US Navy picked us up. By then we didn't like looking at each other.

When we got back to our lives, our lives were a disaster. Dr. Gavin hadn't dropped thirty thousand in our accounts. We were broke, but Gavin had picked us because we were broke. I managed to get back on my feet by selling a lifetime's collection of books, Bud got some help from his granddaughter, one of Pugavitch's friends let him sofa-surf. And so on.

Mainly we couldn't afford therapy. Most of us stopped writing for awhile. The Rev. Dee tried to put some poems together, but found her verse reading more like a boy genius of the 1920s than a twentieth first century hipster. No one asked us about Gavin. Maybe no one knew. I thought about driving to the Carcosa Institute and setting the place on fire, but it wasn't like the building had done anything. Maybe the cook and the handyman were living on some money Gavin had left behind. Good for them.

I don't know about the others, but I really didn't like the open sky. I tried to stay inside a lot or go out only on cloudy days.

Then CNN broke the news about Sharon Runyan. It was a silly death, a grisly death, a death that was made for late night comedians. In Louisville, Kentucky where she not only lived but had set her three vampire novels, a '50s themed restaurant called Greaser's Palace had a dance contest. If you are half-remembering something similar from *The Simpsons* you are right—the whole *Simpsons* plot had been the inspiration for the restaurant. So every time they showed Sharon dancing to death, they showed a clip of Homer and Marge dancing. Real funny. Especially when she started dancing so hard that it literally tore her sides. I think it has been posted a few dozen times on U-Tube with different soundtracks. Let's twist again like we did last summer.

"I'm a two left feet kind of gal."

I e-mailed Pugavitch and told him; I figured one of us would crack. I said I was glad it wasn't me. He e-mailed back: "Honey. It will be you. It will be me. We all got a little Dick in us."

I remembered slurping down the melting Dick Gavin. I hoped Pugavitch was wrong. Ironically, he was next to go.

He had gone to Ontario for a horror con. ConNadian. Very clever. He did his usual over-the-top drag queen shtick at a midnight reading of his story, 'Sweet Sesqua Valley High.' Then he pulled two 9mm Glocks from his bookbag. He shot members of the audience until an off-duty Mountie took him out.

"I have a perfect loathing for guns. I would never pick one up even to defend myself."

There were some fierce anti-gay riots the next three days.

To my surprise no one linked the two incidents. A month passed. The Rev. Dee was touring France. At the Basilica of St. Joan of Arc, she made a scandal by rushing to the altar and proclaiming in flawless French that she was Joan of Orleans. Local police gave chase, but she eluded them "as if by magic." She repeated her performance the next day, and before the officials could be summoned stole a baguette and some sardines from an American tourist. She began making little sandwiches to pass out. By the time the gendarmes arrived she had fed a huge (and growing) crowd. With a good deal of religious awe, the gendarmes did nothing but listen to her sermon. She preached on the need of France to leave the European Union. At the end of her talk she began to rise into the air. Several people recorded her ascent beyond the clouds on various electronic devices.

I got an e-mail from Ghose. "It is the Will of a God. I had no ideas there were gods. I suppose that it makes sense Chaos is THE God."

The bloody riots began in Paris in less than twelve hours. France is still under martial law. The French emergency almost took all the media attention from the Clocktower Sniper. Emulating Charles Stuart Whitman's 1966 feat, Bud DeBill went to the Clocktower of the University of Texas in Austin with a couple of sniper rifles and a couple of boxes of ammo. It bespeaks the state of Texas armament that Bud only had time to take out sixteen before an armed janitor sent him to whatever special hell the children of Azathoth go to.

Finally someone in the media drew the lines between the dots. I was interviewed. Ghose was interviewed. Picassa was interviewed. There was consensus—we were nuts. Dr. Gavin had driven us nuts with drugs. No one explained how insanity had helped the Rev. Dee rise into the stratosphere. But it was OK. We were victims. Unlike Bud and Toadstool we surely wouldn't hurt anyone.

Ghose keeps e-mailing me links explaining Chaos Theory. How one small change can make millions. In Canada concerned Christians are burning gay people alive. In France a right wing revolution is in progress. In Texas private gun sales have gone through the roof. Chaos Theory—I don't really think it's much of a theory at this point. The rest of wait and watch the sky. Someday the Eye will eat through Space again, and See through those of us that are left. I don't know what I will do. Something wacky like dance myself to death, something horrid with a body count, but it will blacken your world.

We made a God. We got what we deserved.

And so will you.

For Denise Dumars and W. H. Pugmire (in memoriam)

Tick Tock

IF ANY HUMANS had lived on in any meaningful way past the Night, John Cardenas' life trajectory would be seen as ironic. John failed out of the University of Texas twenty years ago. He has worked as an exterminator, apartment leasing agent, vending machine stocker, and product demonstrator and for the last four years for Eye-in-the-Sky. If you listened to late night AM radio or to certain podcasts you've heard of Eye-in-the-Sky. If you visited their webpage with its bright purple eye above the pyramid design floating atop a silver saucer and read the free newsfeed you would be up to date on excavations of giant skeletons, proof that we are living in a computer simulation or the Big Foot love commune in Arkansas. Of course, for a few dollars more you could subscribe and find out the REAL TRUTH THAT THE GOVERNMENT DOESN'T WANT YOU TO KNOW. Mainly this was about the plan to Take Away your guns, the tax on the internet, and what really goes on in Area 51. This lively feed of the wacky, the scary and the plain untrue was largely John's work. He got to work from his north Austin apartment, he had a poker game once a week with five friends (of assorted races and sexes), and he had a newer car. He had benefits. It was a great job. Heck, he had basically done this job free years before there was even an Internet. He had run a BBS called Shaved Truths that people with early PCs and external modems would call up and read paranormal news. Getting to be a "reporter" for Eye-in-the-Sky was the answer to a prayer. Not that John prayed. He had evidence that "god" was a meme created by the Babylonian elite to subjugate the masses. But for all of John's friends, it was a great fit.

He got out of bed about nine thirty in the morning. He checked the Eye-in-the-Sky Facebook page, making quips at last night's posters. He read some of the better paranormal pages like Church of Mabus and Shaver Tron and shared their cooler stories. Then about ten after his bowl of Applejacks he began the days "research." He looked at Fortean sites and occult sites and conspiracy sites. He checked Google News every hour. If he found something about the government it went into the paid feed, other stuff went into the free feed. He had lunch at one—always a large vanilla milk shake and a Spicy McChicken sandwich from the MacDonalds three blocks away. He took a multi-vitamin and 2000 units of Vitamin D. At three he checked FaceBook, tweeted some stories that he put on the site and took a little nap. At six he wrote up whatever was interesting to him. He read books on cognition, world history, media theory, the occult and the history of UFO sightings. He also read the classic paranormal writers—Fort, John Keel, Amos Carter, Pauwels and Steiger. He could handle dry academic stuff and mix it well with speculation from the '50s and '60s. On Sundays he called his mom in Flapjack, TX (English) and his grandmother in Mexico City (Spanish). He had a stable and uninteresting life despite the contents of his mind and his odd niche profession. Yet without the aid of ancient texts, special training, or unusual genetics—he was one of the few hundred humans whom, in their own quirky ways, Opened the Gate.

John hosted the poker night at his apartment every other Thursday. On nights when he didn't he drove or walked about fifteen blocks to Don Bowen's small stucco home in the St. Johns' neighborhood. In the summer he walked. Don operated a small used bookstore out of his home called Libby's Used Books. It used to belong to a man named Libby and be in a strip mall. It was one of the few used paperback stores in business. Don also rented out his garage apartment. He had inherited the house from his mom, and his expenses were low. He was John's supplier of old paranormal paperbacks. One night as John drove there he had a funny scare. John was waiting at a light at the corner of two major streets, his car next to a large concrete storm drain. A piece of shiny Mylar (possibly from a balloon) blew into the drain. The silver caught the light from John's headlights. Flash! And it startled him. He almost jumped. He drove on to the poker game and expounded on the incident.

"It scared me because I never look down and to the right when I'm driving. I mean I have driven past that storm drain almost every day for eight or nine years. I never see it—especially if the street's dry and there is no rain going on. The drain could be the entrance to the world of Richard Shaver's deros, or the Xibalba of my Mayan ancestors."

John had decided he was Mayan in 2012; he didn't look very Mayan. Just a plump 35-year-old Mexican-American with a thrift store aesthetic.

"Or," said Don. "A storm drain."

"The point," John continued, "is that the real unknown could be right under our noses and we would never know. Maybe we shouldn't be watching the skies or looking for looking for government conspiracies. Maybe we should be looking at storm drains."

Phillip Blassingame, another poker player, said: "That would make your website a lot less fun—'The Daily Storm Drain Watch'—today a black and white tomcat was seen entering the drain about midnight. Is it a dero spy?"

"That's not what I mean," said John. "I don't mean that the drain is the entrance to another world. I think fear might be. A sudden flash of fear instead of the invisibility of the storm drain. You ever read about how the Aztec shamans couldn't see Cortez's ships?"

Mary Machworter shook her head.

"Supposedly," said John. "Back me up Don, supposedly as the ships sailed up to Mexico, the shamans knew something was up, but they literally couldn't see the ships because they had no scanning pattern for them. When the ships arrived with their cargo of white men and *horses* for god's sakes. They still couldn't quite make them out."

"I'd read the story," said Don. "It's called 'Inattentional Blindness'—look at that YouTube clip where they tell you to watch the basketball and you don't see the gorilla walk by."

"Yeah," said John. "Except I'm saying that the gorilla can't interact with you because you don't see it. What if fear opened a channel? What if it took down another brick in the wall?" He tried to make it sound like the Pink Floyd song.

Mary shook her head again. "But wouldn't that be a bad idea? Isn't it better we don't interact with the gorilla?"

"Maybe the gorilla is the Bringer of Ecstasy," said John. "Maybe that's what he's waiting to do."

Don asked: "So what's your plan? Scare some people with a storm drain and hope God shows up?"

Which in fact was John's plan. He wrote it up on Eye-In-The-Sky as an 'Experiment in Terror.' He would draw people's attention to a hitherto unnoticed object, and see what happened. He bought an Iron Man mask at the Dollar Store, and wedged it in the storm drain. It was shiny, and for the car parked in the right hand lane just visible as a face by headlight. It was far enough back to be a mysterious object. You could see a shiny face in the shadow. He took some photos of the mask, the mask by car headlight, and posted his theories. He parked his car on the cross street. He watched for hours. A couple of cars—once the passenger, once a driver spotted the mask. But that meant nothing. He asked Don to ask his customers if they had seen anything weird in the neighborhood. He asked Phillip, Don's tenant in the garage apartment, to ask folks in the neighborhood if they saw anything weird. Nothing happened. Then a thunderstorm came, and the mask was washed down the drain. Oh well, as many people had said on FaceBook, it was a badly designed experiment.

Two months later when a light rain had once again caused John to take his car, the mask was back. Or at least *a* mask. Or at least a shiny face. John decided that he would examine it tomorrow or at least the first day with rain. Which proved to be Saturday. No mask. Well, that was odd. Then a week later and weather necessitated another car trip. There it was. It looked to be a different mask. There was something odd about its proportions. The following day he went to snap a picture for his blog. No mask. Was someone putting it there at night? Some reader of his page, or a prankster following his own prank? He walked over that night with a flashlight. He couldn't just lie on the street and look in lest incoming traffic roll over him, so he lay upon the top of the drain and leaned over. Three cars honked at him, and one driver shouted abuse. He could see the mask was much further in the drain than before. Perhaps tools had been used to push it in. Also, it didn't look quite right—perhaps it was a different mask? Something was written in a fairly shake hand near the mask. John first thought it was a magical inscription in some eldritch rune, but it turned out to be the words, "Thank You." Followed by another word obscured under the mask. He tried to get some good photos but nothing useable could be made because of the odd angles involved. He talked with Don and Mary and they drove by and looked at it and Don suggested parking his car at the intersection and then using it as a shield from traffic shooting some photos. Mary reminded him to put his hood up and put his blinkers on for extra safety. He did that the next night. The mask had moved slightly, the inscription now read: "Thank You John." John's first hypothesis (after fifteen seconds of Wonder and Fear) was that one of the poker buddies had done this. He had not mentioned the location of his experiment on his blog—and it would be very hard to figure out what storm drain from the picture he had used. He texted his friends, "Haw Haw!" but none of them took credit.

And so weeks went by. John spotted the mask a few times, but the mystery was gone. Besides he had been really busy. Weirdness seemed to be happening all over. There were bell sounds and booms off the Atlantic coast, the slime falls on those cultists in Argentina , and a nerd group claimed that pi was changing, Europa seemed to be leaving orbit, a massive something-or-other had been seen in the Artic, there were Pacific earthquakes. For the first time ever, the "fun" aspect of his job was slipping away. He had never believed all of it, heck maybe not even most of it. He did believe that mainstream politics concealed a good deal of stuff that mainstream science was spotty, and that humans didn't really have a decent metaphysics. He was beginning to wonder what to believe. Not in the sense of his clients who could "believe" in Bigfoot, ESP, UFOs, the Trilateral Commission. No. What to believe in like relativity, politics, love, good and evil. The center had ceased to hold. He was even thinking of getting a real job and foreswearing paranormal studies. Did posting reprints of John Kincaid's article 'Was Bigfoot Lincoln's Father?' help anyone? Had he moved homo saps one centimeter closer to the Truth? Or was he the underpaid projectionist of a one star B-movie in Plato's cave? John was in something of a spasm of self-hate as the light caught him at his storm drain. There were wreathes and candles—lit candles—on the drain. Objects of worship? Thanksgiving? Had there been a accident there, or was it connected in a sick way with the Iron Man mask? He turned on St. John's and pulled his car into a Texan market parking lot. He walked the half block to the drain. There was a wreath of blue and white artificial flowers, three small white candles in jars, and in chalk in big letters—THANK YOU JOHN CARDENAS. He bent down to pick up the wreath. When he touched it a strong shock, not exactly electrical, not anything he had a name for, ran through him. He flinched and nearly fell. He could hear a bell in the distance or was it a bark? A bell-like cry. For no clear reason he thought a very clear thought "the cosmic alarm clock." He pulled out his phone to snap some pictures, and then put it aside in disgust. This was the problem. Focusing on this instead of education in Texas or the garbage island in the Pacific Ocean. If you divert all of human attention, all of human intent, away from mankind, you will break the center. All of the hatred and divisiveness in American politics. All of that decline of a civil civilization increased with more and more News of the Weird. He took the wreath back to his car. He was going to toss it on the green folding table they played poker on. As he drove the remaining eight blocks to Don's house, he had another clear thought—none of his friends did this. Logic may point to his friends' gaslighting him, but this was beyond logic. This was the very crack he had meant to cause. Not with the damn Iron Man mask—with all of it—with eighteen years of focusing on the paranormal. He could still hear the bell. It was getting louder.

He parked in front of Don's house. He left the wreath on his passenger side seat. Don was standing behind his screen door, the lights were on in his front room. Don looked worried.

Don spoke as John walked up the cracked narrow sidewalk to his two step cement porch. "I've got troubles. Your kind of trouble." There was some anger in the possessive pronoun "your."

John already felt defensive. "Yeah, what kind of trouble?"

Don opened the door. "Come in. I'm sorry. I'm scared. I called off the game, but I didn't call you because I wanted you to come over. Come in."

As John walked in, Don took him by the collar and pushed him past the bookstore rooms to the tiny greasy kitchen in the back. Several of the books had been pulled from the shelves, and something black seemed to be squirming under them. When John tried to stop and look at the strange scene, Don pushed him harder. The kitchen had had new green linoleum in Don's mother's day. Now it was shiny and mainly gray. There was a small kitchen table which once had false woodgrain, but now was brown with years of cheap furniture polish. Don had opened two beers, and he had chips and salsa ready on the little table. "Take a load off."

John pulled up one of the plastic backed chairs. "So, what problem you got?"

Don said: "I don't want you reporting this. I don't want to see it on your FaceBook page. I don't want it on Twitter. Got that?"

"Sure, sure. What's happening?"

Don pulled up his own chair. For the next twenty minutes Don rambled on about the brightening of the Pleiades, the mass deaths of men in Tibet, the South Pole aurora phenomena, and the increase in coma cases. John had heard of most of these, in fact he had blogged about most of these. He had no idea where his friend was getting at. He tried to interrupt, to share his new truth that it wasn't right or good or healthy to spend all of one's attention on such things. But Don went on and on, sometimes mentioning his reading habits as a boy and a young man. Finally, he said: "You see I never believed any of it. I saw how there was more weirdness every year, but I thought that was because there was simply a need for it. No, it's breaking."

John asked: "What's breaking? What's it?"

Don said: "Reality. Reality is broken. We can go in my front room and I can show you where it broke. Well a local crack, anyway. The break on this block. The Return of the Old Ones."

"What does that mean?"

"If I cover this table, my mom's old 'breakfast nook' table from Sears with a newspaper, what do you see?"

"A newspaper?" asked John.

Don nodded as if encouraging a simple child. "No. You don't see a newspaper. You see stories Governor said this, the President said that, the Pope said another thing. Two stars are getting a divorce. An embarrassing crime by a celebrity. Unrest in the Middle East. A sale at Jerod's. What do you not see?"

John ventured: "The table?"

Don smiled. "Right. But the table is older and bigger than the news. Mom bought this table in 1969. Dad spread his newspaper on it every day at breakfast. Then Mom did so after his death. Then when I got the house, I keep my PC here and read the news. Stories about millions of humans for decades come and go, but the table remains. Now I read my news on my phone most days. So, what can I see now?"

"The table."

"As a species we are beginning to see the table. And it ain't from Sears, and it ain't made for humans. It's older and bigger. Now I can show you the front rooms."

"Before you show me, can I ask you something?"

"Sure."

"On the way over here I started to hear this bell-like sound. Can you hear that?"

Don looked truly sad. "No, my apocalypse has no bells and whistles."

Jon followed him into the front rooms. Big bookshelves from Libby's Used Books dominated the front room. John knew that Don still had drop-in customers, although most of the business was on line. The room had hardwood floors. Red Oak #3. Many of the books from the Science Fiction section were piled on the floor. Occult and "Metaphysical" likewise. The books moved up and down slowly; they were covering up living creatures. Don knelt down by the biggest pile. "Look!" he said, raising a handful of paperbacks.

On the floor were two black wet looking creatures looking like a cross between a horned toad and an earthworm, they writhed as though in pain. "Look!" he said again. He took his right index finger and pushed through the flesh of one of the beasts. It had the consistency of pudding. A small part of the creature was easily scooped up. It was a homogenous blackness—no internal organs or bones. He flicked the nastiness off his finger, like a man gets rid of a booger. It flicked away and when it hit the floor reshaped itself into a tiny replica of the creature it had been sampled from. It scurried toward its parent, which promptly ate it. Then Don grabbed some of the books. "Look!" he said for a third time.

He fanned the books in front of John. The pages were blank. Old and yellowed but blank. No, that wasn't quite accurate; the front matter, the copyright notices and so forth were intact.

Don's voice began slow and even but broke as he said: "It started two days. Some of the books began sweating ink. At first I thought it was humidity, remember that killer fog we had Monday morning? Oh, that's right, you sleep then. At first I thought it was these two Lovecraft paperbacks. They're side-by-side (or they were). But then I noticed other books. All of my Lovecraft, my Ramsey Campbell, some Stephen King, all of my Phil Dick. Then a few books in the Metaphysical section: *UFOs in Colonial America* by Amos Carter, *The Mothman Prophecies* by John Keel. All my Charles Fort. Then some of my mythology books, an advanced math book I was holding for Phillip. I had no idea what to do, as you can see the books are worthless now. A few other dealers had the same problem. With the SAME titles."

John advised his friend to breathe.

"So," asked John. "Why didn't you report this?"

"I called up KEYE and they put me on hold and I played on my computer. I read the news. Did you know Pi is changing? That's like a prime number missing for god's sakes. There are rumors that some of the dead are returning in Tibet, or that the rash of comas in Australia is much bigger than CNN says. In the face of that weirdness I'm going to report, 'strange paperbacks are losing their ink.'?"

"But the creatures," said John.

"They formed yesterday. Last night one of them crawled on my face while I was sleeping. I don't know it was exploring me, moving mindlessly, or seeking to enter my brain. "

"We need to get you out of here. You can stay at my place."

"Oh, really? How many of these titles do you own?" Don broke into a hysterical laughter.

"OK. OK. Let's get calm. We can get away from this. There's a Motel Six not too far from here. We'll go there, spend the night, and figure this out tomorrow."

"OK," said Don.

They went out to the car.

"What's this?" asked Don picking up the wreath.

"That's nothing. That's some trash I found. It has nothing to do with this," John lied. The ringing sound had grown more intense. John switched the radio on picking an all music FM station. Classic Rock will banish anything for a few minutes. It was ten minutes to the hotel. They had agreed not to watch the news.

Despite the level of fear Don went to a snoring peacefulness quickly. John lay in the other bed thinking that he could do something. If he had helped crack reality, he could do something. He knew he wouldn't fall asleep. And then he was under.

He dreamed of sleeping in his own bed. Seven little men came in his room. Dwarves all wearing Iron Man costumes. They surrounded his bed, singing "High Ho! High Ho!" He couldn't move, but he could talk with them.

"Who are you?"

"Tough one to answer in your language John. We kind of liked your friend's label. The Old Ones. We have been around longer than you people. Anyway we're here to say thanks."

"That's it? You're just seven little men?"

"Then that would make you Sleeping Beauty." There was more than a passing sexual hint there.

"I don't believe you," said John very firmly.

"More to the point, you have ceased to disbelieve in us. We seven have always been here. Oh, we're small potatoes, that's why we could come through a crack as small as you made. See we're even a little human looking—because we've been standing near the Barrier so long. We're not like the big things moving certain moons, or even the Door in the South. We're human enough to want to thank you for tearing the newspaper away. In a sense we're human enough to be sorry for what's about to happen in the motel room with you and your friend."

John woke, covered in sweat. Don still snored peacefully. It was all a dream.

Then John realized that there were seven little men standing in the room. At their feet writhed four of the spiked ink worms. And like so many thousands of humans in that hour, John screamed. Don woke and turned on the light by the bed. He started to laugh at the kids in their Iron Man costumes, but the seven little men took off their masks.

They weren't really human. Not. At. All.

(for Joe Pulver)

Red, Green, Blink, Black

by Don Webb and John Shirley

SOMETIMES WHEN EDWARD looked at his Christmas lights he felt they got brighter, their colors beaming more sweetly just because he was looking at them. It was as if they were aware of him, acknowledging him, as they blinked red and green.

He'd chuckle and think, *Funny, what comes into a man's head sometimes.*

But at first, going back a few years, Edward Johnston had to be coaxed into putting up Christmas lights. He wasn't the "Homes and Gardens" guy on his block, but neither did his yard ever stand out for neglect. Dandelions didn't bloom amidst his grass in the spring, yet he had never had a jogger slow down and admire the trimming of his junipers or smile at the iris blooms. For Edward this felt normal—it was almost a message: Respect me, and do it from a distance.

His dad had been a middle-of-the-roader as well—in all things. Denise, Edward's wife, had come from a more yard-involved family, but after years of dragging Edward to various garden centers had come to accept that if she planted it—he would take care of it. They had moved to south Austin three years ago. The neighborhood was nicer, if perhaps lacking in that intangible quality of charm. Most but not all of the neighbors put up Christmas lights. Edward didn't, the first year. He outlined the front door the second. But to Denise's surprise on the third year he outlined the door and garage and draped some light nets over the junipers. It was nothing that would attract the neighborhood association's prize, but it was as celebratory as most of the homes.

Edward expressed various pro-neighborhood sentiments in a vague way, for the first time in ten years of marriage. But he preferred to keep to himself. He found he was vaguely uncomfortable chatting with neighbors, no matter how likable they were.

I guess that's just me, he thought, when he looked away, smiling but with his lips pursed, to avoid talking to neighbors. *Most people will always be strangers, to me.*

Edward did have one valued trait as far as the neighborhood association was concerned. He walked. He liked to take a brisk half hour walk before retiring. He made himself known to the Watch Committee the first year. He dressed well, was always kind to older folks and minded his own business. He did however call in a burglary-in-progress the first year and stop some drug trafficking the second. He and Denise would show up at the twice-yearly meetings of the neighborhood association—Edward coming along grudgingly. He liked turning people into the police—but he didn't like the earnest, chummy neighborhood meetings. He rarely spoke at them for the occasional advice on bidding for contractors. In short, he and Denise were liked and largely ignored.

The year he put up the lights Edward was very orderly. He turned them on at 6:15 just as dusk began to fall and off at 11:15 when he went to bed. He noticed four houses that kept their lights on all night, and into the day. Their lights were on, trying redundantly to light the day, as he drove off to work at 7:30. *That is inefficient.* Not that Edward would think of talking to them about it; he was a great believer in homeowners' rights. And talking to them would bring that taut feeling of inner discomfort.

Edward grew prouder of his lights every night, but he grew prouder still of his neighborhood. He would tell people at work that they should drive though his neighborhood. He took Denise on walks at night to take in the lights. He found all the lights soothing . . . Except for one house.

There were 36 houses in his neighborhood. Behind them ran the railroad track, in front was a major road. To the east was a dedicated greenbelt, to the west a small strip mall. Edward took careful enumerative note: Eleven houses put up lights, four more had other sorts of decorations. The lights were usually tasteful—simple strings of sparkling white and gemstone green outlining the roof and doors. Some were gaudy, even oddly disturbing—animatronic reindeers jerkily moving their white wire bodies while pulling a sleigh with a grotesquely fat Santa. Still, he could see they were trying to bring a little something more to the display. Not everyone had good taste.

But that one house was like someone prodding him with a thumb—like that kid Erwin had done, when he'd been a boy. Jab, jab, jab, every time he saw the display. It had large white lights on the roof and doors, and in the yard, which sloped up a bit from the street, was an oversized cross with red lights. The cross was about fifteen feet tall, atop the slope, as if a parody of Golgotha. Now Edward was (at least in theory) a Christian. There was nothing obviously sacrilegious about the cross. The red seemed somehow —Edward couldn't quite find the words for it—just too *red.* It was obnoxiously red. The big cross house stood at the corner of the railroad track and the greenbelt. Edward didn't know the residents. Edward's neighbors didn't know them either.

On one of their walks he asked Denise if the cross bothered her.

"It's kind of big. Sort of used car lot."

The big cross house was one of the four houses that kept their lights on all night.

As everyone knows there is a glowing controversy about when to take your lights down. Many people stop on Christmas. Edward was part of the leave-them-up-until-New-Year's set. A couple of the more traditional families choose to keep theirs up until Epiphany.

On January 8, Edward noticed that the big cross house still had all their lights on. An ugly rather overlarge white plastic wreathe had been added to their door. Edward wondered if there had been a death in the household. He called the President of the neighborhood association, Jim Mendoza. No, Jim didn't know the family. They had never been to a meeting. They paid their fee through their mortgage company. Did Ed want to complain about the lights?

"No. I think what people do with their houses is their business."

But Edward decided that he wanted to speak with these people. He wasn't sure why. It wasn't concern; not exactly anger. Not exactly. But the impulse was very strong. Surprisingly strong.

He began by doing a couple of extra walks by the house at night, thinking it'd be better if he just seemed to run into them. But he didn't run into anybody—he saw lights on, but no other sign of life. Then Monday came and they didn't put their garbage out. Ah, that was it, they weren't home. The lights were on some timer.

One night, as they drove by, Denise said: "Why do those people still have that big tacky cross up? Don't they know it's February?"

Something rippled through him, and he said: "I'm shocked at you. You know they have a child dying of leukemia—they are going to keep those lights on every night until their son passes. Hell, Denise, if need be we'll help pay for their electric bill."

"Oh!" She didn't question him. She'd assumed, probably, he'd found this out from the Neighborhood Association.

But of course, it was a lie. A complete lie.

And Edward had said it with true anger. He was puzzled, thinking about it later, as they came home. Hey, he was a nice guy. He had said very few things in his whole life to hurt anyone, and lying wasn't a skill. Yet he said it to hurt her. Her dad had died of cancer. He had really enjoyed his pretense at self-righteousness. It scared him, now, though, and he almost ran to the bathroom, just to be by himself. He sat on the toilet lid, thinking. What if she called him on it? How would he get out of it? It wasn't the kind of thing you could say was a joke. *Funny as cancer.*

But then, why not? It wasn't like she would ever meet them. She had no deep interest in the neighborhood. She seldom even walked. Mostly she spent her time on Facebook with High School chums, usually on her extra-large smartphone, her finger endlessly caressing its screen. He calmed down, flushed the toilet for camouflage, and when he came out she was clicking away furiously on Kandy Krush, but he could see the traces where tears had coursed down her cheeks. His lie had made her weep!

He felt a certain distinct excitement, at that.

As February progressed so did his tendency to get short with her. Both of them worked, and mealtime was shared responsibility. You either cooked on your night or you brought food home. One night she walked in with a bucket of chicken. He began to talk about how although his mom had worked; she always made warm nutritious meals for her family. It grew ugly even before the chicken grew cold. He huffed out for a walk. As he rounded the corner of the block he ran into Mrs. Reynolds, a middle-aged poodle walker. Her light brown Reggie was snuffling at her feet.

"Evening Edward. Hasn't it been a mild winter?"

"Yes'M."

"Do you know those people down the block?" She pointed at the cross house. The cross was so large and vivid he could see it clearly from here.

"I know *of* them," he said. "Why?"

"Well, I was just wandering if they were ever going to take down their lights."

"Mrs. Reynolds, you should know that the Sedners have a sick son—Joseph. He is dying of leukemia. They want it to be Christmas every night until the little boy goes. They wrap up a present a day for him. Of course they are really small things, but he's only eight."

"Oh, my god," she said, a hand over her mouth. "I had no idea."

Great, thought Edward, that doesn't sound like a name. *Sedner*. I am really losing it.

He went and stood in front of the "Sedner" house. A light went on an upstairs bedroom. Maybe they are home. He hurried away; he didn't want to appear to be stalking them.

There was a little coffee house in the strip mall. Edward parked himself there until it closed at midnight. The teenagers of the neighborhood kept staring at him. He overheard one of the boys saying that he was the one who had "narc'd" on his friend last year. It had never occurred to him there might be dark consequences of his report.

When Edward went home, Denise was in bed. He slept on the couch, carefully leaving home before she got up.

The next day, she apologized to him. She had no idea that cooking meant so much to him. He was such a great, reliable guy, she just wanted to make him happy. Edward wanted to break the spell, to say that home cooking didn't mean a damn thing, but he couldn't.

The night after that, Denise made two pumpkin upside down cakes. She asked him if he could take one down to the people with the sick child.

"The Sedners?" he asked.

"Oh, you've met them?"

"Yeah, he works at the electronics store across from my office. A nice guy. Bill Sedner."

"Oh honey, you are so great at meeting people." She gave out a little laugh of self-derision. "I am just so shy."

"It is part of our Christian duty to love our neighbors."

Denise winced. Her family had been fairly religious in a sort of creepy fundamentalist way. As her dad was dying, the minister had told her mom that if the family was nicer to the church, her dad would live. The family gave the church all the money that would have sent Denise to college. But her dad had still died. God seemed to have shrugged, taken the money, and dad's life with it.

Edward went into the den to watch a cop show while the cakes baked. She brought one of the cake pans. "Why don't you take this down to the little boy . . ." She didn't look at him, but her voice was the trying-to-brave voice she used when her mom was acting crazy. He had never heard her use it with him before.

"We can have ours when you get back," she added.

He took the cake.

"Oh, and Edward, tell them he is in our prayers."

Carrying the cake down the street, Edward felt scummy and small and sneaky until he walked up into the glow of the red and white lights at the "Sedner" house. Then the ugly feelings washed away—and he felt really good about making Denise sad. *I hope she cries. I hope I can see her cry.* He marched across their front lawn and walked around the house to the railroad tracks. The train came only once a night and it had made its lonesome visit already. He sat on the tracks and began eating the cake with his bare hands. He was fairly sure he saw a back curtain move at the back of the Sedner house. I'm doing this for you.

After he had gobbled most of the warm cinnamony pumpkin goodness, he began wiping his hands on the weeds by the track. To make pumpkin upside down cake, you made a regular white cake and then poured a can of pumpkin pie filling on the batter. You stuck it in the oven and baked it as though it were a regular cake. The pie filling sank to the bottom and the cake absorbed its moisture, but it was a much wetter cake than most. Edward left orange smears in the grass. He threw the rest of the cake away across the tracks. He stayed outside for several hours, walking slowly up and down, basking in the odd but pleasing feeling he had, here. Finally, tired and chilly, he went home at one. He left a note that morning telling Denise that he had stayed and eaten with the family and prayed with them.

Valentine's Day was approaching. He and Denise usually went to a swanky restaurant downtown. He had been poor mouthing their finances for a week, so Denise had volunteered to cook instead. In fact, she had cooked every meal since his speech—even on the nights that would have been his.

She made a meatloaf in the shape of a heart, used red food coloring to die the mashed potatoes pink and made icebox cherry cheesecake. He came in and began with: "Well if it ain't the Happy Homemaker trying her sensuous best! Oh my, heart-shaped meatloaf!"

In less than two minutes she was crying. In five, she had run up to their bedroom. Edward followed her up, feeling like he had when he'd tracked deer with his dad, and tried to open the door. He had never noticed before that night the bedroom door had a lock on it. *Have to fix that.* He listened to her crying and felt a sickly excitement that became sexual—he wanted to press himself against the door.

He started to do it—then stepped back, startled at himself. His normal state of mind returned to him in a cold rush.

He didn't know what to do. Panic swept over him and he fled the house. He would drive downtown, get flowers, come up with some damn story. He squealed out of his neighborhood, exceeding the speed limit, pretty nearly unprecedented for him.

The first florist had sold all of her roses. The second was closed. He couldn't think of a story to tell Denise—something to cover his behavior, the things he'd said. The muse that had fed him names like William Sedner was strangely silent. He drove around and around and even put more gas in his green Taurus. When he drove home at one, he found that Denise had dead-bolted the front door. He knew he could break-in, at the back, but doubted if that was going to get him straight with her—hell, he'd sneered at her on Valentine's Day. A wife had a right to expect something, some kind of appreciation on Valentine day. Didn't she?

He took a walk, vaguely walking toward the "Sedner" house, raking it all over the coals in his mind.

He resolved to spend the night in his car. Maybe she'd see him and feel bad about it.

As Edward turned back toward the house, two teenagers sped down the street on those low, motorized mini-scooters they like. What were they doing out at this hour? He was sure they were some of the kids that had been watching him at Edgar's Grindhouse.

He didn't want to let them see him sleeping in his car. So he decided to walk around the block. He could do that. It wasn't weird. He was on the Watch Committee.

To his surprise the kids weren't to be seen as he rounded the corner, coming back to his block. *They must have gone into some house.* Well that was good, he could walk his walk some more till he was sure they weren't coming back and then not be too embarrassed at being the jerk husband sleeping in a car. Edward doubted that he was the only married man sleeping in his driveway that night.

He had to figure out what was wrong with him. Work was stressful, but not crazy. His relationship with Denise, after six years of marriage, was not steamy, but it was—or at least until a very few days ago—reasonably content. Maybe it was a medical issue. Maybe he drank too much coffee, or too much beer on the weekends, or some gland was letting him down. At the end of the block the Sedner house blazed forth in its red-neon Yule glory. It took him a moment to break out of his introspection to see what was different.

All the house lights were on.

And the front door was ajar.

He could check this out; he was on the Watch Committee. He wondered if the kids were inside, stealing from the absent Sedners. Of course the right procedure would be to call the police to come and do a safety check. But this was his chance to resolve all this, to meet them. To find out . . . what?

He wasn't sure. But he strode forward purposively, strode up the driveway, over to the door, and called out.

"Bill? Mr. Sedner? Hello?"

Then he remembered that he had *made up* those names. Just because he could get Mrs. Reynolds and Denise to believe them didn't mean he could get the actual neighbors to believe them. But it was OK. Whoever had the lights on and the door open at this hour was probably not the real tenants. He was scaring burglars and hooligans away. Really should call the cops . . .

But he couldn't bring himself to even take his cell phone from his pocket.

Still, it took him almost a minute to walk in. As he came, he kept yelling the names every few seconds. He knew it made no sense, but it felt right. In a vague way, Edward was aware there were only two or three house plans in his neighborhood. This house was the mirror image of his. The stairs were on the right instead of the left, the windows reversed and so on. No one was in the den. They had a TV where Edward had his TV. No one was in the kitchen, or the laundry room. Nothing special about the furnishings. Upstairs, then.

No one was in any of the three bedrooms.

In the master bedroom was something that brought him to a stop. He stared . . .

There were four huge canvasses, covering most of the available wall space. They had somewhat baroque antique gold frames and they were painted a cream color covered with writing. The writing was painted in dark green. At first Edward thought it was Chinese, and then he decided that it looked more like cuneiform. Finally, he decided that he had no idea what it was.

He checked the closets. There were ordinary men's clothes and women's clothes in the master bedroom and in one of the smaller bedrooms. The two bathrooms upstairs were completely empty—not only of hoodlums but of towels or toiletries. They had toilet paper by the johns however.

He went downstairs to check out the downstairs bathroom. Somewhere along the line he had stopped shouting the make-believe names. In fact, he was almost holding his breath. Nope, there was nothing in the downstairs bathroom either.

It occurred to Edward that he could spend the night here. He was locked out of his house, after all. And he had that odd little buzz of pleasure, in being here . . .

Surely, he had clearly driven away the thieves. He deserved a reward, and nobody was coming home at two in the morning. Or if they did, he could say he had found the door open and checked the place out.

He went to the den and sat in what was clearly the husband's chair.

What was this?

He felt in the cracks of the chair. It was a little glass dope pipe with some burnt weed in the bowl. It was cold and had a stale smell. Edward and Denise had smoked a little in college, but given it up as a childish thing. He stuck the pipe in his mouth. He pondered lighting up for a minute, but decided that didn't match his cover story. He stuck it back into the chair.

He knew it would be more economical to shut off the lights, but it scared him to do so.

He went back upstairs to the master bedroom. But—those paintings jabbed at him, like Erwin. They seemed to pull at his eyes, as though his eyes were full of iron fillings and they were lodestone. He kept trying to read the alien script.

Instead he went to the smallest bedroom. The one (in his house) that he and his childless wife had always called "the kid's room." He laid down on the twin bed, not disturbing the covers, and unlike his usually restless nights at home fell immediately asleep.

The transition to dreaming seemed instantaneous. He was standing outside of the Sedner home. The big red cross wasn't a cross anymore, it was one of the strange symbols from the paintings, and it was hundreds of feet tall. Its arcs and angles were collecting some red mist from the night sky. The mist collected and became drops and the drops began glowing as the rolled down the symbol. Suddenly, in his dream, he knew the word for it—the

Ythrig pole. The mist rolled down the Ythrig pole and small creatures, little many legged creatures about the size of a wiener dog with white slimy bodies, wriggled up to the pole and drank the glowing droplets. Sometimes the image shifted within itself, so it looked like a cross with big Xmas lights, again. Then it was the Ythrig pole once more. This was no Christmas symbol—this was for a very different festival. He remembered something about Christmas trees being an appropriation of a pagan ritual. He was about to recall the name of the festival, the way he'd somehow learned Ythrig, but as the word formed in his mind—it hurt him. It hurt him like stepping on shattered glass in the dark. He writhed away from the dream——

He woke confused and sweaty. How could a word *hurt?* At first he thought he was in his own home, that he had had a fight with Denise and was sleeping in the "I'm-in-trouble" bedroom. *No, fuck the bitch, she had tossed him out, he had just been trying to get her juice to run down her face.*

What?

He jumped out of bed. Maybe there was something weird in that pipe—maybe just putting it into his mouth had been enough. Maybe this was some kind of drug house.

He rushed out of the house, hurried home, almost running, slowing only when he saw a police prowler turning the corner. He still just did not want to talk to the cops, though most of the local cops knew him by name.

He was relieved when the cop car rolled by.

Reaching home, Edward got into the car, warming it up inside with the motor on for a while, and then spent the night in his car.

He drove slowly to work at dawn. He didn't want to give her the satisfaction of seeing him in the driveway. At work he called the Ben White Florist and sent a vase full of red roses and blue irises to her job. He texted her an abject apology.

He called Jim Mendoza. Jim's day job was real estate. The neighborhood presidency was a way of snagging clients.

"Hey Jim-bo, remember when I called you about the Christmas light people? I need to get ahold of them. I was on watch last night and saw they had left their front door open. It was kinda late, you know I always walk after eleven. I knocked—but they weren't home. Place was open and deserted! So I closed the door for them, but I want to tell them. What's their name?"

"I've got it right here. Sedner."

I made up that name.

"That's an unusual name. Any idea what he does?"

"No. Let me see. Now that's funny—Edward and Denise Sedner, like you-all."

"Not William? Not William Sedner?"

"Says 'Edward' here. Let me give them your phone number."

The phone rang two times then went to an automated message center that repeated the number. Edward didn't know what to say. Not having bathed, his clothes rumpled, unshaven, he did everything he could to stay in his cubby and avoid the other workers.

After lunch, he got a curt forgiveness note from Denise. He thought, *I should call her* . . . but instead, he decided to google *Ythrig*. A couple of people online referenced it as a fantasy gamer name. An anagram of "Righty." And a reference to *The Night Book of Edward Lamnath, Esq*.

By afternoon coffee break he had found out what little there was to know about Mr. Lamnath (April 12, 1892–April 13, 1973). Lamnath was a figure of rather minor controversy. According to some folks he was a sort of Charles Addams humorist producing two long running columns for the *San Francisco Chronicle*. His columns are collected in Schmulowitz Collection of Wit and Humor (SCOWAH), which is the world's second largest collection of humor and folklore, eclipsed only by the House of Humor and Satire collection in Gabrovo, Bulgaria. He wrote two columns—the *Daybook* (which dealt with Bay Area eccentrics and government boondoggles) and the *Nightbook* (which dealt with spooky stuff). He fits in the long tradition of San Francisco humor from Mark Twain to Eric Kauschen. Everything seemed OK with his life until 1970 when he began obsessing on electricity. He said that the worldwide electrical grid was the body of a very old god from a "galaxy far, far away." Despite the *Star Wars* jokes, he seemed very serious about this. This supposed entity was not taking over computers, as one might expect, but instead the humble electric light. Christmas lights, Vegas, especially lights in spaces that were empty of humans—these were vessels for this consciousness. Its mission was to blanket the world in an ultra-complex web of lights that would allow several other Entities a foothold on our benighted planet. He had given away buttons that read *LIGHT POLLUTION SUMMONS THE OLD ONES*.

At first these occasional cranky columns were seen as failed humor, but when this became his only topic, he was asked to leave the paper. It must have been painful for everyone to watch, he had written for nearly four decades. His death was suitably macabre. A widower for nearly twenty years, his cleaning lady found him naked and covered in strands of Christmas lights apparently in an act of auto-erotic strangulation.

So—at some point he'd heard of this guy? And Ythrig?

But that's not how it had been. It had been so distinctly like something whispering a name in his mind . . .

He suddenly felt sick inside. He would go home, make things good with his wife and then go to the Sedner's home and tear down the lights. If he did it late enough at night, he could get away with it.

The world, or at least his boss had different plans. Mr. Villanueva, smelling of cigarettes and apologies, dumped a huge packet of papers in his cubicle at 4:30. "Sorry but these have to be redone, Eddy boy. Tonight. You've gotten behind the last couple weeks . . . way behind."

"Um . . . yeah sure. Okay."

Had he gotten that behind? Where had his mind been?

He had to get caught up. And honestly, he wasn't in a hurry to try to make things up with Denise in person. The work wasn't brain-hard, just tedious. He texted another apology, ordered a pizza and watched CNN on his computer.

But he'd slept badly, he was tired, and, working alone in the office after hours, he could barely make any progress at all. The papers seemed to swim mockingly away from his vision; as if rain had fallen on them and the ink had run; as if the rain were sweeping them away in a tunnel . . .

At the end of the tunnel was a cross of bloody-red neon. Something twisted around the cross—the Ythrig . . .

He sat up, blinking. He'd fallen asleep on his work.

Take it home, he thought. Get some rest, get up early and finish . . .

Hands shaking, he piled his work papers into a briefcase, shut it with parts of them sticking out, and lugged it quickly to the elevator. He clutched the briefcase to himself in the elevator as a maintenance man came in, pushing a trashcan on rollers. The chubby white-mustachioed man stared at him, and sniffed. Then turned away. He was pushing a trashcan, but he was picking up a bad smell around Edward . . .

I haven't bathed in a while. That's all it is.

He drove home with extra care, afraid his fatigue might end in a car crash—and he nearly drove a car into a light pole, when he saw his house. As it was, jerking the wheel to avoid the pole sent him up on the sidewalk.

The house—Edward's own house—was covered in lit Christmas lights. They blinked red, green—then they blinked out, and everything was blacked out. Then they came back on with red, green, blink . . . blackness.

The door was standing open. He walked numbly up to it, and called out: "Denise!"

The only response were footsteps, somewhere upstairs; and someone spoke in a hushed, unintelligible voice.

Then a strong, suffused red light blinked on—from behind Edward. He thought: *The police?*

But he was afraid to look. That particular neon red . . . .

He turned on the stooped—and saw it. The red cross was there, in his own lawn. And it hadn't been there a few moments before. Perhaps he hadn't noticed it, as it hadn't been lit up? He took a step closer to it . . . and saw there were no wires leading up to it. The enormous neon cross was glowing like a red-hot branding iron—but it was not plugged in.

Then he saw the Ythrig quivering over it, translucently superimposed, with the fleshy grubs climbing up to sip at its psychic secretion.

Edward turned away, overwhelmed, and had a blurry, split second impression of a young male coming at him with a baseball bat.

* * * * *

When Edward woke, he perceived everything through a flashing throb, emanating from the place the bat had struck him on the forehead. He saw he was lying in a tub of water, tied up somehow, in the upstairs bathtub; he saw all this through a filter of throbbing glimmer that came and went just like the blinking rate of the Christmas tree lights draped over the house. The lights. He looked down at himself, saw he was tied up in the green wires of Christmas tree lights, bulbs and all. They were not illumined.

"I went to the Sedner's house, Edward," Denise said.

She was coming into the bathroom, wearing her bathrobe, dragging something he couldn't see clearly behind her.

"What happened . . . here?" he managed. It was difficult to talk. "What have you done to me?"

"I went there to talk to them, to offer my help. No one was there, but the door was open—and Someone was there, after all, really." She sat on the edge of the toilet and crossed her legs. Her face had a strange dreamy contentedness.

"And now," she said, softly. "I understand. My mother was so wrong. Her God is the lord of punishment. It's all about punishment whatever you do, Edward. Do you see?"

"No. Denise . . . Who hit me?"

"Oh—one of the boys. I knew they were angry at you. So, I found them. And here they are . . ."

Edward saw the two teen boys who'd been talking about him in the coffee shop, standing together at the door. One of them was staring in fascination; the taller one was licking his lips, looking scared. "I don't think I'm down with this shit," he said.

Denise lifted up the thing she had dragged into the room—an extension cord.

"I don't fucking know about this shit at all," the taller boy said, taking a step backwards. "I don't wanta do no jail time."

"Those pictures, in the Sedner's house, upstairs, the writing? The house said I could have one. I brought it home. And then I knew exactly what we needed to do, Eddy, my Eddy . . . You humiliated me over and over and now the sweet power tells me, tells me, tells me what I need to do. A sacrifice to the god of Punishment."

Edward looked down at himself, the shock of realization penetrating his pain dazed mind. The green insulation on the wires of the Christmas lights he was tied in had been partly pared back, exposing copper. There were copper scrub pads, he saw, under the exposed parts of the wires, tied to him. He tried to shout an order at her—and couldn't.

Denise stood up, opened her robe and dropped it. She was naked. Then she stepped into the bath, straddled Edward and as the boys shouted at one another and then ran from the house, she reached for the extension cord and the plug for the lights.

"*Denise!*"

The lights worked, for perhaps ten seconds, in a sparking holiday glow, as they both fried in their electrical embrace. Red, green—blink . . .

Black.

for Fritz Lieber

Root Work Saves the World

by Christopher Ropes and Don Webb

> "I am naturally a Nordic—a chalk-white, bulky Teuton of the Scandinavian or North-German forests—a Viking berserk killer—a predatory rover of Hengist and Horsa—a conqueror of Celts and mongrels and founders of Empires—a son of the thunders and the arctic winds, and brother to the frosts and the auroras—a drinker of foemen's blood from new picked skulls—a friend of the mountain buzzards and feeder of seacoast vultures—a blond beast of eternal snows and frozen oceans—a prayer to Odin and Thor and Woden and Alfadur, the raucous shouter of Niffelheim—a comrade of the wolves, and rider of nightmares."
>
> H. P. Lovecraft

I.

THE AIR SMELLED of white people, or more precisely of the Great White Space, so Lucy Downing knew there would be trouble even before she opened her eyes. It was the last day of the shortest month of 1963 by the white people calendar, or the first day of the first month of the year 30,418 of the true calendar. Lucy could smell other things—ginger, High John the Conqueror, candles burning on the altar, and the funk of the Mississippi. Soon there would be knocks on the door. White people coming to buy gris-gris bags, colored folk asking her to write papers for their shoes—and about noon Sarah would come by for her lessons in rootwork, promising that she would never be late again. Lucy took a long sniff. The problem with humans is they don't keep their eyes closed and their nostrils open when they first wake up. *By Their smell shall ye know Them . . .*

Things were moving into the world. Some good things—President Kennedy was going to send the Civil Rights act to Congress today, and bad things—the Klu Kluxers had hung a man in the bayou last night for kissing a white girl. He hadn't actually kissed her, she had just said he did. She had wanted to know if her boyfriend would kill for her. When such a death happens, it creates a gap. Every human, even the white ones, have a unique genetic and neurological purpose—so that if they're pulled out of the matrix, They draw nearer. That's why They love war. But certain deaths at certain times and places are more of an invitation than others. Lucy breathed this in and opened her eyes. She could see the light coming in from under her door, and moved her tired bones. Lucy was 101, but as she liked to say, "Didn't look a day over 83." She had been born a slave, and as far as she knew she was the last of her kind. Of course, she didn't advertise this fact. White people would want to know her secret, and that would make things too complicated. Besides she had pushed the envelope as much she wanted. She wasn't like her teacher Dr. Rufus Miller. He had lived until the overly ripe old age of 153.

Cracker, her white Persian cat, began yowling. Someone was at the back door. It couldn't be Georgia, her apprentice. Georgia was supposed to come at 8 in the morning. It *was* 8 in the morning, so it couldn't be Georgia. That girl had never been on time in her life. Even when Lucy had delivered her 18 years ago.

It was Georgia.

She looked more scared than a body had right to be—even if the Klu Kluxers was burning a cross in their front yard. She ran in wearing the height of white woman dress, a cream colored near-princess pinched-waist coat—Yves St. Laurent's assertion of the super sportive "young natural" look. There wasn't a black woman in New Orleans that dressed as well, as mod, as Georgia. She smelled of Chanel No. 5, and of fear.

"They're going to do it," Georgia said. "They're going to open the Great White Space."

"Quiet, child," said Lucy. "Where did you hear that?

"My momma heard it."

Georgia's momma cooked for Dr. Ward and his family. Ward was rich and smart and had the best families, the best white families, as his patients. He Knew a little—and as Dr. Miller had always said human that Know a little are the greatest danger the human race held.

All sleepiness had left Lucy and she pulled on her pink Sears housecoat and started a pot of chicory coffee. She gave Cracker a little tuna on a plate from the icebox, and she sat the girl down. The news matched the smells of the morning, Thank the Powers, that she was getting a bead on this so early.

"Tell me exactly what you *know*, not what you suspect."

"Momma had to work late last night. Dr. Ward was having a visitor from the east, from Boston or somesuch. This man had thick black glasses and wore a leather coat. He looked like a mad scientist, momma said. Mom gave them sheet cake and coffee and hear them talking about NASA and rockets and such. Then the little guy said: 'Of course if we could open the Great White Space directly we would never fear the Russians again.' "

Lucy asked: "And how did your momma know to listen for the Great White Space?"

Georgia looked at the yellowing linoleum on Lucy's kitchen floor.

"I told what you Taught me last week. About how the scientists in the Gobi Desert opened the Great White Space thirty thousand years ago and it made the plague that turned their skins white and their dicks little and made them mean. Of course it weren't no desert then."

"And what did I tell you about repeating what you Learn?"

"I know M'am, but it's the biggest wonder that all of us have that white folks is the way they are—and Knowing I had to tell."

"Tell what you Know and you won't Know it no more. A Secret has an effect on the manifest universe. Gossip ain't got none. But go on, Sweetie, sounds like Knowledge worked well for us this time."

"Well, momma said that this little guy told Dr. Ward he had worked out a way to blast through to the Great White Space using uranium salts and space-waves. He had found a recipe in Eibon's Book. I thought Eibon's Book was safe since Eibon was colored."

"It don't work that way, Sweetie, it ain't who writes a book—it's that there is a book. Any fool can read a book. That's why we don't commit secrets to books, we tells them—Mouth to Ear. Did Dr. Ward say more?"

"He told this little guy that if the government could provide the uranium he could run a test at the end of February. Can he do that?"

"I don't know. I have never learned much about the Curse of the Gobi."

"Why would they repeat their mistake? What does the Great White Space do?"

Lucy spoke slowly. "About 33,000 years ago a Lyran named Muras founded two centers called Agharta One and Two. One was the seat of learning, Two the seat of power. In the seat of learning they discovered the Great Old Ones and marveled at their power. The Great Old Ones could move through space and time at will. They plunged into the force of No-Thing, which is the Great White space and were annihilated. Whiteness is the force that destroys individuality. That's why white people worship it. The Great Old Ones could let themselves be destroyed at one place and just come into being at another time and another place. The scientists thought if we humans could learn this power we could become masters of the universe. The wiser folks in AghartaTwo said that this would be too much for humans. Most humans found they never have the strength of being to use total annihilation as a way to move about. We aren't made to defy space and time the way Yog Sothoth does. So they forbade experimenting with Great White Space—but the scientists did so anyway. Unleashing vast fields of radiation and making the Gobi a desert. It turned the survivors' skin white, and left them with a desire to conquer the universe. The Great Old Ones have nothing to with this—would you be worried if cockroaches destroyed themselves with a cockroach experiment. Eibon wrote this down in his book—he thought it would stop folks from meddling with it—but he didn't know white folks. White folks love to meddle. They figured out a little and that's why they got the atomic bomb—which removes indivi-duality on a cellular level—that why them poor folks in Hiroshima that lived got awful cancers."

"But why mess with this?"

"Well they already turned them fool selves white and shrunk their dicks—they probably figure they ain't got much to lose," laughed Lucy. "Seriously they are driven by their war-lust. They're just thinking about the ability of sending troops straight from Texas to Moscow in the blink of an eye."

"But they must be stopped. Can't you just go and tell them?"

"Sure, Sweetie—I'll just go up to Dr. Ward's house and ring the bell and say, 'Dr. Ward I'm a poor nigger lady that knows the Secrets of everything and realize that you are about to screw organic life on Earth as your ancestors' ancestors did thirty thousand years ago and speaking for colored people everywhere I am asking you to cease and desist.' "

Even Georgia laughed, then caught herself and shuddered. "You've always said that Dr. Ward Knew things. But . . . does he know what they mean? Is he ignorant of the consequences or . . ." Cracker yowled as a shadow shifted in the corner and vanished. Georgia started and then resumed her question. "Is he actually evil? *Is he one of them?*"

Lucy let out a tired sigh and waved a finger at a newspaper on the countertop. *Dr. Alvin Ward speaks out on Negro hanging*, read the headline. "You don't wanna read that article, girl, but I can tell you one thing. That white man doesn't know what he's up to, not all the way. But when I read that, there was one thing that was perfectly plain to me. What he don't know, he don't care to know." Cracker mewled and put one fluffy white paw over his face. Lucy laid her hand on his head and stroked him. "See, Georgia? Even this Cracker knows there's bad things brewing down on Gentry Lane. Now, listen here, I need you to find out all about that mad scientist type. I figure he's the one pulling Ward's strings, him or someone higher up than he is who sent him. Then come back and I'll see what can be done. Ain't gonna be no goddamn white mad scientist blasting open the Door to the Great White Space while I got breath in my body and the spirits of my kin watchin' my back."

Cracker rubbed up against her hand and purred.

II.

"Breakfast," Regina Ward piped with false perk, as she entered Alvin's book-stuffed bedroom with a still-steaming hot plate of waffles, bacon, and eggs on a platter. Alvin Ward, her husband-in-name-only, groaned and thrashed in his sheets, in the grips of one of his nightmares. Once again, Regina was glad that her bedroom was down the hall.

The couple, if indeed they were one any longer, hadn't shared a bed in many years, but that never bothered Regina. Alvin was a lukewarm lover, and the free space gave her the opportunity to indulge in her favorite pastime: seducing young black men. She smiled, remembering pretty Jackson Hughes from last night. If Alvin knew of her predilection, he couldn't be bothered with it. The preoccupied look that had always been plastered on his face had hardened into the shell of an obsessive who simply didn't care about anything but the object of his mania.

"Honey," Regina called, her voice dry and crusted with bitterness saying that term of endearment. "Wake up; you're having a bad dream." The thrashing ceased, and the whiter than white sheets fell to stillness, and he groaned and rubbed his eyes.

Dr. Ward rolled over and, before reaching over to the nightstand to retrieve his glasses, gave her a withering sneer. Maybe he did know about her "hobby." He still never said anything to her about it, but she couldn't be certain that he wasn't telling others about what she did. She was painfully aware, though not enough to stop, that the men she lay with were frequently among those lynched and gone missing. And it was happening with greater and greater frequency.

"Damn Reese and this entire Great White Space," she heard him mutter, as he waved her towards his bed with the platter of breakfast. She wasn't sure what he meant, but it was of a piece with many of the strange things she overheard in her household, from Dr. Ward as well as his many guests, so she put it aside in her mind, in a corner labeled, "Do not think about this." She set the platter down in front of him and, before leaving, she said: "Enjoy your breakfast, love."

Alvin snarled. "If it's the last thing I do. Which it just might be." Regina rolled her eyes once her back was to him and left. He was getting meaner and meaner, the closer it got to March. She suspected, given his worsening mood and the increasing number of visitors, that something important was nearing. But she had no idea what, nor did she truly want one.

Downstairs, she sent the serving girls scurrying in all four directions, first with a scowl, and then with lashed directives she practically barked at them. Upstairs, Alvin was tossing his breakfast in the trash, and getting dressed to take care of his day's business. A meeting with the press, a call or two to the people who would "take care" of young Jackson Hughes, and then a trip out to the swamps for the Rite.

Last night, the meeting with the scientist-priest had confirmed Alvin's suspicions. If the Great White Space was going to be let loose, February 28th was the day the preliminary ritual had to be undertaken. There would have to be an appropriate sacrifice. He smiled, a smile that would have chilled even his relatively inured wife. The sacrifice had been taken care of already. A young, well-hung stud of a lad named Jackson Hughes. The entities inhabiting the Great White Space would find him . . . delicious.

III.

Reginald Reese grinned as the Klansmen and fellow cultists of the Great White Space dragged the nigger boy in. He was beaten and bruises darkened even further patches of his already night-sky dark skin. The scientist-priest spat and waved them into the clearing in the swamp where he'd been waiting for them. The soggy ground sucked at his feet, the reeds and tall grass and blossoming scum flowers made his allergies hell, but that had to be endured for the sake of the Rite.

The Klansmen bowed almost to Reginald's knees, then tossed the boy down with obvious scorn. In this place, where no animal, no insect life could be heard or seen, the air throbbed with the Greatness and Whiteness of the Beyond, with Yog-Sothoth's own breath and hunger. Reginald knew the secrets that Dr. Alvin Ward did not, the secrets that were borne in the blood of one whose ancestors led the bloody and vile rituals in the Gobi Desert so long ago. They wrote many of the fabled and lost books, lost to all but Reginald and a few others scattered over the globe, in outposts small and large, of whiteness and its superiority over the savages.

Death was coming for them, Reginald knew. A death suited to inferior races, to be food for the gods and for the white men. The white women would be slaves, and the surviving subhumans would be beasts of burden. The wisdom of Yog-Sothoth, the White Space devouring the Blackness of ignorance and superstition; his head swam with the many delightful options he saw in the future, reflected in the brilliant whiteness of the shard of stone that a creature from beyond had passed to him when he was under the tutelage of his late father.

He looked at his watch and cursed. Alvin had better not be running late again, or he would be fed to the hungers from outside. A sharp nod from him was all that was needed to dismiss the Klansmen. Jackson lay at his feet, a lump of humanity with the breath barely left in him. Careful not to touch him, Reginald knelt and gazed at the boy's fearful face, plainly swimming in and out of consciousness. Reese chuckled to see the terror coursing through the boy's veins and nerves every time his mind had some clarity.

After a time, Jackson tried to leap to his feet and found himself staring into the wild eyes of a white madman, and bound hand and foot with swamp vines. He spat at Reginald's face and Reginald merely shifted to the side and the saliva shot past his ear. He knew how he must look to the boy, all patchy white hair, staring bloodshot eyes, redder than their natural blue, and a thin-lipped mouth that twitched with odd spasms every few seconds, completely outside of his control. The face that was his reward for decades of service to the Great White Space must have been a terror to the kidnapped Negro, who must have been slowly grasping what was going to happen to him, even if he was completely unaware of the particulars.

Reginald put his ragged brown loafer on Jackson's shoulder and forced him face-first into the muck. "Do not presume to look into the eyes of your betters, boy."

"Fu-fuck you," Jackson said, trying to keep mud from filling his mouth and forcing the words out between gasps for breath.

Laughing, Reginald shoved him down harder. "You slept with a white woman, didn't you? Naughty, naughty. You know that's above your station, even with a whore like stupid Ward's blonde wife." Fanaticism gleamed like a silver switchblade in his eyes, highlighting the burst blood-vessels in the whites. "You're the thirteenth, boy. You know how many niggers been lynched the past month, right?"

Jackson closed his eyes tightly, and started to pray, a prayer a root-worker and priestess had taught him, a lady by the name of Lucy. He knew exactly how many had been lynched. Twelve black youths in one month, swept away at all times of day by white-robed Klansmen and never seen alive again. Now, he knew the significance of where he was and why. Like Lucy had told him once, the white man hates all superstitions but his own, and unlucky thirteen was something like an umbilical cord between here and something nasty.

Reginald watched the boy pray, and his eyes grew brighter with envy. Not caring anymore about propriety, he grabbed Jackson Hughes by the throat, almost his windpipe, before he loosened his grip and screamed at the hacking and wheezing man: "Where did you learn that prayer?"

"I learned in Sunday School," said Jackson.

Reginald slapped him across his face. "Tell you what boy. I can get these redneck fools to bring me another young buck in an hour. If'n you tell me who told you to pray to the Lord of Shadow, I'll put fifty dollars in your pocket and let you run. If you stay away from here you might grow to be an old coon." Then he lay his hand on Jackson's forehead. It was like cool water on a summer day. He could see himself with a car and a paid-for house and a

TV and a light skinned wife and a paved road. He could see it and feel it. All the pain left his body. He was drinking a Coke and Southern Comfort.

Before he had even thought it through, he said: "Mama Lucy. Mama Lucy told me."

IV.

Mama Lucy had been busy. Georgia had brought her Dr. Reginald Reese's name, and the librarian had found a photo from the *Arkham Advertiser* telling of the sever radiation burns Dr. Reese had suffered during an archaeological trip to the Altai Mountains of Gobi Desert. The article mainly focused on the "new era" of cooperation that the trip supposedly meant between the USA and Red China—but mentioned that all of the Chinese nationals on the dig had died.

It wasn't much of a personal concern. She had no hair, no sweat, no fingernail clippings—not even dust from a footprint. But as Dr. Rufus always said, you got to Work with what you got.

She was making a little doll baby with his face on it. She made it out of white wax. She filed some of the radium paint from her glow-in-dark watch. She added some sand, and on a tiny strip of papyrus wrote the word "djefa" in red hieroglyphs. It meant divinely tasty in the Egyptian language. The Crawling Chaos had lived in Egypt and gods are suckers for nostalgia. She named the doll baby then she gave it a coin from last year's MardiGras—a little brass token that read "Lucky 13 Krew of Thoth" on one side and had the Dixie flag on the other.

She called Georgia.

"Miss Georgia, I am headed to the swamp tonight. I know what they are planning, and I plan to stop them. I'm no fool, the Klu Kluxers ain't going to take kindly from some old black lady watching their hell-raisin'. I know I might not be coming back. I have left a will made out to you honey. You will get everything."

"Mama Lucy, I ain't ready."

"We're never ready child. Life is the process of never being ready, but you are willing to learn, to admit your mistakes, to be brave and to think of others. That does make you ready. The Powers will Teach you the rest as long as you seek the mysteries."

Lucy rode the bus out of town, another old Negro riding in the back, as invisible as thought itself. The bus headed south to Jean Lafitte National Park.

The sun was setting as she got off. The snowy egrets were beginning to roost in the cypress. She could hear the blue herons signing their goodnight song, and the pelicans fighting for fish. As she began trekking into the marshy ground snakes slithered away and she kept an eye out for water moccasins. A big nasty nutria with teeth green from algae grinned at her. She turned on the cheap flashlight she's brought at Woolworths on Canal Street. A little Eastern screech owl leaned out of its nest toward her, but it wasn't a hoot that came out. It was the voice of Jackson Hughes, that little orphaned boy she's helped out ten—no, fifteen years ago. He was saying a prayer to the Dark One of Khem, the prayer for safe passage to the Duat.

Mama Lucy thanked the owl for being a voice in the wilderness, and promised if she lived through the night she would find some field mice for it. Then she heard the local KKK begin singing their hymn, 'Onward Christian Soldiers.' Soon they would be lighting their cross and soon after that Dr. Reese would open the Gate.

V.

"Thank you boy."

Dr. Reese took his hand from Jackson's forehead. Jackson tasted blood instead of Coke Cola. He smelled gasoline. Dr. Reese was hanging a necklace on his neck with little pieces of cotton with Greek letters on them. Fucked again. Why hadn't been able to keep his mouth shut?

"You ain't letting me go," said Jackson.

"I'm giving you a running chance boy. When the Way if Opened your soul just may be quick enough to dart past the Lurker because of that prayer that Mama Lucy taught you. You may be reborn as a human. Heck, you may even get to marry a white woman in your next life. You like white women; maybe you'll be a white woman." Reese laughed long and hard at this.

The Klan had lit their cross.

Onward, Christian soldiers, marching as to war,
With the cross of Jesus going on before.
Christ, the royal Master, leads against the foe;
Forward into battle see His banners go!

But Dr. Reese had begun his own chant:

White obscures the angles

White obscures the planes

White destroys ipseity

White removes my pain.

Yog Sothoth Neblod Zin!

The Grand Cyclops had lit the cross and the gasoline burned bright. Out of the center of the roaring fire came a thick whiteness, pouring like milk in no gravity. Everything it touched merged in perfect Unity. No place, no time, no reason, no rhyme. Just before it Touched with its endless silence was a barrier of sound, the endless screams of souls losing their individuality. The Klansman stopped signing. Some dropped to their knees, others ran. Dr. Reese stepped behind his bound victim, beckoning the Great White Space with the Sign of Kish. Some one ran up from the trees. A little black woman panting. She tossed something in the cross's flames—almost white and colorless by now. It sizzled. It screamed. The same scream (but much louder) escaped from Dr. Reese's lips.

Somewhere—very far away or very near—it was impossible to tell—a tiny black dot or a huge black galaxy—flew forth faster than anything (or slower than molasses in January) and broke through the Whiteness of sameness and caught Dr. Reese. It pulled him back into the thinkable direction. Meanwhile at (possibly) the same time a shot rang out and Mama Lucy hit the damp ground while one of the Klansman began his revel yell. The White surged forward and grabbed most of Jackson Hughes body. Then the White melted back into that everywhere, everywhen it is always going to and retreating from. The fire on the cross went out with a mighty "Whuff!" and the remaining Klansmen began turning on flashlights and wondering what the hell they would tell their pastors, their wives and their kids about tonight.

VI.

For the most part the world of men went on. Georgia had fourteen dreams where Mama Lucy taught her the art. She runs a VooDoo shop in the Quarter, you can visit it today. The USSR and the USA stopped fighting, and the US had to find a new enemy. Some small part of Jackson Hughes soul attached itself to an African American pop singer that became obsessed with becoming a white woman. The US government seized Dr. Reese's files. Dr. Ward met a strange death—but that's another story, and Mrs. Ward gave a good deal of money to the NAACP. As for Cracker, he lived to the ripe old age of nineteen with plenty of catnip and occasionally—just occasionally—Miss Georgia would let him have a little crayfish jambalaya.

(for Basil Copper)

The Waters of Dhul Nun

SUSAN HATED MLANDOTH, TX. The name, she supposed, came from some bad white mispronunciation of some American Indian word for "No the fuck where." She was driving Jose to the tiny local airport. Jose was going back home to Indianapolis, where he made middling bucks in an advertising firm. At least he was going back to 20 inches of snow, whereas she was facing an 80-degree afternoon since she was stuck in Texas in a town where you couldn't drink the water. After Flint, Michigan; Crystal City, Texas; and St. Bernard Parish, Louisiana, toxic water didn't even make the news anymore. She assumed that her oil company's big ass refinery was to blame. It was the major employer in these parts. Everything else services its employees—the tiny bank, the two liquor stores, and the Cat-Fish Parlor. She marveled at how ugly, how pulp-fiction monster ugly the big catfish on the pole that advertised the place was. It was ginormous, and at night its blue neon outline wiggled as though some even more giant creature had hooked it. Even on this overcast day it looked too alien.

At least Exxon was buying bottled water for the town. Which she supposed was a tacit admission of guilt.

It was awkwardly silent in the car. She and Jose were supposed to have a fun weekend, but it devolved into the same old fight. No, she did not know how long this assignment was going to last. No, she didn't think she could tell Mr. Walters that he either had to bring her home or she would walk. She made more money than Jose, which bugged him. Not much more, but more. He was threatening to go all Erin Brockovich on Exxon. He would rat out the company, unless she returned home. She tried to explain that taking on big oil would end both of their careers, but the real story was she was fairly sure that if she just hung on for six months, she would be up for promotion to a Regional Manager. That meant serious money, and that would either make their marriage better or give her enough to live pretty well on her own. Depending on the phase of the moon, Susan was happy with either. Her green car sped by the Tikki House, a quasi-Polynesian BBQ place with its own ugly advertising. It featured this tall wooden figure which was a cross between Groot and an Easter Island head. Again, ugly and creepy. The first night she had been in Mlandoth she thought some barbecue pork with pineapple sounded good. She'd driven here from the Best Western. A group of drunks were standing around the wooden man singing or chanting to it. She was creeped out, running every bad movie scenario of some strange BBQ cult that served long pig, and drove away. She bought damp plastic wrapped turkey and Swiss cheese sandwiches at the 7-11, drive back to the hotel and put the chain on the door.

If only Jose could be supportive of what she was trying to do.

Or maybe he was, but was confused by some blend of machismo and not knowing how to deal with ambiguity. Part of him might be proud, part of him missed her, part wanted to protect her. And there was something about Mlandoth that just seemed some unsafe. Some vibration in the air, some strangeness in the proportions of the architecture, maybe the sound the soda machine made before it dropped your bottle—there was something, some recurrent datum or data that just told your brain that things were strange. Of course, the smell of the refinery and the inbreed look of the locals probably didn't help. Nor that they seemed to worship ugly advertising icons.

Susan knew that after the cold and stiff scene at the airport there would be tentative happy texts full of heart icons, and then hours later after she had turned off the lights in her hotel room, he would call and there would be apologies and promises to never "be that way" again.

Susan went to a MacDonald's for dinner. She didn't like to be out at night. Things would catch her eye. One night when she first arrived in December, she found herself looking at the methane flame that shot out of the vertical flare stack over the refinery. She was walking from her car to the hotel and looked to the West, and there it was. It didn't scare her nor give her ecstasy, she just found herself staring at it. Another night it was a fountain in a little park downtown. Nothing very elaborate, just a fountain that alternately illuminated its water spumes with red, yellow and green. Yet she had watched for fifteen minutes without a thought in her head. Maybe there was something else besides the water that was contaminated. Maybe it was a sound, maybe a quality of light.

Not a town to read Stephen King in at night. Techno-thrillers were OK. She had been jonesing for dope. Now she hadn't smoked weed since college, but alcohol didn't take the edge off.

Of course, she wasn't to ask / hint to the employees at the plant—mainly Baptist whites and Catholic Hispanics that were scared of her powers to audit. She couldn't have asked Jose to bring anything—he was pretty straight edge. She couldn't meet anyone else. She didn't do bars—and didn't have the nerve to walk into the one head shop in town Yidhra's Cauldron. As she ate her oatmeal, two sausage burritos and drank her large diet coke she listened to the four teenage boys in the booth behind her with some jealousy. There was a tall thin half Hispanic boy (probably what her kids with Jose would look like if they ever got to that place in their careers where they could have kids)—his dark blue jeans had worn threads where the knees were. Next to him was a pudgy slug-like kid with black nerd glasses and ginger hair. Across the table was a smaller younger Hispanic, much darker, with a slightly idiotic grin and a muscular Anglo guy with bad acne and a much faded "Don't Mess with Texas!" t-shirt.

Half-Hispanic: "The town is dry, there is no weed."

Glasses: "Well, it's not like we can't get high."

Half-Hispanic: "I tried that once and I didn't like it."

Muscles: "Because you're a pussy.'

Half-Hispanic: "You did it? You reals did it?"

Muscles: "My sister's boyfriend did and said it was ggucchi. All flowers and shit."

Half-Hispanic: "Well, it fuckin' ain't. At least not for me."

Glasses: "Were you purposeful? Did you plan it out?"

Half-Hispanic: "Who would plan that shit? I cleaned out the garage for my old man. It was hot. I forgot and took a drink from the hose. Dad was working a double shift. I lay down in the hammock and sort of vegged. I fell asleep. I woke up at twilight and the tree was trying to eat me and my pit-bull had those octopus things. Testicles."

Glasses: "Tentacles. You have testicles."

Muscles: "No he don't, 'cause he's a pussy."

Glasses: "My point is, you could have known it was going to happen. You could've had some bottled water on hand to drink if it got scary. You could've had friends to tell you to watch out for the testicles."

Idiot giggled.

"So," asked Half-Hispanic. "How *should* we do it?"

Glasses sighed.

Susan thought that kid is going to have a rough go of it, when they read *Lord of the Flies* in senior year.

Glasses said: "First we do the phone drill. You tell your mama you're at Rodrigo's, you tell your dad you're staying with me at my grandmother's house, etc. Then we bike to the Dairy Queen on I 93. We each buy a bottle of Nestlé's. We bike to that place, that creek." He looked at Idiot.

Idiot said: "Arroyo Secca. We go to Indio rock."

"Yeah," Glasses continued. "We go to Indian Rock. I'll bring a big canteen full of town water. We each take a big slug. Then when it comes on we watch the petroglyphs dance. If it gets scary, or when we get bored, we drink the bottled water, wait fifteen minutes and bike back to my grandmother's. We sleep in the storm cellar. I'll convince her the next day, she knew all about it."

Muscles: "Petroglyphs?"

Glasses said: "Pictures, dummy. The pictures they painted on the rock."

That night Jose called and they had make-up phone sex. As Susan lay snuggled in the blankets, he talked about his "research." Jose liked to look things up on the Internet, it made him feel smart. It seems that Mlandoth had some sort of hippy eco-cult in the '60s and '70s. The FBI shut them down with the usual subtlety they showed in Waco and elsewhere. The abandoned houses had been bought up cheap by Exxon. A few of the cultists remained, but Exxon bought the really cheap (maybe even not exactly purchased if you know what I mean) land, to put in a refinery. The water problem started in 2001. Exxon claimed that they had nothing to do with it—maybe it was a parasite. Certainly there were no petroleum byproducts in the town's water. There was a federal investigation. Two of the investigators died suspiciously, and, get this, the Federal government pays for the bottled water. Not Exxon. Your fucking tax dollars at work, right?"

Susan applauded his brilliance and then asked if he had found out what the name meant.

"I couldn't find it. There's the exact same name in Tibeto-Burmese languages but that couldn't be the same source. It means 'Hungry Ghost'—apparently some sect believes that you and I don't have souls. But instead of us all being part of some friendly group soul—all life in this solar system is possessed by a parasite. We're like its legs and arms. Our self-consciousness in an unintended side effect. Of course maybe the hippies had picked up on this. Didn't Timothy Leary have people reading *The Tibetan Book of the Dead*?"

Jose kept talking while Susan fell asleep.

She got the bad news the next day. She had been expecting good news. Her audit showed that four mid-level managers were skimming off some expenses by buying from a company that their wives owned in no-bid contracts. She assumed this would be a promotion and her ticket out of Mlandoth. Instead it was her job to fix it. She would be here at least another six months. Screw it. She took the afternoon off and went to Yidhra's Cauldron. She figured her good (well at least better than average) looks, lean body and blonde hair might give her more purchasing ability than a foursome of teenage losers.

It was a nondescript head shop in a tiny strip mall that also hosted a tattoo parlor, a pawn shop, and a martial arts studio. It was rows and rows of shiny glass pipes, legal herbal pills to give you energy; clean up your urine or make you last longer in bed; and graphic novels. There was a used books area big on sci-fi and old paranormal paperbacks with gee-whiz titles like *UFOs on Colonial America*. Behind the counter were nudie mags and bumperstickers—mainly supporting legalization. Keep on the Grass Man! I've got a HIGH IQ! (made of stylized marijuana leaves). You Can't Beat A Wasted Life.

It was deadsville. Only the gray haired bear of man in a denim jacket that manned the counter (and probably owned the joint) was there. An enormous black dog, probably half-lab and half-Godzilla, snored and farted on the dirty gray linoleum floor. She dropped a few hints about being new in town, looking for people to party with, etc., but no help from the owner. She leaned over the counter a few times so he could ogle her firm breasts. He ogled, but gave out no useful info. She saw he was wearing a turquoise bolo with a rather deformed thunderbird motif.

"What's that?" Susan asked. "Something Indian?"

"Older than the Indians. It's the mother goddess Yidrha."

"Oh," said Susan, thinking this might be the ticket. "Are you one of the town's original inhabitants?"

He smiled. "You know your history."

His tone told her that was *NOT* the question to have asked.

He continued. "I came after the FBI raids. I came in 2001. The EPA was trying to nail Exxon. I was one of the investigators. Who would have thought a doctorate in chemistry would've enabled me to run the best little head shop in Texas?"

Susan asked: "So what's the deal about the water?"

"Nothing," he said. "It's perhaps the purest water in the world, certainly the purest drinking water in North America."

He stepped back from the counter and opened the door to the employee rest room. With exaggerated motions, so Susan could watch clearly, he drew himself a drink in a Scooby Doo glass from the bathroom sink. He put the water to his lips and chugged it down, making an exaggerated sigh of relief when he had finished it. He looked at her with hatred.

"See?" he asked.

"What happened to your fellow investigators?" Susan asked.

"They couldn't handle the purity. The FBI said it was murder-suicide."

Susan was betting on murder. She had a clear shot at the door. She decided to ask one more question.

"If you weren't part of the cult, how come you wear the amulet?"

"Just figured out a lot of it. Mainly by living here. Some by reading poetry, myth. I'm a regular Joseph Fucking Campbell I am. Found the amulet one day when I was walking along I93 picking up cans. Won at the lotto after that bought this place. The American Dream if you ask me."

"Did the amulet make you win the lottery?"

He shrugged. "Who fucking knows?"

"So, it wouldn't hurt me to drink the water?"

"Didn't say it wouldn't hurt you." He handed her a bumper sticker. The Truth Will Make You Flee. "On the house."

"Thanks." She turned to leave.

As she walked out, he said: "It's Mlandoth's Curse. Everywhere, everywhere BUT here. Duhl Nun. Google it."

She resolved to tell Jose her bad news that night, that her stay in Mlandoth would be longer. But he was grumpy and so she told a less scary version of her encounter with the head shop guy. She didn't say that he was one of the EPA scientists, just that he was kooky and told her to Google 'Dual Noon.'

Man could she use some relief besides beer and fast food. The water couldn't be that bad, could it? She had seen the head shop chug it. She could drink some town water and like the kids have her bottle of water as relief. So she tried a little from her motel room faucet. Nothing. A little more, still nothing. A fucking gallon. Nada.

She asked the waiter at the breakfast bar the next morning.

"How much of the bad water do you need to drink to have the hallucinations?"

"I hear not too much. Of course, the hotel has treated water, so anything you drink here is safe."

At work she took gallon jugs of bottled water from the employee supply. After work she drove to Yidhra's Cauldron. She said: "I'd like to buy some of your very pure water. Please empty this bottle and fill it from your sink."

The owner nodded and said nothing.

When he handed her the recently refilled bottle, he said: "I know the temptation is strong. I know you think it doesn't really matter. We all thought that. You know when my friends killed themselves they didn't have guns. All they had was a steak knife from Western Sizzling. Not even a sharp steak knife. It took a while. If you open the doors of perception, remember you can close them again."

"Yeah? Then why didn't you do so?"

"I'm a scientist—or at least I was. I valued objective truth. It's kind of overrated."

"But you're not going to stop me?"

"You could've filled up your bottle at the Shell store on Bowie St. I know you passed it between here and your hotel. You wanted to see me. You needed to see me. I don't know why, but I can guess. I was a loner here once. The one pretty honest guy with a good education. People are weird here; some try the water—others get a little bit on themselves while watering the lawn or washing their cars. Mainly it makes them mean or crooked or just a little dumb. If I was younger or if you came on more desperate, I would make a pass at you."

She marked the refilled bottle TW and the unopened bottle PW for "pure water."

The first night she wasn't brave enough.

The second night she wasn't brave enough.

The third night Jose mentioned that he had had dinner with his ex-wife. She was brave enough.

She decided she would trip out between 8 and midnight. She locked and chained the door of her motel room and pushed a chair in front of it. She sat the room other chair near the bed facing the window. The window faced the west and looked out over most of the city of Mlandoth. There would be pretty lights as 18 wheelers sped north from Mexico toward Dallas / Fort Worth. She put the Town Water to her left, the Pure Water to her right. She reused her large Styrofoam cup from MacDonald's. She lay her Ipad on the bed, so she could watch the time or play games if the mood struck her. She drank half a cup of Mlandoth water. It did taste sweet and pure. She distracted herself with Facebook.

After thirty minutes it seemed her fingers were sinking into the Ipad. It was becoming warm and liquidy—but also velvet. It became a puddle on the bed. Outside a cop car chased a truck. The flashing lights became eyes and the car grew great bat wings, while the truck turned into some kind of rhino / slug-looking thing. The windows became jelly that breathed. This was becoming a little much, Susan thought, but it was also fascinating. She could see the Cat-Fish Parlor sign. It really was a giant, living fish impaled on a pole, twisting in agony. Its blue neon was glowing blood and as drops were being flung in the air glowing insect-bats were sucking it up. The tall god of the Tikki House was looking up at her, and she knew its NAME which hurt her mind to think it, and she wanted to give it small warm gifts. She turned from the window and she saw her pale scabby face in the mirror with its extra line of vestigial eyes. And she opened her mouth with its three rows of teeth and screamed a sound like the strings of cello might make if you struck them with a file. Her longer arm swirled up and covered her eyes (all of them) by circling her head several times. She dropped to the floor, which was covered in soft mushrooms that realized clouds of minty smelling spores. She scuttled back around the bed and stuck her proboscis into the Pure Water and sucked it in—feeling it make millions of tiny bites as it came into her. She cried oily green tears and convulsed.

And slowly.

And slowly.

And slowly the world she knew came back to her, as she lay next to the bed and sobbed. She didn't go work the next morning, and stayed inside until hunger drove her from her room. She took the two bottles with her.

At work she visited the plant chemist and got two specimen bottles. She had a friend at Exxon offices in Houston, a chemist with not one but two PhDs. An old college fling. She sent the bottles to her with a letter saying that one was from land she was thinking of buying, and one was bottled water as a control. Could she do a full analysis of each—they tasted the same, she just wanted to know the water from her well was OK. She poured the rest of the TW water into a toilet.

She didn't know what she was looking for—a strange army drug? A parasite that rewrote the mind? Something she could sell the CIA? Something she could denounce her own company with?

She just wanted to know something. Some solid ground to set her jelly-quivering mind upon.

The next three days went by slowly. She drew her drapes in her hotel room. She threw herself into work—getting done what would have normally taken a week. She had 12 panic attacks. Anything could cause them: hearing loud music from a low rider's candy red car, seeing a cockroach scuttle across the asphalt in the hotel's parking lot, the murmuration of a flock of birds at sunset, a funny looking raisin in her oatmeal. She thought of driving out to Yidhra's Cauldron, but what would she say? The guy had warned her. Maybe the chest-pounding fear would lessen with time. Maybe.

Jose said she sounded distant on the phone.

The results came back. One sample had an amoeba like parasite that had a cellular membrane that gave it great affinity to human neural tissue. The other sample killed the parasite. The bad water was the bottled water. The good water was from the wells of Mlandoth.

Maybe she had mislabeled the bottles? But she knew she had not.

That night Jose called. It wasn't "Dual Noon." It was Dhul Nun, a Sufi saint. Jose read to her from a website: "Dhu'l Nun is known for a famous teaching parable The Khidir, the teacher of Magi, came to Moses and warned him that Allah was pissed off at mankind, and was going to punish them by driving them mad. Allah was going to do this by poisoning the waters. So the wise could hoard up water now, and thus remain sane. Many did so. They sealed the water away in special jugs marked with the six-pointed star of stasis. They were sure they could remain sane. But as they went forth in the world, they noticed that men now spoke in strange ways and they could not understand the actions of men. They noticed that men now acted in strange ways, and they could not understand what men did. And men hearing the wise either grew angry, or full of compassion at these madmen. So one by one, due to loneliness and to economic reasons and to fear of the madmen, the wise gave up drinking pure water and drank the waters of the Earth. They forgot all about their special store of water, and slowly they became like the rest. The rest of mankind welcomed them with open arms—seeing them as madmen who had regained their sanity."

Jose asked: "Does that make any sense?"

Susan said: "I just think he was some old hippy. Too much acid."

Then she told him tales from the office, the usual banter of their couple-hood and Jose was happy.

The next day she drove to Yidhra's Cauldron.

The owner was in same denim jacket over (she guessed) the same yellowed t-shirt. His medallion seemed alive, moving. She tried not to look at it. He looked sad.

He said: "So you drank the water. And you want to know why it caused such terrible hallucinations."

"No. Like you I have access to science, not to mention the lovely little parable you told me. I realize that water stops hallucinations. I realize *that* was the real world. I just want to know why and when. When did the world become that?"

"Don't know for sure. There are a lot of strange forces that game and gambol on this haunted planet. Yidhra gave a Gift to her Children that they could see the real world. The consensus world is ruled by much more terrible gods and goddesses than her. Some it slops through—the death of bees and butterflies, the global heat wave, the extinction of the mega-fauna, violence. Since you seem pretty sane I'm guessing you didn't watch TV news when you could See."

"Which is better?" Susan asked. "Knowing or not knowing?"

The old man was silent. His medallion grew and eye and Winked.

(for Walt DeBill)

The Healing Power of Snow

IT HAD BEEN five years since the serfs of Tibet had risen up and the PLA had aided in their liberation. A peaceful transition to the principles of Marxism was being enjoyed throughout the country, and Lieutenant Chang had every hope of returning home to Shanghai. There was only the small matter of the *gompa* of the Migauo Mountain. Throughout Tibet the superstitious forces of the monks diverted many economic resources toward their practice, even though an intensive process of reeducation had begun. Chang hoped that the center of the region had advanced further but Niyma County was still lost in some fabulous dark age. It had bothered him less when he was at Nagqu City, but as a junior officer the wild had been given to his care. He lived with peasants who had not seen electric light, and almost believed him when he told them that his radio was not an example of Bon sorcery. At times however, when he wondered if he would ever really be warm again, Lieutenant Chang wondered if better fuel and medicine might help the serfs even more than Marxism.

Chairman Mao's orders about the liberation had been strict, there was to be no interference with the religious or cultural practices of the Tibetan people. It was important to do two things: one, to begin regular reeducation, and two, make a thorough listing of the whereabouts of all religious centers and artifacts. Lieutenant Chang was always amazed at the benefice of the Chairman. During the battle of Chamdo, Chairman Mao urged mercy. All of the surrendering army were given lectures on communism, money and train passage back to Lhasa. Most of the PLA had wanted to kill them on the spot; Chang even saw one Tibetan solider bragging that he had cut off the heads of seven Chinese soldiers with his sword and all he got was a lecture. Chairman Mao had insisted that reeducation would lead to enlightenment.

Perhaps Lieutenant Chang was a bad lecturer. Every day he went from farm to farm and village to village (at least when the snow was not piled too high), yet the Tibetans seemed unable to grasp even the basic principles of dialectic materialism. Most spoke little or no Chinese, and he relied on his interpreter, Tsewang. Tsewang was stoic and stocky. That is to say, Tsewang was Tibetan. He had asked him once: "This county Niyama is 'Sun' County. It is one of the coldest places on Earth, why did you name it 'Sun?' " "Because Tibetans like things they can believe in, not things they actually experience." It was one of the few times in two years that he had heard Tsewang laugh.

Today was a good day. It was only chilly, which meant it was July. The fields were making their usual feeble effort. The dried dung fires had ceased to nauseate him, the rancid yak butter was beginning to taste good in tea. No one had asked him if the coming of electricity meant the prayer wheels could be automated. Today was a good day; news had come to him that North Korean forces had reached Seoul a few days ago. The victory of world communism was assured. In March the People's Republic of Poland had claimed the property of the Roman Catholic Church. It was a great blow against superstition. He was going to meet one of the monks. They would not let him climb the hill to the *gompa*. It was his duty to inventory its contents and draw a blueprint. The monks refused to let him go; Chairman Mao said to act like guests in Tibet. Because of their ignorance Tibetans did not realize that Tibet had been part of China since the Yuan dynasty, and because of their superstition did not understand that all people Tibetan and Chinese owned all things—not Buddha or some mountain spirit. Soon he would have to ask for another solider or two to motor-cycle out from Nagqu City and forcibly inspect the monastery.

The monk came early. Tsewang was still at his farm, so the old man sat smiling on the floor of Chang's headquarters. Chang was running his hand-held generator for his radio. The monk watched as he gave his report to his superior in Nagqu City. If he did not obtain permission today, he was to use force. The monk seemed attentive; Chang wondered for the thousandth time if the monk actually knew Chinese.

When Tsewang came he greeted the monk first before Chang. "I have good news, comrade Chang. He says the devil of the mountain wants to speak with you."

"What is this devil?"

"In Chinese I do not know the word. Much of the higher hills of Tibet used to belong to these devils. Before the coming of the Glorious People's Republic, of course."

"Do you believe in these devils, Tsewang?"

"Comrade Chang, I believe in whatever the Glorious People's Republic tells me to believe. I do not know their opinion of the devils of the hills."

If there was any irony or amusement in Tsewang's tone or eyes, Lieutenant Chang could not detect it.

"Ask him why the devil of the mountain has changed his mind."

There were several rapid back-and-forth exchanges in Tibetan. Tsewang seemed puzzled. The monk shook his head sadly.

"The monk says that the devil has only a few more days. He wants to meet a member of the Glorious People's Republic."

"Ask the monk if I may make photographs and sketch the *gompa*."

"There will be time for that when the devil is gone. In fact they will leave the monastery then. Their mission will have ended."

"Do they worship this devil?"

The monk actually laughed when Chang asked the question, before Tsewang translated.

"No, sir. They are sorry for it."

In the early days of his stay in Niyma County, altitude sickness had been a constant problem; aches, nausea and dizziness tormented Chang day and night. On the climb all of these demons returned. He had learned the monastery had been built about the time of the American Revolution; as he, Tsewang and monk reached the top of the hill any dreams of opulence he might have had vanished. The small gray stone building was a few hundred feet above the snow-line. At best it was eight hundred square meters, with two much smaller outbuildings. It bore no windows, no art adorned its walls, no statues stood before it.

The monk spoke to Tsewang.

"The devil lives in an open cell at the back of the *gompa*. The monks respect its wishes but counsel you not to think about what it says. It is an agent of *maya*. This is a word that means illusion."

Chang had had one thousand theories about the "devil." It was well known that the monks practiced magic tricks to ensnare the populace. Many Chinese political officers had likewise mastered sleight-of-hand to demythologize the monks. In many cases the Tibetans did lose faith when they saw they had been duped, others saw the Communists as merely a new sort of wonder worker replacing the monks, as the monks had largely replaced the Bon shamans. Chang was expecting a fearsome statue that perhaps would breathe fire like great and terrible Oz in the communist classic he had seen in Bejing, *The Wizard of Oz*. The devil would no doubt tell him to leave Tibet and take the other Chinese with him. The monk was laying his line of deniability.

"The devil must rest in the snow and can not come to meet you. They have built a screen so that you will not be frightened to look at it."

Chang decided that they didn't have the resources to even build a devil. Of course to terrify the populace, they need only *tell* them that a *monk* had seen the devil. It would be harder to fool an officer of the PLA.

"The monks say the devil speaks Chinese, that I need not witness your exchange."

"I am sure they say all devils speak Chinese," said Chang, and Tsewang repaid him with a laugh.

They crossed to the Monastery. It consisted of a temple with the inevitable Taras and Buddhas. Around the Temple were the kitchen, a small library, and the monks' cells. At the back the roof of one of the cells had collapsed in an avalanche. Chang could feel the cold as he approached. Tsewang seemed glad not to attend him. Maybe his reeducation had not been as thorough as Chang had hoped. But then, on the other hand, Chang had never told him the official opinion of the Glorious People's Republic on devils.

The door opened to a very dimly-lit cell. There was a wooden screen that held back snow and a single rude chair. Chang sat, looking forward to the performance. The room smelled of rot. On the other side of the barrier was a buzzing sound, perhaps a small engine.

He sat. He had not removed his coat, he had not removed his side arm. He took charge of the situation.

"I am Lieutenant Chang of the People's Liberation Army. I am here to help the Tibetan workers throw off the shackles of superstition and ignorance as our mutual country, the People's Republic of China, leads the way to world socialism!"

The buzzing increased. It was sometime before Lieutenant Change realized that it could be broken down as words. The Chinese was archaic. It sounded like the poetry in his mother's books. Good food and good books were his mother's struggle against the harsh truths of the world. In the end they had not saved her from the Japanese.

"I am glad you came. You are more like me than the monks. I can leave this world happy."

"Are you the devil of the mountain?"

"I am one who serves the Laughing One. This body has been trapped here for many years. The monks found me damaged. It is not their way to let stricken beings die alone, so they packed me in snow and recite *The Book of the Dead* for me. I have outlasted them for hundreds of years."

"I do not know the monks maintain the illusion of the devil."

"Humans are made to maintain illusions. Think of the illusions you maintain. Every day you are urged by radio to map all the Tibetan treasures for the good of the Glorious Republic."

"How do you know about my radio? What does it have to do with illusions?"

Chang was embarrassed. Already the trick was working on him. The "devil" knew because the monks knew.

"The Chinese have made a great show of religious tolerance while locating every monk, every golden idol. When they have the troops fully in place blood will stain the snow."

Chang paused. Ever since Poland had done so, he had wondered why Mao was waiting.

"Why do you smell so bad?"

"This body is a fungus and it does not fare well in the extreme heat of this world. When the monks found me they packed me in snow."

Chang paused again. Shouldn't he be claiming to be devil, a monster, some horror to drive the PLA away? He was claiming to be a mushroom. Lieutenant Change was discussing the world with a mushroom.

"Why did you say 'this' planet?"

"This body sprouted on a planetoid near the great comet storm. We prefer the outsides of systems. Our chemistry is different than yours. Slower by far. We hate the warm greenness of this world, its heavy gravity, its thick poisonous atmosphere."

Chang had read 'Yueqiu Zhimindi Xiaoshuo,' Huang Jiang Diao Sou's story of a lunar colony. His mother had liked science fiction. Lu Xun's translations of Verne and Wells were among her favorites. Maybe one of the monks thought that science fiction tropes would work better on a rational thinker than religious ones. How many myths are retold just keep some humans in control of other humans?

"So why does a mushroom come to China? My mother was a great Cantonese-style cook, I bet she had fifty recipes for mushrooms."

"I like you Chang, you are like the Laughing One. I came to mine. Some of the minerals we need aren't found in the asteriod belt and the great comet cloud. Why did you come to the roof of your world?"

"I came because I am liberating the masses. If you need raw materials, perhaps I can arrange trade between the Glorious People's Republic and the Mushroom Men from outer space."

"We have reasons for not trading directly with men. Men have other uses. You for example will prove useful to me."

Chang thought *here it comes*. But the devil said nothing. Chang was enjoying this game very much. He asked another question: "So, mushroom man, how old are you?"

The devil paused, no doubt trying to come up with a good lie.

"This body sprouted on the Plateau of the Third Hieroglyph about the time that humans entered Asia."

A good lie.

"I have enjoyed this game, Comrade Mushroom Man, but I gave up xiangqi and mah-jong for the sake of the revolution. I am not a peasant to be entertained by such theatritics."

Chang rose to push down the screen. Suddenly the room smelled very foul and felt very cold. Then he seemed to be falling.

The old monk stood over him. In the background he heard a monk chanting a sutra. Tsewang stood by with actual worry on his face.

The monk was speaking to Tsewang. Chang lay on a small mattress on the floor of the temple. A younger monk was handing him tea, bitter and oily.

"He says that the devil does not want you to see him yet. The devil wants you to come back in a week. He says you should not do so. The devil will harm you in some way."

Chang had trouble sitting up.

"The monk says the devil can make the air bad with his magic. The monk says that the devil needs you because you are PLA. He says don't return. He says you feel better shortly."

Chang felt numb. Perhaps the monks have some sort of gas or drug. He would come back with troops. This had ceased to be a game.

"Ask the monk why he does not want me to return."

It was a lengthy conversation. Tsewang was having trouble understanding the monk. Finally he shrugged and said: "You will be made to give off something by the devil. It needs some substance from you. The monk said it will pay you for this, but it is better not to be paid by such creatures."

"Why does the monk know so much?"

"The library contains a book, *The Black Sutra* of U Pao. It had been left here by a traveler that came to see the devil a hundred years ago. It is about the reason humans exist. It is about the conspiracy agaist the human race."

"Tell him I want this book. Tell him I will come again with soliders. I will see the man behind the curtain."

Tsewang spoke and the old monk shook his head. Chang had been expecting fear or anger, but the old man looked very sad.

"He says that the book will not help you. It is written in facing pages of Pali and Sanskrit and it is filled with the lies of the devil."

"Bring me the book. Tell him soliders are coming."

When he had left the mountain and could breathe better, Lieutenant Chang was ashamed of his reaction. He had not acted like a man of reason. He had not acted like a Communist.

The book was useless. It was a nineteenth century reprint, the front matter was in English, but that didn't help. He might as well as send the book to Bejing as an early present—he was sure the prediction of the crackdown was correct if nothing else. He hesitated for two days making his report. He enphasized the monk's gas weapon might be of use to the Glorious People's Republic. Ten soldiers were promised him.

The next five days passed slowly. Tsewang suggested that he simply draw the monastery from memory and say there was only a gilded Buddha, some books and a Russian samovar. It would have been more prudent to do so.

When the soliders came, he repeated Chairman Mao's injunctions about acting like guests. He told them he would go into the *gompa* alone, and they should remain outside for an hour. If he did not emerge, they were to enter and take everything of value. He cautioned that the monks' gas weapon was of great interest.

He left Tsewang behind.

"We will not need translators. The voice in the cold room speaks Chinese."

When his troop gained the summit, gasping for air, they found eight monks waiting outside. Each had a small pack. They bowed to him. The oldest monk approached and said in heavily accented Chinese: "Our mission is over. Take what you want."

The soliders inspected the packs—a few trifles, ivory prayer beads, a pint of brandy, playing cards—were taken. Nothing of real value. He told his men to let them depart.

The Temple was unlit. The ghee lanterns had exhausted their fuel. Fire had not been relit. It was cold.

Chang made his way to the devil's cell. He carried a machine gun.

"Chang, you are so like us. So precise. Thank you for coming. I needed you."

"What do you want?"

"I need for this body to leave this planet. You will help."

"Am I going to be paid for this help?"

"I offer you what you think you want. What do you want, Chang?"

"I want truth."

"Of course. The Laughing One deals in truth as a lure."

"A lure?"

"The Chinese have legends, do they not, of forest creatures that tell wizards things for a great price?"

"Those are tales of peasants."

"Are you not a peasant, Comrade Chang? Oh, no, you are a worker. I have trouble with your terminology. You have questions. I have answers. Then you will pay."

"I will pay you nothing. I have the building surrounded."

"Good for you. Ask your questions."

"Do you know the future?"

"I can analyze data."

"Will world communism triumph?"

"World communism will fail. It does not move resources efficently enough. In fifty or sixty of years your country will be the planet's fiercest capitalists."

"Is Chairman Mao a god?"

"Yes. Or he is the mouthpiece of a god. Do you really want to know?"

"I have risked my life not to believe in gods. I want to know."

"When I am gone. I will make you the same offer I made U Pao when I visted Burma. Eat some of my flesh. It will de-hypnotize you."

"How do I know you are not lying?"

"You already know, or you would have trained your machine gun on me."

"What do you mean, I will pay? What do I have—a fcw yuan, a copy of the *Communist Manifesto?*"

"After a great war humans were made as milk cattle. They secrete things that other, more important beings, find useful. They do not understand their secretions because their senses are limited in certain ways. Some of these they call fear, shock, worship. My race serves a similar purpose. Different beings use us or you."

Chang hated the voice behind the screen. He threw the screen down.

Half buried in the snow was crab about four meters tall. Each of his twelve arms terminated in a pincer. His carapace was covered with grey fuzz like the mold on old rice. The head, or at least where the head should be, was a mass of pink entrails heaped in a rough pyramid shape. These twitched. A few eyestalks protruded from the entrail mass. The entrails began to twitch very violently; the buzzing grew very loud.

"Your shock is most helpful. The slow compassion of the monks helped for a long time, but this has finished my healing."

The creature righted itself. Two large chitinous wings opened.

"The body is leaving now."

The wings were clumsy. As the creature took flight, the soldiers outside the monastery took aim. They tore a few holes in the wings, and their bullets shot through the fungalflesh, but the creature continued skyward.

Chang and the soliders agreed there was nothing to report.

A few days later Chang returned to the snow-filled room. The creature had shed some its flesh. He gathered up the flesh carefully.

Chang protested when the crackdown of 1959 came. But he did not protest too loudly. He kept the book and the flesh and remained a good officer. He watched the posters of Chairman Mao grow every year. He heard the songs, took part in the parades, and spoke less and less. His postion in the PLA was secure.

By the time of the Cultural Revolution he was reasonably secure. He was old enough for the Young Guard to spit on, but not important enough to be sent to a reeducation camp. All of the men who had served with him vanished in the night one-by-one. One night he gave up on his fantasy of having the book translated and burnt it. Many times he thought of throwing the flesh away. He ate some one night and watched Chairman Mao on the television that his apartment block in Shanghai owned. The Chairman seemed to go out of focus and a mixture of robotic mouths and slime took his place, but this was fleeting. Perhaps he had only hallucinated.

In 1972 everything everybody knew changed. President Nixon of the United States had come to the People's Republic of China.

Major Chang was allowed to be a bodyguard at the Shanghai Summit. The old enemies the PRC and the US were to agree that neither would establish hegemony over the Pacific. Most party hacks said that the US was afraid of Chairman Mao. After the Cultural Revolution there were few critics of Chairman Mao, but they whispered that he was afraid of Nixon. Major Chang said nothing. On the last day, when the two leaders would share the stage, he ate nothing but the remaining flesh of the mountain devil. It was bitter and dry, like some of the mushrooms his mother had cooked. It did not make him dizzy or numb or nauseous.

He stood in front of the stage as part of an honor guard. Mao had wanted old timers for this event. It was the second time Major Chang had made the news in his fifty two years; he had been one of the smiling young communist soldiers helping captured Tibetans on the train back to Lhasa on the Pathé newreel. Chang was fairly sure the devil flesh had had no effect, but turned once to look at Mao and Nixon.

It is a credit to his bravery that he did not cry out. He merely turned away. In his apartment later he made some sketches of what the creatures that really rule men look like. The drawings were found after his suicide, found to be anti-revolutionary and burned.

(for Philip K. Dick in memoriam)

Pumpkins

PHILLIP BLASSINGAME WAS my customer for many months before he became my tenant. He was a good customer. He was a good tenant. I think he was a good man, perhaps with just too active an imagination. I don't think he meant for it to happen. No, I don't think that at all.

I may have been the real world friend that knew him best. I know he had online friends that were very serious mathematicians with lots of letters after their name, and he had lots of FaceBook occultist friends with names like "Thee Demon Azathoth." The press made a big noise about the latter and most of them seemed to vanish like cockroaches encountering the light. The former was a bit too obscure for them to think about. Of course, I got mentioned in two articles in the *Austin American Statesman* and Libby's Books got mentioned once. Of course, that was at the first part, at the second part; the more plainly horrific part he wasn't mentioned, but that was my fault not his.

Libby's Books was in the wrong section of town for a bookstore. It was at the end of a strip mall in the St. John's neighborhood, which is the likeliest place to meet a crackhead. It had been a bookstore for 35 years. The neighborhood around had rotted. I lived in that neighborhood, on a semi-undecayed block. I had moved into my Mom's house the year of my divorce to take care of her. She had died three years later. I didn't feel much like being a technical writer then, and one day buying vintage SciFi at Libby's I asked if he needed an assistant. Nowadays Libby is in a home and the shop is just me. The rent is low and Libby's secret porn room has enough older male customers to keep the lights turned on. The general room has its regulars—romance, westerns, SF, and the like. About half my customers are white. It is a premier store for "Blerds"—their term, black nerds. There were three main customers—Malcom Briscoe, Abdullah Loggins, LeRoy Green. LeRoy later got a lovely glasses-wearing young woman LaTonia Washington. I met Phillip there. He was in his mid-twenties unlike the teenage blerds, but he was pointing out

Samuel Delany's shorter novels to the blerd tribe. When he came to the counter I complimented his taste. He was carrying a stack of mathematic magazines—Libby would buy anything—but technical journals on higher maths aren't a big seller. I think they had lain there for seven years. He also had a rather shady occult book the *Codex Catamaco*, a "Mayan grimoire" that had been briefly popular in 2012. He looked a little embarrassed, I assume by the occult book. Hell, I sell stained copes of *Nuns in Bondage*—who am I to judge.

He became a regular after that. He bought all of the math from the story, all the weird fantasy Lovecraft, Smith, Klein—even crap like *Lucifer's Aces*. He was a student going for a PhD in "hyperbolic geometry"—go ahead Google it, I did. He drove a shitty car, dressed from Goodwill, and had taped glasses. One day he said he was about to be thrown out from his apartment near campus. I told him I had a room over my garage that I rent cheaply. It was a done deal. He would pony up seventy-five in cash every week and it was just between us.

I liked the pin money and I liked having someone nearby. My friends had largely left the city over the last decade after the tech bubble burst. Phillip tolerated my stinky old tomcat. He came over for chili on Saturday nights and we watched *Dr. Who*. Naturally we talked about time, space and other dimensions. He was a believer; well I guess that's the wrong word, he had a good scientist understanding of M-theory and some unusual notions of access to other dimensions.

"There's more around us than we can see, but perhaps some of it we can interact with. Maybe that the mechanism of synchronicity. Maybe that causes 'serialism.' The phenomena of an unlikely event repeating itself again in a single life."

I like this sort of speculation. It made my ex-wife crazy. So I say: "I've always thought that higher dimension stuff was mental. If I can conceive of a four dimensional solid, I must have a five-dimensional mind."

Phillip looked at me like I was simple-minded and we stopped that line of discussion. He had moved in March and the week before Halloween he confessed his dark secret. I don't drink except in October; I'm crazy for pumpkin beer. So I'd bought a six pack of pumpkin ale, and Phillip knowing my weakness for pumpkin beer bought a six pack of pumpkin beer—and after *Dr. Who and The Navy versus the Night Monsters*, I realized he had

had ten beers. His story was very boozy, but I think I got most of it.

His mom had been in some cult in Los Angeles in the '80s. When he was a kid they either had more money than they could jump over or be literally living out of their car. The cult wanted something from her, some sacrifice, possibly Phillip. She did a ritual and called up the cult's god—"a polychromatic hypersphere" and offered herself in exchange. Phillip saw a mass of glowing globes surround her, and pull her off screaming into another dimension (or as he tried to explain to me—unobservable parts of this dimension). But he knew It would find him some day—tracking on the spirals of his DNA. He broke into drunken tears a couple of time why he was explaining the science of this. He likened human flesh to old style punch cards (for the IBMs I grew up with). He said these multidimensional beings were like vast computers that needed living beings for input. I couldn't follow his explanation, but he was sure it was based on the structure of DNA. He had come up with a comic book solution. He would contact the hypersphere and make a deal with it. Sorcerers had done so aeons ago, and if he could visualize the right model of the creature / god / hypercomputer / Old One he could talk to it.

I let him sleep on the old convertible sofa in the living room. Of course, I didn't believe in monsters from dimension X, but I could believe that the right cultic environment aided by LSD, PCP—and the stress of economic woes in Hollyweird—would let a little boy see his mom's death as an extraterrestrial fantasy. When he woke up, he was embarrassed. He told me a hundred times that he had just been drunk. That he was sharing a plot for a science fiction story. He was a terrible liar, but I could tell it was important to him that I believed it. So, I never mentioned it again.

Sometimes very late at night, four, four-thirty I could hear chants, see strange lights from his room. Well, he didn't seem to be building fires.

Months went by. Christmas brought a little more business to the ship and about Valentine's Phillip showed up grinning from ear-to-ear.

"I just had a long chat with Aunt Jane. I am adopted! Mom had been briefly married in LA and they had adopted me, then dad ran off. I have no DNA ties to her."

The chanting stopped. The weird strobe lights at predawn stopped. He dressed better. He dated. He was elected to some office in the graduate students' association.

Then came April. He sold most of his occult books to the store as well as a ton of the weird fantasy stuff. I even ran an ad in Craigslist for a couple of days, and got some real odd folk to drop by and drop cash. It was a beautiful Austin spring. Bluebonnets filled the roadways, little rainstorms at night. Phillip won a prize at the University of Texas Math department for "groundbreaking work in four-dimensional topology, synthetic geometry and gauge theory, and for his remarkable use of ideas from physics to advance pure mathematics." Which means Phillip really was much, much smarter than me.

On the 30th a hell of a thunderstorm came. I usually kept the shop open to six, nine of Thursdays—but listening to the storm-tracker, I decided to close by four. No sane person would risk hail and / or tornado to buy old paperbacks. Even the pervert crowd has limits. I walked home. It was windy as hell and began to rain just as I turned onto my block. The drops fell fat and cold and with speed. I saw the lights were on at Phillips'. I went up the shaky steps and pounded on his door.

"Are you OK?" I asked.

"Sure," he said. "It's just a storm. UT closed at noon though, the officials are worried about flood."

"You want to come down for chow?"

He thought about it.

"Nah. I've got a little pot of soup going. And thirty pages of a paper due."

"If there's a tornado, you should come down; we'll sit in the bathroom and play chess. There's no windows there."

"Thanks. You guys take weather more seriously than we do."

I ran downstairs—both soaked and cold, I turned the TV on the Weather Station and lost myself in a Robert Silverberg paperback from the '70s. The rain really picked up and the gales shook the stucco covered walls of my little house. The lights flickered, and the storm cell filled up most of the radar screen. I thought about ordering a pizza then decided that would be too tough on the delivery guy. The wind didn't seem to be letting up. A small tornado was spotted in Doublesign about forty miles south of me. Small hail started to fall. Few cars were on the street. A few blocks away on Cameron I heard an ambulance and a fire truck. I made a sandwich of turkey pastrami and American cheese and read some more. The storm began dying down about eight. By ten it was done, the clouds parted and a very slivery full moon made the rain glazed world sparkle. I watched the local news; they said another cell was due after three. It would be the "bad one." I unlocked my backdoor in case Phillip needed shelter. I cracked the windows slightly, crawled under my burnt orange comforter and went to sleep.

The dream was peculiarly vivid.

I was walking in the park next to my childhood home. Sam Houston parks had a football field in the middle, swings on one side and was ringed with Chinese elms. It was a pretty spring day, there were some kids on the swings, opposite my side of the park. The park sloped gently; I was entering from the south east corner. At the northwest base was a small outdoor theater. I saw a clown selling balloons. Everything was exaggerated as it often is in a dream. He had a huge mass of balloons of every color. His harlequin costume had diamonds of every shade. He was tall and thin and looked like Ronald MacDonald or maybe Pennywise from Stephen King's *It.* I knew it was a dream and upbraided myself for such a schlocky image. I walked across the football field and approached the clown. He smiled with his bright red mouth. I could hear calliope music from somewhere, annoying flute like whistles. Knowing this as a dream I walked up to him.

"Hello Donald," he said.

I've always hated *Donald.* I'm Don, just Don.

"Do you want to buy a balloon?"

"Yes, I want all of your balloons."

"Well, my balloons might want you. You can hold them for now."

He handed me all of the balloons. All of their strings had been woven into a rope. As I took them the rope became a semi-transparent sticky cord. It wrapped around my little fist like five times, and then the balloons began to tug me upward. I tried to let go. I grabbed at the rope with other hand and my other hand was stuck by the cord as well. I kicked and tried to force myself down. I was rising swiftly. I was already thirty feet in the air. I was screaming for my dad. The suspension hurt my arms; I felt they were tearing out at the socket. Some people say you can't feel pain in dreams. Some people are wrong. The kids at the swings had run over to watch. The clown was petting a little girl's black hair while looking up at me laughing. The balloons were rising faster now. I was a hundred, maybe two hundred feet in the air. I saw where they were taking me. A massive cloud of spheres rolling against each other. Pulsing, living, vast. Perhaps a mile across. Between the spheres was thick red oil. Some it was falling on my face and exposed arms. It burned like dry ice burns. I had stopped remembering this was a dream. I could remember something on the radio about a UFO. I screamed and screamed.

And woke myself up. The wind was pounding my house and the rain / sleet mix was overpowering loud. I looked at my alarm. Four thirty. I got up and lightening flashed followed by a deafening roar. The bolt must have been in my yard. I was deafened and also confused because when my eyesight came back to me the power had gone off. My old tomcat Shem was howling at the top of his lungs. There was a rumbling outside. Tornado? I couldn't find my smartphone in the dark. I keep a candle in my nightstand with a box of matches I've had to use exactly twice in 20 years, but it was where Mom had kept it. It was one of her rules, like always have a can of soup in your house in case you get sick and don't want to go shopping. I lit the candle. Lighting flashed again four times in a row. One of the blasts seemed to be green, the last one purple. I ran to my backdoor. There was light in Phillip's apartment. How could that be? My lights were out. It was a weird multicolored light. Then I could hear his screams—the storm noises were louder. I paused to pull on pants and ran out into the night. I nearly fell twice as I went up the rain-soaked stairs. At the top, the door was locked. I pounded. I couldn't hear Phillip anymore, just a loud white noise hiss as if all the transistor radios in the world had decided to howl at once. I fumbled the keys out of my pants pocket and put them in the lock.

I hate to admit this, but I hesitated at that moment. The nightmare still clung to me like a wet T-shirt and the beery confession of six months ago seemed very plausible. Then I regained myself. This was my home, my land and had been my mother's home. I threw open the door.

Half the room was filled with glowing spheres rolling against each other over Phillips twin bed. I couldn't see him. Their hiss filled my ears and my mind. They were shrinking. Lightning struck the mass—or shot out from the mass through the roof. This knocked me down the stairs. It took a few minutes to get back on my feet and back into the apartment. There was a jagged hole through the roof, the mattress of the bed had caught fire and the fire had been extinguished by the rain. The room stank like burned hair, cat litter and bus exhaust. I could barely hear anything, but over the ringing in my ears I made out the sound of a fire truck. Suddenly there were strange lights in my front yard. Red and blue.

It was the fire truck a neighbor had called. The firemen were rushing my down the stairs. I couldn't understand them, but I made them understand that I was the landlord looking for my renter. They had huge flashlights and searched Phillip's flat. They found nothing, but there were strange burnt organic masses on the bed. He could've been vaporized. Over my protests they took me to the hospital. I tried calling Phillip and left a message. It turned out his phone was sitting on the dresser and quite unharmed.

It was a great story for the paper. Local Man Vaporized by Lightning. I threw away the stinking mattress and my insurance paid for fixing the roof. Otherwise there was strikingly little damage. I got a nasty letter from the city about renting without a permit, but in light of the disaster they declined to press charges. I was interviewed by the local paper. And it was forgotten.

I had real problems sleeping after that. My doctor tried three levels of sleeping pills—it pretty much took industrial strength. To my surprise I had no nightmares—at least nothing beyond the going-to-school naked sort of thing. After the roof was fixed I kept the apartment locked up. My neighbors were nice; they brought me a few casseroles and even walked over to my shop and forced themselves to buy something.

In the summer Libby died and left the store to me. I figured his son would protest the move, but he lived in Florida and didn't care. He didn't even go to the funeral. Over the next few months I visited Phillip's Facebook page and sent messages to all 111 of his friends that he had died of lightning and gave a link to the article in the *Austin American-Statesman* article. Some of his occultist friends made dire remarks about his passing on Walpurgisnacht. Some of his math friends thanked me. Once nice girl even said she was sorry for my loss, I called UT of course. I was hoping to track down his Aunt Jane. After all he had left behind a computer, a dresser full of poor grad student clothes and some books. I never found her. In August Shem wandered over to Cameron road and spent the ninth of his nine lives. It took me a couple days to find the body. I scraped it off the road and buried it in my back yard.

When October rolled around, I drank my pumpkin beer every night and felt sorry for myself. I was sad because I could tell no one. I had my own theories of course. I think his years of trying to visualize the hypersphere had caught Its attention. It came at a time when the world is open—April 30 and Halloween are the traditional times. I thought about writing to paranormal researcher, but I wouldn't want the questions. I was 60 and for the first time in my life, I began to feel tired. I decided to sell Phillip's books. I had no right to do this of course, but I wanted closure. I gave his clothes and his computer to the Salvation Army.

The blerds bought them all. They wanted to do something in memory of his passing. LaTonia pointed out with all the horror Phillip liked to read—a big Halloween bash might be the best memorial. They could show movies at the Community Center, and decorate the neighborhood. Only after they left the store did I realize they had taken the two spiral notebooks that Phillip kept with his books. I had glanced through them once. They were full of very precise drawings of spheres, cubes, tesseracts, and hyperspheres as well as mathematical formulae—several references to John Milnor's seven dimensional manifolds—I tried Googling that and just felt dumb, although I did learn the term from differential topology "Exotic sphere." Oh well, I thought those kids are a lot smarter than me, maybe they could have meaning there. Maybe they could bring a positive spin on everything.

The kids put out flyers promising a haunted house and a party. They bought all the pumpkins from St. Mark's Methodist Church pumpkin patch. They painted some of them, made strange jack o'lanterns of others. They exhausted the Party Pig's supply of faux spider web and draped it everywhere in the six-block radius. They put up fake tombstones and big statues of "elder gods." They encouraged folks to decorate their yards, and they put up posters with Phillip's pictures everywhere. They even bought candy for low-income households to give out and helped kids get costumes.

They invited everyone in a six-block radius to the event. They pestered me every day until I said I would go. On Halloween night the moon was cantaloupe full and as lovely as the night Phillip was taken away. The party was being held in the community center about three blocks from my home. My street was alive with trick-or-treaters. I walked down to the community center. In twenty years in this neighborhood I had never seen as much Halloween activity. Cars drove slowly down the streets, young couples walked arm-in-arm.

The pumpkins were everywhere. The kids must have bought hundreds of them. But they weren't right somehow. They were oddly spaced. Some in clusters, some singly. Some of them had been died green, red, or purple. They didn't have faces. They had mathematical symbols carved in them—illuminated from within by small white candles. Some of the symbols were complex and looked more like the seals of demons from magic books.

These were the spheres from Phillip's notebooks. The trick-or-treaters, my neighbors and me were inside a model of the hypersphere that had carried Phillip away. Just as I turned to run, the jack o'lanterns began to roll toward me. A couple rose into the air. One flew into me. I could smell the pumpkin guts and the wax from the candle splashed on my face, near my eyes. I could hear screaming. I tried to keep running and then there were more of them. One flew between my legs and spread me open and lifted me off the ground. They all spun and I was being put with small children, and then dogs and cats. And we were all screaming, howling. Lights began flashing over the surface of the pumpkins—white, green, red, purple, and orange. They pressed harder and blood began to act as a lubricant. I could feel they were dragging us upward and away—away from the world of four dimensions and five senses. My nose was broken, and I saw bits of children's mask in the spinning red goo.

We were being made into the hypersphere god. We were being broken up and reassembled. I was coming into contact with Phillip's mind (well parts of it) and his mom and a thousand human (and prehumen) sorcerers that had called to this Old One. My limbs were torn off and my memories and that rather vague thing I had called a soul. The assimilation was painful in ways humans have never known pain. And it

It

It

It took much, much longer to do so than we could have imagined in our worst nightmares.

(for T.E.D. Klein)

The Codex

HISTORICAL NOTE: Robert H. Barlow began corresponding with H. P. Lovecraft at age 13. Lovecraft made several trips to Barlow's home in Florida and collaborated on six stories with him. Upon Lovecraft's death in 1937, the 19-year-old Barlow was named Lovecraft's literary executor. Barlow turned from weird fiction to anthropology and became an expert in Mexican folklore and the Mayan codices. His zeal at tracking down obscure codices as well as working with living informants is still talked about. He became Chairman of the Anthropology Department at Mexico City College. One of his last students was William S. Burroughs, whose studies of the Mayan codices influenced his avant-garde writing. Barlow killed himself with sleeping pills on January 1, 1951. Burroughs shot his common law wife nine months later on September 1, 1951. He later claimed he was led to this act by an entity he called the Ugly Spirit.

"MR. BURROUGHS DISAGREES with some of the current thought on the codices," said Professor Barlow. A couple of students sniggered. Burroughs was older, suspected of being a drug user and a homosexual, and had weird theories about addiction and control. Others were impressed with his cool mineral calm, Midwestern voice and Ivy League vocabulary.

A poster board Christmas tree from Barlow's far-off youth in Florida hung in the room marking the season. Its green had faded; its lights and ornaments had grown dim.

"I make them for books of the dead," said Burroughs.

"But they deal with the extreme past, not some future state," objected Miss Jimenez.

"Exactly," said Burroughs. "If reincarnation is a fact, you want to orient yourself toward the future. You do that by looking backward to before death. Not just your last death, but a time before death. Before the ball games and the biological courts. That's why the codices stretch back four hundred million years."

"But that amount of time can't have any meaning," said Bill Peabody.

"Why does time have to be 'meaningful'?" asked Guy Smith. "Does 'In the beginning' have any meaning?"

Professor Barlow smiled. "Now you're beginning to think mythically. You have to drop your Western thinking if you want the Mayan world to open to you."

Smith, Burroughs and Carsons smiled. The rest of the class looked angry. Maybe angry at having Western rationality spurned, but some were angry that the professor favored the queers. Well, there was a rumor at least.

A bell rang and students ran from class.

"Feliz Navidad!" yelled Barlow. "Remember to get your reading done over the holidays!"

Carsons, Smith and Burroughs remained. Barlow looked at them quizzically. He avoided the gay ex-pat community. It would be professional death. But he liked Burroughs. Burroughs was a writer, unpublished of course, but he had the kind of mind that can focus on anything without flinching. When details about Mayan or Aztec religion came up that made the other students shudder, Burroughs merely looked thoughtful. He couldn't help but think about Burroughs ideas of pre-death as reflecting the sort of thing that Lovecraft had written about. All of the stuff he had believed in when he was 13 and wrote Howard for the first time. Of course real anthropology wasn't based on subjectivity. He had thought of sharing his prize, Lovecraft's handwritten MSS of *The Shadow Out of Time* with Burroughs, but the sexuality question bothered him. It had been so painful when he had confessed to Lovecraft during the last visit. And there had been—well—mistakes with students.

Audrey Carsons asked him: "Dr. Barlow, you seem to hint at things sometimes. We're interested in the real secrets."

"There are no secrets Mr. Carsons, only speculations."

Burroughs said: "My Uncle Ivy made millions on speculations. Speculations just mean you got there first. Poison Ivy they called him."

"Speculations are more guarded for a scholar than a Wall Street type, I'm afraid. What speculations are interested in?"

"We want to know about Death. Ah Pook and Zushakon. We want to know about Ix Tab or Yig Tab, the serpent goddess in charge of snares—catching a soul in her coils for its next reincarnation."

"Those names don't appear in the official codices," began Barlow.

"We're not interested in the well-thought of translations," said Guy Smith. "We're interested in the ones that Work."

"You're talking about magic," said Barlow. His other vice, one that Lovecraft thought terrible. A vice that had to hidden from the scholarly world.

"Yes, that could be a word for the technology we're looking for," said Burroughs.

"I won't discuss anything like that on campus. Maybe you could drop by my apartment over break. There is another Codex, one that has a problematic history that talks about the ideas you are interested in. Of course I'd have to swear you to secrecy."

"Of course," said Burroughs. "I wouldn't have it any other way."

He regretted inviting them. Barlow felt it was a set up. But who's conning who? Two years ago he happened across a small bookshop in Tlatilōlco, frankly a weird neighborhood for a bookshop. It was stuck between a barber's shop and a taquería—it had books overflowing its overstuffed shelves. Mainly modern novels in English, French and Spanish—random volumes from encyclopedias, books brought into the city by tourists, cheap occult books on palmistry and the lore of the tarot—in short, junk. Barlow had been about to leave when the shop keeper, a well-dressed woman in her thirties, asked if he needed help finding anything. Her English had almost no accent; her skin tone was very light.

"No. I don't think you would have what I am interested in."

"Señor, we do have what you are interested in, that I know. My uncle's shop is a trifle unorganized."

At that moment he spotted a fading copy of the June 1936 copy of *Astounding Stories* with Lovecraft's 'The Shadow Out of Time' providing the (inaccurate) cover illustration. The Great Race of Yith (as faded as his Christmas tree) menaced a well-dressed white man. Barlow broke into a big smile and picked up the magazine, which lay atop a stack of books. Beneath it was the Codex Catamaco. The word "Codex" was a magnet to his iron. He snatched the thin light brown leather covered book up. The front matter had been torn away. It looked as if the book originally had about a hundred pages. The paper quality was poor, rough and brown. It had probably been printed during the war. The last seventy pages were a Mayan codex with *interlinear English translation*. Like most scholars, Barlow assumed that the language would someday be deciphered, but certainly nothing like this level of translation existed! The book's back matter was mainly in place —including an index which included topics that were well known to any Mayaologist—and others of a more tantalizing nature such as Charles Hinton, the mathematician that had done significant work on the Fourth Dimension. Of course, all such rogue references were conveniently pointing to the missing pages in the front. But if the volume were a hoax or a joke, it had been an expensive one—buying the type for the Mayan ideographs would have cost a pretty penny. Trying not to look overly excited he asked the book's price. The young woman looked over its condition, and told him to simply take it—her store didn't sell damaged goods. He picked up a copy of Norman Mailer's 1948 bestseller *The Naked and the Dead*, no doubt brought in as summer reading by a tourist, and paid a few pesos for it. It seemed wrong not leave something.

Barlow had almost run home with the book. He came back the next day. He had expected the shop to vanish, or the "uncle" to be some seedy character from a Lovecraft story. Instead Sr. Gonzales was a stout middle aged businessman fond of Mark Twain with no idea whom he had bought the codex from. He tried to get Barlow to buy some books on palmistry. The shop lasted another year and either closed or moved. Nothing of interest ever showed on its shelves.

The remaining book was in four parts. The first was the tale of the arrival of the death god Ah Pook on Earth via comet 400,000,000 years ago. He fell in the northern polar regions where he fought two other death gods Kisin and Zushakon. The three divided deaths on this world. Ah Pook taught humans how to die in order to be reborn with their memories, more-or-less intact. They had to carefully not remember their deaths, or they would die again. Zushakon, a centipede god that lived in a lightless world, collected criminals—evil beings that were sacrificed to him in a grisly manner—whose souls he would use as a sort of garment. The text gave dubious translation of Zushakon as the "Ugly Spirit." Kisin was less picky. He / It simple fed on death and rot of all sorts. The three gods fought for over a million years, calling on the aid of other beings from exploded stars.

The second part dealt with the creation of humans and other races—the Insect People, the Vegetable People, the Fungus People, the Hairy People and finally humans by the Death Gods as sources of food or "vessels" for their servants / allies. Each of these groups was given various worlds or planes of existence, but they could trade certain gems, drugs, and metals with each other—if they paid a high tax to the Death gods. Barlow had never read any mythological speculation of this sort—frankly the "gods" were being treated more as a sort of space alien. It certainly reminded him more of Lovecraft's fiction than true mythology. Humans should love or fear their gods, but not be nihilistic or sarcastic towards them. He read with a start that the Fungi People had been given an extra cold planet to live on. This was too close to Lovecraft. Why had that copy of *Astounding* been lying conveniently atop the pile of books? But that wouldn't have meaning for anyone other than him in Mexico City. The effort to place it in a bookstore in a neighborhood that he had visited perhaps twice, and hope that he would spot the magazine AND pick up the doctored book beneath required millions-to-one odds.

The third part of the book was similar to *The Tibetan Book of the Dead.* It explained death as a long journey began at the invitation of one of the Death Gods. It was a hazardous journey, where every mistake you had made in your life counted against you. The three gods were going to try and trick you, but if you slipped last them you were out of "time" and in eternity. Ix Tab, goddesses of snares and hanging, tried to trick you by inverting future and past. You might be cagey enough to avoid two fornicating peasants thinking that was the road to be born as a peasant, but you could touch a rotting dog body and be sucked into the corpse to live the dog's life in reverse. On one of the glyphs "Ix" was translated "Yig." Now that had to either be a hoax or the biggest coincidence ever, because Lovecraft had made up that name as a god for one of his clients.

The fourth part of the book was about control, both magical and political. The Mayans used (and still use) a slash-and-burn system of agriculture. If you wait too long to burn the shoots, rains will make them too damp to burn. If you plant too early drought can ruin your crops—if you plant too late the big downfall could wash away your seeds. A few days either way and a year's crop is lost. So the priests are given great control calendars—this way they will seem to be gods. The priests are instructed to have a continuous circle of festivals so that the population never learns how to read the signs of the year—thus they need the priests—probably why there is no number higher than twenty in spoken Maya today. After this realpolitik, came a time travel spell that enabled the priests to go back in time and make contact with the Death Gods.

Barlow was ashamed of it, but he wanted to try. He had had two questions for Lovecraft. One was about the real source of the *Necronomicon.* The other had been about boys—about sex with boys. Both answers had been disappointing.

Now Burroughs and his friends had mentioned Zushakon, a name not attested in the three "official" codices. Likewise (and more suspiciously) "Yig". He knew Burroughs was said to be an heir to the Burroughs adding machine company. He might have resources that could produce the book—but how could he have got it to Mexico in 1948?

Burroughs was a weird cat. He claimed to know another writer Jack Kerouac, whose *The Town and the City* came out last year. Burroughs even said one of the characters in the book was based on him (Will Dennison). He had a wife, Joan—another book character for Kerouac Mary Dennison—who was strung out on speed to contrast Burroughs fondness of opium products. Mexico was good for Americans with a monkey, even one of Barlow's fellow teachers kept powdered codeine and sugar in a box of bicarbonate of soda and would stir spoonfuls of it to his tea at staff meetings. A "wife" was good cover in homophobic Mexico City.

Barlow hadn't been to find out anything about Guy Smith or Audrey Carsons. They were young beautiful wild boys—they had Midwestern accents as well. All three seemed to be remittance men. Barlow had decided that they would spill the beans on the codex caper.

His apartment was huge. He had two setting rooms, kitchen, full bath and a large bedroom. He showed Burroughs and the boys into the inner sitting room, which served as library. They were book people all right. Burroughs picked up and glanced at several anthropological texts as well as his collection of William Hope Hodgson and Arthur Machen. Barlow offered them Mexican hot chocolate and sweet tortillas. Small talk was talked largely until twilight fell. The boys had come at teatime.

"So Professor, what can you tell us about Zushakon?" asked Guy Smith.

"He was a centipede god living in a dark realm beneath the earth—probably somewhere in the United States," he added with a smile.

"America is an old and evil land," said Burroughs. "There was serious shit there before the Indians came."

Barlow continued. "When the priests convicted someone of a serious crime, they said the Ugly Spirit had chosen him. They didn't want to piss off the Ugly Spirit—so they treated the criminal real courteously—until his execution. Then they would heat a copper centipede shell long as the miscreant was tall. As they heated the shell, they skinned the criminal alive and then forced him into the shell now glowing cherry red. As he died great bells were rung that had a special property—probably due to infrasound—that made the room suddenly become black. When the anomalous darkness vanished, it was always found that the victim's body was gone from the shell."

At this point loud knocking came from Barlow's outer door. He rose, and after closing the door to his library, answered the door.

Burroughs and the two boys could hear much of what went on.

On the other side a drunken American male voice—high with anger kept denouncing Barlow for "having made him this way" and saying he would "tell the dean" and be sure Barlow was "ridden out of town on a rail."

The ranting became repetitive, so Burroughs began telling his friends about Bishop Landau, who had burned all of the Mayan codices to kill their civilization. Burroughs said four codices escaped the fire. The whereabouts of three of them are known: Paris, Dresden, Madrid. The angry voice became more incoherent and Audrey Carsons said perhaps they should intervene. Burroughs said no. It sounded like a lovers' spat.

The front door slammed. There were five minutes of pure silence, then Barlow appeared at the door. His face was white as the chalk he taught with.

He walked in and slumped down in a large rattan chair.

"It is all over," he announced.

Burroughs and the boys looked at him.

Barlow said: "As an old teacher of mine used to say. The Unnamable."

"The boy may change his mind," said Burroughs. "He's just seeing what he is—and wants that monstrosity to reflect on you."

Audrey Carsons asked: "What will you do now?"

Barlow said: "I used to be a publisher and writer. I'm going to do that again. And I think I'll try my hand at magic."

Burroughs and the boys stared. The wild boys had a hungry look, Burroughs had his mineral calm.

"The rite involves time travel. I think we should do it on New Year's, magic should always follow the path of least resistance," said Barlow.

"What do you mean?" asked Guy Smith.

"New Year's is a hole in time. It is a weak point between the year that was and the year that will become," said Barlow.

Burroughs said: "This year was when the future started. L. Ron Hubbard gave us *Dianetics*, so we will be able to fight Control, and Dr. von Braun said that humans are going to the Moon. Time became looser this year; maybe we can gain technology to make it looser still."

Burroughs and the boys left with Burroughs doing a routine about German pornography.

The festivities were well under way when the three returned to Barlow's apartment. Burroughs eyes were wet with a recent fix, the boys hungrily munching on chocolate having smoked some tea earlier. Barlow looked like hell. Normally thin, now he was gaunt and pale. It looked as if he had not seen the light of day since they had been with him three weeks ago. He showed them into the library. The books were gone and huge sheets of white butcher paper hung on the walls covered in Mayan ideographs. Burroughs recognized some of them as god names: Ah Pook, Kisin, Zushakon, Ix Tab, Ix Chel. The guys were giggling and pawing each other. Burroughs motioned them to be quiet.

"All true magic begins in silence. Sound is about being controlled by another, silence is about controlling yourself."

Barlow smiled wanly and motioned them to the four chairs sat in a row. He went to his bedroom and returned with a clay pot filled with a smelly tar-like liquid. He signaled silence. With a small paintbrush he painted a crescent moon on the floor around Burroughs and the buys, and then a trapezoid around his chair. He offered them a pipe.

"I found the recipe in the *Codex Catamaco*. It is a time travel drug. It contains Diviner's Sage and hallucinogenic mushrooms. Traditionally Mexicans eat twelve grapes at the strokes of midnight to being good luck for the next year. We are going to use the church bells as way to leave time."

Burroughs lit the pipe and took a long drag. He gave it to the boys, and then to Barlow. Barlow turned off the light and went to his chair. The room was very dark lacking any outside windows. A small amount of yellow light slipped in under the door to the first sitting-room. Mariachi music blared up from three floors below. Fireworks were popping and yells of ¡Feliz año nuevo!" gave proof of the festive night. The smoke was nasty and disorientating. Red, yellow and purple lights appeared as mini-comets in the room. Barlow began ringing small bells and chanting something in Mayan.

Everyone felt dizzy, sick, and crazy. Sounds hurt, the lights burned their flesh. Then a few blocks away a mighty cathedral bell rang. The colored lights vanished. A man was standing in the room in front of Barlow, his shadow limed by the faint light.

Barlow spoke. "Howard. I gave your papers to Brown. Augie is publishing you and Robert and Smith and Long. I . . ."

Another deep bell sounded and the shadow vanished. The light seemed to pour back out of the room, the darkness became thicker, a dull dry vibration. Then everything came into focus, the four men were sitting on two pieces of worn yellow linoleum. Three in a crescent moon, Barlow in his trapezoid. In front of them was a jungle scene of 400,000,000 years ago. The lush vegetation of the Devonian Age was populated by many crawling arthropods, but no birds flew. A few small four-legged creatures—looking more like fish than reptiles crawled in the underbrush. About a hundred yards away, a mass of twisted burnt metal the three or four times the size of the *Hindenberg* was the center of a small village. Barlow rose and began walking toward it. The three other men tried to rise up but found themselves paralyzed.

"I'm sorry gentlemen, but I could not trust you. You came into my life knowing too much, knowing Names that you shouldn't know. I don't know if you are pawns of some fate that is moving me, or the magicians making it happen. You are invited here as witnesses only."

Burroughs tried as hard he could to move. He realized that this was a mental construct; they weren't "really" sitting in chairs behind a smear of some magical tar—that was how their minds had reacted to the drugs and the incarnation. As Barlow walked forward their perspective changed. They seemed to drift after him always about ten feet behind. They heard the buzzing of the jungle, but occasionally sounds of New Year's Eve seemed to issue from the trees.

Near the village was a cultivated area. Dark green vines ran everywhere. They looked like the gourd vines Barlow knew from Florida except that they grew dark green people. The vegetable people moved feebly. A group of red skinned dwarves scurried around them extracting a thick blue fluid from their veins. Closer to the village were insect people. Human-looking with the heads of praying mantises and insect pinchers instead of hands. These creatures lived in huts that looked like spun silk, possibly somehow extruded from their bodies. They were engaged in worship, their high whining insect voices forming words very similar to the chant Barlow had uttered to get here. Barlow advanced to the ruined spacecraft. He put his hands on its metal surface and pictures began to form in their minds. The ship had escaped a nova taking with it criminal creatures that were almost indescribable. These felons ate addictions—addictions to sex, to magic, to death, to hatred. These were a form of a nearly immortal parasite that humans called "gods"—but they had not yet put on human forms. No nice smiling Zeus, no Jesus on the sticks, no Thor throwing a hammer. These creatures were ugly. They were making vessels to be born in—the insect people, the vegetable people, the fungal fliers, even mewling weak humans.

Something stirred inside of the spacecraft. It beckoned Barlow inside. Inside was dark, cold outer space dark, the dark It needed because of the fear and pain that had been associated with the nova light. In the darkness a mass of centipedes crawled ceaselessly upon a shapeless god. The god talked to Barlow inside his own mind. "I NO DIE. YOU NO DIE. I TAKE YOU HERE BEFORE I GIVE DEATH TO YOUR RACE. You serve me in the future. There you die maybe a million times. I sleep while you die making your world hotter. Eventually you will make your sun go nova, then we move on. I ask nothing for my gift except a few million deaths, and the burnt remains of your world. WHEN NOVA COMES I LEAVE."

Barlow felt sick with the touch of the other mind. This was too alien. No wonder man had invented the god-idea not to see the criminals. He didn't want this bargain, but he realized he had accepted it long ago on Earth. He had been a Mayan priest writing the forbidden codex. He would be this again writing the words that this creature needed to control its human dogs, its vessels. He turned to go, but something exploded from the centipede mass. Black thick liquid with a nitrous smell. It smelled like jism in the back of a YMCA, like furtive nasty sex. The black stuff fell over him, each spot becoming an eye—sometimes human, sometimes faceted insect eyes, sometimes like an octopus. Deep red erogenous sores appeared around each eye filling him with ugly desires, lusts that had nothing to do with the sane life of earth. The fetor was overpowering. Some of the eyes began to weep a gooey stinking yellow matter.

"YOU DIE MAYBE A MILLION TIMES THAT IS WHY WE MADE YOU. DEATH MADE YOU."

Barlow turned to go, looking very inhuman as the eyes grew and blinked and wept. He could feel egg-like masses forming in his groin. This was what evil meant—a totally alien impulse toward living as something foul and eternal. This creature, this

Death and Control god had been running the whole rotten game on Earth for millions of years. The roulette wheel was fixed in the house's favor. Any priest, any magician that came along and asked for immortality was source of the virus that would wipe out everything. It didn't matter if the priest was some Madison Avenue advertising magician or an inbred rural local like Howard liked to write about. He left the spaceship. The insect people ran up to him and licked the dripping yellow matter from his eyes with black thin whip-like tongues leaving sexually-thrilling the sores on his being. Soon he would be addicted to that pleasure. He pushed on, seeming to walk toward his three witnesses in their chairs. As he approached, they seemed to recede. He understood that he must walk them back to the original co-ordinates so that they could return to Mexico City. Burroughs had half risen from his chair, sticking his right hand beyond the magical barrier. Some of the black jism had spattered on him as well. A tiny dot. A cancer for his soul. As Barlow walked past the vegetable people, they smiled idiot smiles, opening their mouths to laugh at him, a think green saliva drooling from their green lips, the red skinned dwarves urged him on with menacing gestures—he was upsetting the calm of the vegetable people, spoiling the blue drug they were collecting. Barlow walked back to the place where they were.

Suddenly the last cathedral bell rang. It was the New Year and they were all in Barlow's library. He sprang out of chair. The eyes were gone; he was simply the pale haunted gringo he had been before the magic. He ran from the library back into his bedroom. They could hear him opening a bottle of pills. They could a faucet turned and off. They still couldn't move. A few minutes later they could hear him lie on his bed. After an hour the paralysis slowly left them. Burroughs went into Barlow's bedroom. On the stale dirty bed, Barlow lay fully clothed and dead.

"We couldn't move until he died. He held us in place by the spell," said Burroughs. He went to the phone and called the Mexican police to tell them that they would find a dead American professor, a suicide. The three left the apartment, not closing the door behind them.

It was two in the morning, and in certain sections of the city parties for gay ex-pats had just begun. Burroughs' wife stirred in her sleep, dreaming a dream that humans weren't meant to have.

for C. L. Moore in memoriam

The Future Eats Everything

IT WAS THE day of the flood that Matthew D. Smith discovered that the human world faced a menace, always has faced this menace, and will lose out to it.

Central Texas had been enduring a three-year drought. The weather was so hot and so dry that even the staunchest of the "global warming" deniers had begun to doubt. The Catholics had prayed to Mary, the Protestants to God, the Muslims to Allah, the Wiccans to the Goddess, and the Thelemites had practiced sex-magick for rain. Someone or something had heard the call. Matthew pictured this as an old man in a white robe saying: "Me-damnit! I'll give these S.O.B's rain!" It had begun with a lightning storm about eight the night before. Matthews and his wife kept their windows open all night—if you haven't heard rain in many months, it is a sleep-inducing bliss to hear it. Several times in the night Matthew had awakened from vague and uneasy dreams to the sound of a huge downpour. At 5:15 the automated voice of Doublesign Data Systems Inc. had called and told him that work would start two hours late. "Great I can sleep late," Matthew thought. Then at 5:25 the Austin Independent School District automated voice called Kathleen and told her that school would not start until noon. Then at 6:30 his assistant called and asked him if the message was for real that work was delayed. And finally at 6:45 Kathleen's principal had called her to see if she had got the 5:25 message.

Common sense told Matthew that he should allow extra time to drive from his south Austin two-story brick home to the one-story white stucco building in Doublesign. But the sweet sound of rain told him to sleep longer. After all he had driven the same back-road route for nine years and the roads had never been closed. There had been one snow and two other floods in that near-decade and there was no problem. Matthew took his old black Chevy pickup out at eight, waited for the school traffic to ease up and headed south. He noticed that no cars were streaming north of Austin on FM 118. Perhaps that was only an early morning problem. The sky glowed a lovely gray mother-of-pearl color. Matthew always drove to work in the dark; it seemed almost like a luxury to be driving so late in the day. About a mile out of Austin, two orange and white sand-filled trashcan-style roadblocks were set up with a protruding ROAD CLOSED sign. But there was space enough to drive between them. He could see another car a quarter of mile ahead where the road twisted through a grove of live oak. If that guy could make it, he could make it. He was, damnit, a man; even if his big blonde wife sometimes disagreed. Matthew drove his car very slowly between the roadblocks, he car very gently brushing one of them.

After his car rounded the bend, he saw the river, which was a surprising sight because there had never been a river there in nine years. There wasn't a creek there, or even a dry creek bed. It was scarcely a dip in the road. The cream-colored Lexus he had seen seconds before was making a difficult three point turn to head back to town. Matthew saw that he could have to turn in the same spot, so he waited for the Lexus to navigate its turn. He pulled up slowly to the fast moving river. It was at least waist high in the oaks, and Matthew could see that where the road dipped there was an angry muddy gap in the pavement, and he could see hunks of asphalt falling off into the foaming white water.

This would be a perfect picture to put on Facebook. Matthew pulled a little off the road. No other cars were coming; apparently others were not as foolhardy as him. He left his white Chevy pickup and walked up to the crumbling shoreline. He slipped in the tall wet grass twice. He planted his feet on an exposed limestone ridge and focused his phone at the exposed red earth bank, thinking how it looked like a wound. He hoped the cloudy morning light would provide sufficient light for his picture, when he saw a really big bug break out of the earth. At least a foot in length and half as much in width, the pallid segmented being looked like a cross between a trilobite and a cockroach. It had seven legs on each side of its thorax, and a pair of crablike pincers, and glistened with mucus. It had tiny mammal-like eyes, with light blue irises. As it pushed through the earth, Matthew saw that it had a few brothers or sisters climbing up on the grass heading toward him at fast scurry. He broke into a run, fell, got up and ran some more. He lost his iPhone in the process. He got his pickup turned around in record speed and was going down the empty highway at 70mph, before he could even order his thoughts.

What the hell were they?

Should he go back and get pictures?

Who should he call?

Is there any money to be made from this?

Should he keep his trap shut so that he didn't look like a nut?

Matthew thought of Gordon, the science teacher on *Sesame Street*, who never saw any weird phenomena that other kids and Muppets saw. So, he became the voice of skeptical reason—he was always wrong, of course, but he was supposed to the smart, credible adult. Kathleen would know; she taught high school science.

Matthew thought his wife would be all practical and skeptical. Instead she was thrilled. She tossed back her mane of blonde hair and demanded that they drive out to the site right now.

"Look, the road is still closed; if you wait until the morning, it will be open again. This could be our Discovery."

He definitely heard the big "D."

It was a scary drive. Rain had continued to fall all day, albeit much more gently, and the road was slick. There was no oncoming traffic, apparently no one else was foolish enough to risk the drive. He didn't pull his car into the red mud of this morning. He figured it would be way too squishy. Kathleen practically flew out of the car, carrying the giant flashlight she had bought for emergencies. She found one of the creatures almost instantly. "Matt, hold the flashlight while I snap some shots."

The pale fleshed trilobite (or whatever the fuck it was) didn't seem to like the light. It began pulling itself toward the scar in the earth.

"Matt, grab it."

Matthew made a grab, dropping the flashlight. The bug hissed at him, and he jumped back. It had three rows of sharp looking teeth—translucent and like shark's teeth, but much smaller.

"Ok. Maybe don't grab. Can you get the flashlight back, Sweetie?"

Matthew recovered the flashlight and kept the scurrying bug in the center of the beam. It climbed over a gray green rock as it headed toward the mud. Matthew swung the beam in long gentle arcs. No other creatures were in evidence.

"Move the light back to that rock."

Matthew did so, and he observed what Kathleen was about to comment on.

"Something is written on the rock."

Something was. A piece of gray plastic with a word in black letters was embedded in the siltstone. XUTHLTAN. Matthew picked up the stone. He tried to knock the plastic tag off, but he could see that it was truly embedded in the rock.

"Hey, it's really in there. Why would a rock have a piece of plastic stuck in it?" asked Matthew.

"I don't know. Time travel maybe. Maybe some future person journeyed back to trilobite times and dropped his portable Xuthltan in the muck, probably when of these little fuckers hissed at him."

Her large brown eyes were shiny with excitement. This was suddenly the sexiest moment in the marriage in the last ten years. Matthew stepped forward, but Kathleen said: "Look!"

They were everywhere. Matthew could see at least twelve of the bugs all headed toward him and Kathleen. Suddenly they all started to whine like summer locusts. Each bug had a slightly different pitch, and each seemed to be modulating its tone. As he grabbed Kathleen by the waist, he thought they might be talking. He had the presence of mind to shove the rock into his pocket.

* * * * *

The warm Texas sun ruled for the next three days. Flood water receded. The middle-class neighborhood of Onion Creek dealt with property damage and the poor neighborhood of Dove Springs dealt with homelessness. The closed streets were opened, and Matthew found the strange insectile visitors had vanished. No tiny claw marks in the drying mud. All that was left were a few badly lit photos and memories of a night of fear and lovemaking. Kathleen pointed out that in an era of Photoshop, bad pictures didn't mean squat.

But there was the rock.

Five years ago, as Kathleen was getting her degree at the University of Texas, she had dated a man named Randall Wong. Randall worked in the Accelerator Mass Spectrometry lab, was a careful and thoughtful lover—and was dating three other co-eds. Like catnip these AMS lads are—— Anyway all the girls dropped him but Kathleen, who remained his friend (at least on Facebook). He had said to her in a PM just weeks ago: "If you ever need any Carbon 14 dating, just ask me."

Matthew wasn't too keen on all of this. In his heart he knew—or was at least 85% positive—that Kathleen and Randall had had a little affair last year when he had had to work in Dallas for six weeks. But she seemed so excited by the mystery. It had led to the first time they'd made love in five years. Besides he still cherished the hope that "solving" the mystery would mean leaving his dead-end day job. At least Kathleen could stop dogging him about that.

He was (of course) quite surprised. It's not that often you see plastic encased in siltstone. Kathleen told him that she couldn't tell him about the artifact but hinted her uncle in the CIA needed to know. As Uncle Fitz did payroll this would be unlikely.

Randall didn't like the results.

"Look, don't tell anyone the University lab had anything to do with this. I could lose my job. This will bring every nutcase out of the woodwork for miles."

Kathleen and Matthew had met him at the Kirby Lane café. They looked up from their pancakes and said "Why?" almost at the same time.

"I'm not giving you the printouts. I'm not giving you nothing. The plastic is from now, which shouldn't be a surprise. The matrix was laid down about three million years from now."

Randall dropped the stone on the café table. Before they could speak, he said: "No. Just no. No, I don't understand it. No, I don't want the publicity. No. Stuff like this ends careers. Investigate if you want, you're a High School science teacher—and you do whatever it is you do. But for me. No."

Randall walked out.

Matthew and Kathleen stared at each other.

Of course, the next step was the Internet.

"Xulthan" was the name of a government official in the Maldives, a word for an evil village in a short story by Texas writer Robert E. Howard, a character in a multi-player online game, and a church in a bad Austin neighborhood.

Austin it was then. The phone number from the website had been discounted. Matthew decided to visit on Saturday, he told his wife to stay home "in case there was any trouble." Matthew didn't know what trouble you could have with people that had artifacts embedded in siltstone millions of years from now. The internet wasn't really of advice for that one.

The Church of Xulthan was part of a cheap-looking row of shops in East Austin. It shared its parking lot with a pawn store, a 7-11, a store that sold replicas of famous perfumes, a tattoo parlor, a loan office, and a botanica. Some guys were working on a white car near the door. The light was off, but Matthew could see someone inside—an old white guy in faded blue jeans and a dirty white t-shirt. He had a long scruffy white beard and a blue baseball cap. He was watching a tiny television. Matthew knocked on the thick glass of the shop window. The old man looked up and gave him a wide grin, perhaps one of idiocy. The guy got up and ambled to the door. The church had four rows of rusty folding chairs facing a pulpit. There were bookshelves on two walls. A cash register and what could be a baptismal font. The old guy turned on the overhead fluorescent lights and unlocked the door. He smelled like he had not bathed in a while, but there a cinnamon-y odor coming from the church itself.

"May Xulthan eat your woes!" said the old man.

"Hello," said Matthew.

"Come in," said the old man. "The Grand Chronopastor is not here, just me. Are you here to buy a book? Light some incense, say a prayer? Or just shoot the shit?"

Matthew saw the open fake marble pillar he had guessed was a baptismal font was full of gray plastic tokens with the word Xulthan printed in black letters. These were identical to the one embedded in the stone he was carrying in his left pocket. Matthew pointed at the container as he walked in.

"What are those?"

"Prayer stones," said the old man, "they're free if you are a member, and a buck (tax included) if you ain't."

"What do you pray to?" asked Matthew.

"Well, I ain't much of a theologian," said the old man. "I'd say they was bugs. Hardy bugs of the future, I'd say. Makes more sense than praying to a dead Jewish carpenter, if'n' you ask me."

"Why's that?" asked Matthew.

"Well, what can a dead Jewish carpenter do fer you? Build something in the past? Heck, that's over two thousand years ago. Let's say you wanted some bookshelves. You could pray 'Dear Jesus, make me some bookshelves and hide them so I can find them!' Well even if he did make them and hid them real good, you'd have to get on a jet and head off to the Holy Land and try and find them. And if you did find them, they'd be two thousand years old—and what kind of shape do you think they would be in then, I ask ye?"

Matthew wasn't prepared for this line of reasoning. So he asked: "So what can future bugs do?"

"What do bugs do anyway? Eat of course. They can eat up your problems if you chant on 'em."

"What do you mean?"

"Well, Praise Xulthan! I had two no-good sons. Never took care of me. When they was out of jail, they would literally rob me out of house and home. Took my car. Took my tiny savings from the bank. Hell, tried to sell that silver jar that held their mother's ashes. I used to live over there on Chicon. One day I walked past this place. Door was open on account of the AC not working. They was all prayin' and chantin' up a storm. Xulthan! Xulthan! Xulthan! And rubbing these little doodads. Then one of them jumped up and said, 'Praise Xulthan! My husband's gone!' And she showed everybody her ring finger and there was no wedding ring on it. I came in and asked just what the holy hell was going on."

"And these bugs had eaten her husband?"

"Of course I didn't believe it at first. But I was hurting so bad from the way my no-good kids had done me. I dropped down and started chanting along with the rest of the morons. I chanted for three days—took the talisman home and chanted. Then I looked up. I used to have a framed picture of Ed in his graduation robe in a little frame. It was gone! I looked around my house—it ain't very big, so this did not take me very long. There was nothing belonging to Ed. There was still some of Mark's stuff, so I went back to chanting, and guess what?"

"Mark's stuff disappeared too?"

"Well, eventually. He called me on his cell phone. All I got was a land line. He called me and told me his house was full of roaches that were hissing at him, could I come over and help him? I told him I could've had he not stole my car. I said I'd ride over in the bus tomorrow. Told him he could've called his wife except that she was smart enough to leave his ass. Hung up. Unplugged the phone. Chanted for three hours. Next day I took the bus to his neighborhood. Different family living there. Looked like they been there for a spell. They had a swing hanging from the sycamore in the front."

"Don't you feel bad?"

"No. That's the beauty of it. The bugs are just trying to get here. They're in some crazy war with flying octopi or something in the future. When the Reverend Nadis first found them they were 100 million years away. Now they're thirty million."

"Closer than that," said Matthew.

"You've got Word?" asked the old man with a look of holy awe, his backwoods crazy set aside for a moment.

"No," said Matthew. "I don't know why I said that."

"They can come through inattention, through synchronicities, through certain shapes, as well as the shape waves of the mantra. Their name isn't really Xulthan. That just has the right vibrations. You must meet Reverend Nadis."

Matthew felt the hairs on the back of his head stand up. He didn't want to meet Reverend Nadis. He looked over at the books for sale. Most were used paperbacks on the paranormal—*The Truth About Mummies*, *The Truth About Werewolves*, *UFOS in Colonial America*, etc. There were a few antique hardbound books with hard to read titles in German and French. Money. Money could buy time. Little church like this must need money.

"I would like a couple of the Xulthan talismans. And let me make a little contribution toward the Church."

Matthew took a twenty out of his worn black wallet. Kathleen had given it to him four years ago for Christmas. He never bought wallets for himself, he hoped that she would notice and get him another.

"You don't have to give us anything. Sure, we look like nothing now, but the time will come when only this little church in this little strip mall is the only thing standing."

Matthew could picture what the man was saying. This stupid strip mall on a grey featureless plain surrounded by the bugs. They must have intelligence to have worked this. Somewhere there would be their vast cities, their haunted hives where they fought another incomprehensible race. And their fight used pure human selfishness as a weapon. Matthew stood there, shocked at the vision—it as though he was really seeing it. He could almost hear their hissing song.

"It gets through to you, don't it?" said the old man, his eyes now full of intelligence. Matthew wondered if *this* were the Reverend Nadis. The old man went on. "I see you have a wedding ring, that means you'll be wanting two of the calling cards. Here you go."

The plastic felt slimy in his hands. Almost as if they were alive. He felt—or imagined he felt—the rock twitch in his pocket.

"How long? How long have you known about them?" asked Matthew.

"Now that, sir, is difficult to explain. Working with them plays hell on your time sense. If you started with a lot of enemies, then, how hollow your mind would get. On the one hand you would know them, remember them. But on the other hand you would have a great hollowness in your mind. Things echo in hollow spaces, you know."

Matthew turned to leave.

"Come again!" The old man's voice had gone all hick and stupid again.

Matthew said: "I won't. I'll throw your plastic prayer stones away, and I'll forget this place."

"Doesn't matter," the old man said. "Just you coming starts another cycle in motion. Don't you even want to show me the rock in your pocket boy?" He laughed a little.

Matthew turned his back and stepped out of the shop.

"Praise Xulthan!"

On the way back to his house Matthew edited and re-edited the story he would tell Kathleen again and again. He stopped at McDonald's and had a large chocolate shake. He would tell her about the talisman's supposed ability to make people disappear. He would portray the old man as a crazy hick. Overdo the accent when he told his wife—make him sound East Texas, bayou country. He wouldn't mention the vision, and of course nothing about the bugs. The whole thing should be a dead end. He thought about throwing away the talismans, but found he didn't want to handle them. He needed to see Kathleen laugh at them. She was so sensible. She was a Science teacher for god's sake. Then after she had destroyed their magic by a good laugh, he could drop them in his document shredder. It was strong enough for credit cards, and these were little smaller than that.

By the time he drove home he was all smiles and sheepishness. It had been such a waste of time.

"So he really chanted his sons away?" Kathleen asked.

"He was a crazy old man in a closed down storefront. He was probably homeless. You should've seen the junk they had for sale."

"But you bought two of the cards?"

"I offered him twenty bucks for them. I figure the guy needed to eat."

"And he turned your money down?"

"I told you he was crazy."

She looked at the cards, shrugged; lay them on the kitchen counter.

She spent longer than usual on her computer that night. He felt sure she was chatting with Randall. He took a long bath, listening for the sound of her going to bed. When he left the tub about midnight, the calling cards were gone, and she had taken the rock out of his pants pocket.

A day passed, and then a week and the memory of the strange bugs and the stranger church were obscured by bills and problems at work. WDS lost two technicians, so everyone had to pull an occasional extra shift. Matthew drew Sunday morning. He crept out of the house at 6:45 and drove into Doublesign. He took great pride in not waking Kathleen, although she got two months off in the summer plus Christmas, fall and spring breaks. He stopped at the Sac-n-Pac store and bought his diet Dr. Pepper and multi-vitamin packet and let himself in at work. The mainframe was up, the satellite systems were (mainly) up, he checked the night log and the e-mails. He put coffee on and raided a banana from the bosses' fruit bowl. He began file maintenance, when he heard something in the server room. Probably rats (rats had given Arjay a huge fright a couple of months ago). He ignored it, and then he heard someone say something. He jumped out of his chair. Should he dial 911 or confront? Probably kids from the Discipline Alternative Program.

He moved to the back and threw open the white painted door. The servers were warm, happy and alone. He stepped and walked up them.

Something fell from the ceiling behind him.

He turned.

It was one of the bugs larger than before. Two feet long, with he saw seven sharp legs on each side, and two crab like pinchers. It was bigger, he knew somehow, because it had eaten its way closer in time. Two more were crawling along the walls, their blue human like eyes focused on him. One spoke, not a hiss this time, with his wife's voice: "Xulthan!" Matthew could see the three rows of glasslike teeth clearly reflecting the yellow, green and red lights of the servers.

Two scurried out from under the server rack. One spoke with the slightly Chinese accent Randall Wong effected: "Xulthan!" Another hissed.

Then they rushed him. It was quick, but not quick enough.

for Matthew Carpenter

The Hollow Man

by H. P. Lovecraft and Don Webb

IT WAS LATE Saturday afternoon and Frank Riley was vacillating from the touristy thrill of actually sitting in a London Pub, the Nellie Dean, and a deep feeling that his drinking companion he had idolized all of his fannish life was quite barking mad. The Nellie Dean Pub stands on the corner of Dean Street and Carlisle Street, in the heart of London's Soho district. Frank had spent more than his advance on *Cult of the Ghoul* to fly to World Horror Con here in Blighty. The first day he had met Karl Ramsey, one of the great old men of English horror. Aickman, Campbell, Undercliffe, Basil Cooper—Karl Ramsey had given all of them a run for their money. Now dark age spots marked his transparent skin, his fair was thin and white and didn't cover the skull underneath very well. Frank began to tear into a package of crisps, but stopped; he could hear Martha telling him to watch the salt. He noted (with some dismay) that Ramsey has ordered two more pints. The English capacity of beer, even the capacity of octogenarians, startled him. At home in Amarillo he and Martha killed a six-pack on Friday nights; that plus the SyFy channel made for an adventurous night.

"You see, it is all about hollowness. Horror writing, I mean," said Ramsey. "If your mind is full of day-to-day thoughts then there is no room for horror. Take that Paki over by the Budweiser sign."

Frank didn't know if calling people from the Indian subcontinent "Paki" was kosher. Frank taught Middle School and spent long time removing racial slurs from his kids. Also he didn't like the fact the bar has small neon signs for Budweiser and Miller. That would be appropriate for a bar on Western Ave. back home.

"He's thinking about paying his bills, can he afford another beer, will his wife belabor him for drinking when he gets home. Horror to him might be three blokes with a knife."

"Well, that would be horror for me," said Frank.

"No, that would be *fear* for you. Horror doesn't happen in your regular thoughts; most people think of their thoughts like an unending movie. But there are gaps between thoughts, or times when thoughts stop then run backward. It is in those gaps that horror comes in. Real horror hollows you out, makes you useful to old Hasty, let's not mention his name too quickly."

"I'm afraid I don't follow you."

What Frank was really afraid of was not knowing how to get back to his hotel on Exposition Street. The notion of Soho had seemed colorful. Frank didn't know the endless sex shops had been vanishing since the 1980s. Frank knew his world from books.

"Precisely, you're *afraid*," Ramsey said the word in high tone, the same bullying tone some of Frank's bigger students used. A tone Frank had known all his life. "But you are not horrified, you're worrying about getting back to your hotel. You want to check the passport in your pocket even though you checked twice in the Tube and once here. You're concerned about meeting me can help your career. But you are not horrified."

Frank was beginning to feel insulted. He didn't know why the older man wanted to make fun of him. *I'll finish my beer and go.* He said: "So what is true horror? Seems like everyone at the Con's got a different answer."

"Horror is encountering a will stronger than your own and feeling it take up residence in your mind. At first it makes you think things you don't want to think. Then it makes you feel things you don't want to feel, then it makes you be a thing you don't want to be."

"Ever written about that?" challenged Frank.

"It's all I write about. I've heard it said that when a writer dies someone discovers that all his stories are the same."

"Actually," Frank said. "You read it. Henry James' 'The Pattern in the Carpet'. James has an older writer," he gestured at Ramsey, "tell it to a younger writer." He pointed out his sad pudgy face.

"I don't remember reading 'The Stain on the Rug' but the idea is sound. When I was a young man in the advert trade I found out about Hollowness. Ads work that way a little—slipping into mind in the gaps. But it was worse. Even my first story to *Science Fantasy* was about me. You know Ballard had a story in the same issues. Poor old sod."

About four good gulps and the beer will be gone. Don't let him start crying.

"I had to write about hollowness, so I borrowed a name from an American. You'd think that Americans would be hollow, but in fact they are more crammed full of trivia than anyone. I took *Necronomicon*. It means 'Place of Dead Roads' I think. Anyway, it is about hollowness."

* * * * *

In London there is man who screams when the church bells ring. He lives all alone with his streaked cat in Gray's Inn, and people call him harmlessly mad. His room is filled with books of the tamest and most puerile kind, and hour after hour he tries to lose himself in their feeble pages. All he seeks from life is not to think. For some reason thought is very horrible to him, and anything that stirs the imagination he flees as a plague. He is very thin and grey and wrinkled, but there are those who declare he is not nearly so old as he looks. Fear has its grisly claws upon him, and a sound will make him start with staring eyes and sweat-beaded forehead. Friends and companions he shuns, for he wishes to answer no questions. Those who once knew him as scholar and aesthete say it is very pitiful to see him now. He dropped them all years ago, and no one feels sure whether he left the country or merely sank from sight in some hidden byway. It is a decade now since he moved into Gray's Inn, and of where he had been he would say nothing till the night young Williams bought the *Necronomicon*.

Williams was a dreamer, and only twenty-three, and when he moved into the ancient house he felt a strangeness and a breath of cosmic wind about the grey wizened man in the next room. He forced his friendship where old friends dared not force theirs, and marveled at the fright that sat upon this gaunt, haggard watcher and listener. For that the man always watched and listened no one could doubt. He watched and listened with his mind more than with his eyes and ears, and strove every moment to drown something in his ceaseless poring over gay, insipid novels. And when the church bells rang he would stop his ears and scream, and the grey cat that dwelt with him would howl in unison till the last peal died reverberant away.

But try as Williams would, he could not make his neighbor speak of anything profound or hidden. The old man would not live up to his aspect and manner, but would feign a smile and a light tone and prattle feverishly and frantically of cheerful trifles; his voice every moment rising and thickening till at last it would split in a piping and incoherent falsetto. That his learning was deep and thorough, his most trivial remarks made abundantly clear; and Williams was not surprised to hear that he had been to Harrow and Oxford. Later it developed that he was none other than Lord Northam, of whose ancient hereditary castle on the Yorkshire coast so many odd things were told; but when Williams tried to talk of the castle, and of its reputed Roman origin, he refused to admit that there was anything unusual about it. He even tittered shrilly when the subject of the supposed under crypts, hewn out of the solid crag that frowns on the North Sea, was brought up.

So matters went till that night when Williams brought home the infamous *Necronomicon* of the mad Arab Abdul Alhazred. He had known of the dreaded volume since his sixteenth year, when his dawning love of the bizarre had led him to ask queer questions of a bent old bookseller in Chandos Street; and he had always wondered why men paled when they spoke of it. The old bookseller had told him that only five copies were known to have survived the shocked edicts of the priests and lawgivers against it and that all of these were locked up with frightened care by custodians who had ventured to begin a reading of the hateful black-letter. But now, at last, he had not only found an accessible copy but had made it his own at a ludicrously low figure. It was at a Jew's shop in the squalid precincts of Clare Market, where he had often bought strange things before, and he almost fancied the gnarled old Levite smiled amidst tangles of beard as the great discovery was made. The bulky leather cover with the brass clasp had been so prominently visible, and the price was so absurdly slight.

The one glimpse he had had of the title was enough to send him into transports, and some of the diagrams set in the vague Latin text excited the tensest and most disquieting recollections in his brain. He felt it was highly necessary to get the ponderous thing home and begin deciphering it, and bore it out of the shop with such precipitate haste that the old Jew chuckled disturbingly behind him. But when at last it was safe in his room, he found the combination of black-letter and debased idiom too much for his powers as a linguist, and reluctantly called on his strange, frightened friend for help with the twisted, mediaeval Latin. Lord Northam was simpering inanities to his streaked cat, and started violently when the young man entered. Then he saw the volume and shuddered wildly, and fainted altogether when Williams uttered the title. It was when he regained his senses that he told his story; told his fantastic figment of madness in frantic whispers, lest his friend be not quick to burn the accursed book and give wide scattering to its ashes.

There must, Lord Northam whispered, have been something wrong at the start; but it would never have come to a head if he had not explored too far. He was the nineteenth Baron of a line whose beginnings went uncomfortably far back into the past—unbelievably far, if vague tradition could be heeded, for there were family tales of a descent from pre-Saxon times, when a certain Lunaeus Gabinius Capito, military tribune in the Third Augustan Legion then stationed at Lindum in Roman Britain, had been summarily expelled from his command for participation in certain rites unconnected with any known religion. Gabinius had, the rumour ran, come upon a cliff side cavern where strange folk met together and made the Elder Sign in the dark; strange folk whom the Britons knew not save in fear, and who were the last to survive from a great land in the west that had sunk, leaving only the islands with the megaliths and circles and shrines of which Stonehenge was the greatest. There was no certainty, of course, in the legend that Gabinius had built an impregnable fortress over the forbidden cave and founded a line which Pict and Saxon, Dane and Norman were powerless to obliterate; or in the tacit assumption that from this line sprang the bold companion and lieutenant of the Black Prince whom Edward Third created Baron of Northam. These things were not certain, yet they were often told; and in truth the stonework of Northam Keep did look alarmingly like the masonry of Hadrian's Wall. As a child Lord Northam had had peculiar dreams when sleeping in the older parts of the castle, and had acquired a constant habit of looking back through his memory for half-amorphous scenes and patterns and impressions which formed no resonance with the healthy things of daylight. Lord Northam's father counseled the lad to pay no attention to dreaming as the "mind goes mad" every night, but to seek after healthy sport and the Church of England. It proved unsatisfying; a searcher for strange realms and relationships once familiar, yet lying nowhere in the visible regions of earth. Filled with a feeling that our tangible world is only an atom in a fabric vast and ominous, and that unknown demesnes press on and permeate the sphere of the known at every point, Northam in youth and young manhood drained in turn the founts of formal religion and occult mystery. Nowhere, however, could he find ease and content; and as he grew older the staleness and limitations of life became more and more maddening to him. During the 'nineties he dabbled in Satanism, and at all times he devoured avidly any doctrine or theory which seemed to promise escape from the close vistas of science and the dully unvarying laws of Nature. Books like Ignatius Donnelly's chimerical account of Atlantis he absorbed with zest, and a dozen obscure precursors of Charles Fort enthralled him with their vagaries. He would travel leagues to follow up a furtive village tale of abnormal wonder, and once went into the desert of Araby to seek a Nameless City of faint report, which no man has ever beheld. There rose within him the tantalizing faith that somewhere an easy gate existed, which if one found would admit him freely to those outer deeps whose echoes rattled so dimly at the back of his memory. It might be in the visible world, yet it might be only in his mind and soul. Perhaps he held within his own half-explored brain that cryptic link which would awaken him to elder and future lives in forgotten dimensions; which would bind him to the stars, and to the infinities and eternities beyond them.

Lord Northam saw the coming of the new century with dismay. All of the comforts of electricity and modernity, he saw as things that would further obscure the link he wished to make with Otherness. He fell into a grey depression in London, seldom leaving his quarters. He was preparing to return to his age-haunted castle where at least he felt some spark of the vital past, when news of seven-day wonder came to him. He could not recall later how he had heard of the mountebank's lectures. He had few friends. He did not listen to the idle chatter of his servants. He pursued the daily papers with little enthusiasm. Yet somehow the notion grew in him that he should make his way to Exhibition Hall and attend the talk of Dr. Farouk from America.

Dr. Farouk was speaking on the current bugaboo, the Fourth Dimension. Lord Northam had expected him to be an Egyptian and was surprised to see that the scarlet-coated lecturer was an American Negro. He had never seen a Negro before at close range, although such did exist in London. Dr. Farouk performed a few demonstrations with electricity creating and catching lightning in glass tubes, where it twisted and sought escape. Lord Northam was unsure the import of these actions even though Dr. Farouk kept up a running monologue in his deep voice. Dr. Farouk began to talk of Charles Hinton and the Fourth Dimension. Hinton had pursued the lecture circuit some years with his popular "What is the Fourth

Dimension?" Lord Northam had read Hinton's *Scientific Romances* with some interest—one of the few modern works that seemed to reach him as well as the medieval romances that dominated his mind.

Dr. Farouk claimed that Hinton's visualization method failed because it was based on too *regular* a concept of space. Hinton had tried to sell a set of multi-coloured cubes with his lectures. He explained that by using the phenomena of "flashing colors" and careful arrangement of the cubes one could visual a *tesseract*, a word Hinton had coined for a hyper-cube, could be glimpsed in the mind's eye. Dr. Farouk had investigated the adyta of eld, especially those of Egypt and realized that the Egyptians had developed such visualization tools. Tonight Dr. Farouk would show off his remanifestation of these tools based on drawing from the tomb of the Pharaoh Nephren Ka. He needed a volunteer from the audience.

Later Lord Northam would be at a loss as to why he had done something as vulgar as putting up his hand. He found that he could not look away from Dr. Farouk's eyes. He rose (as if one in a trance) and walked to the stage. He noted the smell of the lime lights. He noticed an ancient smell akin to incense that emanated from Dr. Farouk. Perhaps all Negroes smell of the mysteries of shadowed Khem. Lord Northam could not look into the audience. He could not look away from Dr. Farouk. Dr. Farouk guided him to a chair by a small table. On the tables lay several irregular frustums of faience blue, carnelian red, antique gold and a star-flecked black. Dr. Farouk stood behind him and grasped his hands. Lord Northam gasped; save for his mother and one fumbling attempt at romance, no one had ever touched his hands. He had a horror of contact. The doctor forced him to arrange and stack the frustums. Suddenly he felt as though he were going to fall off the edge of an abyss, somehow the doctor had hypnotized him and lead him to the edge of a cliff. But he regained his composure and saw the mass ahead of him caused him to see a tunnel or opening into a realm of indistinct color. He could see the frustums; he could see Dr. Farouk's very black hands and very red sleeves. But he could also see a tunnel leading in a direction that he had no name for. The most extraordinary thought flashed though his mind, *I have come thorough this tunnel.* He slumped forward, or more accurately he slumped in the direction of the tunnel, for which there is no word; and he fainted.

Frank Riley had been so engrossed with Ramsey's tale, he had forgotten his worries about returning to his hotel. He noted mastery in the choice of "Exhibition Hall", which stood where his modern hotel did. Maybe one of vendors at the Con had a copy of the 1955 *Science Fantasy* Ramsey's first published story had appeared in. Ramsey had stopped his narrative with some remarks about meeting J. G. Ballard at the office of *Science Fantasy.*

"Oh, my dear chap, I've meandered a bit. You will need to catch the Tube back to the convention," said Ramsey.

"Oh no not at all. I was hoping to hear the rest of the story. You say this reflected an experience you had?"

"Yes. I was going to tell you about hollowness. Well Hinton's fourth dimension is where it begins. He conceived of it as fourth spatial you know, that the H. G. Wells time-as-a-fourth-dimension rot."

"I don't think I follow."

"Well at least you're not *afraid* you don't follow, eh? I live near here, I've got a set of the Hinton cubes. Something of an antique I would say. You could come to my flat and hear the rest of the poor old man's fictional autobiography, eh?"

As they made their way through the streets, Frank Riley thought about how sheltered his life had been. He was not unlike Lord Northam. He had always had a strange fascination with things past, far away or mysterious. He never had been further than his aunt Vera's home in Roswell, New Mexico in the physical world, but he had spent his secret youth in volumes of fantasy, and less than savory occult tomes. As a young man he went to the college in nearby Canyon, Texas and decided to face reality. He became a social studies teacher. He married another teacher, a woman without imagination. When after the birth of their second child he had confessed his "dark" side. He had feared an outright condemnation and had hoped against hope for a "Me, too" moment. But he was unprepared for her seeing dollar signs. What he could be, the next Stephen King. He should write. So he wrote. Maybe Karl Ramsey was like him.

Frank Riley was not an experienced traveler. By the time he arrived at Ramsey's flat he realized that he had not been paying attention to the route. He would have a time heading back to the hotel. No one used buses in Amarillo, and as for the subway his link was reading about "Underground Horror" in Stephen King's 'Crouch End.'

Inside were blown-up posters of Ramsey's book covers: *The Dweller in the Loch and Other Unwelcome Guests*, *The Geometry of Satan*, *Jests of Azathoth*, *The Tunnel to the Past*, *The Bell in the Tower*, *The Moonchild*, *The Doom that Came to Chelsea.* Their lurid reds and yellows screamed against the cream colored paint. Ramsey offered him some port. Another first for Frank Riley. It reminded him of Walmart's knock-off cough syrup. He liked the quiet of Ramsey's flat, and could dream of a quiet home something his kids never allowed. His wife had an unfortunate interest in DIY home repair shows.

"Your place is very quiet."

Ramset smiled at the compliment. "I had two layers of cork insulation put in. I wager it's the quietest place in London."

He had removed a yellowing digest size magazine from his bookshelves. On its cover a man and robot studied Mayan looking ruins at twilight with two moons in the sky. Ramset said: "Oh the cubes!" Ramsey went to a backroom and emerged with a double handful of what seemed to be truncated pyramids: blue, yellow, black, and red. He poured these on mahogany end table near Riley's couch. Riley picked up one of the blue ones to look at it. It was covered in hieroglyphics; he could make out a tiny scarab and a foot cloth near a star. He thought grandly, *I am having an adventure.*

* * * * *

There was an unpleasant ammonia smell. Lord Northam jerked his head away. He lay upon a must-smelling bed in a cheap grey room. Dr. Farouk was holding a small brown vial to his nose.

The doctor said: "Sprit of hartshorn, or you may know it from Pliny as 'Hammonicus sal.' "

"What happened? Where am I?" asked Lord Northam.

"You are in London in a cheap boarding house off of Regent Street. I am staying here during the British part of my tour. As far as what happened, you saw very deeply in the past, and the shock of the length your world-line seems to have distressed you."

"What do you mean? I want to leave."

Lord Northam rose from the musty-smelling bed, became dizzy and fell back.

"Lord Northam, you are too weak to travel. Besides your re-awakening has just begun."

"Re-awakening?"

"*Certe Lunaeus Gabinius, tibi veni.*"

Lord Northam once again passed out.

Lumaeus Gabinius stood among the people of the Elder Sign. He had forsaken Rome for what these people knew. Augustus, wanting to out shadow his father Caesar, had made himself a god; Julius had only been a demi-god. But these people offered him something more. That was merely a title, good for coins and statues. The quiet folk, that the rest of the Britons feared, offered him immortality. He had lived with them for three months since he had been expelled from the Third Legion. He had seen them make normal fire become columns of green flame that was cold and misty to the touch. He had drunk a black milk that let him pass though stone into cavern that had never known the light of day. He had bedded their unspeaking women, who smelled more of earth-worm than human lust. The old priests taught him things about the Cosmos that would have sounded fantastic even in Alexandria. He knew jealous gods had destroyed the home island, sinking it into the sea, drowning thousands who dared the black magic.

Only one doubt plagued him. These folk didn't look as fully human as he would like. Their skin was pale. They were short. On some of them were moist brown patches that looked like the slimy stretchy skin of earthworms. On nights of full moons they wor-shipped lusty Derketo, and when the moon was gone they wor-shipped Shudde M'ell, a worm they claimed kinship with. Lumaeus Gabinius was a brave man, which is why he was military tribune, but he feared that he was being tricked. The little people said they were offering him immortality because he lied to his Legion about their proximity to their camp. In fact, he doubted if his fellow Romans would have ever seen them, so sly in their movements they were. If had not been his habit of taking quiet walks to be alone with his sense of wonder, he would have never seen the one he had taken as his wife. She still had not spoken to him and he was unsure if she even had the power of speech. He feared that they were using him.

Winter had come and the Legion had dug in at Lindum. There was little meat and the caves of the quiet folk were the coldest places Lumaeus Gabinius had ever been. The Birthday of Mithras was coming up, and priests whispered to him that he must make a choice. He could live forever, or his adopted folk would likewise cast him out.

He agreed to the terms they gave him.

He could become be a vessel of Hastur. On the Winter Solstice as the longest night of the year began, they would whisper Hastur's true name to him, and Hastur would begin to live within him. The priests assured him that he would scarcely notice. Human beings are nothing but a thin sort of volitional substance covering a screaming abyss of nothingness. Hastur would live in the abyss, while giving his human form long life. Eventually he might grow tired of the centuries, but there was a way of escape to a new form, when the pressure of Hastur grew too great within.

They drank their black milk, from what horrible cow he never knew, and passed though the small hillock. The milk made them into a sort of nasty vapor that could pour thought the porous limestone. Inside the dark chamber they made two great columns of the green cold fire. The brought out bells. Thousands of bells. The treasure of their sunken land. They hung the bells everywhere in the great cavern. As the Priests made certain signs and whispered certain words the bells began to chime. At first it was the small silver bells, then the bells of brass and bronze. Then the large iron bells clanged forth. Then huge bells made of metal Lumaeus Gabinius did not know. The noise, the infernal clang and crash and roar, began to be a voice, a voice of a god! The tintinnabulation became moaning and groaning. No hand struck these bells, no wind stirred them to their fantastic shriek. Each of them making music from their hollowness. From their emptiness they were filling the cavern, whose shape amplified their roar. Lumaeus Gabinius felt his flesh being torn away, his bones shaking apart. This was their treachery—they were sacrificing him to Hastur. When the pain of the sound had grown so intense that his sight was giving way, his woman, his wife approached him. There were tears in her eyes. She stretched upward to him. How had he not noticed how very short these people were? She stretched upward to him and whispered Hastur's true name in his ear.

* * * * *

Frank Riley had almost worked out the puzzle of the frustums. If he could just twist those two on the outer row. It reminded him of hours wasted in his youth in Rubik's cubes, but the Rubik's cube didn't make his mind feel funny. He noticed that Ramsey had paused in his reading. Somehow all of his story was part of what he was arraying. It was an angular plane he was laying the faded toys on. But that made no sense; how could you lay cubes on a story line? He was all confused. He felt feelings he had when he was five and his mother made him put up his Hot Wheels.

"Of course at that point of the story," said Karl Ramsey, "I had to cheat a bit. I couldn't really come up with a secret name. So I had him pass out like I had done with Lord Northam. But you cheated like that in *Cult of the Ghoul* when Marsden faints at the ghoul festival."

"Oh my god, you read *Cult of the Ghoul*? What did you think? Karl Ramsey read my book." Frank was embarrassed even as the words left his mouth. That port was strong stuff.

"It was adequate. Your next work will be weirder," said Ramsey.

Adequate? Well why did you invite me round to your flat? Oh my god, he's queer. Think of all those Monty Python skits. He's going to make a pass at me.

"Don't be *afraid*, the worst thing that can happen to a writer is that the first thing they write is the best," said Ramsey. "Anyway it's getting late, and I shall skip a few pages of pages. Lord Northam realizes that Lumaeus Gabinius hadn't really obtained a very nice sort of immortality. Hastur had entered via his true name into Lumaeus Gabinius's mind or soul or whatever it is that humans have. The tribe worshipped him as a god, but he had a dilemma, you see. Hastur was eating away at his insides. Oh, he was a god of sorts, he could make the rain come, produce earthquakes, foresee the future and other abilities that his human mind didn't even have a name for. I'll start where the story is back in Edwardian London."

* * * * *

Williams had grown uncomfortable in dealing with the old man. His long account of visiting the nameless city had thrilled him, but he could ascribe some of the whispered details as the old man's sickening mind. But when he had begun the tale of the Roman Williams had begun to wonder if Lord Northam was hinting that he was the Roman. It would be a harmless tale, a silly thing to believe in perhaps. Certainly Williams viewed most of the religions of the world as equally silly tales, but he had hoped that something more useful would occur. When he had seen the light in the old man's eyes upon seeing the *Necronomicon*, his dream was that the old man Knew something. That he would take Williams aside and show him the signs, tell him the words, help him exit this dreary reality that would day make him a bank clerk or an underpaid librarian. Williams brought the old man soup everyday, and butcher's scraps for Pharaoh, a rather distinguished title for such a decrepit beast.

The old man's tale dwelt with the aging of Lumaeus Gabinius. The Roman dwelt with the Little People, for hundreds of years. The Romans left. The Angles, Saxons and Jutes came. The Danes came. He grew old and weak, but his greatest fear was the disappearing of the Little Folk. They fled into further and further and more dismal valleys and moors. Yet once a year they made their way to what came to be called London. Fewer and fewer children were born to them. Some went to live with fully human men and bore them strange fey children. Men who became artists or alchemists or sorcerers. By the time of Arthur's court they're scarcely a hundred. Lord Northam told Williams of the night Lumaeus Gabinius met Merlin. As he wheezed out his story, he traced a symbol in the air that passed between the two.

Williams had seen the symbol in the *Necronomicon*. In one great rushing moment, Williams realized the truth of the old man's tales. The bookseller had said there were perhaps five copies of the work. He interrupted the old man's story.

"Tell me, why did Dr. Farouk give you the vision of Lumaeus Gabinius?"

"He was an aid to Hastur. He intervenes when too much is forgotten."

Frank Riley had tuned Karl Ramsey out. The use of "Hastur" was trite and uninteresting. Frank knew all of his references—Chambers, Bierce, Derleth, Bradley, Martin—all of them. The old man claims this is some allegory to his life. But the cubes, now they were interesting. He had it now! He moved the four largest to the top. That was counter-intuitive, one would think the biggest pieces should be on the bottom. As he lay down the last piece a tunnel began to form. It hung in midair, not displacing the air but becoming another space—a direction of space we are taught not to see, but it is there all the time. *Christ, the whole human race is in denial about an entire direction!*

Frank slumped forward, or more precisely in the direction we don't talk about. Just before he lost consciousness, he saw something about Karl Ramsey, but he couldn't quite make out the words for it. But he didn't like it.

The pounding in his head said "HANGOVER!" Frank had never been a big drinker. A few keggers in college, a couple of New Year's Eve parties, once at his cousin Mary Lou's shindig on the shores of Lake Meredith. His skin hurt. The staleness of clothes nauseated him. Suddenly he realized that he was on Ramsey's couch. Oh god. He sat up quickly, which was a mistake. He struggled to keep his lunch from yesterday down. Martha would be mad that he had not called. His Blackberry was back at the hotel.

He decided to just to head out and catch a cab.

"Oh, Sleeping Beauty has awakened!" said Karl Ramsey

"I'm really sorry, sir, I have been a terrible guest. I'll just let myself out."

"Nonsense. A little too much beer and port and no dinner. Let me make you toast and tea and I'll take you to the Tube."

"Thank you. I could use advice on which trains to take."

The tea was warm and sweet, the toast soggy with English butter. Ramsey asked him questions about which panels he would be on this afternoon. He asked about the flight back tomorrow. Frank Riley talked about what an honor it was to have meet Ramsey. They joked about some of the characters at the Con.

"Are you a religious man, Mr. Riley?" asked Ramsey.

"Well, I suppose in a vague way. My wife is a Southern Baptist, but I am an Easter and Christmas sort of fellow."

"So, you are not used to being up early on Sundays."

"On the contrary, I write while she and the boys pray."

"Better still, without religion you must have big hollow dark spot for your fantastic stories to echo around in."

Frank didn't like the game of comparing Karl's fantasy of Roman secrets with real writing. This guy had lost the good solid wall between reality and fantasy.

"I suppose. If that's a good thing, that is," said Frank.

As they made their way to the Tube station Ramsey repeated the stops that Frank would need to make slowly. Frank began to feel reassured. They paused by a huge church near the station. Karl Ramsey seemed to be waiting for something; he checked his watch as compulsively as Frank had checked his passports the day before.

"Mr. Ramsey, how did the story end? I don't think it is in any of your collections," asked Frank.

"Merlin told Lumaeus Gabinius that he would grow more and more thin as Hastur ate away at him from within his soul-mind-body complex. He would face a very long and painful spiritual death of constant gnawing away. When he could take it no longer, he would have to utter Hastur's true name into a suitable vessel, a descendant to carry on the incarnation."

"I suppose Williams with his dreaminess and his *Necronomicon* was the descendant."

"That was Lord Northam's plan, but our hero escaped and burned the foul book. I'm afraid I overdid the end. I even had the Jewish bookseller to be another aspect of Dr. Farouk. But I was new to writing and I wanted to explain in dramatic terms what had happened to me."

Karl was mad. Frank Riley tried to think of another question, but the church bells drowned him out. The cathedral's bells were a thousand times louder than the recording they played at High Plains Baptist Church back home. Karl's story about a man, who yelled when the bells clanged, made sense. Karl Ramsey smiled and, seeming to understand Frank's need, leaned in very close.

Then he whispered Hastur's true name into Frank Riley's ear.

(This "collaboration" with Mr. Lovecraft is written in honor of the late Dr. Karl Wagner)

RAMBLE HOUSE's

HARRY STEPHEN KEELER WEBWORK MYSTERIES

(RH) indicates the title is available ONLY in the RAMBLE HOUSE edition

The Ace of Spades Murder
The Affair of the Bottled Deuce (RH)
The Amazing Web
The Barking Clock
Behind That Mask
The Book with the Orange Leaves
The Bottle with the Green Wax Seal
The Box from Japan
The Case of the Canny Killer
The Case of the Crazy Corpse (RH)
The Case of the Flying Hands (RH)
The Case of the Ivory Arrow
The Case of the Jeweled Ragpicker
The Case of the Lavender Gripsack
The Case of the Mysterious Moll
The Case of the 16 Beans
The Case of the Transparent Nude (RH)
The Case of the Transposed Legs
The Case of the Two-Headed Idiot (RH)
The Case of the Two Strange Ladies
The Circus Stealers (RH)
Cleopatra's Tears
A Copy of Beowulf (RH)
The Crimson Cube (RH)
The Face of the Man From Saturn
Find the Clock
The Five Silver Buddhas
The 4th King
The Gallows Waits, My Lord! (RH)
The Green Jade Hand
Finger! Finger!
Hangman's Nights (RH)
I, Chameleon (RH)
I Killed Lincoln at 10:13! (RH)
The Iron Ring
The Man Who Changed His Skin (RH)
The Man with the Crimson Box
The Man with the Magic Eardrums
The Man with the Wooden Spectacles
The Marceau Case
The Matilda Hunter Murder
The Monocled Monster
The Murder of London Lew
The Murdered Mathematician
The Mysterious Card (RH)
The Mysterious Ivory Ball of Wong Shing Li (RH)
The Mystery of the Fiddling Cracksman
The Peacock Fan
The Photo of Lady X (RH)
The Portrait of Jirjohn Cobb
Report on Vanessa Hewstone (RH)
Riddle of the Travelling Skull
Riddle of the Wooden Parrakeet (RH)
The Scarlet Mummy (RH)
The Search for X-Y-Z
The Sharkskin Book
Sing Sing Nights
The Six From Nowhere (RH)
The Skull of the Waltzing Clown
The Spectacles of Mr. Cagliostro
Stand By—London Calling!
The Steeltown Strangler
The Stolen Gravestone (RH)
Strange Journey (RH)
The Strange Will
The Straw Hat Murders (RH)
The Street of 1000 Eyes (RH)
Thieves' Nights
Three Novellos (RH)
The Tiger Snake
The Trap (RH)
Vagabond Nights (Defrauded Yeggman)
Vagabond Nights 2 (10 Hours)
The Vanishing Gold Truck
The Voice of the Seven Sparrows
The Washington Square Enigma
When Thief Meets Thief
The White Circle (RH)
The Wonderful Scheme of Mr. Christopher Thorne
X. Jones—of Scotland Yard
Y. Cheung, Business Detective

Keeler Related Works

A To Izzard: A Harry Stephen Keeler Companion by Fender Tucker—Articles and stories about Harry, by Harry, and in his style. Included is a compleat bibliography.
Wild About Harry: Reviews of Keeler Novels—Edited by Richard Polt & Fender Tucker—22 reviews of works by Harry Stephen Keeler from *Keeler News.* A perfect introduction to the author.
The Keeler Keyhole Collection: Annotated newsletter rants from Harry Stephen Keeler, edited by Francis M. Nevins. Over 400 pages of incredibly personal Keeleriana.
Fakealoo—Pastiches of the style of Harry Stephen Keeler by selected demented members of the HSK Society. Updated every year with the new winner.
Strands of the Web: Short Stories of Harry Stephen Keeler—29 stories, just about all that Keeler wrote, are edited and introduced by Fred Cleaver.

RAMBLE HOUSE's LOON SANCTUARY

A Clear Path to Cross—Sharon Knowles short mystery stories by Ed Lynskey.
A Corpse Walks in Brooklyn and Other Stories—Volume 5 in the Day Keene in the Detective Pulps series.
A Fair Californian—Novel by Olive Harper about a young woman's quest for gold — a quest that turns into something completely unexpected.
A Jimmy Starr Omnibus—Three '40s novels by Jimmy Starr.
A Niche in Time and Other Stories—Classic SF by William F. Temple.
A Shot Rang Out—Three decades of reviews and articles by today's Anthony Boucher, Jon Breen. An essential book for any mystery lover's library.
A Snark Selection—Lewis Carroll's *The Hunting of the Snark* with two Snarkian chapters by Harry Stephen Keeler—Illustrated by Gavin L. O'Keefe.
A Young Man's Heart—A forgotten early classic by Cornell Woolrich.
Alexander Laing Novels—*The Motives of Nicholas Holtz* and *Dr. Scarlett*, stories of medical mayhem and intrigue from the '30s.
An Angel in the Street—Modern hardboiled noir by Peter Genovese.
Arthur Leo Zagat—*Summer Camp for Corpses, The Corpse Factory* and *They Dine in Darkness*. Three volumes of weird horror stories.
Automaton—Brilliant treatise on robotics: 1928-style! By H. Stafford Hatfield.
Away From the Here and Now—Clare Winger Harris stories, collected by Richard A. Lupoff
Beast or Man?—A 1930 novel of racism and horror by Sean M'Guire. Introduced by John Pelan.
Black Hogan Strikes Again—Australia's Peter Renwick pens a tale of the '30s outback.
Black River Falls—Suspense from the master, Ed Gorman.
Blondy's Boy Friend—A snappy 1930 story by Philip Wylie, writing as Leatrice Homesley.
Blood in a Snap—The *Finnegan's Wake* of the 21st century, by Jim Weiler.
Blood Moon—The first of the Robert Payne series by Ed Gorman.
Bogart '48—Hollywood action with Bogie by John Stanley and Kenn Davis
Building Strange Temples—Collection of Mythos writings by Don Webb.
Butterfly Man—1930s novel by Lew Levenson about a dancer who must come to terms with his homosexuality.
Calling Lou Largo!—Two Lou Largo novels by William Ard.
Cathedral of Horror—First volume of collected stories by weird fiction writer Arthur J. Burks.
Chalk Face—Curious supernatural murder thriller by Waldo Frank.
Cornucopia of Crime—Francis M. Nevins assembled this huge collection of his writings about crime literature and the people who write it. Essential for any serious mystery library.
Corpse Without Flesh—Strange novel of forensics by George Bruce

Crimson Clown Novels—By Johnston McCulley, author of the Zorro novels, *The Crimson Clown* and *The Crimson Clown Again.*
Dago Red—22 tales of dark suspense by Bill Pronzini.
Dark Sanctuary—Weird Menace story by H. B. Gregory.
David Hume Novels—*Corpses Never Argue, Cemetery First Stop, Make Way for the Mourners, Eternity Here I Come*. 1930s British hardboiled fiction with an attitude.
David&Son: Peregrine Parentus and other tales—Collection of tales and memoirs by Avram Davidson and Ethan Davidson, some published for the first time. Introduced by Grania Davidson Davis.
Dead Man Talks Too Much—Hollywood boozer by Weed Dickenson.
Death in a Bowl—1930's murder mystery by Raoul Whitfield.
Death March of the Dancing Dolls and Other Stories—Volume Three in the Day Keene in the Detective Pulps series. Introduced by Bill Crider.
Deep Space and other Stories—A collection of SF gems by Richard A. Lupoff.
Detective Duff Unravels It—Episodic mysteries by Harvey O'Higgins.
Devil's Planet—Locked room mystery set on the planet Mars, by Manly Wade Wellman.
Dime Novels: Ramble House's 10-Cent Books—*Knife in the Dark* by Robert Leslie Bellem, *Hot Lead* and *Song of Death* by Ed Earl Repp, *A Hashish House in New York* by H.H. Kane, and five more.
Doctor Arnoldi—Tiffany Thayer's story of the death of death.
Don Diablo: Book of a Lost Film—Two-volume treatment of a western by Paul Landres, with diagrams. Intro by Francis M. Nevins.
Dope and Swastikas—Two strange novels from 1922 by Edmund Snell
Dope Tales #1—Two dope-riddled classics; *Dope Runners* by Gerald Grantham and *Death Takes the Joystick* by Phillip Condé.
Dope Tales #2—Two more narco-classics; *The Invisible Hand* by Rex Dark and *The Smokers of Hashish* by Norman Berrow.
Dope Tales #3—Two enchanting novels of opium by the master, Sax Rohmer. *Dope* and *The Yellow Claw.*
Double Hot & **Double Sex**—Two combos of '60s softcore sex novels by Morris Hershman.
Dr. Odin—Douglas Newton's 1933 racial potboiler comes back to life.
E. C. R. Lorac—*Black Beadle, Case in the Clinic, The Devil and the C.I.D.* and *Slippery Staircase*. Classic Golden Age murder mysteries.
E. Charles Vivian—*Evidence in Blue*, *Accessory After*, *The Lady of the Terraces* and *Ladies in the Case*.
E. R. Punshon novels—*Information Received*, *Crossword Mystery*, *Dictator's Way*, *Diabolic Candelabra*, *Music Tells All*, *Helen Passes By*, *The House of Godwinsson*, *The Golden Dagger*, *The Attending Truth*, *Strange Ending*, *Brought to Light*, *Dark is the Clue*, *Triple Quest*, and *Six Were Present*: featuring Bobby Owen.
Ed "Strangler" Lewis: Facts within a Myth—Authoritative illustrated biography of the famous American wrestler Ed Lewis, by noted historian Steve Yohe.
Édouard Letailleur—*Three Eerie Mysteries, Vol.1: A Crime in Sologne*, *Perkane the Night-Demon* & *Crier for the Dead*, translated into English by Dr. Georges T. Dodds.
Evangelical Cockroach—Jack Woodford writes about writing.

Fatal Accident—Murder by automobile, a 1936 mystery by Cecil M. Wills.
Fighting Mad—Tod Robbins' 1922 novel about boxing and life.
Five Million in Cash—Gangster thriller by Tiffany Thayer writing as O. B. King.
Food for the Fungus Lady—Collection of weird stories by Ralston Shields, edited and introduced by John Pelan.
Francis M. Nevins—Three omnibus volumes of novels featuring his legal sleuth Loren Mensing and scam-artist Milo Turner: *Publish and Perish / Corrupt and Ensnare*, *Into the Same River Twice / Beneficiaries' Requiem* and *The 120-Hour Clock / The Ninety Million Dollar Mouse* — and the short story collection *Night Forms*.
Freaks and Fantasies—Eerie tales by Tod Robbins, collaborator of Tod Browning on the film FREAKS.
G. Firth Scott—*Possessed*, a haunting occult novel from 1912.
Gadsby—A lipogram (a novel without the letter E). Ernest Vincent Wright's last work, published in 1939 right before his death.
Gelett Burgess Novels—*The Master of Mysteries, The White Cat, Two O'Clock Courage, Ladies in Boxes, Find the Woman, The Heart Line, The Picaroons* and *Lady Mechante*. Recently added is A Gelett Burgess Sampler, edited by Alfred Jan. All are introduced by Richard A. Lupoff.
Geronimo—S. M. Barrett's 1905 autobiography of a noble American.
Gordon Eklund—*Second Creation*, *Retro Man* and *Stalking the Sun*: three volumes of the author's best short stories.
Go Forth and Multiply—Anthology of science fiction tales of repopulation, edited by Gordon Van Gelder.
Gunnar Johnston—*Soria Moria Castle* and *Perilous Discovery*.
Hake Talbot Novels—*Rim of the Pit, The Hangman's Handyman.* Classic locked room mysteries, with mapback covers by Gavin O'Keefe.
Hell is a City—William Ard's masterpiece.
Hollywood Dreams—A novel of Tinsel Town and the Depression by Richard O'Brien.
Homicide House—#6 in the Day Keene in the Detective Pulps series.
House of the Restless Dead—Strange and ominous tales by Hugh B. Cave
Inclination to Murder—1966 thriller by New Zealand's Harriet Hunter.
Invaders from the Dark—Classic werewolf tale from Greye La Spina.
J. Poindexter, Colored—Classic satirical black novel by Irvin S. Cobb.
Jack Mann Novels—Strange murder in the English countryside. *Gees' First Case, Nightmare Farm, Grey Shapes, The Ninth Life, The Glass Too Many, Her Ways Are Death, The Kleinert Case* and *Maker of Shadows.*
Jake Hardy—A lusty western tale from Wesley Tallant.
James Corbett—*Vampire of the Skies*, *The Ghost Plane*, *Murder Begets Murder* and *The Air Killer* – strange thriller novels from this singular British author.
Jim Harmon Double Novels—*Vixen Hollow/Celluloid Scandal, The Man Who Made Maniacs/Silent Siren, Ape Rape/Wanton Witch, Sex Burns Like Fire/Twist Session, Sudden Lust/Passion Strip, Sin Unlimited/Harlot Master, Twilight Girls/Sex Institution.* Written in the early '60s and never reprinted until now.
Joel Townsley Rogers Novels and Short Stories—By the author of *The Red Right Hand: Once In a Red Moon, Lady With the Dice, The Stopped*

Clock, Never Leave My Bed. Also two short story collections: *Night of Horror* and *Killing Time*.

John Carstairs, Space Detective—Arboreal Sci-fi by Frank Belknap Long

John G. Brandon—*The Case of the Withered Hand, Finger-Prints Never Lie,* and *Death on Delivery*: crime thrillers by Australian author John G. Brandon.

John H. Knox—*Hands Out of Hell, Man Out of Hell,* and *Reunion in Hell.*

John S. Glasby—Two collections of Glasby's Lovecraftian stories: *The Brooding City* and *Beyond the Rim*. Introduced by John Pelan.

Joseph Shallit Novels—*The Case of the Billion Dollar Body, Lady Don't Die on My Doorstep, Kiss the Killer, Yell Bloody Murder, Take Your Last Look.* One of America's best 50's authors and a favorite of author Bill Pronzini.

Keller Memento—45 short stories of the amazing and weird by Dr. David Keller.

Killer's Caress—Cary Moran's 1936 hardboiled thriller.

Knowing the Unknowable: Putting Psi to Work—Damien Broderick, PhD puts forward the valid case for evidence of Psi.

Laughing Death—1932 Yellow Peril thriller by Walter C. Brown.

League of the Grateful Dead and Other Stories—Volume One in the Day Keene in the Detective Pulps series.

Lords of the Earth—A novel of meddling dabblers in the occult invoking the ancient powers of Atlantis. J.M.A. Mills' sequel to *The Tomb of the Dark Ones.*

Mad-Doctor Merciful—Collin Brooks' unsettling novel of medical experimentation with supernatural forces.

Malcolm Jameson Novels and Short Stories—*Astonishing! Astounding!, Tarnished Bomb, The Alien Envoy and Other Stories* and *The Chariots of San Fernando and Other Stories.* All introduced and edited by John Pelan or Richard A. Lupoff.

Marblehead: A Novel of H.P. Lovecraft—A long-lost masterpiece from Richard A. Lupoff. This is the "director's cut", the long version that has never been published before.

Mark of the Laughing Death and Other Stories—Shockers from the pulps by Francis James, introduced by John Pelan.

Mark Hansom Novels—*Master of Souls, The Ghost of Gaston Revere, The Madman, The Shadow on the House, Sorcerer's Chessmen* & *The Wizard of Berner's Abbey.*

Max Afford Novels—*Owl of Darkness, Death's Mannikins, Blood on His Hands, The Dead Are Blind, The Sheep and the Wolves, Sinners in Paradise* and *Two Locked Room Mysteries and a Ripping Yarn* by one of Australia's finest mystery novelists.

Miles Burton novels—*A Smell of Smoke, Death Leaves No Card, Situation Vacant* and *Death Paints a Picture.*

Mr. South Burned His Mouth—Gentry Nyland's only novel: a thriller.

Molly and her Man of War— Romantic novel with a difference, by Arabella Kenealy.

Money Brawl—Two books about the writing business by Jack Woodford and H. Bedford-Jones. Introduced by Richard A. Lupoff.

More Secret Adventures of Sherlock Holmes—Gary Lovisi's second collection of tales about the unknown sides of the great detective.

Muddled Mind: Complete Works of Ed Wood, Jr.—David Hayes and Hayden Davis deconstruct the life and works of the mad, but canny, genius.

Murder among the Nudists—1934 mystery by Peter Hunt, featuring a naked Detective-Inspector going undercover in a nudist colony.

Murder in Black and White—1931 classic tennis whodunit by Evelyn Elder.

Murder in Shawnee—Two novels of the Alleghenies by John Douglas: *Shawnee Alley Fire* and *Haunts*.

Murder in Suffolk—A 1938 murder mystery novel by the mysterious 'A. Fielding.'

My Deadly Angel—1955 Cold War drama by John Chelton.

My First Time: The One Experience You Never Forget—Michael Birchwood—64 true first-person narratives of how they lost it.

Mysterious Martin, the Master of Murder—Two versions of a strange 1912 novel by Tod Robbins about a man who writes books that can kill.

Norman Berrow Novels—*The Bishop's Sword, Ghost House, Don't Go Out After Dark, Claws of the Cougar, The Smokers of Hashish, The Secret Dancer, Don't Jump Mr. Boland!, The Footprints of Satan, Fingers for Ransom, The Three Tiers of Fantasy, The Spaniard's Thumb, The Eleventh Plague, Words Have Wings, One Thrilling Night, The Lady's in Danger, It Howls at Night, The Terror in the Fog, Oil Under the Window, Murder in the Melody, The Singing Room.* This is the complete Norman Berrow library of locked-room mysteries, several of which are masterpieces.

Old Faithful and Other Stories—SF classic tales by Raymond Z. Gallun

Old Times' Sake—Short stories by James Reasoner from Mike Shayne Magazine.

Pair O' Jacks—A mystery novel and a diatribe about publishing by Jack Woodford

Pawns of Destiny—Psychological drama by Kay Seaton.

Perfect .38—Two early Timothy Dane novels by William Ard.

Prince Pax—Devilish intrigue by George Sylvester Viereck and Philip Eldridge

Prose Bowl—Futuristic satire of a world where hack writing has replaced football as our national obsession, by Bill Pronzini and Barry N. Malzberg.

Ralph Trevor novels—*Murder in Silk*, *Front Page Murder*, *Easy for the Crook*, *The Deputy Avenger*, etc.

Red Light—The history of legal prostitution in Shreveport Louisiana by Eric Brock. Includes wonderful photos of the houses and the ladies.

Researching American-Made Toy Soldiers—A 276-page collection of a lifetime of articles by toy soldier expert Richard O'Brien.

Ripped from the Headlines!—The Jack the Ripper story as told in the newspaper articles in the *New York* and *London Times.*

Ronald S. L. Harding—*One Dreadful Night* and *Library of Death*.

Rough Cut & New, Improved Murder—Ed Gorman's first two novels.

R. R. Ryan Novels — *Freak Museum, The Subjugated Beast, Death of a Sadist, Echo of a Curse, Devil's Shelter* and *No Escape*. Introduced by John Pelan.

Roland Daniel Novels — *Ruby of a Thousand Dreams*, *The Girl in the Dark*, and *A Roland Daniel Double: The Signal and The Return of Wu Fang*.

Ruled By Radio — 1925 futuristic novel by Robert L. Hadfield & Frank E. Farncombe.

Rupert Penny Novels — *Policeman's Holiday, Policeman's Evidence, Lucky Policeman, Policeman in Armour, Sealed Room Murder, Sweet Poison, The Talkative Policeman, She had to Have Gas* and *Cut and Run* (by Martin Tanner.) Rupert Penny is the pseudonym of Australian Charles Thornett, a master of the locked room, impossible crime plot.

Russell Gray—*Hostesses in Hell* and *My Touch Brings Death.*

Sacred Locomotive Flies — Richard A. Lupoff's psychedelic SF story.

Sam — Early gay novel by Lonnie Coleman.

Sand's Game — Spectacular hardboiled noir from Ennis Willie, edited by Lynn Myers and Stephen Mertz, with contributions from Max Allan Collins, Bill Crider, Wayne Dundee, Bill Pronzini, Gary Lovisi and James Reasoner.

Sand's War — More violent fiction from the typewriter of Ennis Willie

Satan's Den Exposed — True crime in Truth or Consequences New Mexico — Award-winning journalism by the *Desert Journal.*

Satan's Secret and Selected Stories — Barnard Stacey's only novel with a selection of his best short stories.

Satans of Saturn — Novellas from the pulps by Otis Adelbert Kline and E. H. Price

Secrets of a Teenage Superhero — Graphic lit by Jonathan Sweet

Sex Slave — Potboiler of lust in the days of Cleopatra by Dion Leclerq, 1966.

Sideslip — 1968 SF masterpiece by Ted White and Dave Van Arnam.

Slammer Days — Two full-length prison memoirs: *Men into Beasts* (1952) by George Sylvester Viereck and *Home Away From Home* (1962) by Jack Woodford.

Star Griffin — Michael Kurland's 1987 masterpiece of SF drollery is back.

Stakeout on Millennium Drive — Award-winning Indianapolis Noir by Ian Woollen.

Strands of the Web: Short Stories of Harry Stephen Keeler — Edited and Introduced by Fred Cleaver.

Suzy — A collection of comic strips by Richard O'Brien and Bob Vojtko from 1970.

Tail of the Lizard King / Kaliwood — Two novellas by Adam Mudman Bezecny paying homage to the sleaze genre.

Tales of the Macabre and Ordinary — Modern twisted horror by Chris Mikul, author of the *Bizarrism* series.

Tales of Terror and Torment Vols. #1 & #2 — John Pelan selects and introduces these samplers of weird menace tales from the pulps.

Tenebrae — Ernest G. Henham's 1898 horror tale brought back.

The Alice Books — Lewis Carroll's classics *Alice's Adventures in Wonderland* and *Through the Looking-Glass* together in one volume, with new illustrations by O'Keefe.

The Amorous Intrigues & Adventures of Aaron Burr — by Anonymous. Hot historical action about the man who almost became Emperor of Mexico.

The Anthony Boucher Chronicles — edited by Francis M. Nevins. Book reviews by Anthony Boucher written for the *San Francisco Chronicle,* 1942 – 1947. Essential and fascinating reading by the best book reviewer there ever was.

The Barclay Catalogs — Two essential books about toy soldier collecting by Richard O'Brien

The Basil Wells Omnibus — A collection of Wells' stories by Richard A. Lupoff

The Beautiful Dead and Other Stories — Dreadful tales from Donald Dale

The Best of 10-Story Book — edited by Chris Mikul, over 35 stories from the literary magazine edited by Harry Stephen Keeler.

The Bitch Wall — Novel about American soldiers in the Vietnam War, based on Dennis Lane's experiences.

The Black Dark Murders — Vintage '50s college murder yarn by Milt Ozaki, writing as Robert O. Saber.

The Book of Time — The classic novel by H.G. Wells is joined by sequels by Wells himself and three stories by Richard A. Lupoff. Illustrated by Gavin L. O'Keefe.

The Broken Fang and Other Experiences of a Specialist in Spooks — Eerie mystery tales by Uel Key.

The Strange Case of the Antlered Man — A mystery of superstition by Edwy Searles Brooks.

The Case of the Bearded Bride — #4 in the Day Keene in the Detective Pulps series.

The Case of the Little Green Men — Mack Reynolds wrote this love song to sci-fi fans back in 1951 and it's now back in print.

The Charlie Chaplin Murder Mystery — A 2004 tribute by noted film scholar, Wes D. Gehring.

The Cloudbuilders and Other Stories — SF tales from Colin Kapp.

The Collected Writings — Collection of science fiction stories, memoirs and poetry by Carol Carr. Introduction by Karen Haber.

The Compleat Calhoon — All of Fender Tucker's works: Includes *Totah Six-Pack, Weed, Women and Song* and *Tales from the Tower,* plus a CD of all of his songs.

The Compleat Ova Hamlet — Parodies of SF authors by Richard A. Lupoff. This is a brand new edition with more stories and more illustrations by Trina Robbins.

The Contested Earth and Other SF Stories — A never-before published space opera and seven short stories by Jim Harmon.

The Crackpot and Other Twisted Tales of Greedy Fans and Collectors — The first retrospective collection of the whacky stories of John E. Stockman. Edited by Dwight R. Decker.

The Crimson Butterfly — Early novel by Edmund Snell involving superstition and aberrant Lepidoptera in Borneo.

The Crimson Query — A 1929 thriller from Arlton Eadie. A perfect way to get introduced.

The Daymakers, **City of the Tiger** & **Perchance to Wake** — Three volumes of stories taken from the influential British science fiction magazine *Science Fantasy*. Compiled by John Boston & Damien Broderick.

The Devil Drives — An odd prison and lost treasure novel from 1932 by Virgil Markham.
The Devil of Pei-Ling — Herbert Asbury's 1929 tale of the occult.
The Devil's Mistress — A 1915 Scottish gothic tale by J. W. Brodie-Innes, a member of Aleister Crowley's Golden Dawn.
The Devil's Nightclub and Other Stories — John Pelan introduces some gruesome tales by Nat Schachner.
The Devil's Saint—1924 fantasy novel by Dulcie Deamer.
The Dirges of Maldoror — O'Keefe's illustrated English translation of Lautréamont's *Les Chants de Maldoror.*
The Disentanglers — Episodic intrigue at the turn of last century by Andrew Lang
The Dog Poker Code — A spoof of *The Da Vinci Code* by D. B. Smithee.
The Dumpling — Political murder from 1907 by Coulson Kernahan.
The End of It All and Other Stories — Ed Gorman selected his favorite short stories for this huge collection.
The Evil of Li-Sin — A Gerald Verner double, combining *The Menace of Li-Sin* and *The Vengeance of Li-Sin*, together with an introduction by John Pelan and an afterword and bibliography by Chris Verner.
The Fangs of Suet Pudding — A 1944 novel of the German invasion by Adams Farr
The Finger of Destiny and Other Stories — Edmund Snell's superb collection of weird stories of Borneo.
The Gold Star Line — Seaboard adventure from L.T. Meade and Robert Eustace.
The Great Boo-Boo — Curious 1892 politico-satirical fantasy by Henry S. Wilcox.
The Great Orme Terror — Horror stories by Garnett Radcliffe from the pulps
The Hairbreadth Escapes of Major Mendax — Francis Blake Crofton's 1889 boys' book.
The House That Time Forgot and Other Stories — Insane pulpitude by Robert F. Young
The House of the Vampire — 1907 poetic thriller by George S. Viereck.
The Illustrious Corpse — Murder hijinx from Tiffany Thayer
The Incredible Adventures of Rowland Hern — Intriguing 1928 impossible crimes by Nicholas Olde.
The John Dickson Carr Companion — Comprehensive reference work compiled by James E. Keirans. Indispensable resource for the Carr *aficionado*.
The Julius Caesar Murder Case — A 1935 retelling of the assassination by Wallace Irwin that's more fun than Shakespeare's version.
The Kid Was a Killer — Caryl Chessman's only novel, based on his own experiences.
The Koky Comics — A collection of all of the 1978-1981 Sunday and daily comic strips by Richard O'Brien and Mort Gerberg, in two volumes.
The Lord of Terror — 1925 mystery with master-criminal, Fantômas.
The Man who was Murdered Twice — Intriguing murder mystery by Robert H. Leitfred.
The Melamare Mystery — A classic 1929 Arsene Lupin mystery by Maurice Leblanc

The Man Who Was Secrett — Epic SF stories from John Brunner
The Man Without a Planet — Science fiction tales by Richard Wilson
The N. R. De Mexico Novels — Robert Bragg, the real N.R. de Mexico, presents *Marijuana Girl, Madman on a Drum, Private Chauffeur* in one volume.
The Night Remembers — A 1991 Jack Walsh mystery from Ed Gorman.
The One After Snelling — Kickass modern noir from Richard O'Brien.
The Organ Reader — A huge compilation of just about everything published in the 1971-1972 radical bay-area newspaper, *THE ORGAN*. A coffee table book that points out the shallowness of the coffee table mindset.
The Place of Hairy Death — Collected weird horror tales by Anthony M. Rud.
The Poker Club — Three in one! Ed Gorman's ground-breaking novel, the short story it was based upon, and the screenplay of the film made from it.
The Private Journal & Diary of John H. Surratt — The memoirs of the man who conspired to assassinate President Lincoln.
The Ramble House Coloring Book — Twenty illustrations to color in, each adapted from one of Gavin L. O'Keefe's cover designs.
The Ramble House Mapbacks — Recently revised book by Gavin L. O'Keefe with color pictures of all the Ramble House books with mapbacks.
The Secret Adventures of Sherlock Holmes — Three Sherlockian pastiches by the Brooklyn author/publisher, Gary Lovisi.
The Secret of the Morgue — Frederick G. Eberhard's 1932 mystery involving murder and forensic science with an undercurrent of the malaise that's driven by Prohibition.
The Sign of the Scorpion — A 1935 Edmund Snell tale of oriental evil.
The Silent Terror of Chu-Sheng — Yellow Peril suspense novel by Eugene Thomas.
The Singular Problem of the Stygian House-Boat — Two classic tales by John Kendrick Bangs about the denizens of Hades.
The Smiling Corpse — Philip Wylie and Bernard Bergman's odd 1935 novel.
The Sorcery Club — Classic supernatural novel by Elliott O'Donnell.
The Spider: Satan's Murder Machines — A thesis about Iron Man.
The Stench of Death: An Odoriferous Omnibus by Jack Moskovitz — Two complete novels and two novellas from 60's sleaze author, Jack Moskovitz.
The Story Writer and Other Stories — Classic SF from Richard Wilson
The Strange Thirteen — Richard B. Gamon's odd stories about Raj India.
The Technique of the Mystery Story — Carolyn Wells' tips about writing.
The Tell-Tale Soul — Two novellas by Bram Stoker Award-winning author Christopher Conlon. Introduction by John Pelan.
The Threat of Nostalgia — A collection of his most obscure stories by Jon Breen
The Time Armada — Fox B. Holden's 1953 SF gem.
The Tomb of the Dark Ones — Adventure in Egypt where ancient forces are roused from æons of slumber. A J. M. A. Mills novel from 1937.

The Town from Planet Five — From Richard Wilson, two SF classics, *And Then the Town Took Off* and *The Girls from Planet 5*

The Tracer of Lost Persons — From 1906, an episodic novel that became a hit radio series in the '30s. Introduced by Richard A. Lupoff.

The Trail of the Cloven Hoof — Diabolical horror from 1935 by Arlton Eadie. Introduced by John Pelan.

The Triune Man — Mindscrambling science fiction from Richard A. Lupoff.

The Universal Holmes — Richard A. Lupoff's 2007 collection of five Holmesian pastiches and a recipe for giant rat stew.

The Werewolf vs the Vampire Woman — Hard to believe ultraviolence by either Arthur M. Scarm or Arthur M. Scram.

The Whistling Ancestors — A 1936 classic of weirdness by Richard E. Goddard and introduced by John Pelan.

The White Owl — A vintage thriller from Edmund Snell

The White Peril in the Far East — Sidney Lewis Gulick's 1905 indictment of the West and assurance that Japan would never attack the U.S.

The Wonderful Wizard of Oz — by L. Frank Baum and illustrated by Gavin L. O'Keefe.

The Yu-Chi Stone — Novel of intrigue and superstition set in Borneo, by Edmund Snell.

They Called the Shots — Collection of authoritative articles by Francis M. Nevins exploring the action movie directors of the late silents through to the late 1960s.

Time Line — Ramble House artist Gavin O'Keefe selects his most evocative art inspired by the twisted literature he reads and designs.

Tiresias — Psychotic modern horror novel by Jonathan M. Sweet.

Tortures and Towers — Two novellas of terror by Dexter Dayle.

Totah Six-Pack — Fender Tucker's six tales about Farmington in one sleek volume.

Tree of Life, Book of Death — Grania Davis' book of her life.

Trail of the Spirit Warrior — Roger Haley's saga of life in the Indian Territories.

Twelve Who Were Damned — Collection of weird menace tales by Paul Ernst.

Two Kinds of Bad — Two 50s novels by William Ard about Danny Fontaine

Two Suns of Morcali and Other Stories — Evelyn E. Smith's SF tour-de-force

Two-Timers — Time travel double: *The Man Who Mastered Time* by Ray Cummings and *Time Column* and *Taa the Terrible* by Malcolm Jameson. Introduced by Richard A. Lupoff.

Ultra-Boiled — 23 gut-wrenching tales by our Man in Brooklyn, Gary Lovisi.

Up Front From Behind — A 2011 satire of Wall Street by James B. Kobak.

Victims & Villains — Intriguing Sherlockiana from Derham Groves.

Wade Wright Novels — *Echo of Fear, Death At Nostalgia Street, It Leads to Murder* and *Shadows' Edge*, a double book featuring *Shadows Don't Bleed* and *The Sharp Edge*.

Walter S. Masterman Novels — *The Green Toad, The Flying Beast, The Yellow Mistletoe, The Wrong Verdict, The Perjured Alibi, The Border Line, The Bloodhounds Bay*, *The Curse of Cantire*, *The Curse of the Reckaviles*, *Death Turns Traitor*, *The Wrong Letter*, *The Death Coins*, *The Nameless Crime*, *The Tangle*, *The Baddington Horror*, *The Hooded Monster*, *The Mystery of Fifty-Two*, *Back from the Grave*, *The Secret of the Downs*, *The Rose of Death*, *The Silver Leopard*, *The Avenger Strikes*, *The Hunted Man*, *2.L.O.* and *The Man Without a Head*.

Wayne Rogers—*Satan's Sin House* and *Death Rocks the Cradle*.

We Are the Dead and Other Stories — Volume Two in the Day Keene in the Detective Pulps series, introduced by Ed Gorman. When done, there may be 11 in the series.

Welsh Rarebit Tales — Charming stories from 1902 by Harle Oren Cummins

West Texas War and Other Western Stories — Western hijinks by Gary Lovisi.

What Was That?—Ghostly murder mystery from 1920 by Katharine Haviland Taylor.

What If? Volume 3 — Richard A. Lupoff introduces three decades worth of SF short stories that should have won a Hugo, but didn't.

When the Bat Man Thirsts and Other Stories — Weird tales from Frederick C. Davis.

When the Dead Walk — Gary Lovisi takes us into the zombie-infested South.

Whip Dodge: Man Hunter — Wesley Tallant's saga of a bounty hunter of the old West.

Win, Place and Die! — The first new mystery by Milt Ozaki in decades. The ultimate novel of '70s Reno.

Writer, Volumes 1, 2, 3 & 4— A *magnus opus* from Richard A. Lupoff summing up his life as writer.

Wyatt Blassingame — Four volumes of collected stories: *The Tongueless Horror*, *The Unholy Goddess*, *Lady of the Yellow Death* and *Mistress of Terror.*

You'll Die Laughing — Bruce Elliott's 1945 novel of murder at a practical joker's English countryside manor.

You're Not Alone: **30 Science Fiction Stories from *Cosmos Magazine***, edited by Damien Broderick.

RAMBLE HOUSE

www.ramblehouse.com

flyingspiderster@gmail.com

10329 Sheephead Drive, Vancleave MS 39565 USA

Made in the USA
Monee, IL
03 November 2021

81370922R00215